DAZZLING DEATH

DAZZLING DEATH

A COSMETIC CRIMES MYSTERY

ARLENE KAY

For my husband

Praise for Dazzling Death

"A Dazzler of a mystery! Well-drawn characters, a plot with plenty of twists and turns, and a satisfying ending."—Leslie Wheeler, award-winning author of the Miranda Lewis Mysteries and The Berkshire Hills Mysteries

Chapter One

From the moment she appeared in Harbor Bay, Michigan, Teagen Doyle captivated the town. I wasn't jealous—not really. After all, she was still what passed for a celebrity in our seaside spot, even though her days as the star of a totally forgettable soap opera were long gone. Besides, Teagen was no ingenue. Her bio on Wikipedia said she was thirty-six, although my business partner Gemma Watts and I pegged her at closer to forty-five. Meow! I should have followed the counsel of my brilliant Aunt Violet and erred on the generous side. Violet, a renowned painter and cosmetics mogul, merely smiled and pronounced Teagen "interesting."

"We need more colorful characters in Harbor Bay," Violet said. "And you must admit that Teagen is a great advertisement for skin care and judicious use of cosmetics. Try a friendly approach with her."

I was chastened by my aunt's words, even though I still believed that the Doyle glow owed more to the services of a skilled surgeon and stylist than nature itself. My name is Marketta Davis, and as the proprietor of POPPET, a cosmetics emporium, I know quite a bit about the beauty biz. I've also learned the virtues of tact. When my customers gushed about Teagen's artfully streaked hair and unlined face, I managed to nod and keep my opinions to myself. My business partner Gemma Watts was less circumspect.

"Ten to one she wears extensions," Gemma said. "Good ones, though. That mane of hair is too full to be natural. Probably goes to Chicago or Manhattan for them. Isn't her hubby one of those billionaire business tycoons?"

Violet stopped stacking the Laura Mercier display, turned around, and gave us an enigmatic smile.

"Do you know him?" Gemma asked. My aunt was a major player on the international social scene who seemed to know most of the big shots worth knowing. She was notoriously private about her personal life and ignored even my feeble attempts to pry information from her.

"We've met. Of course, he's older than her. Brendan must be pushing sixty by now, but he's still a remarkably vital man." I detected a gleam in my aunt's eyes as she reminisced. Curious. As far as I knew, Teagen had swanned into town without her husband, citing his business commitments elsewhere. Harbor Bay housed several of the uber-wealthy set, and according to our faithful customer and real estate confidant, Doogie Kinkaid, she was temporarily housed with one of them. Doogie handled most of the high-end properties from Harbor Bay to Traverse City and was never shy about broadcasting carefully edited bon mots about his clientele.

"Teagen, I mean Mrs. Doyle, is staying with Madge Stone in her glorious waterfront compound." Doogie sighed, and I swear dollar signs appeared on his eyeballs. I'd never visited the Stone manse, but, naturally, Aunt Violet had. She described the ten-acre lakefront parcel as "comfortable," which meant anything from glamorous to glorious. Madge had homes elsewhere, of course. Winters in Harbor Bay weren't everyone's cup of Earl Grey unless ice-skating, skiing, or sledding were on the agenda.

When Doogie dropped into Poppet the next day for a massage and facial, Gemma skillfully extracted tidbits from him about his famous clients. My partner, a vivacious redhead, was a friend to many and a foe to the unlucky. Fortunately for Doogie, he fit firmly in the former category.

"Your muscles sure are tight, Doogie. Too much tension. All that partying with the rich and famous." Gemma's hot stone massages and line of patter drew clients from Traverse City to Grand Rapids. Most of them also left Poppet with a bundle of products that fed our bottom line.

"Aw, Gemma, you flatter me. I'm not one of the in-crowd. Not really. Just a convenient dinner guest when they need an extra man or an occasional escort." He grinned. "Besides, I enjoy those gals, and mostly they just want a little company. I supply them with the attention their husbands don't and whip up the occasional feast when they're hungry."

Doogie, a man of ample proportions and a big heart, made friends easily. I envied him that trait. No one in Harbor Bay had a bad word to say about him, even his business competitors. Doogie was a friend to most and an enemy to no one. Plus, he knew when to keep his mouth shut and when to emote. Upscale clients would have dropped him like the proverbial hot potato if their secrets leaked out.

Gemma sighed. "Ah, what woman doesn't need an extra man or occasional escort?" She winked at Doogie. "If you meet anyone who meets our standards, send him my way."

As I listened to the lively chatter between Gemma and Doogie, I examined my conscience. My own social skills were limited, even though I tried mightily to be friendly. Just call me a Dale Carnegie washout. According to Gemma, a woman who seldom minced words, some people considered me "snobbish or standoffish," descriptors that were patently untrue, hurtful, and totally unfair. Aunt Violet merely patted my cheek and told me not to worry. "Anyone who really knows you appreciates what a kind, generous soul you are. As for the rest—that's their loss."

I'd once been dubbed Marketta Davis, the Golden Girl of Harbor Bay, after a string of successes ranging from Prom queen to Valedictorian, and best of all, acceptance at the prestigious Art Institute of Chicago. Away I sailed to the Windy City, leaving Harbor Bay and its inhabitants in my rear-view mirror. I was convinced that my path to artistic stardom was preordained, but it was not to be. That dream was shattered when the Art Institute sent me packing. Words like "pedestrian" and "derivative" were used to describe my painting, a painful experience that still seared my soul and humbled me. No more "Golden Girl" for Marky Davis. With the help of Aunt Violet, I put aside my ego, returned to Harbor Bay, and focused my energy on building POPPET, our upscale beauty boutique. Although I still lusted for artistic glory, my life was good even on a much smaller stage.

Doogie flashed a wad of cash and paid his bill. Naturally, Gemma pounced on that. "Since when did you become a high roller, Mr. K?" she asked.

He waved away her comment, "Don't get excited, sweetheart. This is nothing special. Just some folding money that's going straight into my savings account. Bet you didn't know that I'm a cardsharp. Doogie the demon, that's what the losers call me." His grin was so beatific that we both forgave him for bragging. Gemma immediately changed tactics.

"Okay, spill. Tell us what Teagen Doyle's really like."

I joined Gemma in double-teaming poor Doogie. "Yeah, come on. We're dying of curiosity. She always looks so perfect that it's intimidating."

He threw back his head and guffawed. "Funny thing. Just today, Mrs. Doyle was asking about you, Marky."

I am seldom speechless, but, on this occasion, I found myself bereft of words. Fortunately, Gemma filled the void.

"OMG! Don't tell me she's opening her own salon. This town can't support two beauty emporiums."

Doogie shook his head. "Not to worry. Teagen asked personal stuff. Seems the local ladies heaped praise upon your artwork, but especially your sleuthing. She's not a competitor, Marky, she's an admirer."

That really puzzled me. I'm no detective, even though I had recently been thrust into three homicide investigations. Doogie must have misinterpreted Teagen's interest.

"Let me get this straight. She's not opening a business in Harbor Bay."

"Not quite. Teagen's really into health things—potions, pills, the whole works. Her hubby has the cash, but she has the dream. She swears that's the secret to her incredible vitality and beauty."

Gemma stopped counting out his change and pursed her lips. "Sounds to me like Mr. Doyle wants his wife to have a hobby. Keep her busy while he hits the hot spots. I read on the internet that he's a womanizer."

Scurrilous comments about our customers can be downright dangerous. Gemma, who considers the internet to be the fount of all knowledge, sometimes forgot that. Doogie's eyes widened as he sputtered out a defense of his friend. The timely arrival of Aunt Violet diffused what could have been an explosive situation. My aunt, an elegant woman of a certain age with boundless reserves of charm, quickly assessed the situation and acted. She grasped his hand and turned the full wattage of her personality upon

Doogie.

"What's this?" she said, "No one told me that our favorite customer had an appointment."

If he were a spaniel, Doogie would have wagged his tail with joy. Instead, he hugged my aunt and forgot all about Brendan Doyle. "I'll bet you tell everyone that. How do you do it, Violet? You look radiant."

His use of hyperbole was legendary, but in this instance, praise was warranted. Violet Davis was a vision, resplendent in a deep blue Chanel jacket, cashmere turtleneck, and charcoal slacks. Her flawless makeup and raven hair made lesser beings like Gemma and me fade into obscurity.

"You know the Doyles, Violet. Lovely people." Doogie glared at Gemma as if daring her to dispute that.

"Yes indeed," Violet said. "Quite the power couple. I'm having dinner with them this evening. You're invited, Marky. Should be very entertaining. Kim will be joining us, too. Seems she knows Teagen from her modeling days."

Kimberly Stevens, wife of the irascible lawyer Lionel, was an elegant addition to our Harbor Bay crowd. I'd cheered her transformation from downtrodden housewife to prominent business executive and animal advocate. Surprisingly, that success had saved her marriage and enlivened her husband's dour personality. Lionel was hardly the life of the party, but his scowls and snubs had noticeably lessened with his wife's business success.

I should have savored my chance to meet Teagen Doyle, but instead the invitation aroused every one of my insecurities. Wardrobe choices were limited, and my accessories consisted of hand-me-downs from my mother plus several statement pieces crafted by local artisans. The waif look would be woefully inadequate when contrasted with the glitz and glamor of my hostess and her set. Fortunately, once more, Aunt Violent rode to the rescue. She unzipped her Louis Vuitton garment bag and produced a treasure trove of goodies.

"Voila, my dear Niece. Check out these outfits and make your choice."

I was speechless, but Gemma was not. She surveyed the array of silks and satins with a gimlet eye and chose a tawny jumpsuit with a matching cashmere jacket. "Here. This goes with those lovely blonde locks of yours, princess. Add the gold belt and you're all set."

Violet nodded. "Perfect choice, Gemma. I have a necklace that will complement the outfit. Simple but elegant. That's the look we're shooting for. Nothing garish. After all, Marky has youth and beauty on her side. That's something Hollywood hokum can't compete with."

Under the circumstances, my only option was to submit with good grace. My mother advised me to always be myself, but my very best self. No need to challenge Violet's offerings. or dispute her fashion taste when I knew she was right. We agreed that she would swing by and fetch me around six-thirty pm, in time for cocktails. Meanwhile, Gemma shooed me away to prepare my hair and makeup for the big moment. Her haste aroused my suspicions.

"Got a hot date, have you?"

"Maybe." She grimaced slightly. "Not that hot. Benny's Mom is making dinner. If I survive that we're going to catch a movie." The mother in question was a formidable matron who doted on her odious son, Deputy Sheriff Benny Soto, and regarded any other female as an interloper.

"She knows you're engaged, doesn't she?"

Gemma shrugged. "Sort of. Until we set a date, she'll keep her hopes up."

She wasn't the only one. I loved Gemma and shuddered at the thought of her being wedded to a creature like Benny. His imperious ways and limited intellect earned him the secret scorn of all who knew him. As Gemma often observed, when it came to the marriage market, the pickings in Harbor Bay were woefully small. Besides, my credentials as a matchmaker were scarcely sterling. I had yet to solidify any lasting relationship for myself despite several attempts. My current squeeze, a political science professor from the University of Michigan, had hinted at a possible future for us but never actually popped the question. Roddy Park had the looks of a film star housed in the mind of an intellectual. Sentient females of all ages lusted after him, but he remained unaffected and vaguely puzzled by their attention. We'd met and connected during a sizzling summer session at a prep school where murder headlined the curriculum. Somehow, amidst the mayhem, we found a mutual attraction that blossomed into something more. I couldn't define it and dared not share my dreams even with Gemma and Aunt Violet.

I thought of Roddy while fluffing my hair and applying a light cosmetic touch. Good thing I was going solo to Teagen's party. No need to compete with a glamorous television star, even if she had passed her sell-by date. Roddy was an intellectual, but he was still all male. Such sentiments made me cringe since they were unworthy of me as a feminist and emancipated woman. I brushed them aside and made my way out of Poppet. Violet's massive Mercedes was parked outside, awaiting me like Cinderella's magic coach. The

Chapter Two

I'd seen photos of Madge Stone's opulent estate but had never ventured into the gated enclosure that protected it. *Architectural Digest* (*AD* to hipsters) had featured a four-page spread extolling the excellence of design and the sumptuous water views of Stonegate, Madge's palatial pad. As we neared the entrance, my description of it was understated elegance, a dwelling that exuded timeless beauty and a healthy respect for the surrounding landscape. This was some place that I could happily call home, unlike the unsightly McMansions that had sprung up like toadstools in Harbor Bay's other fashionable spots. The Stone family had deep community roots as well as deep pockets. They had neither the need nor the desire to impress their neighbors.

"Lovely, isn't it?" Violet said. "You'd scarcely realize the size of the property, let alone its price tag. Now don't be shy. You'll like Madge. She's unpretentious and genuinely kind. An animal lover like you, Marky. Madge supports more charities than you'd guess, not that she'd brag about it. She has a menagerie of pets, mostly rescues, and somehow manages to keep them all in check."

Those bona fides from my aunt allayed my concerns. Violet was a keen judge of character who was never swayed by an individual's wealth or position. She'd seen the good, bad, and the ugly in her many international ventures and had learned to sift the wheat from the chaff.

"What about her cousin?" I asked. "She must keep a very low profile because even Doogie seldom mentions her."

Violet hesitated. "Letty Briggs has rather a sad story. At one time, she had a promising acting career, but it fizzled. After that, everything went downhill. Pills, alcohol, the whole routine. Madge took her in and probably saved her life."

"Wow, what happened to her?"

My aunt pursed her lips. "The usual. Letty fell head over heels for a man who betrayed her. Rumors surfaced that she even tried to commit suicide, but there was no proof." She wagged her finger at me. "Let that be a lesson to you, my girl. Value yourself and don't let any man or woman take your self-esteem. Dr. Roderick Park is lucky to have you."

"His family has some deep pockets, I understand, but Roddy supports himself."

"Admirable. Wealth alone doesn't ensure happiness. Just read the tabloids." Violet lifted my chin, "You dear Niece are a pearl without price."

As usual, her pep talk buoyed my spirits. I felt a surge of optimism stirring within me.

"I'm still astounded at even being here," I said. "Any advice?"

Violet smiled. "Just enjoy yourself. These are potential customers, but more than that, they're potential friends. And we all need that."

A butler greeted us at the door, took our wraps, and led the way into the great room, where a dozen or so women gathered. Although he was garbed in traditional livery and sported a British accent, his manner was cordial and not off-putting. Violet called him Ian.

A civilized hum of conversation filled the room as our hostess approached us. According to Wikipedia, Madge was a fifty-nine-year-old childless widow and former nurse with a law degree that she applied to championing various good causes. Biographies have their uses, but they tended to be sterile recitations of facts. Nowhere did those words capture the warmth of Madge Stone's greeting or the joy in her smile. She wore a beige caftan embroidered with red braid and an arresting gold necklace depicting a crouching cat. I recognized it immediately as the *Cartier* panther, a pricey bauble that made a statement about her love for animals, exquisite taste, and ability to indulge it.

"I'm not a hugger," Madge said, "but I feel that I know you already, Marky.

Violet does brag a teeny bit about you."

My aunt shook her head dismissively and grinned at her friend. "All of her exploits are the unvarnished truth. My niece is a gifted artist and entrepreneur."

"You forgot to mention sleuth." A nicely modulated voice in a faintly mocking tone announced the arrival of Teagen Doyle, celebrity, and honored guest. I may have backed up a step, but I couldn't be sure. No doubt Ms. Doyle inspired awe and insecurity among most of those she met, especially women. She towered over my five feet seven frame, willowy and elegant in a peach concoction that must have cost the earth. Garments aside, it was her enormous green eyes that mesmerized me. Teagen might have played Medea in another life. How many moths had perished after having been lured to her flame? I wondered.

Violet was unfazed by encountering this vision. She gave the actress a friendly greeting and embraced her as casually as if she were her next-door neighbor. "Lovely as ever, Mrs. Doyle. That hairstyle suits you."

Teagen's auburn tresses were artfully arranged in what the tabloids call a messy bun. Most women would have looked disheveled; on her, it was sublime.

Madge sighed. "She puts most of us to shame. Look at my mop of hair. Must be that elixir she keeps bragging about. Of course, you don't play second fiddle to anyone, Violet." She herded us to the dining room table and performed introductions. One of the guests especially intrigued me. Madge put her arm around a slim woman with casually styled blonde locks and a classic profile. "This is my cousin, Letty. She's the power behind all my good works, especially the animal charities. No one can wheedle money from donors like Letty. It's magical."

Letty's slim cheeks flushed as her cousin praised her. "Don't believe Madge. I'm just her assistant and factotum. Madge has all the computer skills. I still write everything longhand. Bad case of carpal tunnel syndrome that won't go away." She backed up as if she were trying to make herself invisible. I did a quick inventory of Letty's face and fashion. Despite her self-effacing manner with a light cosmetic touch, she would have been lovely, even beautiful. Her nondescript beige shift and unvarnished nails contrasted sharply with the eye-popping diamond gracing her left hand. Madge's cousin was indeed a study in contrasts.

I felt an immediate kinship with Letty. Humility was in short supply in this gaggle of

high-powered women. Besides, any animal lover automatically made my friend list.

Dinner was a casual affair if platters of crab, lobster, and caviar qualify. I was relieved to be seated next to my friend Kim, who playfully squeezed my arm and winked at me. "Loosen up, Sweetie. You look amazing. Every woman here envies you."

Kim, lovely, sophisticated Kim was surely joking. Several of my fellow guests were occasional customers of Poppet, but they patronized the shop when Violet was around. Gemma and I were regarded merely as the hired help. Not Kim. We'd bonded over our love of animals and the resolution of her late son's death. Sitting near her was a confidence booster for me, particularly when I caught Teagen Doyle staring at me with an odd expression on her exquisite face. I tried to remain neutral, but the woman's gaze was disquieting. No reason to delude myself. In this august gathering, I was closer to the hired help than the higher-ups.

No surprise. Dinner was sublime. I tried to skip dessert but was seduced by the tantalizing sight of crème Brule, served in individual cups. Madge and her other guests attacked the sweet treat with gusto, but Teagen abstained. Small wonder that she'd kept her enviable face and figure intact.

"This dessert is fabulous," Violet told Madge. "I should have followed Teagen's example, but I couldn't resist."

"Don't give her too much credit," Madge laughed. "She's highly allergic to dairy. Nuts too. Teagen succumbs to other temptations often enough."

Afterwards, we gathered in the great room, a cavernous space that truly justified its name. As I sipped a Perrier, I noticed that once again Teagen Doyle was staring at me. Her gaze was both intense and unnerving. I pretended not to notice, but to no avail. The woman was magnetic, with a force field that left me powerless in her thrall. Letty Briggs stayed on the fringes of the group, giving the guest of honor a wide berth. I wondered if it was natural reticence or some personal animus between them.

Aunt Violet gently elbowed me. "What's wrong, Marky? You look ossified."

I shook myself and flashed a very unconvincing grin her way. "It's Teagen. She creeps me out. Maybe I'm just awed by her or something."

Violet frowned. "Oh, pish tosh. Let's go talk to her. Teagen is human, just like everyone else. You'll see."

She didn't drag me over to the guest of honor, but I must admit that I wasn't eager to observe the social niceties. Fortunately, Madge intervened. Her warm smile melted the ice encasing my brain and made me a bit braver. Marky Davis was no coward. Not really.

"You haven't met Teagen yet, have you? I know she's dying to meet you." Madge clutched my arm and steered me toward her guest. Her technique was reminiscent of the herding instinct exhibited by my collie, Fantasia. I heard my aunt chuckle as she witnessed the scene.

Face to face, Mrs. Doyle was less intimidating than I'd feared. For one thing, I noticed some tiny lines around her eyes that weren't visible from afar. Call me petty, but it helped to find that this idol had feet of flesh after all. Her steely gaze, about which the press so often rhapsodized, was magnificent though. She pinned me in place as firmly as if I were a trapped butterfly. Teagen extended an impeccably manicured hand and gave me a perfunctory handshake.

I tend to babble when I'm nervous, and this occasion was no exception. "I'm one of your fans, Ms. Doyle. So nice to meet you."

Violet interrupted before I embarrassed myself by gushing. "My Niece is a double threat, as I've mentioned. Art and artistry in cosmetics. You two have much in common."

Teagen's tight smile said that she very much doubted that. However, she managed to nod pleasantly as she surveyed me from head to toe. "Madge boasts about some of your exploits. Rather unusual to combine crime solving with business acumen and painting."

"A young woman of many talents," said Violet, gazing fondly at me. "Do tell us all about your new venture, Teagen. Health potions, I understand.

Brendan must be proud."

Teagen stiffened at the mention of her husband and shrugged. "I suppose so. He's off on one of his European jaunts, otherwise he would have joined us."

"Where to this time?" Violet asked. "Some exotic spot, no doubt."

Teagen shrugged. "I'm not certain. You of all people understand how whimsical my husband is."

A look passed between them that was fraught with meaning. Unfortunately, I couldn't decipher it, and my aunt showed no reaction. Not one bit.

Madge shook her head. "Honestly. I don't know how the two of you manage such demanding careers. Maybe now you can settle down in Harbor Bay and just relax." She patted her friend on the shoulder. "Tomorrow, we start house hunting in earnest. I know just the spot for the Doyles. Beauty and seclusion."

When Violet asked what they had in mind, I envisioned a palatial pad comparable to Madge's. Harbor Bay had several gated communities where the rich and nearly famous congregated. Teagen dismissed that theory immediately.

"Nothing special. Something simple. Just a pied-à-terre."

"Doogie Kinkaid is handling things," Madge said. "You know how efficient he is. I expected him to join us tonight, but he landed some hot prospect from Chicago and had to cancel."

We chatted a few more minutes before Madge led her guest away after urging us to mingle. Before they left, Teagen turned to me. "I'd like to discuss something with you. Business. I'll call tomorrow."

That startled me, but I managed to keep my composure. "Sounds good."

Violet gave me a knowing look. "Seems like you were a hit, my dear. Teagen doesn't warm up to most people. Comes from being in the limelight, I suspect. Make the most of it."

Before I could answer, a disturbance akin to a hurricane-force wind blew in. Conversation paused as a man I immediately recognized as Brendan Doyle entered the room. Correction. He commanded the room and every bit of space in it. It seemed to shrink around him. Doyle aroused the carnal instincts of every sentient female, me included. An effect that was not lost upon his wife. Six plus feet of testosterone-infused presence was complemented by a sculpted body and a shock of flaming red hair with a matching beard. As he advanced toward us, I noted the piercing blue eyes that had likely eviscerated many a business competitor or wooed a willing female. He was indeed a force of nature and a fitting partner to his lovely spouse. For once, internet rumors that touted his appeal appeared to be true.

"Brendan, you old devil." Madge planted a sisterly kiss on his cheek. "We didn't expect you so soon. Wasn't Europe exciting enough for you?"

"Couldn't bear being away from my bride any longer." Brendan put his arm around Teagen and embraced her. His faintly lascivious wink was tempered by a boyishness that only augmented his charm. "Besides, I've got some things to attend to in Harbor Bay." He glanced at the dining room table. "Any scraps left around here? I'm famished."

Madge crooked her finger his way. "Come along with me, you reprobate. I'll fix you a plate."

Before he joined her, Brendan spotted Violet and let out a yell. "Violet Davis! What in the world? And who's this lovely lass standing beside you?"

My aunt remained perfectly poised, seemingly immune to his charms. "Didn't you know? I live in Harbor Bay now, and this beauty is my Niece, Marketta."

A look passed between them. A knowing look that suggested a bond stronger than mere acquaintance had once existed. That didn't surprise me one bit. Although she seldom mentioned it, Violet had left a trail of broken hearts from Paris to Harbor Bay. She maintained a dignified silence about any liaisons, past or present, but occasionally she supplied a tidbit or two. My aunt was old school that way.

As I shook Brendan's hand, I saw that Teagen had pursed her lips into a pronounced moue, leaving no doubt that she was all too familiar with her husband's antics. For my part, I pegged the exuberant Mr. Doyle as a harmless flirt, a sprightly Irish setter with a surplus of energy who needed to be brought to heel.

Madge soon led him away, but Teagen didn't follow. She swallowed twice and, speaking in a hoarse whisper, told me that she'd see me the next day at Poppet. It was a command more than a request, but curiosity led me to accept. Violet laughed as the redoubtable Mrs. Doyle vanished into the crowd without saying another word.

"Quite a conundrum," she said. "Seems like you passed the Teagen test."

"Huh?" Sometimes, under stress, my vocabulary lags a bit. I was still transfixed by the intensity of her presence and the message it conveyed.

"She's quite discerning. Makes her mind up about people immediately and never alters it." Violet brushed a stray hair from my shoulder. "Obviously, she wants something. Might be business or personal. Either way, it should be quite intriguing."

As the party gradually disbanded, we thanked our hostess and prepared to leave. Madge pulled us aside and, after checking for eavesdroppers, spoke sotto voce.

"Take care of Teagen, won't you? I know I can count on your discretion, Violet."

My aunt clutched her friend's hand. "Naturally. She's quite a close friend, I gather."

Madge nodded. "Yes. We've been like sisters since grade school. And something's bothering her. She won't confide in me, but for some reason, she wants to see your niece."

My mind buzzed with possibilities. What in the world could I, an erstwhile artist and cosmetic purveyor, offer this gorgeous celebrity? Teagen Doyle had everything—fame, fortune, and a smoking hot hubby with a roving eye. Maybe that was it. Something told me that her philandering spouse was at the core of whatever troubled Teagen. If so, as one of love's unlucky losers, I was scarcely the person to consult. Every time I thought of Dr. Roddy Park, I pinched myself, hoping that this time I'd finally struck romantic gold. But Teagen Doyle had found the mother lode in Brendan, a titan of industry who obviously adored her. Or did he? Appearances were often deceiving, and I couldn't forget the gleam in his eyes when he spied my aunt.

As we buckled ourselves into Violet's Mercedes and sped off, I debated which version of the story was true. Little did I know that the answer would present itself that very next day.

Chapter Three

From the moment she arrived at Poppet that next morning, Gemma Watts rapidly worked herself into a frenzy. She demanded a word-for-word account of everything that had transpired the previous evening. Teagen's wardrobe, attitude, and conversation were her primary interest, although she also demanded a description of Madge's mansion and other guests. In typical Gemma fashion, she gave me a capsule version of the life and trials of Letty Briggs.

"She starred in one of my favorite soaps. Always played the girl next door. Then suddenly poof! She disappeared." Gemma scratched her head. "Come to think of it, Teagen Doyle was on that same show. Crazy, huh?"

When I mentioned that Teagen planned to drop in during business hours, Gemma clutched her heart and fanned herself vigorously.

"Oh, my goodness!" She grabbed a magnifying mirror and inspected every inch of her face and hair, looking for flaws and who knew what else. A lesser being would have suffered a panic attack.

"Calm yourself, partner. Mrs. Doyle is human just like the rest of us." That statement was a blatant lie, but it had the desired effect on Gemma. She powered down and perched on one of our makeup stools.

"Should we offer her a latte? Maybe I'll pop over to the patisserie and score some scones or croissants. Seems like the polite thing to do."

That made me laugh. Considering Teagen's svelte physique, I doubted that carbs ever touched those perfect lips. Her abstemious habits were on full display last evening when that yummy crème Brule appeared. Unlike the rest of us gluttons, Teagen turned aside without even sampling the tasty treat. Perhaps Brendan Doyle satisfied any cravings she might have.

Gemma wasn't easily deterred. She spent an inordinate amount of time speculating about just what Teagen wanted from me. Certainly not beauty advice. I recognized that and so did she.

"No offense, Marky, but the Teagen Touch is one of the top beauty blogs in the universe. Not that she hawks her own stuff. Her personal makeup artist does a how-to that's surprisingly good. You know, applying eyeliner for that cat eye look of hers and sharing her other beauty secrets."

Gemma meant no harm. I knew that and yet I couldn't help feeling the teensiest bit hurt by her comments. I prided myself on being a beauty resource specialist, even though I didn't plaster my face all over the internet. Teagen Doyle might want my advice, or perhaps she wanted to assess the business climate in Harbor Bay before launching her supplements. Gemma was more focused on dishing the dirt than fantasizing about business. She segued seamlessly into her next line of inquiry without pausing to catch her breath.

"So, what was Brendan Doyle like? If he's half as magnetic as the tabloids report, I'll bet you were bowled over." Gemma's eyes widened as she visualized that titan of industry and major hottie. I suspected that she was more intrigued by his physical attributes than his business balance sheets.

"To be frank, he's overwhelming, both physically and personally. Sort of like a gale force wind sweeping away everything in his path. That's my initial impression, but it's not conclusive. I barely had a chance to assess him. Ask Aunt Violet. She's known him for years. Who knows, maybe he'll join his wife when she stops in here."

That possibility made Gemma nearly fall off the stool. "OMG! I won't survive meeting both at once!"

At that moment, Aunt Violet sauntered into our store. Despite a barrage of questions from Gemma, she merely smiled enigmatically and fired up the espresso machine. "I got a text from Madge this morning. She and Teagen will swing round at about noon. That passes for early hours in their world."

I gulped, fearing the worst but hoping for the best. "Any idea what she wants?"

"Don't worry. According to Madge, this is strictly a business meeting. Just relax and treat her like any other customer. Fawning never works with someone like Teagen. Celebrities tire of it, and they aren't moved by flattery."

"What's the deal with her hubby?" Gemma asked. "Any chance he'll show up too?"

"I doubt it. This business venture is strictly her domain. I think Teagen wants something of her own that is separate from him." Violet grinned. "Not that she'll turn down any seed money he offers. That would be quite ill-advised."

Although we busied ourselves helping several customers, I couldn't help glancing at my watch more than once. When the magic hour arrived, Teagen Doyle alighted from Madge's Rolls and entered Poppet as if she were once again strolling the red carpet. Today, she had abandoned her finery, choosing to wear a simple white silk jumpsuit that clung to her like a second skin. On most women, it would have looked outrageous. She managed to carry it off with aplomb.

Gemma gaped conspicuously until I elbowed her in her side. "No fawning. Remember what Violet said."

She recovered and managed to greet our distinguished guests with some semblance of dignity. Word of mouth was deadly in a small community, and Harbor Bay was no different. A gaggle of local women slowly drifted into the store, trying mightily to act nonchalant but staring at our captive celebrity. Violet flashed them a warm smile and immediately led them away from Teagen. "Why don't you go into the conference room, Marky. Gemma and I will serve our customers."

Teagen glided into our newly refurbished conference area, which had formerly served as a storeroom. Once again, I breathed a silent prayer of thanks for my aunt and her sense of effortless chic that had transformed a utilitarian spot into a mini-French salon. Our guest nodded her head in approval.

"Nice touch," she said, accepting an espresso. "I like plenty of sweetener in mine. A vice I know, but so be it. No dairy, of course."

How refreshing to find that this paragon of beauty had at least one flaw!

Teagen sipped her drink and immediately got down to business.

"I need your help," she said. "Kim says you're trustworthy and Violet adores you."

I was speechless. A feeble nod was all I could manage, and even that took effort. What kind of help could I offer this goddess of cinematic glory? She knew more about beauty than I could ever hope for, and her face and figure proved it. Perhaps she was interested in art. I was on firmer ground there. Portrait painting was a specialty of mine after all. I'd already snared a few commissions in Harbor Bay and elsewhere and hoped for more.

Teagen leaned over and whispered so softly I could barely hear her. Her expression radiated anxiety and something else. When she clutched my hand, her fingers felt like icy harbingers of doom.

"It's a stalker," she whispered. "I think someone's trying to kill me."

My eyes widened, and my throat felt dry. Surely, I had misunderstood. Was this some sort of Hollywood hoax or prank? She strengthened her grip until I winced in pain.

"I don't understand. What can I do? I'm no detective. You must know plenty of professionals who could help you. Your husband must have a security force."

"That's just it." Teagen leaned back in the fauteuil and relaxed. "Don't you see? The press would love to pounce on this. Brendan has spies everywhere. He already thinks I'm hysterical and seeking attention." She ran her fingers through her hair. Anyone else would have looked ravaged. It only enhanced her looks.

"The establishment leaks like a sieve. *TMZ*, *Page Six*...you name it. They'd salivate at even a hint of scandal. I can't take that chance. Brendan's too clever, too well-connected. He'd use it against me in a divorce action. You know, aging spouse feigns danger to thwart husband's infidelity." She lowered her head. "I've had several episodes in the past. All hushed up, but proof exists."

"Episodes?" This entire scene had gone from weird to fantastic.

Teagen closed her eyes. "Psychiatric ones. Mostly due to exhaustion, but we managed to keep them private. Not good for one's career to be considered a risk, you know. That's why I can't involve Brendan. He'd pop me into some nice place for rich loonies."

I was in a quandary. Should I find some tactful way to disengage or risk encouraging this woman? My curiosity was aroused, but the situation seemed surreal.

"Why do you think you're in danger? Has anything specific happened?"

Teagen opened her purse and extracted a sheet of paper. It was heavy vellum with the name Teagen Doyle engraved at the top. "I know you think I'm being a diva but suspend judgment for a moment."

She adjusted a pair of gold reading glasses on the tip of her nose and recited a litany of events that on the face of it sounded mighty suspicious. If only Aunt Violet would join us. She was a shrewd judge of character. Far better than I.

"I've always known that Brendan played around," Teagen said with a shrug. "It's not unusual in our set, and it was something I was prepared to accept even though it hurt my pride. The watchword, though, was discretion. Lately, his little dalliances have become more public. Fodder for the tabloids."

"I still don't understand. Seems like he's in more danger than you are. Why not get a divorce?"

"That's just it. Brendan is a big-time Catholic. Doesn't believe in divorce despite the irony. Apparently, the sixth commandment is optional in his book. Plus, he has political aspirations. There's a senate vacancy looming in Michigan, and he's been approached. With me, the loving wife at his side, he's probably a shoe-in."

She still had me stumped. Why kill his wife if Brendan Doyle wanted to seek public office? Previous pols had long ago lowered the bar for infidelity.

Teagen continued as if everything was perfectly normal. "I have a stalker, some creep who sends me lewd messages on Facebook and always seems to know my phone number even though I change it. Brendan must give it to him. I'm sure of that. Besides, before I moved here, my home was broken into. Nothing important taken except personal items like photos and letters." She lowered her eyes. "Some underwear too. Disgusting."

"Can't the authorities help? After all, there are anti-stalking laws in most states."

She shook her head. "I tried that. Basically, they said, until something happens, they can't act. Great endorsement for the cops, isn't it? Become a corpse, and then they'll act. Besides, they immediately questioned Brendan. He went ballistic, of course, and threw a fit."

I paused, waiting for her to say something, anything, that involved me.

"Look. You know Harbor Bay and everyone in it. Just keep an eye out for strangers and tell me anything that you might hear. Anything at all."

During the summer season, our sleepy little town ballooned into a city on steroids. That's when anyone could infiltrate the community, especially if Teagen's new venture generated publicity.

I shrugged helplessly. "I'll do what I can, but I can't promise anything. Do you have any information about your stalker? Like a description, age, gender, race. You know the drill."

She shook her head. "Just a creepy feeling. Like I'm being followed. Madge noticed it too. Yesterday, someone delivered two dozen red roses to me." She frowned. "I loathe roses. Anyone who knows me wouldn't do that. Besides, how would anyone know my address?"

The name Doogie Kinkaid immediately sprang to mind. That garrulous gent had likely spread the word about Teagen to a few select pals who probably shared the scoop with their friends. Before long, the entire town of Harbor Bay knew the whereabouts of Teagen and probably her breakfast menu. Nothing was sacred in a village that thrived on gossip.

"It's a puzzle," I said. "Why not find a reputable private investigator? They're pros at this. Besides, how would I explain being around you all the time? We scarcely move in the same circles."

Teagen raised her voice and stared me down. "I heard you were smart, but obviously I was misinformed. Forget I said anything." She abruptly gathered her purse, rose, and stalked out the door. Fortunately, Poppet was empty by that time, except for Gemma, Aunt Violet, and Madge. The trio shared looks of amazement as they watched Teagen exit our store. Madge hurried after her friend, leaving me to piece together a narrative.

Gemma didn't mince words. "What happened? You didn't insult her, did you, Marky? You know how blunt you can be."

That remark left me speechless. Talk about the pot and the kettle! Gemma Watts was infamous for blunt remarks that often bordered on outrageous. By contrast, I was Miss Milquetoast, Marky Davis, good girl.

Violet calmly strolled over to the door, locked it, and flipped on the closed sign. "Let's regroup. Can you fill us in, Marky, or was your talk confidential?"

I repeated Teagen's conversation word for word. In retelling, it seemed even more bizarre. Perhaps the woman was having a psychiatric break. More likely, she was merely a drama queen, a diva seeking attention from a wandering spouse.

Gemma folded her arms. "Sounds to me like she's nuts. No normal person would ask a beauty expert for help. Not if she was really scared. No offense Marky but you're no Sherlock Holmes."

For once, my partner was correct. Although I'd stumbled into danger before, it was strictly by accident. I had no wish to embroil myself in the affairs of an entitled, fading celebrity. I turned to my aunt for approval.

"I agree that the entire episode seems strange," Violet said. "Madge did say that Teagen was uneasy. Who knows what her motive was? Brendan can be quite a handful, and this may be her way of getting his attention." She patted my knee. "You were wise to extricate yourself from the drama, Marky. I'll speak with Kim tomorrow. Maybe she has some insight on this situation."

At that moment, a most pleasant interruption occurred. A text from Roddy Park reminded me that he would arrive the next day. I breathed a sigh of relief as visions of romance supplanted those of intrigue.

A sound night's sleep put the entire episode with Teagen Doyle into perspective. No need to overreact. The celebrity crowd was prone to exaggeration if the tabloids and internet sites were even half accurate. Teagen probably felt neglected in our sleepy little burg and wanted to make a big splash. She was welcome to the attention, but she could do it without my help. I felt relief tinged with a touch of regret. Truth be told, Teagen's glamorous world held some allure for me. Life in Harbor Bay was lackluster, especially from New Year's to Easter when so many residents fled to warmer climes. I paired an espresso with a solitary slice of toast and one scrambled egg. Moderation in most things was Aunt Violet's watchword, and her face and figure were proof positive of its efficacy. Curbing the desire to stuff my face, I harnessed my faithful collie, Fantasia, instead. A brisk two-mile walk would make me feel virtuous and satiated. It would prepare me for my date with Roddy Park as well. He was surrounded by nubile coeds who most likely flung themselves at his head. No sense in suffering by comparison.

As soon as I returned to Poppet, my cell phone buzzed. The number was unfamiliar, cloaked in anonymity. It was likely Spam, but something made me respond. I recognized my caller's throaty voice immediately. Teagen Doyle. How in the world did she get my private number?

"Ms. Davis," said she without identifying herself. "I called to apologize and ask your indulgence. I behaved very badly yesterday. You see, I've become used to everyone doing my bidding. Except Brendan of course."

Curiosity and a touch of malice overwhelmed me. "Mrs. Doyle?"

Teagen proceeded as though I hadn't interrupted. "I thought things through and spoke with Madge. I have a proposition that might appeal to you. Something that would solve both our concerns."

I should have stopped her straight away, but I stayed silent. Call it cowardice, or curiosity. It was a mixture of both.

"Madge says you occasionally paint portraits. Suppose I commission one of me. That would provide you with a handsome fee and a way to observe things on site."

The proposal was crazy, totally outrageous. I loved it! Teagen Doyle was an artist's dream, lovely, mercurial, and ruthless. Any of my painting peers would leap at the chance. Aesthetics aside, the prospect of a sizable fee also appealed to me. Poppet could certainly use an infusion of cash.

I tamped down my enthusiasm, knowing that luminaries like Teagen expected serfs like me to leap to their tune.

"That sounds feasible. Perhaps we can meet to finalize the details?"

The relief in her voice sounded genuine. "Oh, thank you, Marky. Madge suggested we meet for dinner at that French bistro in town. I forget the name."

"I have a guest with me this weekend," I said.

"No problem. Bring him or her with you. My treat." Teagen radiated charm now that her ends had been achieved. "How does eight o'clock sound? And bring Violet if she's available."

"Perfect. I'll ask her."

Gemma gasped when I shared my news. Aunt Violet was more contained.

"OMG," Gemma said. "You're hooked. You're going to do it? She trapped you, snookered you into getting involved."

"Don't be so hasty, Gemma. Marky's career could get a huge boost from Teagen and her friends. Recognition, maybe even fame. She deserves it." My aunt patted my arm. "It certainly wouldn't hurt to listen. See what conditions Teagen imposes."

"You'll come with me tonight?" Having Violet along would soothe my jumbled nerves.

Gemma stood, hands on hips. "And what about the delectable Dr. Park? I'd never expose him to a barracuda like Teagen. Benny is strictly off limits around her."

I bit my tongue. No need to mention that bumbling Benny Soto was unlikely to attract Teagen's notice. He was passable until he opened his mouth and exposed his idiocy to one and all. Gemma doted on him and excused his forays into the bizarre as charming eccentricities. In truth, the man was a boob who brandished his badge and gun as a substitute for intelligent conversation. I prayed that Gemma would realize that before she took the plunge and became Mrs. Soto.

"I'm sure Roddy can resist Teagen's charms," Violet said. "After all, he's surrounded by coeds all week and hasn't succumbed. Why don't we focus on the situation at hand? Perhaps Teagen's being honest. Her life may be in danger."

I had a sudden inspiration. "If Brendan Doyle is plotting against his wife, I need a chance to assess him. Why not include him in the painting? I'd get a chance to study him."

Violet clapped her hands. "Excellent, Marky. He's quite egocentric. I'm positive Brendan would love the chance to be painted by you. Just be prepared for his nonsense. He's quite the ladies' man."

Time passed quickly as we serviced an influx of customers that day. Normally, I loved bus tours filled with affluent riders who swarmed our little hamlet. Most were female, cash-laden, and eager to try the potions and services Poppet featured. Roddy's arrival and our tete-a-tete with Teagen complicated matters. I'd envisioned having a leisurely afternoon to pamper myself and had even saved a special outfit that might catch his eye. Nothing risqué, of course. Despite his incredible looks, Roddy focused more on intellect than appearance, but as Gemma reminded me before she shooed me up to my apartment, he was still a man. Looking my best wouldn't hurt.

I prided myself on my hair. It wasn't vanity, simply reality. Nature had gifted me with wavy, natural blonde locks that most men noticed. A cosmetic touch enlivened my eyes, and a hint of blush made my cheeks bloom. A red silk slip dress and stilettos completed the look. It wasn't often that I glammed up, and seeing Roddy was worth the effort. I dared not try to compete with Teagen. I knew my limitations, and that was a bridge way too far.

When I entered Poppet, I heard grunts and groans of pleasure that sounded orgasmic. That didn't worry me. He was stretched out on a table, savoring a neck and shoulder massage from Gemma. Professor Roddy Park was tall, trim, and gorgeous with perfectly fashioned features and a wealth of glossy black hair worn in a ponytail. Best of all, this monument to masculine beauty was oblivious to his impact on women. Unlike many men, he had no clue that he was catnip to every sentient female within fifty miles. Roddy lived and breathed politics. Ask him the names of the current President's cabinet secretaries, and he could rattle them off immediately. Offer an opinion on the Supreme Court, and he could cite their decisions chapter and verse. But when it came to art or fashion, he was a total philistine.

"Enjoying yourself?" I asked.

Gemma snickered, and Roddy leapt to his feet. "Gosh, Marky. I didn't see you there. Gemma took pity on my poor, stiff muscles." He stretched. "That felt magical. After grading papers all day, I was stiff as a board."

"Lucky you, Marky." Gemma whooped at the double entendre. "No woman wants a man who's too relaxed. I hope Benny's the same way."

Roddy looked me up and down and smiled. "Wow! You look great. Tonight, must be special."

I took his hand and led him into our office. Naturally, Roddy had no clue who Teagen Doyle was, but he had keen instincts when it came to danger. I summarized Teagen's plans for me in a few sentences.

Roddy went on high alert. "Hold on, Marky. That sounds like a dicey situation. I don't know anything about his wife, but I have heard of Brendan Doyle. All those money moguls are tough customers, and getting involved in marital squabbles isn't smart. Stay out of it."

I dismissed his comments with a shrug. "My cover's perfect—painting a portrait of his wife. What man could resist that? Besides, the exposure would boost my credentials as an artist, not a detective."

Roddy's frown told me he wasn't happy. That's when I fired the big guns. "Aunt Violet knows about it, and she approves." I ruffled his hair. "Aw, come on. Don't be a fuddy duddy."

He shook his head but couldn't help grinning. "Okay, but I'll be watching both of you tonight. No one expects a dull professor to be involved in skullduggery, so that's my cover."

Roddy was anything but dull; however, I welcomed his input. "Come on," I said. "We don't want to be late for the party."

Teagen reserved a private room at Giverny, the bistro that passed as a hot spot in Harbor Bay. When we arrived, the other guests were already seated, and several appeared to be well-lubricated. Magnums of champagne, La Grande Dame Veuve Clicquot, were placed on the table, thereby loosening tongues and good sense. When Doogie Kinkaid, seated between Teagen and Madge, saw us, he tipped his glass in a toast.

"Hail to the artist," he chirped. His eyes widened when he spied Roddy. "And who is your handsome escort?"

Teagen Doyle immediately rose and welcomed us. Her emerald frock, complemented by a necklace and earrings of the same color, was nothing short of spectacular. Almost any woman would have suffered in comparison, and I was no exception. Her lovely eyes slithered up and down Roddy's body like a serpent recalling scenes from the Garden of Eden. Most men would have quickly succumbed to her spell, but he merely nodded politely and took his seat. I glanced across the table at my aunt and noted a bemused expression on her face. Violet was unfazed by high drama especially power plays between the sexes. She'd starred in plenty of them herself.

I scanned the room for Roddy and was glad to see him engrossed in a spirited discussion with Lionel Stevens, acerbic spouse of my friend Kim.

Letty Briggs was absent, and I wondered if Teagen had excluded her or if Letty had avoided the gathering on her own. The atmosphere between the two had seemed icy the other evening. Doogie would probably know the full story.

One of our party was less sanguine. Brendan Doyle shot a malevolent look at his wife and took a healthy swig of his champagne. He nudged Madge and whispered something inaudible in her ear.

Madge laughed and playfully elbowed him. "You're such a reprobate, Brendan. Now behave yourself for a change."

I stole a glance at the tempting buffet laid out behind us. Fresh fruit, ahi tuna, oysters on a bed of spinach, and petit fours beckoned with a siren song. Teagen urged her guests to partake, although she stayed apart from the crowd. The woman probably never stuffed herself with the gusto I was suddenly feeling, and that likely explained her enviable figure. Doogie, Brendan, and Roddy had no such inhibitions. They piled their plates high with the tempting spread. I edged in behind my aunt and tried to be abstemious or at least appear to be. No petit fours for this girl. No sir! Violet smiled and nodded approvingly. She knew me too well to be deceived.

After dinner, Teagen rose and addressed her guests. Her speech was charming, self-deprecating, worthy of a professional actor. She described her new business venture, Teagen's Tinctures, and praised me for accepting a commission to paint her. All the while, I watched Brendan Doyle's reaction to his wife. His smile looked forced, and he cast his eyes down as she spoke. When Teagen saluted him for his unflagging support, Brendan rose and bowed. The entire scene felt scripted. It resembled a set piece in a fourth-rate melodrama rather than a genuine moment. If he had evil designs upon his wife, it wasn't apparent to me, but then I suspected that Brendan, the hero of many boardroom dramas, was an actor almost as accomplished as his wife.

Madge urged us to mingle as waiters circulated with after-dinner drinks. I reached for Perrier. Teagen and Madge immediately cornered Roddy, plying him with questions about his favorite subject. Violet and Brendan exchanged pleasantries, and I found myself blocked from eavesdropping by Doogie Kinkaid's considerable girth.

"Which is it, Marky?" he asked. "Painting or sleuthing?"

"Pardon me?"

"Don't play the innocent, my girl, I hear things. People confide in me."

I'm not duplicitous by nature, but I can rise to the occasion if needed. "Stuff it, Doogie. Don't ruin my fun. You know how much painting means to me. This might be my big chance for recognition. I have no other agenda."

Doogie winked at me. "Okay. If you say so." He smirked as he stepped aside.

I gave his lapel a vigorous tug. "Hold on. Not so fast, mister. Say what's on your mind for once."

Doogie's expression was avuncular and a tad patronizing. "Dear girl—so pretty, yet so young and naive. Listen closely to Uncle Doogie. Not once in her star-studded, privileged life has Teagen Doyle ever helped another woman. Especially one as lovely as you. Teagen is a user, a charming entertaining one, it's true, but quite cold-blooded. After you've served your purpose, she'll discard you like yesterday's rubbish."

His words shocked me, and I couldn't help gasping. "Why, that's a horrible thing to say! How do you know that?"

He tweaked my chin and whispered. "I understand her because I'm the same way. Birds of a feather, you know. Have you wondered why Letty Briggs didn't join us? It's a cautionary tale worth knowing." With that, Doogie waddled off to join the duo surrounding Roddy, leaving me flummoxed.

I wasn't alone for long. My aunt Violet, trailed by Brendan Doyle, soon joined me.

"I believe you've met my niece, Marketta, Brendan. She's a triple threat—

talented artist, entrepreneur, and loyal friend."

Brendan Doyle took my hand and stared me down with those piercing blue eyes. "You're such a tease, Violet, leaving out one very important feather in Miss Marky's cap."

Violet's smile never faded. "Whatever do you mean?"

"I've been told on good authority that Marketta Davis is a super sleuth, with quite a track record."

I was too intimidated to try my aw-shucks routine, so I opted for candor. "Someone has been teasing you, Mr. Doyle. I've had some success unraveling puzzles, but that hardly makes me a super sleuth."

He moved closer, uncomfortably so, and whispered in my ear. The scent of liquor was on his breath.

"Don't believe everything Teagen says. My wife is delusional. Charming but delusional. And it's Brendan. All my friends call me Brendan, and I think we're going to become very good friends."

I was gob smacked, unable to react to what appeared to be an opening salvo in seduction. Fortunately, Aunt Violet once again intervened.

"Leave this child alone, Brendan. Can't you see she's already spoken for?" She nudged toward Roddy. "And may I say, Professor Park can give you a run for your money any day."

He didn't like hearing that. Brendan Doyle, the supreme alpha, was unaccustomed to being challenged, and he bristled at the thought. He turned toward Roddy, as if sizing his rival up. "Hmph," he huffed. "Just remember this, my dear Violet. Money talks more than muscles."

"Is that so?" Violet laughed. "Maybe he has both."

He stalked away and joined the gaggle surrounding Roddy. Brendan nosed into the group, parting them like Moses at the Red Sea. The comparison between the two men was interesting to observe. Both were tall and trim, although Brendan was twice Roddy's' age. His body language suggested a Doberman pincher prowling the perimeter to reclaim territory. From my experience walking Fantasia, I'd seen his canine counterpart trying to assert his status as top dog. Despite the onslaught from this captain of industry, Roddy remained perfectly poised, a confident Labrador Retriever eager to befriend everyone. Unlike Brendan, he exuded a sweetness that had first drawn me to him.

"Quite a picture, isn't it?" Kim Stevens sidled up to me and discreetly pointed toward them. "Boys and their toys. Even Lionel's getting into the act at his age." I sized up my lovely pal's elegant attire, perfect makeup, and gleaming hair. Her brow was furrowed, but that did little to diminish her beauty.

"You don't seem worried that Teagen will steal Lionel away. Seduce him."

"Ha!" Kim's retort said it all. "Good luck with that. Lionel's flame flickered out some time ago. Thank heaven for prurient novels. They feed my imagination and nourish the soul."

She blushed as if that was more information than she'd intended to share. "Don't mind me, Marky. I'm lucky, and I know it."

I hastily switched topics. "What's your take on this business venture—Teagen's Tinctures?"

Kim bit her lip as she formed a response. "Sounds like a winner to me if Teagen's behind it. She's the best advertisement for her products, anyway. Believe it or not, she got Lionel to invest. Major miracle! You know how tight-fisted he is with his money. He's absolutely besotted by her."

"She is glamorous. Somewhat competitive with her hubby, though. I suppose that's natural with two big egos in one family. What's your take on Brendan?"

Kim shrugged. "Your typical bad boy with a master of the universe complex. I met tons like him when I was modeling. Oh, he's one hot number to be sure. Just don't get too close to the flame or you'll be scorched."

When Roddy finally extricated himself from his fans, he ambled over to join us. I'm not the jealous type, but I'm no fool either. Feeling the "Teagen Touch" would excite any of us lesser beings. I could tell by his evasive manner that something was up.

"Enjoy yourself?" I asked with only a hint of malice. "You made quite a hit with our hostess."

His expression smacked of guilt and something else—star dust. "A very pleasant group; Friendly to an outsider." Roddy ducked his head after that fatuous statement.

Kim sensed the storm signs and excused herself.

"What did Teagen have to say to you?" I made it a casual, throwaway question.

Professor Park stammered a bit. "Well, we were discussing her business plan. You know, tactics and advertising. Teagen is very persuasive. I must admit I was impressed. She's much smarter than people might think."

There was more to it. "And…? Where do you fit in?"

"It's very tentative. She asked if I'd consider being the face of her men's line. I'm not quite sure what that entails. She was probably just being kind."

"Oh, like Nacho Figueras for *Polo*, and Daniel Henney for *Burberry*? Those ad campaigns made them international celebrities. The University of Michigan may not be big enough for you after that."

His confused look told me he had no idea what I was talking about. "You're teasing me, I know. Teagen probably won't pursue it again."

I snorted. "She'll probably pursue you, though. I understand she likes younger men. The money might be tempting. She can afford to offer plenty."

Roddy's normally even temper began to fray. "It was just talk. A throwaway conversation. Before we got into it, her husband intruded. I felt guilty even though nothing was going on. He's a major donor to the university, you know. Endowed a chair at the business school." Roddy took my hand and squeezed it. "Come on, Marky. This isn't like you. Don't spoil a nice evening. You're involved with her, too. Painting and all."

"Doogie said she uses people, especially men."

That made Roddy grin. "I have nothing to offer except my political advice. Your friend Lionel is a different matter. He must have ponied up some big bucks the way they were talking. He's a partner or something."

Before I could react, our hostess joined us. She bent over, flashing just a hint of decolletage Roddy's way. Even though he's modest, Roddy is all man. He glanced down and stared at her bare white flesh with something approaching awe.

"Oops," Teagen drawled. "Wardrobe malfunction. Happens to the best of us." She put her arm around me and whispered. "Let's discuss our venture tomorrow at your place. Does noon sound about right?"

I stammered a reply. After giving me a quick hug, she turned to Roddy. "Will you still be around, Professor?"

He nodded. "It's our semester break at the University. I hoped to spend it with Marky."

Teagen ignored any reference to me. Instead, she treated him to a blinding smile. "Great. Perhaps we can firm up my proposal then. I'll make it worth your while. Financially."

That was a double entendre if ever I heard one. Teagen whisked away and soon began chatting with Madge and Kim. I noticed Brendan Doyle glowering at her from the other side of the room. I try to avoid frowning. It promotes wrinkles, you know. This time, however, I indulged in a full-blown scowl that consumed my face and distorted my features.

Roddy was oblivious, but my fit of temper didn't escape Doogie Kinkaid. "Don't be upset, my fair lady," he crooned. "You've just gotten a dose of the Teagen Treatment. It's meaningless, believe me." He looked Roddy squarely in the face. "Although I totally understand the temptation." Doogie went on to say that the former storefront of Fanny's Fudge would house the new venture. "After extensive renovations, of course. Full steam ahead. Work starts tomorrow, and Ms. Doyle is paying premium rates for a fast finish."

I swallowed my pride and asked. "Have you found them a place to live yet?"

He dismissed that issue with a wave of his meaty paw. "No worries. They're bunking down in Madge's guest house until we find something. Teagen's very particular, but she always gets what she wants. Always." Doogie left us after slapping Roddy on the shoulder.

"Curious fellow," Roddy said. "Full of subliminal messages. No matter. Here's one that anyone can decipher." He pulled me close. "Let's ditch this shindig and discuss things back at your place. We've been apart way too long."

He was right. That was one message that I couldn't refuse.

Chapter Four

After a night with Roddy, I felt renewed. Doubts about Teagen Doyle and her intentions were swept away by the tender lovemaking of Professor Park, whose expertise was not limited to politics. As Gemma frequently reminds me, I have a checkered past when it comes to relationships. Exercise caution, I told myself. Don't commit to someone until you are certain. Aunt Violent brushed off my doubts. She lived by another credo—follow your heart and let the chips fall where they will. Faint heart had never won the romantic sweepstakes, and my dear Aunt had won the love lottery plenty of times. Her current suitor, a United States Senator, was so besotted by her that he bombarded her with gifts, texts, and invites to snazzy affairs. Since she was famously tight-lipped about her relationships, I had no idea where the romance stood.

While Roddy jogged around Harbor Bay, I prepared myself to do battle with the formidable Teagen Doyle. I took my lovely Fantasia for her morning walk during which I rehearsed every possible scenario that might confront me. Fantasia, my faithful canine companion, urged me on with tail wags and doggy kisses. She buoyed my confidence, which faltered in the face of perfect creatures like Teagen. One glance at my watch confirmed that I had just enough time for a beauty blitz before our encounter. To my dismay, when I sailed into Poppet, I found a beaming twosome awaiting me. Roddy, accompanied by that paragon of perfection, Teagen Doyle, was sipping espresso and exchanging bon mots. He wore an arresting outfit of a college sweatshirt and shorts. Exercise had only highlighted his taut muscles and sculpted abs. Sweat became him in a manner that activated every one of my senses and several areas too private to mention. Apparently, Teagen shared my reaction. While she managed to fawn over Dr. Park without drooling, her admiration was openly on display.

"We bumped into each other on the square," Roddy said, "Mrs. Doyle wanted espresso, and I needed a caffeine fix myself."

She slapped his arm playfully and a tad suggestively. "Please. Call me Teagen. Mrs. Doyle is some stodgy old woman."

Roddy blushed. "You're anything but stodgy. And certainly not old."

I fought to retain my composure. Suppressing the tart response nestling on the tip of my tongue was difficult, but I managed.

Fantasia tried to greet Teagen but was immediately rebuffed.

"Don't worry," I said. "She's very gentle."

"It's not that. Animals annoy me. All that saliva and flying fur." Teagen curled her lip. "Ugh. It's so unsanitary."

I was offended on behalf of my beautiful collie and the entire animal kingdom. Fantasia showed more class and breeding than either Teagen or I did. She backed away and focused her attention on Roddy, who buried his head in her thick coat.

"You'll have to excuse me while I get dressed." I retrieved Fantasia's lead and turned to Roddy. "Come along, Professor. We can share the bathroom while you get cleaned up."

Teagen's smile was forced. "Of course. Take your time. I'll browse your shelves while I wait."

My business partner seldom resembles a savior, but when Gemma Watts swept into Poppet, I swore that she had sprouted wings. "You guys sure start early," Gemma said. "Is this a private party or can I join in?"

"We were just leaving," I said. "Do you have time to give Mrs. Doyle a massage while she waits?"

What Gemma lacks in formal education, she more than compensates for with emotional intelligence. She immediately sized up the tense situation and diffused it.

"Delighted. Come with me, Mrs. D." She led Teagen toward a treatment room while giving me a broad wink.

I sped up the stairs to my apartment without speaking. *"Don't play the jealous card, Marky. Roddy doesn't owe you anything."*

"So. Did you guys have a chance to discuss her business proposal?"

Roddy stripped off his clothes and headed for the shower. I admit that sight caused me to momentarily lose my train of thought. His physique might have been sculpted by Michelangelo himself, although, unlike the famous statue of David, who had limited assets in the pleasure department, my guy was well-endowed.

"Teagen didn't bother with details," Roddy said. "We didn't discuss money, although she assured me it would be 'substantial'. Her words, not mine. Of course, to a lowly assistant Professor, any infusion of cash is tempting."

I chose the high road, refusing to speculate about fringe benefits or other perks that might snare the unwary. Some things defied description and couldn't be reduced to monetary terms. While he showered, I grabbed my blow dryer and valiantly attempted to tame my unruly mane. One of the advantages of youth and good health was the need for only a minimal cosmetic touch. In minutes, I was camera-ready prepared to confront any romantic rival. I reminded myself that Roddy valued achievements and intellect, not glitter and glitz. Besides, Teagen was twenty years his senior. Despite those reassurances, some malevolent imp inside me whispered. *Maybe so, but Teagen Doyle is a bonified celebrity who exceeded those lofty standards.*

As he combed his thick black hair, Roddy teased me. "Cheer up, Marky. We can make this a joint venture. Profit for both of us. Working together again would be fun."

His enthusiasm was contagious, even though I recalled that our last collaboration involved a double murder. I summoned a weak smile and prepared to join the merriment.

Gemma's magical massage had improved Teagen's disposition. The tincture titan was all smiles as we gathered around the conference table. "Now let's get down to business. Dollars and cents." She brushed aside my protests when she mentioned a jaw-dropping fee for my services. "No arguments, Marky. After all, you'll be doing double duty."

Roddy, who knew little about my sleuthing, looked puzzled but maintained a poker face. I suddenly realized what a demon he must be at the card table. Teagen and I established a flexible schedule that would allow me to attend to Poppet and still maintain a presence at her studio. Her plans for Roddy were less structured. Photoshoots would be built around his teaching duties, although public appearances for both print and live campaigns were required. I noticed that his discomfort lessened every time she touched his hand or squeezed his shoulder. Familiarity with Teagen did not breed contempt. Enter Gemma once again to lighten the atmosphere.

"Roddy will be the male face of Teagen's Tinctures," she said. "I get that. But who will attract the ladies? That's where your biggest customer base will probably be. Is Marky the cover girl? She'd score big with millennials."

Teagen stiffened. "Hardly. I am the face of Teagen's Tinctures. The public expects it after all, and my appeal spans all age groups." She beamed at Roddy. "I think we'll be an unbeatable team, don't you, Professor?"

Roddy nodded. His eyes widened when Teagen mentioned the fee that his services would command. "Wow! You make it sound very tempting, Mrs. D. Is your husband on board with all this?"

A thunder cloud darkened Teagen's expression, but she managed to suppress her feelings. "Brendan has no part in this venture. It is all mine from start to finish."

"I understand Lionel Stevens is an investor," I said. "He's acerbic but a very savvy businessman. Gives sound advice if you can overlook his personality."

"What personality?" Gemma quipped.

A smug expression spread across Teagen's face. "Not to worry. I've handled men like him before. I'm very adept at handling men."

I had no doubt of that. Roddy must have been deafened by dollar signs because he missed the subtext of that remark. Teagen was confident that she could impose her will on everyone, especially the males surrounding her. I wouldn't bet against her.

She vanished just before Poppet's official opening after promising to phone later with more details. There was a prolonged silence in our store as each of us processed the whirlwind that was Teagen Doyle. I made a mental inventory of my painting supplies and debated just how I would pose my client to showcase her to her best advantage. Her physical beauty wasn't in doubt, but the challenge was how to penetrate the woman's inner psyche. I recalled her avaricious look when she glanced at Roddy. Gemma understood, although Roddy, like most men, was transfixed by her personality and beauty. I was positive that my aunt Violet could dissect Teagen with the precision of a surgeon's scalpel.

Our first customer that day was my pal, Kim Stevens. As a former runway model, she knew as much about cosmetics as I did. Kim headed straight to the Dermalogica shelf and selected several products.

"I ran out of my exfoliating powder," Kim said. "It's part of my daily routine. Always front and center in my shower."

"No wonder your complexion is perfect," I said. No need to exaggerate. At forty-five, her skin was poreless and wrinkle-free.

"Don't tell me Lionel exfoliates too," Gemma teased.

Kim laughed. "Nope. I'm afraid that ship sailed long ago. Men are so lucky. They can hide the ravages of time under a beard or mustache."

Roddy looked bored by our comments, even though we'd discussed this issue before, and I'd packed a hefty supply of *Kiehl's* for men in his suitcase. He reluctantly used them just to please me, but his interest in potions flagged until he met Teagen Doyle. As more customers drifted in, he edged out of Poppet and disappeared. Paranoia overtook me as I visualized an assignation between him and his new employer. Aunt Violet's arrival put a stop to such notions. Her calm demeanor soothed the green-eyed monster within me, forcing me to confront my insecurities.

"I ran into Madge just now," she said. "Sounds like Teagen is charging ahead with her plans." I was never adept at hiding my emotions. My woebegone expression immediately gave me away. Violet put her arm around me and hugged. "Don't tell me she reneged on having you paint her portrait."

Gemma immediately jumped in. "Guess again. Marky's worried about her man. If Teagen Doyle targeted Benny, I know how I'd react. No ordinary woman can compete with a celebrity."

"Nonsense," Violet said. "Marketta Davis bows to no man or woman.

Right, Poppet?"

I eked out a smile that didn't fool her for one moment.

"She offered very generous financial terms—to both of us."

Kim leaned in. "What's Roddy's role in this? Teagen talked about finding a male model, but nothing had been firmed up."

I forced myself to be brave. After all, as a business owner with customers to serve, I had to behave professionally. Tears were never appropriate in the workplace. Everyone knew that. Gemma lowered her voice and whispered. "He's it. Dr. Roddy Park is the male face of Teagen's Tinctures. How about them apples?"

Our door chimes announced the arrival of a deadly duo. Deputy Benny Soto trailed the impressive bulk of his mother as she marched into the shop. Josephine Soto defined the term *femme formidable.* I normally avoided both for different reasons. Benny was an abhorrent pest, and his mother, a redoubtable matron who could squash me like a bug. Today, their presence was a blessing and a welcome distraction. All discussion of Teagen and Roddy ceased as we froze in place. Even Gemma, the putative fiancée of Benny, was cowed.

Benny wasn't hideous if you favored the brash, oleaginous type. Gemma rhapsodized about his body beautiful and macho manner; however, she was far too honest to praise his intellect or sterling career prospects. Mrs. Soto was the proprietor of our local bookstore, and despite her vagaries, she was an intelligent woman and avid reader. Her devotion to Benny must be attributable to blind maternal love rather than rational thought.

"Today is Mom's birthday," Benny said, gesturing to Gemma. "Pick her out something nice. The sky's the limit."

We were all aware of the paltry salary paid to deputies in Harbor Bay. Obviously, Benny's sky was very limited indeed. Gemma was normally fearless, but Josephine reduced her to a shadow of her feisty self. Aunt Violet immediately intervened by squiring Mrs. S. around Poppet and explaining our range of products. Kim seized the opportunity to make her escape after promising to call me later. That respite allowed me to cast aside my fears about Roddy. To calm myself, I recited my mantra: *You are a strong, independent woman who will not be defined by the actions of a man, even a gorgeous intellectual.*

Those words inspired confidence and helped me survive the storms in my rocky relationships. But talk is cheap. My romantic adventures seldom ended well, or as Gemma pointedly observed, "You have rotten luck with men."

When Benny and Josephine completed their mission, I was curious.

"I haven't met your new boss yet, Benny. What's she like?" Our beloved former Chief now headed a far larger force in Traverse City, and the local council had wisely decided to recruit an outsider to fill his shoes.

Benny frowned, but before he could utter a word, Josephine Soto jumped in. "Seems like they should have picked from within," she sniffed. "No good comes from using strangers, especially females from Detroit."

"Her name is Aubrey Miles," Josephine grunted. "Funny kind of name for a woman, but what can you expect these days? Decent boys like Benny get shoved aside."

I'd read her CV in the newspaper and knew that Chief Miles held a law degree and a slew of commendations. Comparing her credentials with Benny's lackluster resume was a fool's errand. Benny, basking in the glow of maternal devotion, patted his mom on her back.

"You know how mothers are about their sons," he smirked. "Nothing and no one is good enough for them."

Gemma's normal exuberance had faded away, even though Mrs. Soto was delighted with her gift. Violet had given Benny a generous friends and family discount on a bottle of Jo Malone cologne. The hibiscus scent was light and lovely, just the right touch for a no-frills woman like Josephine.

"What's your problem?" I asked Gemma when they left. "You scored a home run and made Benny look like a hero."

"She hates me," Gemma moaned. "Didn't you notice how she ignored me? She thinks I'm not good enough for him."

Violet laughed. "Don't be discouraged. You're competition for his mother. He's her little boy, remember. Besides, Benny would be lucky to have you. Think of all you've accomplished."

The thought of anyone doting on Benny repulsed me, but I wisely said nothing. If Gemma found another love interest, I would be ecstatic. Come to think of it, I'd never met Roddy's parents, although he assured me they would adore having an artist in the family. Who knew what their reaction would be?

I shared Teagen's financial offer with my aunt, knowing that as an astute businesswoman she could evaluate it.

"Hmm," she said. "Generous terms indeed. Make sure you get that in writing. Artists can be too casual about money and get taken advantage of."

I'd avoided mentioning Roddy's offer, but Gemma had no inhibitions. "What's your take on Teagen?" she asked. "Is she hot for the delicious doc or just horny in general?"

Violet wagged her finger at Gemma. "You bad girl. Teagen is unique, an aging beauty in an industry that idolizes youth. Who could blame her for flirting with a young man like Roddy? Good for both of their egos. Besides, I suspect part of her scheme is to antagonize Brendan. His womanizing gets more flagrant every year, and it's got to sting."

"She thinks he wants to kill her," I said. "Is that realistic or pure fantasy?"

"Brendan is egotistical," Violet said, "but hardly homicidal. He has too much to lose. Teagen probably just wants attention. Madge says she's the ultimate drama queen."

Gemma paused. "Wait a minute. I thought Madge was Teagen's best pal. Doesn't sound like it to me. I'd never smear my besties that way."

"She didn't mean anything by it, but Teagen can be quite a trial. Remember, she's been Madge's house guest for a month. No wonder the poor woman needs to vent."

I felt uneasy about becoming involved in the Doyles' drama but was too craven to extricate myself. Besides, I'd be on-site to police Roddy and Teagen's romantic escapades if any.

"She plans to do a lecture on tinctures," I said. "Most people know nothing about them."

"Great idea," said my aunt. "I guarantee it will be an SRO crowd. People are more curious about Teagen than tinctures, but they'll learn about both. I assume she'll feature it on her podcast as well. All part of smart advertising."

No more was said about Teagen or her designs on Roddy. We spent a few minutes debating painting techniques and locations instead. Aunt Violet's paintings commanded six-figure prices, but mine were more down-market. Way down. I checked my watch, wondering what time Roddy would want dinner. A text answered that question. Teagen was formulating her business plan and wanted his input. She'd order dinner in for both from our local vegetarian spot.

Gemma, who had no qualms about reading other people's messages, glanced at his text and sighed. "Oops. The Professor's flying the coop. Mark my words, this is only the beginning. That woman will have him eating out of her hand or worse before you know it."

I tried to maintain my composure. Gemma meant well, but her comments stung. Perhaps it was because they had the ring of truth.

"I'm sure it's only business," I said. "After all, he's not a prisoner. Roddy's free to do whatever he wants. I plan to use my free time wisely. Maybe I'll make some preliminary sketches of Teagen. You know, different expressions or poses."

"Splendid idea," Violet said. "Focus on your needs and keep cool."

Good advice was far easier to dispense than apply, but keeping busy helped to dispel my doubts. I pasted a faux smile on my face and focused on realigning our shelves. Several matrons ventured into Poppet and peppered my aunt with more questions about Teagen Doyle than our beauty products. Violet handled their inquiries with panache as I knew she would. When Madge Stone ambled into our store for a facial and hot tissue massage, I seized the initiative. Carpe Diem and all that. She was as close to the mare's mouth as I could ever get.

In contrast with her houseguest, Madge favored a decidedly casual look. Her hair was skinned back in a low bun, her face was makeup-free, and she wore no jewelry. Admittedly, her tracksuit was Italian cashmere, a Bruno Cuccinelli creation that I'd lusted after in last month's *Vogue*.

"Are you ready to feel rejuvenated?" I asked her. "Gemma will be right out." Madge accepted my offer of an espresso and eased into a leather fauteuil.

"You have no idea how much I needed this," she said. "Teagen really keeps me hopping, and with Brendan popping in and out at all hours, I'm at my wits' end." Her smile was kind as she said. "I understand Dr. Park has signed on as the face of the male line. A good choice, I think."

I nodded and turned away to stem the tears that suddenly flooded my eyes. What was happening to me? I'd always been an ice princess, not a blubbering fool.

"Don't let it concern you, dear. Teagen's little enthusiasms usually don't last long. Brendan was irate when he heard the news, and I suspect that was part of her plan. After all, even the great financier can be challenged by youth, brains, and beauty. Your professor has them all."

Madge was trying to be kind, but her words didn't comfort me. Roddy and I had a special connection, at least I'd thought so until a femme fatale beckoned to him. Since Teagen entered the scene, he'd gone from lover to lapdog in record time.

Gemma flung open the treatment room door and greeted her client. "Come on in. We'll spend the next hour energizing you." She gave me a conspiratorial wink as she left. Knowing Gemma, I was confident that she would extract more information from Madge than I could ever hope to. People responded to Gemma's friendly manner in a way that I envied. My questions might be considered prying, but Gemma's were called friendly curiosity.

"Any dinner plans?" I asked Violet. "There's a new Italian place in town that's gotten a lot of buzz."

"Sorry, sweetie. I can't." My aunt didn't provide specifics. She never spoke about her private life, and I respected that. Still, I was curious. Senator Robert Jenkins, her very close friend, was rumored to be in the area.

"Won't Roddy be back soon?" Violet asked.

I shook my head. "Business meeting. Command performance."

She nodded and changed the subject. "Chief Miles is appearing at our library this evening. Sort of a meet and greet. Might be interesting. We were lucky to hire such an accomplished woman in our small town. You have much in common."

That was a lifeline. Rather than moping around my apartment, brooding about Roddy, I would do something productive. Gemma was certain to attend to support the odious Deputy Soto, so I wouldn't be an orphan. I had never met Chief Miles and was eager to do so. Let Roddy see that Marketta Davis was an independent woman who waited for no man. Brave words. They were better than tears, even if they rang hollow.

*　*　*

The Harbor Bay public library, a venerable structure almost a century old, hosted an array of well-attended community events. During the winter, it was a beacon of light and a literary hub that kept our town connected. Tonight's event was a case in point. To buoy up my spirits, I spent extra time primping before leaving Poppet. Looking good was my best defense against the curiosity or pity of my neighbors. Our community grapevine far outpaced anything in the digital universe, and Teagen's activities generated gossip, speculation, and envy. News of her and her new boy toy had probably spread like wildfire. The size of this evening's crowd proved that my fellow citizens were equally curious about Aubrey Miles.

Lionel Stevens, acting mayor, convened the meeting by welcoming everyone and reciting Chief Miles's impressive CV. The content of his remarks was fine, but Lionel's delivery left half the audience in a stupor. He droned on until someone in the back of the room hooted, "Hey, Lionel. We came to hear the chief, not you."

Aubrey Miles gripped the podium and addressed her constituents. She was petite, almost dwarfed by Lionel's lanky six-foot form, but her message rang out with the authority of a much larger person. I surmised from her large brown eyes and slight accent that she was probably a native of one of the Island countries.

"I'm a proud American," she said, "born in Jamaica, educated in the United States, and a veteran of the US Marine Corps. My husband and I are delighted to join your community and hope to interact with each one of you over the next few months." She pointed to a tall, dignified man in the front row, introducing him as her spouse, Emil. "My priorities include community policing, crime prevention, and fair, courteous treatment for our citizens."

That prompted a round of applause from the audience. As Chief Miles concluded her speech, the doors flew open, and a hush came over the crowd. Teagen Doyle, accompanied by her devoted swain Roddy Park, swept into the room as if it were the red carpet. Teagen looked radiant. Her wide smile and gracious wave acknowledged the acclaim of her adoring subjects. Roddy had a dazed look on his face that I'd never seen before. Was he now a Stepford husband or merely a knight errant serving his feudal lady? Teagen's crimson caftan certainly appeared regal. She had omitted wearing a crown, however she achieved the same effect with eye-popping diamonds that sparkled in her ears and rings. She settled gracefully into a front row seat and prepared to hold court.

Gemma tapped me on the shoulder and whispered. "Gotta hand it to her. That dame knows how to make an entrance." When I turned toward her, I saw Benny Soto had a triumphant smirk on his face. That provoked me.

"Impressive boss you have, Benny. Law degree and military service. Hard to compete with those credentials."

The smirk vanished as Benny threatened to erupt. Gemma forestalled that by whispering some sweet nothing into his ear.

A flustered Lionel Stevens recovered the microphone, and after acknowledging the arrival of our newest celebrity, he urged the audience to mix and mingle. "Our next event features Teagen Doyle debuting her new business, Teagen's Tinctures."

While Teagen held court, I scooted over to the smaller group surrounding Aubrey Miles. She was someone whose accomplishments I admired. I hoped to befriend if she was a kindred spirit. Besides, she had a husband and was unlikely to have designs on other men.

"I've heard of you from my predecessor, Ms. Davis." Her impish grin told me that the report had not been complimentary. "And I've often admired your Aunt's paintings at the Detroit Institute of Art. She tells me you are also a talented artist."

Her overtures were pleasant, and after exchanging a few words, I gave her my card, invited her to visit Poppet, and made a swift and dignified exit without once catching Roddy's eye. On the library steps, I encountered a disheveled Brendan Doyle whose breath smelled strongly of alcohol. He reached out his arm, grabbed me, and twirled me around like a marionette. "Leaving so soon," he asked. "You're missing the greatest show on earth—my wife and her latest flame. Who knew she preferred the intellectual type?" He planted his cheek next to mine. "Or does your boyfriend have hidden talents?"

I didn't fear Brendan, but his behavior flustered me for several reasons. That gibe about Roddy's hidden talents hit the mark. Surely, he hadn't...he wouldn't...I gave Brendan a sharp jab in the side with my elbow and broke away. "Your wife was asking for you, Mr. Doyle. Everyone wants to meet the man behind her success. You should join her."

He hesitated. "Maybe I will. It's my money, you know. Mine." He beat his chest as if he were auditioning for a King Kong role. "I pulled strings to get her that television part. She's nothing without me."

Brendan staggered toward the library entrance and disappeared. For Roddy's sake, I hoped the evening wouldn't end in a brawl. On the other hand, maybe that's just what my campus Casanova needed to bring him to his senses.

Chapter Five

The next morning, Harbor Bay was abuzz with news. By leaving early, I'd missed all the excitement. Brendan Doyle's assault on Roddy Park was thwarted by Roddy's karate skills and the timely intervention of Chief Miles. Brendan's drunken charge provided the crowd with entertainment but little else. He was hauled off in a police cruiser by Benny Soto and released shortly thereafter in his wife's custody.

Gemma's account of the fracas was more colorful but less accurate. She portrayed Benny as the hero who averted mayhem and saved the day. Kim reported that Chief Miles had been calm and professional as the event unfolded. Teagen's tears were staunched by the strong arms of her newest employee, who led her away and into her Jaguar. I hadn't discussed the matter with Roddy. He hadn't returned last night, and that was just as well. For all I knew, Teagen was sampling those hidden assets Brendan had alluded to.

"I missed quite a show at the library," Aunt Violet said. "Brendan must feel humiliated, but I'll bet Teagen savored every minute. Great publicity for her product launch."

When Doogie Kinkad joined us, I exercised my superpowers and didn't beg for a crumb of information. Besides, I knew with Doogie it wasn't necessary. He would gladly share everything he knew.

The big man beamed as he laid a box of fresh croissants on the counter. "Ladies, my treat. After last night, we all need something sweet."

Gemma immediately dug in, but I shook my head and slowly sipped my latte.

"You must feel proud of your man, Ms. Marky. Very impressive display, I must say. Who would have guessed that he had beauty, brains, and brawn?"

"I missed the whole thing," I said. "Bad timing on my part."

Doogie gave me the side eye. "And so modest too. He wouldn't take any credit for defending himself. Said it was no big deal. I mean, Brendan's a bit long in the tooth, but he's still a bear of a man."

Fortunately, I could count on Gemma to pursue the matter. "How did it end? Benny made me go home after they hauled Brendan away."

"They bundled Teagen into her Jag, and Roddy drove her back to Madge's. Then I played host to Roddy for the night." Doogie turned to me. "He didn't want to disturb you, Marky. Such a considerate guy."

There was an edge to his remark, but I ignored it. Doogie was infamous for stirring things up. He would delight in describing my reaction word for word to his many pals.

"You're so considerate, Doogie. Maybe you should operate a B&B." I patted his shoulder. Doogie, Teagen, and Roddy could all go to blazes. Fantasia needed a long walk, and so did I. Let Roddy Park stew for a while or spend his time blotting Teagen's tears. I followed Aunt Violet's advice and attended to my own needs. When all else failed, I could always count on my canine companion to support and defend me. Fantasia twirled around doing a delighted doggie dance as I fastened her harness. We sprinted toward the town square and followed the walking path through the park.

That's where he found me. Roddy jogged up behind us and shouted, "Hold up a minute, Marky. Wait for me." Fantasia was delighted to see him, but my reaction was more measured. Roddy wore his usual college sweatshirt and shorts and appeared none the worse for wear despite his nocturnal antics.

He motioned to the bench adjoining the path and put his arm around me. "You're not mad at me, are you? Things kind of got out of hand last night."

"So, I heard." I inspected his face. "Let's see. No cuts or bruises. Looks like you came out the winner."

Roddy flushed. "It wasn't much of a contest. Mr. Doyle was so drunk he could hardly move. I don't know why he acted that way."

"Jealousy is a bad thing," I said. "Remember what it did to Othello. Beware the green-eyed monster and all that." *Note to self: follow Shakespeare's advice.*

"Mrs. Doyle isn't like they say. She's actually very sweet. Considerate too. I think working with her will be fun. You'll see."

Could Roddy really be that dense? I knew that he underestimated his impact on women, but Teagen was anything but subtle. The bland look on his face answered my question. Dr. Roddy Park was indifferent to the verbal cues other men immediately picked up on. I'd seen him ignore the overtures of lovelorn prep schoolgirls and matrons alike. Even a celebrity might find him difficult to tempt unless she joined Mensa or dangled a Jeopardy slot his way.

"What did Doogie have to say?" I asked. Frankly, I often regarded Mr. Kinkaid as the embodiment of Iago himself, a catalyst for disruption and mayhem.

Roddy shrugged. "Not much. Just stuff about Mrs. Doyle's life and her husband's girlfriends. She's so gorgeous. Hard to believe he cheats on her."

My sour expression finally tipped him off.

"But of course she's an older lady. My Mom's age, almost."

"You still want to work with her, I suppose." I knew the answer before he responded.

"Gee, Marky, I can't afford to pass it up. Besides, I signed a contract already. And you'll be there to keep me straight, won't you?"

"Just be careful. Please. Teagen's hot for you, and she's persistent. Used to getting anything or anybody that she wants."

"I'm not interested in her. Not romantically, at least. You're the only woman in my life."

Those words perked me up, allowing me to recall that my other mission involved sleuthing. "She thinks her husband wants to kill her. Did she mention that?"

Roddy's eyebrows shot upward. "No! Absolutely not. Mrs. Doyle told me she loved her husband even though he didn't always treat her right. That's why she's so keen on this tincture business." He checked his watch. "Oops! Gotta run. We're doing a practice session this afternoon."

"Practice?" All sorts of salacious thoughts rampaged through my brain.

From my experience, Dr. Park's technique was quite perfect. He didn't need any practice.

Roddy laughed. "Oh, you know. Her podcast will tape tomorrow, and she wants to include me. Sounds interesting."

"Indeed." I swallowed the tart response on the tip of my tongue. "Enjoy."

* * *

I joined Teagen's team the next day, just in time for her podcast. Despite the tight time frame, she had assembled a professional crew and a stage that combined homey appeal with a touch of glamour. Madge was at her side, although Brendan Doyle was nowhere to be seen. Roddy, that poster boy for male health, was garbed in a flannel jacket, t-shirt, and cords straight from the *Ralph Lauren purple* label catalogue. I'd never seen them before, but I knew how pricey every item in that line was. I had to assume that Teagen had thoughtfully provided his costume. Teagen herself was at her film star best, doing a charming imitation of one's folksy next-door neighbor straight from a Hollywood set.

I'd brought my sketch pad and charcoals along to craft some casual poses of my client. She had no unflattering angles or awkward looks. Every inch of Mrs. Brendan Doyle was perfection itself and a pleasure to draw. As Madge nodded encouragement, Teagen gave a history of tinctures, their uses, and the holistic practices she employed in formulating them. She was cagey enough to avoid a hard sell, telling her audience that although tinctures had transformed her life and improved her health, they weren't a magic cure. Her only goal was to educate her seven million followers and share her experience. Toward the end of the podcast, she introduced Roddy, a busy professor in need of Gingko for memory support and Chamomile to reduce stress. As credits rolled, viewers were given her website, where more information could be had.

"Great job," Madge said. "Perfection as usual."

Teagen tried and failed to look modest. The woman expected compliments, and she got them from everyone except her bombastic spouse.

"What was your take, Marky?" she asked. Did I detect a note of insincerity in her question, or was my paranoia running amok? Either way, it didn't matter. I tried my best to be positive and honest. A touch of hypocrisy didn't hurt either.

"Very interesting," I said. "I never thought much of tinctures before, but you gave me something to consider."

She turned to Roddy. "How was your debut, Professor? I thought you were marvelous. The female listeners are sure to comment on you."

Roddy beamed at his benefactor but said nothing. His silence was fortuitous because at that moment, Brendan Doyle lumbered into the room bearing a tray of iced lattes with an espresso for his wife. In typical Teagen fashion, each elegant cup was made of delicate white porcelain emblazoned with the initials TD. Her personal cup was adorned with her trademark shamrock. Brendan glared at Roddy but planted a tender kiss on his wife's cheek. "Another triumph, my darling? Let's toast to your continued success."

Madge's look was quizzical. "Are you a barista now, Brendan? Man of many talents."

His response was boyish and quite endearing. "Nope. I found these on a tray in the foyer. Didn't want the ice to melt, so I decided to be a helpful hubby for a change instead of a monster."

Roddy was clearly uncomfortable. He ducked his head as this marital drama played out, but I leaned in. This was a welcome chance for a caffeine fix and some sleuthing.

Teagen's gracious smile was forced, but she played her part to perfection. "You're anything but a monster, Darling. More of a mischievous little boy." She cautiously tasted her drink and pronounced it delicious. I agreed. My first sip of the precious brew confirmed her assessment. Madge and Roddy followed suit. Teagen invited a post-mortem critique of her podcast from Madge and Roddy as I scanned my phone for comments from her listeners. All were very positive, although more focused on Professor Park than on Teagen or her tinctures. Suddenly, one comment caught my eye. "Each man kills the thing he loves." It was a line from one of my favorite poems by Oscar Wilde. Was it a warning for Teagen or merely a joker trying desperately to sound literate? I never got an answer. Teagen Doyle dropped her porcelain cup and clutched her throat. As the cup shattered, the ebony drink spread on her designer duds. She gasped and slid to the floor.

"Oh, my Lord," Brendan yelled. "Do something." He ran to his wife, bleating her name in a frenzied appeal for assistance.

Madge was an oasis of calm in the storm. She grasped her friend's hand and took her pulse. "Call an ambulance, Marky, while I get her pills." She pointed to a petite CHANEL clutch bag resting on the table. "Grab that for me, Roddy. It's got her smelling salts in it."

As she snapped open the bag, I noticed it contained an EpiPen as well as smelling salts and assorted pills. Madge noticed my surprise.

"She's a bit of a hypochondriac, but Teagen does have some serious allergies. She lives in fear of going into anaphylactic shock. You can appreciate how vulnerable she feels."

Our local paramedics were fast and efficient. They arrived promptly and peppered Brendan with questions that he was unable to answer. Fortunately, Madge intervened. "It was something in her drink. Teagen is extremely sensitive to caffeine, and if she overdoes it, her heart acts up. Palpitations. Her doctor warned her that this could happen."

I watched everyone closely, especially her loving husband. No one else had experienced any ill effects from the drinks, and it made me suspicious. Under the guise of cleaning up, I salvaged a large part of her porcelain cup that still contained half of the espresso. The saucer was intact, and I scooped that up, too, and placed it in my tote bag. Roddy rolled his eyes and gave me a conspiratorial wink. I wasn't sure what to do with the evidence until the name Aubrey Miles flashed before me. Cops had access to forensics and laboratory facilities. Let her check it out. If she dubbed me a fantasist, so be it. I'd been called worse by Benny Soto and his ilk.

Teagen's lids fluttered, and she snapped open those famous eyes. "What happened?" She looked incredulously at the paramedics who surrounded her. "I'm perfectly fine. No need to make a fuss. Please, Madge, tell them."

"She's very sensitive to caffeine," Madge said. "Gets palpitations and sometimes faints. She's highly allergic to a host of things."

The paramedic looked dubious. "Her EKG is back to normal now, but I'd still recommend having the hospital check it out. Caffeine intoxication can be serious, even deadly."

Brendan Doyle agreed. "You shouldn't take any chances, my Love."

She placed her hand on his shoulder. "Please. No publicity. People will link it to my tinctures. I got overexcited, that's all."

After Brendan relented, the paramedics reluctantly left. I busied myself with gathering up the remaining cups, saucers, and utensils. "Let me handle this," I said. "No need to fuss."

Roddy followed me out to the kitchen. "What's this? Little Miss helpful. Auditioning for a server's spot, are you?"

I hushed him and pointed to the cabinets. "Check them out. Look for suspicious ingredients but be subtle."

"What's suspicious? Poison or something?"

I stood on tiptoe and scanned the products on the shelf. "No. Something innocuous. Anything that Brendan Doyle may have spiked her drink with." We didn't have much time. Madge or Doyle himself might catch us in a compromising situation that would be difficult to explain.

I turned on the faucet to muffle our conversation.

"OMG! There it is!" I pointed to a nondescript container pushed far back on the shelf. It had no brand name, only the inscription, Powdered Caffeine, food grade.

"Is everything all right, Marky?" I heard Madge coming and grabbed Roddy.

"Kiss me," I yelped.

"Huh?" He complied, although he obviously thought I was barmy.

When Madge entered the kitchen, we were locked in an embrace passionate enough to curl my toes.

"You crazy kids," she said, waving her hands in the air. "Come on, love birds. Cut it out. Teagen's ready to continue."

I managed to eke out a guilty smile and follow Madge into the conference room. To my surprise, another visitor had joined our group. Doogie Kinkaid sprawled out on the sofa as he chattered nonstop to Brendan Doyle. When he spied us, Doogie beamed.

"Well, well, well. Caught canoodling in the kitchen, Ms. Marky. The Professor's under contract to Teagen, remember. Aren't you supposed to be painting, you naughty girl?"

"What brings you here, Doogie? Hawking real estate to some poor soul?" By confronting Doogie, I hoped to conceal my guilty grin. It didn't deceive him, and the grim expression on Teagen's face indicated that she was not amused. I loathe cliches, but the expression "If looks could kill" was apropos in this case.

"I saw the ambulance and got concerned," Doogie said. "You know I take care of people I adore." He turned to Teagen. "And you, Mrs. Doyle, are one of them."

Unadulterated praise seemed to mollify her. Teagen immediately brightened and resumed the critique of her podcast as if nothing was amiss. I took advantage of the opening and made my excuses.

"I'm due back at Poppet," I said. "Are you available later for a formal sitting? I've got several ideas about the portrait to run by you."

Teagen gave me her noblesse oblige nod and dismissed me like the social inferior she considered me to be. I told myself not to take it personally. Pampered celebrities were accustomed to fawning sycophants and retainers who could be replaced at will. Still, her attitude rankled me. I fumed all the way back and stomped into Poppet.

Aunt Violet ignored my mood, although I was positive that she sensed trouble. As usual, Gemma was more forthcoming.

"What's got you all lathered up?" she asked. "Catch Roddy making time with his boss?"

"Hardly," I said with as much hauteur as I could muster. "Things just got complicated."

Violet lowered her reading glasses and stared at me. "Don't let Teagen get under your skin. I'm sure she regards you as competition. Remember your watch words—youth and beauty. Use them as leverage."

I updated them on Teagen's health scare and the suspicious substance in the cabinets. The name Brendan Doyle figured prominently in our discussion.

"Curious," Violet said. "That was rather clever if your suspicions are correct, and very subtle. Brendan is a business shark, but in my experience, a move like caffeine poisoning is simply not his style. Have you considered that Teagen might have exaggerated things?"

Gemma snapped her fingers. "I'll bet she faked it or poisoned herself. Not enough to kill her, just enough for sympathy. That happens all the time on television shows. Check it out!"

I knew nothing about caffeine poisoning, but the internet was abuzz with information. Pure caffeine had both beneficial and deadly properties. Its use had to be strictly monitored, and the amount used limited. Several deaths had been attributed to caffeine intoxication, mostly those of young athletes who used it to enhance performance. Apparently, although the substance itself was bitter, the taste was easily disguised in sugary drinks. Red alert! I'd seen Teagen heap sweetener into her coffee in our conference room. Someone who knew her habits could easily take advantage of that. Someone like Brendan Doyle. To top it off, pure caffeine was readily available from health food stores and internet suppliers.

Gemma's suspicions were also worth considering. Teagen herself might have procured the substance and dosed her drink. After all, she was a creature of the media, conversant with staging dramatic scenes. Her rapid recovery was somewhat suspicious. If her objective was to garner attention, it worked like a charm on Brendan Doyle.

I mentioned the nasty comment from a podcast listener. Neither Gemma nor my aunt took it seriously because, as Violet observed, the internet emboldened all types of lower life forms to assert themselves with impunity.

Our store was almost closed when a new customer appeared. Chief Aubrey Miles stuck her head in the door, asking sheepishly if it was too late to purchase something.

I believe in kismet, fate, or plain good luck. The remnants of Teagen's drink were nestled in my tote, and this was the ideal opportunity to approach the chief.

"I'm out of foundation," she said. "Have anything for darker complexions?" She instantly won my heart by fawning over Fantasia. "What a beauty. She must be your store mascot."

I freely admit to my prejudices. Anyone who ignored my beautiful collie was automatically on my suspect list. Teagen Doyle's reaction was a case in point, but Chief Miles passed the test with flying colors.

Before Gemma could intervene, I pounced. "Absolutely. Let me show you this Armani product. I love it, and we've gotten great feedback from our customers." I was a big fan of the brand, particularly the Power Fabric. When I tested it on Aubrey Miles' face, she agreed. "It's perfect. Just right for my routine."

My courage evaporated when she stared pointedly into my eyes. This woman was not easily fooled. Only an idiot would believe my tale about Teagen's coffee mishap. Even I thought it was convoluted. Teagen Doyle was a prima donna who exaggerated every aspect of her life and thrived on drama. I refused to aid or abet her in that effort.

Gemma sauntered in from the conference room and instantly chatted up the chief. "Lots of excitement in Harbor Bay since the Doyles showed up. Any thoughts about today?"

Aubrey frowned. "Today? Rather peaceful, I thought. Help me out, I'm stumped."

"You know. Teagen Doyle's mystery ailment. They called the paramedics and everything. Marky was there." When Gemma unloads, she spares no one and nothing. "We wondered if it was attempted murder."

Gone was the affable cosmetics customer. Chief Miles now sported the blank expression and stony stare beloved of all cops. "I'll have to check that out." She paid for her purchase and strode rapidly out of Poppet without any further conversation.

"You blew it," I scolded my partner. "Now she thinks we're the town gossips. Subtlety, Gemma. Try it sometimes."

Very little fazes Gemma. She shrugged and gave me a sly grin. "Wait 'til Benny hears about this. I better call and warn him." Off she scampered to the storeroom to alert her beloved. Meanwhile, Violet glided up to console me.

"Don't be too hard on Gemma," Violet said. "I admit she can be frank, but you know that most of the time she's right on target. Besides, I just spoke with Madge. After you left, Teagen and Brendan had quite a tiff. She accused him of trying to kill her, and he stormed out. More drama."

"Was Madge suspicious?" I asked. "Of Brendan, I mean. I almost confided in Aubrey Miles but thought better of it. She's probably heard that I meddle in police business, and I'd like her to consider me as a possible friend, not an irritant."

Violet patted my cheek. "Smart thinking. The entire incident today was probably overblown, although that container of powdered caffeine is troubling. What did Roddy say?" Violet watched me closely.

"We're in limbo now. Lots of sweet talk, then he disappears back to the arms of his employer. I swear, Teagen looks at him as if he's her favorite canape."

Violet looked pensive. "Hmm. I wouldn't worry. He seems very levelheaded. Just keep your eyes wide open and your lips sealed."

Words to live by. After we closed Poppet, I hurried upstairs to freshen up. I intended to look my best before tackling Teagen Doyle. Competing with her glamour and allure was a loser's game. I was ill-equipped for that contest, but I had to keep my spirits high. Truth be told, despite everything, Teagen was an engaging subject, and I was eager to paint her portrait.

Any artist would savor the challenge and vie for the opportunity. That didn't mean I was her doormat or serf, however. I arranged my hair in a messy bun, reapplied makeup, donned black leggings, and a silk shirt. Gold hoop earrings and a simple gold chair completed my outfit. I peered into the mirror, pleased with the result— my version of casual chic. *Take that, Teagen Doyle.*

Before leaving, I filled Fantasia's water bowl and sprinkled chicken on her kibble. No sense in skimping on that good girl's dinner. I grabbed my sketch pad and assorted tools, carefully placing them in my carry-all. Armed for battle, or the equivalent, I drove to the storefront that housed Teagen's Tinctures. The crowd of friends and hangers-on had dissipated, leaving only her red Jaguar in the parking space. I tapped at the door, pushed it open, and called out. "Hello. Mrs. Doyle. I'm here to discuss your portrait."

The front room was empty, but I saw a light in the rear of the structure. Teagen called it her salon. She'd outfitted it à la Francaise with a table, several bergères, and a sensuous velvet recamier. That's where I found them, reclining in splendor on that opulent hunk of French furniture. Teagen Doyle was draped gracefully on the sofa with her head on the curved headrest. She was cradled in the strong arms of Roddy Park.

* * *

My reaction fluctuated between shock, chagrin, and embarrassment. Aunt Violet's voice rang in my ears: *Retain your dignity, don't make a scene. You are better than that.*

No one could fault my behavior. I didn't weep or hurl obscenities until afterwards. In retrospect, the scene was more comical than carnal. Roddy leapt up, calling my name, but Teagen didn't move a muscle. Her face bore a grin that would shame a Cheshire cat.

"Excuse me," I stammered. "I called out, and no one answered. You're busy, so I'll catch you later." I pivoted and strode out of the salon, mustering every ounce of composure that I possessed.

Roddy sped after me. "Wait, Marky. Stop. Things aren't what they seem."

"Huh!" I ducked under his outstretched arms and headed for the door with Teagen's voice ringing in my ears.

"Let her go, Roddy, come back here," she purred. It was a sultry command that made him stop short. I exited Teagen's Tinctures with a heavy heart and a mountain of regrets.

* * *

I tried to be brave, but couldn't hide the tears from my aunt. Poppet was usually deserted after hours, but Violet had stayed to accommodate a late-night delivery.

"Back so soon?" she said. After seeing my distress, Violet outstretched her arms and enveloped me in a warm hug. "Tell me what happened."

I recounted the seamy scene at Teagen's Tinctures and Roddy's pitiful attempt to explain. She wasn't surprised or even outraged. Apparently, seduction was Teagen's modus operandi when dealing with desirable men of all ages.

"She's insecure," Violet explained. "Sex is the only weapon in her arsenal. At least the only one she feels comfortable with now that she's getting older."

Mother had taught me to respect my elders, even shameless vamps like Mrs. Doyle. That didn't mean I wanted to work for her. She had violated any contract, either expressed or implied, by targeting Roddy Park. We were quits. Finis. Over.

"I'm through with her and her stupid tinctures," I said. "She can have Roddy, Brendan, and even Lionel if she wants them."

Violet raised her eyebrows at that last name. "Lionel? Even Teagen has her limits, although Kim would probably surrender him without firing a shot." Then she posed the question she had used so often in dealing with my tantrums.

"Have you considered the downside of quitting? Painting her portrait would burnish your artistic credentials. Besides, what about those death threats? Quite an intriguing puzzle, don't you think?"

For once, my wily aunt's tactics failed. I looked her squarely in the face and said, "I don't believe that nonsense. As far as I'm concerned, she can burn in hell." Then I stomped up the stairs into my apartment and slammed the door. Roddy had no keys, so he'd have to bunk in with his employer or beg Doogie Kinkaid for shelter. I ignored the stream of texts he sent, turned off my phone, and after attending to Fantasia, bundled into my bed. Anger was a soporific that lulled me straight into the arms of Morpheus.

Chapter Six

Roddy ambushed me the next day as I was walking Fantasia. The big lug waited on the park bench until we approached then sprang into action.

"Marky—wait a minute!"

For once my guardian Fantasia let me down. Instead of growling at this predator, she woofed in doggy delight and rolled over for a tummy scratch.

"See," Roddy pleaded. "Fantasia still loves me. Won't you let me explain?"

"Sure," I said standing hands-on hips. "Be my guest."

He patted the bench seat. "Sit down. Please. That scene yesterday wasn't real. It was staged, planned."

"By whom? Are you some type of method actor? Stravinsky would be proud of you, Professor. You really got into your character."

"Mrs. Doyle wanted to improvise, you know, add some zest to her You tube videos. It was pretend. That's all."

I considered the possibilities. Roddy was either obtuse or a facile fibber. Since he was a brilliant scholar, I opted for door number two.

"Did Brendan enjoy your scene setting? Quite a hard sell convincing him it was all pretend. The man doesn't share anything including his wife. Her lipstick was smeared over your new shirt too. What a shame."

Shame was the operative word. Roddy ducked his head and tried once more. "Look, I admit I was flattered. After all she's a celebrity, someone you see on television. But Teagen, Mrs. Doyle, is an older lady, almost my mom's age. Plus, she's scared out of her wits. That thing with the espresso freaked her out. She really believes her husband wants her dead."

He squeezed my hand. "Anyway, she wants to see you this morning. To explain things. Everyone always says how fair you are. At least listen to her."

I felt myself weakening. Violet would handle things calmly, dispassionately. No jealous scenes, no tears. I could probably do the same without compromising my integrity.

"Okay," I said. "I'll drop over about ten am." I tugged his ear. "Make sure you're on your best behavior, lover. Save your acting for another time."

It took Gemma only minutes to wheedle the story of last evening's drama out of me.

"I knew it!" she brayed. "Didn't I tell you that woman's a barracuda? A real maneater." She gave me a steely glare. "Don't tell me you bought Roddy's excuse? Method acting? Phooey!"

"Calm down, Gemma," Violet said. "Let Marky handle this herself. Roddy must be smart, and savvy or he wouldn't have been snapped up by Michigan. It's one of the nation's premier universities after all."

Gemma narrowed her eyes. "There's a difference between book smart and street smart and I'll bet the Professor has never tangled with the likes of Teagen Doyle before. Cute coeds don't count."

Let Gemma gloat, I told myself. I'd already devised a plan. When I faced Teagen, I'd skip the drama and focus on two things: her portrait and the threats to her life. Depriving her of a scene, would be payback. Besides, I was very curious about that powdered caffeine.

When I entered Teagen's Tinctures my putative employer greeted me with a friendly hug. There was an air of faux contrition in her manner as she gushed apologies and explained yesterday's sordid scene. As usual, Madge Stone stood by her side. Professor Park was nowhere to be seen.

"Don't worry," said I. "Roddy explained everything. I'm focused on painting your portrait. It's not often that such a lovely subject is my client."

Teagen looked crestfallen as if she had been deprived of a dramatic scene. I considered that a major victory. "Thank you," she murmured. "Very understanding of you."

"Before we start, I have a question. When I was washing up the other day, I saw a container of powdered caffeine in the cupboard. Any idea where that came from?"

She furrowed her brow. "Not a clue. Madge?"

Madge shook her head. "Are you certain, Marky? I can't imagine how it got there."

"Roddy saw it too. I only asked because that stuff is very dangerous. Even a teaspoon of it can send someone with a sensitive heart into cardiac arrest. Of course, some athletes use it to improve their workouts. Perhaps Brendan knows the answer."

Madge looked troubled. I recalled that in another life before snagging her wealthy spouse she had been a nurse. Small wonder that she hovered over Teagen like a guardian angel.

"You aren't suggesting…" Teagen clutched her throat.

"Hush dear," said Madge. "Marky's question was perfectly reasonable. You have serious allergies after all. Dairy and nuts are your kryptonite."

I'd set the cat amongst the pigeons to use that old British expression. Miss Marple would be proud. We then dispensed with further discussion about death or philandering and focused on painting. Teagen had definite preferences but my assurance that she would look ravishing allayed her fears. When I asked if Brendan would be included in the painting she bristled.

"Certainly not. The finished product will be featured on my website. He has nothing to do with Teagen's Tinctures."

I shared my concepts and the preliminary sketches of her that I had made. We had a productive, civilized discussion at the conclusion of which, we enjoyed tea and sandwiches.

"No lattes for me today," Teagen joked. "Strictly herbal tea."

That remark piqued my curiosity. "Madge said you had a host of allergies. Must be quite a burden."

Teagen grinned and patted her pocket. "Not so much. I always keep my faithful EpiPen nearby. Believe me it's come in handy plenty of times. Some foods are my sworn enemies, but most restaurants accommodate allergies these days. Besides, I love to cook."

"She's a Cordon Bleu graduate," said Madge. "Le Grande Diplome" if you can believe it. "Highest distinction they have. Nothing but the best for our girl." She shot a look of admiration at her friend.

"Roddy didn't believe me," Teagen simpered. "I promised to cook one of my specialties just for him tomorrow evening."

Adult women shouldn't simper. It's unseemly behavior especially when the offender in question has seduced the love of your life.

I chose to ignore the taunt and soldier on. "You're so accomplished. No wonder women envy you. Incidentally, the other day you mentioned several incidents had frightened you. What were they?"

Teagen hesitated but Madge urged her on. "Don't worry Sweetie. Marky wants to help you."

"I feel so silly," Teagen said. "Probably paranoid. One time in Chicago a car almost ran me down. Luckily it swerved at the last moment, but I was terrified."

Madge squeezed her shoulder. "Go on. You know there's more. Tell her about the medication mix-up."

"It was probably my own fault. I take pills for my nerves. Have for years. This time they looked strange. Different color and shape. Madge checked with the pharmacy, and they couldn't understand what happened. Somehow amphetamines were substituted for my normal pills." Teagen shrugged. "Just a mistake, I guess."

Madge snorted. "Mistake my foot! With her heart issues, she might have died."

I tried to keep things low-key. "What did Brendan say?"

"Oh, you know how men are. He dismissed both incidents. Said I was dramatizing things. He picked up the pills himself and as for the other, he said I walked around in a daze most of the time."

"This is sensitive, but I need to ask you. Is Brendan planning to divorce you?"

Teagen bridled at the use of the "D" word. "Certainly not! We love each other passionately."

Madge played savior once more. "Brendan adores Teagen. He'd be lost without her."

Their defense of him puzzled me. I forged on telling myself that a detective's lot was not an easy one. "Then, pardon me, but who else would want you dead? Some disgruntled suitor, or jealous wife? Maybe an obsessed fan. You did say someone was stalking you."

"It sounds so foolish," Teagen said. "There's probably a logical explanation for everything; Forget I even mentioned it."

Those were my sentiments exactly. Artists were often confronted with difficult, demanding, or fanciful clients. Come to think of it, half of the artists I knew behaved that way too. Violet's advice was to ignore the drama and forge ahead. That was my tactic in dealing with the mercurial Mrs. Doyle.

"Why don't you change into one of your favorite outfits and we'll have our first sitting. It may take several sessions before I 'm ready to tackle your portrait in earnest."

That suggestion seemed to mollify her. Just when I thought things had settled down, Roddy Park drifted into the salon. Teagen immediately raced to his side and flung herself into his arms. "Oh Roddy. I'm so glad you're here. I already feel safer."

This was no rehearsal. It felt much closer to a love scene. Perhaps a galloping case of coitus interruptus.

Roddy didn't resist her overtures. In fact, he appeared to welcome her embrace. Only the arrival of Doogie Kinkaid spoiled the tableau.

"My word!" the big man said. "What have we here?" His saucy grin told me that he had plenty of ideas. By tomorrow, the entire town of Harbor Bay would teem with speculation. Teagen's smile was angelic, but she never loosened her grip on Roddy. The expression on his face was a mixture of awe and ardor. When she stood on tiptoe, he bent down to meet her lips.

I knew how those tender touches felt, and it sickened me. No need to delude myself. The professor was smitten, and our romance was in his rear-view mirror.

As I hastened to collect my belongings, another player emerged. Brendan Doyle burst into the room bellowing like an outraged bull. I couldn't repeat all the scatological terms he hurled at Roddy, but several showed true imagination. The lovebirds pulled apart as Teagen made a tearful plea to her hubby. Madge stretched out her arms traffic cop style but Doogie, who savored drama at the expense of others did nothing.

"You slut," Brendan shouted. "Cuckolding me in plain sight! I'll break this scheming bastard's neck right in front of you." His eyes bulged as he lunged toward Roddy. Perhaps I could have stopped him. At the very least I might have pleaded for calm. In the end I did neither. Rodrick Park, PhD was on his own. Who knew? A sound thrashing might knock some sense into him.

Brendan, fueled by anger and angst launched himself at Roddy, pinning him in a headlock. They tumbled to the floor and wrestled until Madge dumped a vase of water on their heads. That temporarily stunned the duo allowing Roddy to break free from his assailant. The room was filled with Teagen's shrieks, Brendan's curses, and Madge's appeals for sanity. Doogie stayed far from the fracas enjoying every moment and surreptitiously snapping photos with his iPhone. I edged out of the room and sped as far away from Teagen's Tinctures as possible. Poppet was my refuge and from now on it was a male-free zone. I raced up the stairs to my apartment, hastily removing every trace of that treacherous teacher's possessions. When I returned to the store, suitcase in hand, Gemma immediately sensed my dilemma.

"Giving him the boot, are you?" she asked. "I'm sorry Marky I really am. I thought for sure he was the one." Gemma gave a philosophical shrug. "Give me that suitcase. I'll haul it over to Ms. Doyle's place and dump it on the stoop. That'll give him the hint, the big creep."

I couldn't stop her, not that I tried. Gemma, Fantasia, and Aunt Violet were the constants in my life. When all else failed they were there for me just as I was for them. Meanwhile I had a business to run and a life to live. The memory of Roddy Park would soon fade into the past along with my other romantic misadventures. I freshened my makeup, fluffed my hair, and fixed myself a strong espresso. As Scarlett O'Hara famously said, tomorrow was another day.

Chapter Seven

The following day, I immersed myself in work. After consulting with my aunt, I crafted an impersonal, businesslike missive to Teagen enclosing the preliminary sketches I had made, thanking her for the opportunity to paint her, and politely declining to do so. No mention of the detective work or her other stratagems. I now realized they were ploys, pathetic bids for attention that had totally bamboozled me. After all, she was an actress, far more skilled than the critics had ever given her credit for. Complete silence from Roddy—no calls, texts, or impassioned pleas. That suitcase must have convinced him of the futility of doing so. Gemma had run right into him as he exited Teagen's Tinctures. According to her, the scene was a triumph for wronged women everywhere.

"I looked that pompous prick right in the eye, shoved the suitcase into his hand, turned around, and walked away. Never said a word."

"Really?" I asked. "That took guts."

Gemma showed a bit of swagger. "Guts, I have plenty of. He didn't deserve any explanation, the bastard."

I swallowed my pride and pasted a bland smile on my face. Soon, he and Teagen would be dining à deux in her cozy little nest. I prayed that both would enjoy a case of galloping indigestion. "Let's face it. Most men couldn't resist Teagen Doyle. Roddy's no better or worse."

Gemma frowned. "Don't make excuses for him. You're the gold standard, even Benny admits that. Dr. Park might have brains, but he blew it."

Thanks to Doogie, the news of Teagen's latest adventure spread throughout Harbor Bay with record speed. He didn't share his photos on social media, but a few select pals had seen them. Kim Stevens was the first. She swooped into Poppet and enveloped me in a hug.

"Oh, Marky! What a mess. I'm glad you extricated yourself from that drama. Violet told me." She pinched my cheek. "Keep your chin up, girl. You deserve the best."

To avoid my errant scholar, I chose a different route for Fantasia's morning walk. Harbor Bay boasted a lovely waterfront filled with picturesque shops and fishing fleets. The harbor, set on Little Traverse Bay, was a sheltered tributary feeding into the shores of mighty Lake Michigan. The brisk wind was bracing, a perfect tonic for beating the doldrums. It refreshed me and renewed my fighting spirit. Fantasia sensed my feelings and gave me an extra canine caress.

It seemed that every customer who entered Poppet that day gave me the side-eye. Violet dismissed my paranoid notions and urged me to ignore them. Gemma took a more practical approach.

"So, what if they know he dumped you?" she said. "Makes them buy more out of guilt or sympathy. Either way, we make a profit."

When Deputy Benny Soto called for Gemma, he showed his snarky side. "Another rumble at that rich woman's place. Your boyfriend sure knows how to pick 'em."

That gibe caused me to lose my celebrated self-control. "I suppose all that education gave Professor Park an advantage." I turned his way. "You wouldn't know anything about that, would you, Benny?"

He puffed up cobra style but couldn't summon an adequate reply. Gemma hustled him out the door before her sweetie put me in cuffs.

The next evening, Teagen planned to debut her new tincture business at our community hall. I knew my fellow citizens. They were agog, transfixed by celebrity. Every seat would be taken. According to Doogie, newscasters from Detroit and Chicago would also join us. Despite the whiff of scandal and my very public rejection, I wouldn't miss the event. In fact, the staff of Poppet, including Fantasia, would be represented. I took special care with my appearance. A cashmere twin set garnished with a simple string of grandma's pearls would set the right tone—tasteful but upscale. No sense in trying for glamour. Teagen Doyle had that market sewn up tight. But as my aunt often remarked, youth was something film stars could replicate but not duplicate, no matter how many surgical procedures they used.

"Come on, Princess, get a move on." Gemma pranced around the room, clad in an outfit that skirted the bounds of propriety. Her auburn curls were adorned with a streak of pink that contrasted sharply with her orange outfit. Oddly enough, this strange pairing worked on her.

"Where's Violet, by the way?"

I explained that my aunt was enjoying cocktails with Madge and Leticia. "Don't worry. She'll join us for the show."

Although I'm not much of a drinker, I felt a sudden urge to down a glass or two of Scotch straight up. That whim soon passed. I loathed the taste of the nasty stuff and needed to keep my wits about me.

Gemma's eyes sparkled. "Will Brendan show up? I'd love to see another brawl. Naturally, Benny will be there to keep order, so we've nothing to worry about."

In my experience, Benny Soto's intemperate actions were likely to escalate a minor fracas into a full-scale riot. I buttoned my lips in the interest of friendship and kept that thought to myself. Fantasia sensed the excitement as she slipped gleefully into her harness. Teagen loathed dogs, so the presence of my loving collie was a subtle gesture of contempt that fortified me.

As expected, a crowd was milling about, jockeying for prime seats. Among them, I spied a mismatched duo, Josephine Soto arrayed in a shapeless shift, and Chief Aubrey Miles, looking svelte and stylish in a beige pantsuit. Kim signaled us from the front row, pointing to two vacant seats.

"I got here early and saved them," she said, squeezing my shoulder. "Remember, Marky, keep cool. Everything is theater to Teagen."

Promptly at eight pm, the festivities started. To my surprise, the master of ceremonies was the normally laconic Lionel Stevens. He cleared his throat, peered over the podium, and greeted the crowd. Kim shrugged when I glanced her way.

"Lionel's a major investor, so he insisted on doing this. Keep your fingers crossed that he makes his remarks short and sweet."

After he droned on for an interminable amount of time, I realized that he had disregarded his wife's advice. Lionel's fulsome tribute to Teagen would have shamed a saint. When he finally concluded, the doors flew open, and the Teagen show commenced.

She was a vision in Titian. Even I had to admit that. The glitz and glamour that might have appeared gaudy on a lesser being were perfectly suited to her.

"Wow!" Gemma sighed. "You've got to admit that dame knows how to stage a show. Take a gander at those jewels. Wow."

Teagen had perfected the royal wave, a back-of-hand, slightly twisting gesture designed to embrace her fawning subjects without any physical contact. With few exceptions, it appeared to work. She gave gracious smiles to a favored few, such as Madge and Aunt Violet, but pointedly avoided acknowledging Gemma and me.

My best pal elbowed me in the ribs. "OMG! Look who's trailing behind her in the fancy duds."

I knew the answer but couldn't resist looking. The splendid male specimen in her wake was Professor Roderick Park, my own lost love. He sported a handsome suede jacket and moss green corduroy slacks that I'd never seen before. No doubt they were yet another pricy token of Teagen's largesse. Roddy looked toothsome, but I much preferred him in his weathered hoodie and jogging togs. The distaff side of the audience cast lustful looks his way while the men squared their shoulders and stole glances at Teagen.

She ascended to the stage, grasped the microphone, and proceeded to deliver a self-effacing and charming presentation.

"As a newcomer to this wonderful community, I want to thank all of you for your warm welcome and share some products that have been a passion of mine for decades." Teagen held up a bottle. "Tinctures—learn about them and the way they can improve your life. I can honestly say that without tinctures, I would not have survived in the competitive world of Hollywood. They saved me and may be of value to you." She winked. "As we become better acquainted, I'll share some of those celebrity scoops. But on to business now."

She then gestured to a bag overflowing with samples and informational material. "My associate, Dr. Roderick Park, will share some of these products with you. Consult my website if you find them helpful and want to order more."

Roddy leapt to his feet, stopping at each row to offer products. When he reached us, Gemma stomped on the toe of his highly polished boot.

"Oops. So sorry, Professor. Didn't mean to spoil your new boots."

He winced but said nothing. Kim, ever gracious, chose several samples and nodded her thanks. I stayed cold and unrelenting as a marble sculpture while Roddy quickly moved on and completed his task. Teagen opened the floor to questions, handling even the most fatuous remarks with panache.

When the strains of a Mozart concerto wafted into the room, Teagen bid us farewell and glided down the aisle. Gemma was disappointed by the lack of drama. Without Brendan Doyle's theatrics, a civilized atmosphere prevailed. I was thankful for that. While Gemma lagged with her fiancé, I joined Kim, Violet, and Madge. Letty Briggs had disappeared into the throng, so the four of us and Fantasia adjourned to Madge's estate for a post-mortem and some choice hors de ores. Everyone agreed that Teagen's performance was a triumph worthy of a star. Tact ruled the night, and Roddy Park was not mentioned, although his ghostly presence inhabited the room. I'd lost at love before, but somehow this episode really stung. Thanks to the encouragement of Kim and my aunt, I managed to rise above the fray.

Chapter Eight

I had something to look forward to that next evening—dinner with Kim and Aunt Violet at one of our favorite bistros. No chance of encountering the lovebirds since Teagen was preparing a feast and playing domestic goddess. I was positive that she owned a stunning designer apron that would challenge anything in Martha Stewart's wardrobe.

After closing Poppet, I groomed myself for success. The impact of a facial and cosmetic touch was therapeutic. I entered Entre Nous feeling refreshed, able to face the harsh, cruel world without flinching. As usual, nothing escaped my aunt's notice.

"You look lovely, Marky," she said, commenting on my silk pantsuit. "Red is your color. Bold and beautiful."

Kim agreed. "Red says, 'Notice me. I'm here.' Quite the power statement."

I lapped up their compliments like a frantic feline. My self-confidence had been sadly depleted, and positive comments helped to restore it.

"Let's chat about something new," I said. "What's the latest political scandal?"

Violet shared a few choice tidbits; information that had no doubt been gleaned from her close friend, the Senator. Kim chimed in with a discussion of the latest weight loss drug and its celebrity devotees. "Everyone was using it, but suddenly that stopped. Side effects, you know. Rather ghastly ones." She shuddered.

Before she provided details, Kim's phone suddenly rang. "It's Lionel," she said, rolling her eyes. I watched her face, noticing her expression change from bored to stunned. "Oh no," she cried. "That can't be true."

A range of possibilities flew through my mind. Lionel Stevens was scarcely an alarmist. We'd often joked that Kim needed to check his pulse to ensure that he was even alive.

Kim clutched her phone like a lifeline as she shared the news. "Teagen's dead. They're questioning Roddy Park about her murder."

* * *

"Dead?" My mouth gaped open, and for once, I was speechless. "Murder?" Even the normally unflappable Violet Davis gasped.

"Lionel didn't know any details. Apparently, Brendan found Roddy stooped over Teagen, clutching her arm. Madge was with him, and she called Chief Miles."

"Roddy wouldn't kill her. He couldn't." My response was understandable but trite. With the right provocation, any human being could commit murder. Only a fool believed otherwise. A fool in love like me.

"We should leave," Violet said, flinging some bills on the table. "Gemma may know more details by now. Benny will be sure to crow about it and spread the word."

She was right. Everyone in the restaurant would soon be scrutinizing us, hoping to gauge any reaction. Poppet was our safe space. I phoned Gemma and told her to meet us there. Pronto. Over snifters of Brandy, we calmed down and discussed what little information we had. When Gemma burst into the room wide-eyed with russet curls askew, her excitement was palpable.

"Benny gave me the scoop," she said. "Not everything, but enough."

I fought for self-control. If Roddy confessed, I would have to accept it. Until then, I would defend him vigorously. Innocent until proven guilty, the mantra of every defense attorney and her criminal client.

Violet urged Gemma to calm down. "Tell us exactly what Benny said. How was Teagen killed? Until they do an autopsy, everything is conjecture."

Gemma hesitated. My partner loved drama, so I knew she was gearing up for a star turn. "Benny was with the chief when the call-came in. Madge

Stone called. They rushed over and found Roddy bending over Teagen's body and Brendan wailing like a Banshee. Paramedics rushed in, but it was too late. Get this—Teagen was practically naked!"

I gulped. That suggested a crime of passion. I knew from personal experience just how passionate Dr. Park could get.

"What was she wearing?" Kim asked.

Benny's descriptive powers were limited, but Gemma pieced together enough information to fill the gaps. "Not much. Some kind of frilly white apron and fishnet hose. You know the kind of thing you see in porno flicks."

OMG! Teagen was posing as a French maid, the fantasy of many a man. I'd never once considered tarting myself up that way. Who knew that staid, sensible Roddy Park would be enticed by such behavior?

"I suppose she cooked dinner?" Roddy always had a hearty appetite for food and other delicacies.

Gemma shrugged. "Who knows? The place was a mess, though—dishes scattered everywhere. Benny had to wrestle Brendan away from her body."

Violet waited before speaking until she had absorbed all the information. "Not surprising that Chief Miles wanted to question Roddy. That makes sense, but I doubt that he was arrested. Too premature without forensic evidence."

Kim jumped up. "If Madge was there, she'll know everything. Let me find her. I'm sure she needs a friend to comfort her about now."

Violet nodded. "Good thinking. Report back as soon as you learn anything. And see if Lionel knows anything else." She patted my hand. "Meanwhile, Marky and I will go straight to gossip central. Doogie Kinkaid."

I was torn with indecision. Doogie would insist on trading information for a piece of my heart. That was his quid pro quo. Violet brushed aside my misgivings and gave me a shot of tough love.

"You can't evade things, dear niece. Like it or not, you're in the thick of this. Besides, we may be overreacting. Perhaps it wasn't a homicide after all. Teagen had plenty of medical issues, remember, and she'd attempted suicide several times before."

True enough. Only yesterday, Teagen mentioned her allergies and use of sedatives. Besides, she was no spring chicken. Despite her glamorous façade, Mrs. Brendan Doyle was a middle-aged woman susceptible to several ills.

I glanced at my watch. It was already nine pm. Would Doogie be roaming about or snugly tucked into his comfy bed? When Violet summoned him, the question was answered.

"He'll be right over," she said. "Play it cool. You know what a chatterbox Doogie is. Act saddened over Teagen's death but confident that Roddy wasn't involved. And of course, be sure to feed him."

My talent for duplicity was limited but goaded by my aunt, I rose to the task.

When Doogie lumbered in bearing a bottle of Courvoisier, he eyed the tray of appetizers before glancing our way. "Ladies," he said with faux sorrow. "On such a sad occasion, I decided to break out the good stuff. In Teagen's honor, of course." He filled his plate as Violet poured the Cognac into Baccarat snifters.

"Ooh," Doogie gave a little squeal. "Special indeed. I see the Napoleonic crest on these."

We solemnly toasted Teagen Doyle, a woman of many motives and varied talents. Then Violet segued into the matter at hand.

"What do you know, Doogie? As you can expect, my niece is distraught. Teagen was a client of hers after all."

He nibbled a canapé before responding. "I wasn't there, of course, so this is all second hand. According to Madge, Teagen was quite infatuated with your young man, Marky, and he returned the sentiment. Tonight was what she called her seduction special. Champagne, caviar, and lobster thermidor with scallops. That was one of her signature dishes." He chuckled. "We always knew when she was smitten. Out came the lobster and caviar, and off came her clothes."

I bit my tongue to suppress the vile comments that I longed to make. Teagen was a succubus, a beguiling seductress on the prowl. Good riddance to her and her professor paramour. While I fumed, my aunt carried the conversational load, charming Doogie with her usual panache.

"Brendan had his flings, so I suppose it was only fair. Sauce for the goose and gander, you know. Besides, I'm sure Roddy was flattered, but I doubt that he took her seriously." Violet gestured toward me. "Not when he had a lovely young lady like Marky waiting for him."

Doogie sipped his Cognac before replying. "According to Madge, they found Roddy almost on top of her. OF course, he claimed to be giving her CPR, but Brendan didn't buy his act. Not with her top down and those fish nets torn." He flashed a look of faux sympathy my way.

"How odd that Brendan and Madge showed up," Violet said. "Seduction scenes don't normally involve onlookers."

"That's just it," Doogie said. "They got a tip. At least Brendan did. Someone told him Teagen needed help."

My suspicions told me that the call had probably originated with Teagen herself. Ever the drama queen even unto death. That ominous text flashed into my mind. "All men kill the things they love." Had Roddy become obsessed with his employer or was Brendan the culprit? Jealousy festered and corroded the soul. Othello felt the sting of that green-eyed monster and look where that led.

Doogie left after polishing off every scrap of food and draining his snifter of Cognac. Afterwards, I felt puzzled and out of sorts, but Violet banished my blues with a hug. "Get some sleep, Marky. We'll get more answers tomorrow. Besides, we need a clear head to confront whatever arises."

As usual, she was right, but that didn't improve my sleep that night. Nightmares plagued me as I saw Roddy in manacles with Teagen scantily clad in her French maid attire, standing over him, cackling maniacally.

Chapter Nine

I didn't like Teagen Doyle, but I didn't wish her dead. She was spoiled, manipulative, and unkind. Her sudden death was probably an accident, and Roddy wasn't in custody. He was merely being questioned. That made sense. After all, he was the last person to see her alive, and no matter what Brendan Doyle said, Roddy had no reason to harm her.

When I checked my phone, I saw a text from him. It was succinct, almost brusque. "Can we talk?" it said. I responded immediately. "Meet me at Poppet."

I whisked him into the conference room as soon as he arrived. Despite his ordeal, the wayward scholar seemed remarkably chipper and looked untouched by his time in the big house. Roddy held out his arms to me, but I backed away. "Have a seat, Professor. We need to talk."

"Marky, I don't know what to say. Nothing went on between me and Mrs. Doyle, I swear." He gulped. "Things just got out of hand. It was supposed to be dinner. A business meeting. When I got there, she was wearing this caftan thing. Sort of like a robe. Before I knew it, she slipped it off and came out in that outfit carrying a platter of lobster thermidor, a dish of caviar, and some vegan corn fritters."

I raised an eyebrow. "Lobster Thermador is quite a dish, but so was Teagen."

He shook his head. "No. It wasn't seductive, it was kind of sad. I mean, she was an older lady, close to my mom's age. Nice looking, but still… I tried to be polite. The meal was delicious, and I love caviar, not that I can afford it on my salary. Then things started getting weird. She started asking me things…"

"What kind of things?" I noticed that he couldn't look me in the eye. The man was lying, or at least downplaying his tete-a-tete with Teagen. I'd seen photos of his mom and, trust me, she looked nothing like Teagen Doyle. Mrs. Park looked…well…motherly.

"You were saying," I refused to let him off the hook. This was truth-telling time.

"She asked personal things. Sex stuff." Roddy stammered as he said that.

"Go on." I stood hands on hips and glared at him.

"Ah, Marky, this is embarrassing."

If he expected mercy, he was sadly mistaken. He'd caused me plenty of embarrassment. Payback was bound to hurt.

Roddy recovered his poise and plowed through his confession. "Okay. She asked what positions I liked and stuff like that. Then she moved over and sat in my lap." He closed his eyes. "Before I knew it, she'd unzipped my pants and was, you know, reaching for me."

I wished Gemma was with me. She would have found the truth without being blinded by affection. I reminded myself that Dr. Roderick Park was thirty years old, and with his luscious looks, he had been fending off frantic females for most of his adult life. He was scarcely the neophyte he pretended to be.

"How far did she get?" My tone was neutral, almost unemotional. I played the Grand Inquisitor, Torquemada, in drag.

Roddy squirmed in his seat. "Not very far. I swear. Suddenly, she started grabbing her throat, saying that she couldn't breathe."

That changed the picture. Teagen was prone to any number of allergies. Was her death a terrible accident rather than murder? Roddy's face contorted as he recalled the grisly scene.

"She gasped like she was choking. I remembered her EpiPen, but at first, I couldn't find it."

Madge said that Teagen never let that EpiPen out of her sight. Hard to believe that even during a seduction, she changed her ways. "Then what happened?"

Roddy closed his eyes, as if he were reliving the traumatic event. "I looked around and finally checked her purse. I found it there under a bunch of makeup and stuff. She was still able to speak then."

"And…" I felt an immediate kinship with dentists. Extracting the full story from Roddy was as difficult as pulling teeth.

"She tried injecting herself, but it didn't seem to help. It dropped to the floor. She got all pale and kept gasping for breath." He shuddered. "I tried CPR, but that was when Brendan and Madge burst in. All hell broke loose. He started screaming and pulled me away. Mrs. Stone phoned 911. I guess she used to be a nurse or something because she told Mr. Doyle to find another EpiPen while she did CPR."

No wonder Roddy was shaken. Watching someone die would traumatize most people.

He gulped and continued the tale. "Anyway, the paramedics and the cops got there about the same time. They loaded her into the ambulance, and that was the last I saw of her."

"What about Madge and Brendan?"

"Mrs. Stone put that caftan thing on Teagen before the ambulance came. I think she was trying to, you know, preserve her dignity. Mr. Doyle went in the ambulance with his wife."

The whole thing sounded like an unfortunate accident to me. Roddy was probably not a suspect, but I still wanted to know more. Gemma could learn the police angle from her boy toy without any trouble. Benny Soto freely leaked information without a thought to confidentiality. Aunt Violet was a confidant of Madge Stone, a far more reliable source than Benny. Between the two of them, I might piece together where the situation stood. Then, I would approach Chief Miles. She needed to hear that Teagen feared for her life. It had little to do with me and nothing at all to do with Roddy. If her death was accidental, the issue was moot; however, coincidences bothered me. How likely was it that a woman who sought out a sleuth would lose her own life shortly thereafter?

"Can I still stay with you, Marky? Chief Miles told me to hang around at least until the coroner's inquest." The look in his eyes reminded me of a puppy who had misbehaved and sought forgiveness.

"Of course you can stay, unless you're stuck on Doogie's hospitality. He probably pulled out all the stops for you."

Roddy frowned. "He was very solicitous. Maybe too much. I felt rather uncomfortable."

That gave me an idea. "You need to find Doogie and talk to him. Tell him you're worried about being blamed."

"I'm not sure about that. What excuse would I give?"

I fought the urge to pinch the good professor's cheeks. "Use your noggin. Who cares what you tell him? Pretend you need his advice. That always works. If anybody has his finger on the pulse of Harbor Bay, it's Doogie. Just keep his fingers off you while you're at it."

He shrugged. "Okay. I'll think of something, I guess."

I propelled him toward the door. "Look. It's lunchtime right about now, and Doogie always drops in at the Patisserie. I'm sure he'd welcome company, especially if it's yours."

My next contact was Gemma. She had just finished a couple's massage and was taking her break. Unlike me, Gemma was a wizard at the massage table. She managed to soothe the crankiest customers with her magic hands and cheerful chatter.

"Wow," she said as she dried her hands. "Everyone is buzzing about Teagen. Most think she was murdered, although some admit she may have overdosed on those tinctures of hers." She scrutinized my face. "Okay. Out with it. Is the professor guilty or is he back in your good graces?"

"He's no killer, you know that. Besides, I bet it was an accident. While she was whipping up that seduction dinner, she probably mixed something into it that made her sick."

Gemma eyed me. "Maybe, but Brendan Doyle told everyone that your boy did it out of jealousy. What do you call it, unrequited love?"

"Ha. Brendan has the best motive of all when it comes to jealousy. What does Benny say?"

Gemma rolled her eyes. "That boy has plenty of theories, but facts, I'm not so sure." She grinned. "So, tell me. Are we on the case? It's only fair since Teagen hired you."

Gemma was my Watson on two other cases, although she insisted on top billing as Sherlock. I could count on her to pursue fearlessly, often recklessly, whatever leads we might uncover.

"Your assignment is to get the scoop from inside the investigation. Use any tactics necessary. Benny is a sucker for flattery and other inducements."

"Got it." Gemma saluted and dove for her iPhone. I stepped away to give her privacy and spare myself from the nonsensical sweet talk she spoon-fed to Benny. Thank heaven my business partner was honest. She would have made a spectacular con-woman.

Aunt Violet didn't need any prompting. Her lunch with Madge Stone had produced some tasty tidbits on Teagen's death. When she swept into Poppet, dressed in head-to-toe aubergine, my aunt's usually calm expression had changed.

"What did Madge say?" I violated every stricture of good breeding by plunging right into the main event. My mom and Emily Post would both have been aghast.

"Madge was puzzled. Teagen was extremely cautious about food allergens, almost paranoid. With good reason as it turns out." Violet hesitated. "The meal she prepared, the one called seduction special, was one she had made dozens of times. Madge doubted that Teagen used any ingredients that would harm her. Unless…"

We exchanged looks, reluctant to state the obvious. "Unless she planned a dramatic final act and deliberately sprinkled something in the mix." Violet shook her head. "I can't believe that Teagen would harm herself. She loved life and enjoyed causing a scene. More likely, she planned to be rescued by Roddy amid a flood of publicity for her business venture and sympathy from Brendan. Remember, she had her EpiPen at hand."

I closed my eyes as I considered the possibilities. Teagen played the damsel in distress to perfection. Her plea for help against a potential killer had fooled even me. Roddy would have been putty in her beautifully manicured hands. If that was her plan, she had overplayed things big time.

"When will the coroner determine a cause of death? If it's accidental, that clears Roddy, doesn't it?"

"One would suppose so," Violet said. "All the publicity puts Chief Miles under a lot of pressure. Madge said that Brendan is beside himself with grief. He's using every contact he can to exert pressure on the authorities. Lucky for him, he has her to console him. She's known both for years. At one time, I even thought that Madge and Brendan might get together. She was obsessed with him back then. Of course, that was before she met her husband, and Teagen came on the scene. Ancient history."

"That's strange. He and Teagen were so competitive. He wasn't a model husband from all that I've heard. Lots of affairs on both sides."

Violet contradicted me with a wave of her hand. "Few things are that clear, Marky. Brendan and Teagen had a complicated relationship. Game playing, flirtations, all of that only fueled their desire for each other. They lived for drama."

I knew nothing of the ways of the rich and famous, but Violet inhabited their world. I felt naïve and callow, way out of my depth. If I intended to help Roddy, a crash course in upper-class mores was in order.

"Teagen hinted that her husband wanted to kill her. Was she wrong?"

My patient Aunt sighed. "We've discussed this before, Marky. Brendan is all bluster, but he doesn't have a mean bone in his body. Except in business matters, of course. Then he's a shark. Men don't rise to those heights without cutting a few corners." She grinned. "And a few throats."

"I plan to approach Chief Miles and tell her what I know. It's my civic duty."

I ignored Violet's raised brows and basked in self-righteousness. Marketta Davis, pillar of rectitude. My motives were pure, my conscience clear. After all, I didn't even like Teagen Doyle. Sharing information with the police was the right thing to do.

"Before you go," Violet said. "Check in with Kim. Remember, Lionel was Teagen's business partner. He might have some useful ideas."

Lionel Stevens was one of the least imaginative humans I had ever encountered. The crotchety counsel barely breathed a word to me, but Kim might have pried some information from him. I texted her asking to meet at the patisserie. My visit to Chief Miles could wait. I needed fuel to sustain me, and a few extra calories wouldn't hurt.

Kim arrived there ahead of me. She'd managed to snag a secluded booth at the back of the restaurant where we could avoid eavesdroppers. Lunch time generated a crowd of hungry patrons, who eagerly consumed quiche, croissants, and soup with undisguised zest. I sailed past curious customers without stopping to chat, although I nodded to Doogie. He was ensconced in his usual spot, engaged in what looked like a serious discussion with a certain handsome Professor.

Kim pulled out a chair next to her and beckoned to me. "Have a seat, Marky. I'm dying to hear any news." Like my aunt, Kim exuded an understated elegance that defied age or time. I tried to emulate them, but usually came up short. Gemma maintained that style was innate. You either had or you didn't. As an artist, I easily detected the appropriate form or subject. As a woman, it was more difficult. I veered from gamine to femme fatale without ever capturing the right look. Kim knew instinctively what suited her, and it showed.

"How's Roddy holding up?" Kim asked. "Lionel said they don't have enough evidence to charge anyone at this point. You know my dearly beloved. He's thinking more about the monetary end than a homicide. After all, Teagen's Tinctures without Teagen can't survive, and he's a major investor. Fortunately, he'd insisted on getting insurance. What they used to call a key man policy." She shook her head. "I'm so out of date. The term now is key person policy."

That was normal business practice, but it still shocked me. Would the police see it as prudence or a motive for murder? Lionel was cagey but scarcely homicidal. The stark reality was that Teagen's Tinctures couldn't exist without its namesake.

Kim gestured toward the table where Roddy and Doogie were speaking in low tones. "Looks like he has at least one supporter, although I question Doogie's motives. He falls in love so easily."

"Roddy's innocent," I said. "I haven't forgiven him for drooling over Teagen, but he didn't kill her, no matter what Brendan says. Besides, it was probably an accident."

Kim's face radiated compassion. "I'm sure you're right. It's hard to believe that Teagen is really gone. She was such a force of nature. I always thought she was indestructible."

I fought to control my emotions and failed. "Humph! She was a bit long in the tooth to be flaunting herself at every desirable male, especially one young enough to be her son. That whole French Maid costume sounds ludicrous!"

"Don't forget Teagen's background. Those film people live in an alternate universe," Kim said. "Face it, Marky. Most men would be flattered by the attention, and I suspect that no matter what you think, Professor Park is aware of his effect on women."

Her words echoed those of Aunt Violet. My judgment was fatally flawed when it came to my love life and my penchant for bad boys. Bearing that in mind, I forged ahead anyway. "Lionel must have contacts at the coroner's office. What's the latest?"

Kim hesitated. "They're calling it homicide even though it might be an accident. Teagen had what they called elevated levels of dairy and nuts in her system." She shuddered. "Now I feel guilty. Teagen always dramatized everything, and I thought that this allergy story was just another bid for attention. She flashed that EpiPen around like a talisman. Called it her good luck charm."

"I guess she was wrong," I said. "Either way, Roddy should be in the clear. Trust me, he has zero experience cooking anything. His mother and sisters spoiled him, waiting on him hand and foot. Besides, Teagen made a big deal about preparing her special seduction dinner herself."

Kim cleared her throat. "That's somewhat misleading."

"What do you mean? Madge said she was a diplomate of Le Cordon Bleu. Top marks and a certificate to prove it. I saw the picture."

Now, Kim looked distinctly uncomfortable. She paused and sipped her latte before commenting. "Look, Marky, I tried to explain before. Teagen lived in an alternate universe where fantasy became reality."

"You mean she lied?"

Kim squirmed in her seat. "Exaggerated. Teagen did enroll at Le Cordon Bleu in Paris, but she got bored. The process became tedious, and she dropped out. That diploma was an arranged marriage, so to speak. They got the publicity, and Teagen gained another star in her crown. Brendan was so proud. Always bragging about his wife, the chef."

That opened my eyes to yet another possibility. If Teagen didn't prepare the meal, who had? There were only three or four restaurants in Harbor Bay that served high-end fare, and one of them must have whipped up Teagen's lavish feast. That widened the suspect pool considerably.

"Okay, Marky," Kim said. "Out with it. I can see the wheels churning in that fertile mind of yours."

I'd hatched a scheme that just might work. By deputizing Kim, Aunt Violet, and Gemma, we could scour the likely restaurants and find the source of Teagen's last meal. Stealth and duplicity were needed, as well as a pinch of luck. No establishment would freely admit lacing that dinner with allergens unless it welcomed a whopping big lawsuit from Brendan Doyle.

"I have another question," I told Kim. "Roddy said she injected herself with that EpiPen. Why didn't it work?"

Kim shrugged her shoulders. "Who knows? I've never needed one, thank goodness. You could always ask Madge. Remember, she was a nurse at one time."

I had no medical knowledge, but I thought EpiPens saved people's lives. Madge could probably explain things, but better still, I could scour the internet for information and consult my old standby, Web MD. Gemma's contact at the hospital might also know something.

"I'm trying to keep a low profile," I said. "There must be plenty of information about EpiPens out there without asking Madge. Remember, she was Teagen's BFF, and Brendan clings to her like a limpet. She may blame Roddy."

Kim rolled her eyes. "Don't forget Letty Briggs. She's another dependent of Madge's." She shivered. "There's something weird about that girl. I know it's unkind to say so, but she's terribly cold. I think she'd be capable of eliminating anyone she disliked without turning a hair."

Letty Briggs. The self-effacing cousin was an enigma to me. "What's her story? Is she dependent on Madge for money?"

"Hardly," Kim laughed. "Believe it or not, Letty is an heiress. Her family owned that large Chicago department store chain. You know, the one that took up an entire block of Michigan Avenue. She uses Madge as a crutch, unfairly, I think, but Madge has a soft spot for strays, human and animal." Kim squeezed my hand. "Remember, Marky, Madge, and most of the people in Harbor Bay are very fair. They won't turn against Roddy without proof, no matter what Brendan says. I think most people resent well-connected outsiders pushing their agenda."

I watched Roddy and Doogie end their tete-a-tete and exit the Patisserie. Doogie was all smiles, but Roddy appeared somewhat shaken. Perhaps my errant Professor should stick to politics and leave the sleuthing to me. He was manifestly uncomfortable with extracting information from the unsuspecting.

Fortunately, Gemma had no such qualms. As soon as Kim and I reached Poppet, she hustled us into the conference room. Aunt Violet was already in there, calmly sipping Oolong tea and paging through the latest edition of *Architectural Digest*.

"Boy, do I have news," Gemma said. She was gloating, awash with triumph. Violet merely raised an eyebrow, but I was less patient.

"Stop stalling," I said. "Out with it."

Gemma pouted. "Ah, you're no fun at all. When I think of what I had to do to get this scoop…" She trailed off, leaving me to speculate but sparing us from lascivious details.

"Okay, Benny overheard Chief Miles on a conference call with the District Attorney."

I couldn't resist sniping. "You mean he eavesdropped."

Gemma dismissed that comment with a wave of her hand. "Big deal. No time to quibble. Anyway, the DA wanted a quick arrest, probably to shut up Brendan Doyle. It seems he has the Governor's ear, and things are heating up."

I closed my eyes, visualizing Roddy in an orange prison jumpsuit. Bright colors flattered him, so the picture was not unpleasant.

"Does that mean they have more evidence?" Violet asked. "Have they definitely ruled out accidental death?"

Gemma shook her head. "Nope. I guess the chief held her own and said that the inquest hadn't even been held yet. Called it "premature" or something like that. Anyway, they're putting a rush on the testing." She eyed us closely as if expecting a round of applause.

"I have some news as well, and it may be the answer to Teagen's death." I avoided saying the word murder. After all, until compelling evidence was presented, accidental death was still the most likely cause. When they heard the Cordon Bleu scam, both Violet and Gemma gasped.

"Unbelievable," Violet said. "Certainly shines a new light on Teagen's death. I agree that we should divide and conquer. I'm friendly with the owners of two of our premier dining spots. With a bit of persuasion, I should get the information we need."

Gemma scratched her ear. "I don't know the big shots, but I'm pals with a couple of waiters in those ritzy joints. Believe me, they know everything that goes on. More than their bosses know."

Even though my dear friend often engaged in unfounded class warfare, I realized that in this instance, she made a valid point. "Okay," I said, "Let's divide up and get to work."

I assigned tasks based on the food preferences of my crew. Aunt Violet was a Francophile who had lived in Paris for years. That endeared her to Pierre LePenn, the owner and chef d' cuisine of the Bistro Versailles. Kim shared fashion tips with Rene Marcel, partner in Maison Blanc, and I was a regular customer of the Patisserie. Gemma agreed to do her bit by ingratiating herself with the head waiter at French Fare, a bakery and gourmet coffee spot.

"Timing is essential," I said. "The mills of justice may grind slowly in most cases, but not if Brendan Doyle keeps agitating everyone."

When Roddy sauntered in later, Gemma gave him the side eye. "Found a new sponsor, have you, Professor? I hear that Doogie is very generous with his friends."

He flushed but held his ground. "Ah, come on, Gemma, I just had lunch with him. Marky made me do it."

Gemma snorted a rather vulgar reply, but I was eager to learn what he'd found out.

"What was he hiding? I know him, and Doogie had that guilty look on his face. He knows more about Teagen's death than he admits."

Roddy bit his lip. "You'll be disappointed. He spent almost the entire meal asking me about the menu that night. It was ghoulish. He wanted details about every bite we ate."

That seemed odd even for Doogie. Of course, he was a gourmand as well as an accomplished cook himself. Was this some sort of bizarre food foreplay?

When he heard that Teagen had not prepared the meal, Roddy was astounded. He wrinkled his brow in thought. "Come to think of it, everything was ready when I arrived."

"Wasn't there a mess in the kitchen?" Gemma asked. "Most people aren't tidy when they whip up a big spread."

"Not that I recall. The table was set with crystal and china. I remember that. But Mrs. Doyle was more interested in putting on a show." He locked eyes with me. "You know what I mean, Marky."

"So Doogie didn't give any clues. Anything at all?"

He shook his head. "Nope. Guess I'm not much of a detective."

I was curious about the police involvement. "Anything more from Chief Miles?"

Roddy froze. "She asked me to drop by tomorrow after lunch. I'm sure it's just routine. Nothing to worry about. I haven't hired an attorney or anything."

That remark sent chills up and down my spine. How naïve could Roddy be? Even the most basic cop shows advised suspects to consult an attorney. Perry Mason would be aghast! I thought of a wily man from Chicago with whom I'd shared a few moments. Killian Blaine would have scoffed at Roddy's casual manner. Of course, Killian was a shark, the type of lawyer you'd want as an advocate but not an adversary.

"You can't go alone," I said. "I'll go with you. They may be laying a trap for you."

Gemma laughed. "You're no lawyer, Marky. Maybe Lionel will go."

"Roddy's entitled to have a representative present. If they read him his rights, all bets are off. Besides, Lionel might be more hindrance than help. You know what a fuddy duddy he is."

Just then my aunt joined us. She agreed that Roddy needed someone with him but insisted that I was not the one.

"I'll phone Kim right away," she said. "Lionel can at least protect Roddy's rights. Besides, police are more cautious with a lawyer present."

"Chief Miles said it was just a chat. That doesn't sound too ominous." Roddy's voice sounded less confident than it had previously.

Violet patted his arm. "I'm sure it will be fine. However, better safe than sorry. There's a reason that cliché has endured so long."

We agreed to change the subject to more pleasant topics. Gemma described her encounter with Benny's family, and Violet charmed us with several anecdotes about famous and infamous people she had known.

Bright and early the next day, we implemented our attack plan. Violet, as usual, was miles ahead of us. She had already chatted with her contact at Bistro Francais. "Pierre assured me that neither he nor any of his staff prepared Teagen's seduction special."

Gemma grimaced. "How do we know he's not lying?"

"Simple," said my aunt. "The electrical system malfunctioned that day and the restaurant was closed for forty-eight hours. Besides, I can vouch for his character." Violet was too refined to smirk, but her expression said it all.

I had to do my part, so I sped down to the Patisserie the moment it opened. The scent of newly baked croissants and fresh ground coffee wafting from the kitchen was maddening. Discipline, I told myself, reciting Aunt Violet's mantra. That stricture usually suppressed my instincts to indulge in useless calories, but in this instance, it failed dismally. I ordered two almond croissants and a double Cappuccino and settled into a vacant booth. My timing was perfect. Since the lunch crowd had yet to arrive, Marie Dubois, owner and pastry chef, ambled over to chat. Like most of Harbor Bay, her number one topic was the death of Teagen Doyle. Marie's approach was oblique, but her aim was clear.

"You must be distraught, Marky," she said in her charming accent. "So sad about Mrs. Doyle and your young man."

I played innocent, a challenging role for me. "Yes. Professor Park was traumatized by the whole event. You can understand that."

Marie nodded. "Mrs. Doyle was such a vibrant woman. A great loss."

"You shared an interest," I said. "Teagen was a diplomate of Le Cordon Bleu just like you."

Marie raised her perfectly plucked brows in surprise or possibly sarcasm. "She never mentioned that, but of course I was not one of her intimates."

"Oh. I thought you helped her with that lobster Thermador. Roddy said it was superb, and I thought immediately of your special touch."

As if she sensed a trap, Marie immediately rose and said with a forced smile, "Alas, Mrs. Doyle did not contact me." She spread her hands out in a gesture of sorrow. "If only she had, Teagen might still be with us. We take special care with food allergies."

That terminated my feeble attempt at engaging Marie, leaving me to commiserate by downing more calories than any sane woman should even consider. When I returned to Poppet, Gemma greeted me with a triumphant smile.

"Guess we know who's the real Holmes," she said. "I got the scoop from my pal at the Boulangerie. Wait till you hear!"

I wasn't resentful. Not really. Gemma was far more adept and less scrupulous than I was when it came to extracting information. "Hold the news until Aunt Violet and Kim get here. No sense repeating things."

She pouted but agreed to restrain herself. When Kim and my aunt entered our store, I waved them into the conference room and poured Pellegrino. I could tell by their expressions that their search had been fruitless.

"Let me go first," Gemma said. "My informant knew all about Teagen and her phony cooking claims. He said it was a big joke, and all the food guys knew about it. They buttoned their lips in case Brendan Doyle came after them. No one wants to tangle with him."

"Informant?" Kim said, laughing. "Sounds very official. I'm afraid I came up empty. My friend said Teagen never even dined at her restaurant. It seems that Brendan flirted with Renee at some cocktail party and that caused a big scene." Her smile brightened. "But I do have some good news. Lionel agreed to accompany Roddy to the police station." She checked her Rolex, "In fact, they should be there right now."

Gemma scoffed. "Bet that wasn't easy. What'd you offer him, Kim?"

"Cut it out," I scolded my partner. "What about Alain, Aunt Violet?"

Alain DuMonde was a Michelin-starred chef who operated a bistro in a neighboring town.

She frowned. "We had a very nice chat this morning. He knew all the gossip, of course, but he assured me that Teagen never approached him about preparing that meal. She told him she had a secret weapon, or some such nonsense. Bragged about it. Typical Teagen, ever the drama queen."

I puzzled over the secret weapon comment. If Teagen didn't prepare her final meal, who did? Despite all her frivolity, there was one unavoidable fact: Teagen was dead.

"Maybe Lionel had some luck with Chief Miles," I said. "We're running out of suspects."

Kim scoured the shop for any eavesdroppers. "There's good news and bad news. Lionel just called me."

"Didn't he text you?" Gemma narrowed her eyes. "I'll bet he doesn't know how."

"Don't listen to her," I told Kim. "What did he say?"

"Roddy wasn't arrested or even cautioned. Aubrey Miles questioned him closely but was professional and polite. Lionel's words, not mine. It seems that the meal did contain significant amounts of dairy and nuts. Teagen was highly allergic to both of those things and would never have ingested them knowingly. Roddy, like most men, never noticed the ingredients. He just enjoyed the meal."

"What about those tinctures?" I asked. "Did they test those things?"

Kim shrugged. "I doubt that they had time to do that. The lab rushed the results on the meal because Brendan bellowed so to everyone, from the forensic staff to the Governor. He's like a freight train when he gets going. That man stops at nothing to get his way."

The whole thing didn't make sense. According to Roddy, Teagen used her EpiPen, another of her secret weapons, or so she thought. Surely that would have saved her. So, who prepared that seduction special? Perhaps Teagen did learn a few things at cooking school and tried to impress Roddy.

"We made the national news, you know." Kim unfolded a newspaper from her tote and pointed to a headline from the *Chicago Tribune.* It sounded more like tabloid journalism than the typical prose from that venerable newspaper. *"Teagen's last tip—beloved star's death stumps authorities."*

Gemma immediately grabbed her iPad and scrolled down the headlines from the more sensational media outlets. "Yep. Harbor Bay is on the map again, but not in a good way." She pointed to a photo. "Great shot of your professor, Marky. He is a handsome devil, I must admit. And get this—-one reporter squealed about that French Maid outfit Teagen wore. I wonder how that got out."

"Probably a morgue attendant or one of the paramedics. Remember, *TMZ* pays good money for tips like that." Kim sighed. "Brendan must be livid."

I shivered, wondering what impact this scandal would have on Roddy's career. Political science was a rather dry subject, but murder raised the profile of anyone associated with it and not in a good way. Tenure was the golden fleece that every fledgling academic frantically pursued. Competition was keen, and Roddy's notoriety might arouse all sorts of opposition.

"Don't worry," Violet said. "It still looks like the whole thing was merely a tragic accident. Talk to him when he returns. Maybe he'll recall something Teagen said or did that might be helpful."

Gemma leered. "Yeah, Ms. Marky. You must have some sexy number that would catch the Professor's eye. He liked the French Maid outfit, so play Mata Hari and grill him good."

When a bus loaded with affluent tourists disgorged its riders in front of Poppet, they flooded our store with checkbooks in hand. That gave me a reprieve from Gemma's snide suggestions and the worrisome state of my personal life. Fantasia shot me her pleading stare, reminding me that she was woefully in need of exercise. So was I. A brisk walk would clear my head and allow me to think. We maintained a steady pace as we circled the town square and headed toward the waterfront. I deliberately altered my route to avoid any sighting of Roddy Park. My feelings for him were uncertain, far more conflicted than I had thought possible. He was still someone I cared for, but his feckless behavior troubled me. Ever since his encounter with that faded femme fatale, Teagen Doyle, Roddy had acted like a total wimp! A niggling doubt assailed me. Was it possible? Had Roddy conspired with someone else to kill his benefactor? I shrugged that off. He had no motive even lust. Teagen had been more than willing to share her favors, and as for money, she'd already advanced him a substantial sum. Above all, he was a rationalist, an intellectual who was far too clever to murder someone while he was in the room.

When my iPhone buzzed, I answered automatically without checking the ID. It took only a second to identify the caller's deep baritone and faintly mocking tone.

"Making headlines again, Ms. Davis? Murder follows you around like a dark cloud." The voice of Killian Blaine, crack attorney and ultimate alpha male, was unmistakable. He lived in Chicago, so it was inevitable that the Doyle case would attract his notice. Gemma drooled over him, describing Killian as a "Total Hottie." An accurate assessment, but she forgot to mention that he was also a serial womanizer who disrupted lives and broke female hearts with abandon. I'd managed to fend him off, although the attraction between us was palpable. We'd dabbled in romance and a bit more until Roddy inserted himself into my life once more. Now I was vulnerable, and like a predator smelling blood, Killian had once again swooped into my life.

"Still building your empire?" I asked. "Surely a mundane, small-town murder is beneath a man of your talents."

"Not so mundane," he said. "Brendan Doyle happens to be a client of mine, you know, and a pal as well. He filled me in on all the grisly details, including the involvement of your very close friend, Roderick Park, and you, too, Marketta Davis. Imagine my surprise when he described you as the artist, amateur sleuth, and busybody who was in his late wife's employ."

"I wouldn't take Brendan's word for things," I said. "He's still a suspect, you know. Besides, Teagen's death was a tragic accident, not homicide."

"Really? My sources dispute that."

"You're not practicing criminal law these days, I trust. Surely there are still conglomerates to menace, or hostile takeovers awaiting your golden touch."

Killian was impossible to discourage. He relished a challenge, especially if it generated sensational headlines. My barbs didn't faze him one bit. He laughed. He guffawed as if my feeble jests were comic gold.

"Maybe you need an attorney, Marky." He used his silky-smooth voice that promised far more than it delivered. His track record with women, celebrated in the society columns and *Page Six,* documented the wily rogue's many escapades.

"No thanks. I'm satisfied running my little business and painting. I have no interest at all in Mrs. Doyle's death, no matter what Brendan told you."

"Hmm. Doesn't sound like the Marky I know and admire. You and I have unfinished business, Ms. Davis. Count on it." Before ringing off, he made one final retort. "Are you engaged to this murder suspect. I understand he's a professor or something exciting like that."

Killian had a gift for annoying me. That deliberate bit of sarcasm left me unable to ignore him. "My personal life is off limits to you, Mr. Blaine. From what I hear, not much has changed. You have plenty of excitement in your own life to deal with."

"Ah, still keeping tabs on your old admirer. Splendid! That means you're not engaged, and there's still hope for me. We solved a murder together not long ago, remember? History could repeat itself."

"I'm not interested in *old* admirers. I prefer younger men. And you were more hindrance than help during that last fiasco."

"Ouch! Still have that rapier-sharp wit, I see. No matter. We need to have an attorney-client conference very soon. I'll check my schedule. Don't mind Brendan. He won't harass you anymore. I told him that you were strictly off limits."

With that, he terminated our conversation, leaving me curious and conflicted. I didn't need Killian Blaine to fight my battles. Why didn't he just leave me alone?

Chapter Ten

I couldn't face Gemma after Killian's call, so I sought out my aunt. She'd understand how dangerous the man was, but wouldn't assign blame or be swayed by his blarney.

Violet chuckled when I shared my battle of wits with him. She wasn't even surprised.

"I wondered when he would surface," she said. "You put a dent in that man's ego, and he's unaccustomed to that. Rejection is not Killian Blaine's style."

"Suppose he shows up here?" I fretted. "He could make trouble."

Violet patted my cheek. "Only if you let him, dear girl. Take the imitative and plan. He'll swoop in when you least expect him, probably with Brendan Doyle. He's back in Chicago for the week, you know. Madge told me."

"What about Roddy? How would I handle two men? They might fight."

"Honestly, Marketta, that's a delicious problem. Two very attractive men vying for your attention. Most women would relish that challenge." She placed both hands on my shoulders. "Before it comes to that, I suggest you think long and hard about your relationship with Dr. Park. Seems like you've been fighting all his battles for him."

That observation stung even more because it was true. "He needs my help. How could I abandon him? After all, I introduced him to Teagen."

Violet shook her head. "Stop that. He's a grown man more than capable of making his own choices. You told me yourself that he has a brilliant mind. Teagen didn't force herself on him. Not really. He was flattered by the attention and the prospect of fame. Face it."

I bowed my head and would have closed my ears if time permitted. A gift from Festive Flowers forestalled my reaction and alerted Gemma to my plight.

"Wow!" she said as she signed for the flowers and tipped the deliveryman. "Must be for you, Violet. Oh look. Orchids and succulents with oriental lilies. Someone shelled out a bundle. for this."

I grabbed the accompanying card before she read it. The inscription confirmed my suspicions about the sender. It read, "Some women, like pearls, are without price."

"Must be from that Senator", Gemma said. "Come on, Violet. Fess up. Benny won't even spring for carnations, let alone orchids."

My aunt was neither deceived nor sidetracked by Gemma's antics. "You're wrong, Gemma. These beautiful blooms are for Marky."

"What! You mean the Professor upped his game?" Gemma gasped. "Well played, partner. Who knew he had that many bucks to splurge with?"

Blushing during emotional moments had always plagued me. My cheeks burned as I spun away from Gemma. "Don't mention this to Roddy. Please. You know how private he is."

Killian Blaine had surpassed himself this time. He knew that I adored orchids and lilies, and his message was clear. He made all the moves that won female hearts. I didn't delude myself. This wasn't a sentimental gesture. Those flowers were probably ordered by his assistant and charged to his corporate account as a tax deduction. They were too lovely to discard, even though I yearned to hurl them into the trash. While Violet positioned them in the entryway of Poppet, I texted Mr. Blaine, thanking him for his thoughtful gift. My mother taught me that lack of social graces and ingratitude were simply not acceptable.

When Roddy ambled in, he made a beeline for the orchids. "Something even Nero Wolfe would have enjoyed, right Marky?" I glared at him. His manner was exceedingly cheerful for a man teetering on the edge of oblivion. Lionel's assessment of the meeting must have been accurate. I was surprised to see that Roddy wore the upscale ensemble that had come courtesy of Teagen. Somewhat insensitive, I thought, in view of his sponsor's sad end.

Aunt Violet's advice rang in my ears. What were my feelings about Roddy? I am a strong woman. Too strong at times, according to some men. I could never be satisfied with a partner who was not equally strong. On the other hand, I valued sensitivity over the caveman approach of alpha males like a certain Chicago attorney. Surely there was a happy medium, although it had eluded me thus far.

"How did your interview go?" I asked.

Gemma snickered. "Well, he's not in cuffs yet. Benny said that Lionel showed some gumption for a change. Right, Professor?"

"He took good care of me," Roddy said. "Chief Miles didn't give me the third degree or anything, but she was thorough. That's one woman I wouldn't want to cross."

Violet gave him a thumbs-up. "What kind of questions did she ask?"

He shrugged. "You know. Mostly about the meal. Who made it; how it tasted. That kind of thing."

I knew there was more to it. Roddy was clearly being evasive, and it probably had to do with that French Maid costume and the EpiPen. "Did she mention Mrs. Doyle's attire at all?"

"The tabloids are buzzing about that French Maid angle," Gemma said. "You should read the comments on social media. Most people think you were sampling more than lobster." She grinned. "They think you offed her in a fit of passion."

"That's not true!" I'd never seen Roddy become so emotional. "Mrs. Doyle flirted with me, but that's as far as it went. Before anything happened, she got sick."

"What about the EpiPen?" I asked. "Any update on that?"

He shook his head. "Nope. Listen, I've got to drive to Ann Arbor today. My department chair wants an update."

I offered to go with him, but he declined. Then I recalled that his boss was female and realized that he was better off pleading his case alone. That gave me time to plan my meeting with Chief Aubrey Miles. Recalling my aunt's warning, I kept that scheme to myself. My conscience was clear. It was my civic duty to share information with the authorities. If by chance it helped

Roddy, so be it.

* * *

Fortune may favor the brave, but bad luck shadowed me that day. The first person I saw upon entering the police station was Benny Soto, whose sneer and pompous manner were on full display.

"What do you want?" he growled. "Do you have an appointment?"

"I have information for Chief Miles."

He yawned. "She's unavailable. We don't like amateurs meddling in murder cases here, especially girlfriends of the prime suspect."

"So, it is a murder inquiry? Thanks for the heads up." I waited until he was distracted by a phone call and slipped into the hallway. Aubrey Miles was seated at her desk, hunched over her computer screen. She glanced up and gave me a warm smile.

"Ms. Davis. Please come in and sit down."

At that moment, a very flustered Benny Soto flew into the room. "I'm sorry, Chief. I told her you were busy."

"No problem, Deputy. I wanted to chat with Ms. Davis anyway. You can leave us alone."

Benny stomped off, dangling his handcuffs. Was he frustrated by missing his chance to use them or his truncheon on me?

"I know all the tropes about cop coffee," Chief Miles said, "but this is Nespresso. My private stash."

Suddenly, I became tongue-tied, unable to frame a coherent sentence. Something about Aubrey Miles' calm exterior confounded me. She smiled and waited me out.

"You told Deputy Soto you had information for me. How can I help?"

I regained my poise and most of my dignity. "It's about Mrs. Doyle and that last meal."

She raised her eyebrows and nodded encouragement. "Yes…"

"She didn't prepare it. All that Cordon Bleu stuff was hype. Someone else, some secret ally, did it. Teagen couldn't cook at all."

Chief Miles made a note. "You're suggesting that this person may have intentionally or accidentally added the dairy and nuts that killed her."

Nerves make me babble, and this was no exception. I shared every scrap of information we'd gathered and added a theory of my own.

"I think Teagen Doyle sprinkled nuts and dairy into that meal. Deliberately."

That did astound the chief. "Are you suggesting suicide?"

"Not exactly. Look, Teagen was a drama queen. Everybody who knew her says that. I think she staged a big show, expecting to be saved by her EpiPen. She always bragged about it. Anyhow, she must have miscalculated and used too many allergens." I gulped. "Anyhow, you know the rest."

The chief frowned. "But why would she do that? Why take the risk?"

It sounded irrational to someone who had never known that faded star. I believed that it was not only possible but probable. I tried to explain the Doyles' fractured relationship, but ultimately suggested that Madge Stone might have valuable insights to share.

Aubrey Miles' expression was unreadable. Did she think I was delusional or deceitful? I couldn't tell. "That's very interesting, Ms. Davis. I applaud your public spirit. Too bad more citizens don't step up and do the right thing." She rose and shook my hand. "I'll follow up on that information right away. Incidentally, I'd give Brendan Doyle a wide berth if I were you. He's highly motivated and very litigious. Any suggestion that his wife poisoned herself might make him explode or sue." She checked her watch. "He's coming here this afternoon with his attorney from Chicago."

Unless I was mistaken, the lawyer in question was Killian Blaine, that suave sender of the flowers gracing Poppet. I thanked the chief and sped back to my loft to spruce up my appearance. I'd feign surprise when he showed his smug self, but in this instance, forewarned was indeed forearmed.

* * *

Gemma gave me the gimlet eye when she saw me. "What's the special occasion? If you're expecting the Professor, you're out of luck. He couldn't reach you, so he called here."

No wonder. I'd turned off my iPhone at the police station and forgotten to turn it back on.

She paused, expecting me to beg for information. When I shrugged, Gemma plucked a Post-it note from her pocket. "Here it is. Tell Marky I'm spending the night in Ann Arbor. More meetings with my Department Chair.' Hmph. Sounds mighty fishy to me. Bet you that boss is female and Dr. Dreamy plans to sweet-talk her or more."

Sometimes Gemma's cynicism irritates me even though she's usually right on target. "Oh Gemma, give it a rest. He's fighting for his career after all."

"What about his love life? Doesn't that count?"

Before our argument escalated, an unexpected customer joined us. Letty Briggs acted diffident, almost timid, as she approached the counter. Although her attire was casual, I detected traces of the high-profile socialite she had once been. Her unadorned face, graced with spectacular cheekbones, needed very little enhancement. Waves of thick blonde hair fell to her shoulders. Even the drab linen jumpsuit she wore highlighted an enviable figure.

"Madge traded her appointment time with me," she said in a whispery voice. "I hope that was okay."

Gemma consulted her schedule. "Sure. Mrs. Stone booked a Swedish Massage. Does that work for you?"

Letty nodded. "Absolutely. Some unexpected guests dropped in, so I jumped at the chance to take her place."

I had a sneaky suspicion about those guests. "Mrs. Stone is so hospitable," I gushed. "Even strangers feel welcome at her lovely home. She's been a great comfort to Mr. Doyle, I'll bet."

Letty spoke through downcast eyes. "I suppose. Sometimes people take advantage of Madge, but she never complains. My cousin is very kind. She cares a lot about Brendan."

I locked eyes with Gemma, telegraphing a silent message. Her nod assured me that during the fifty-minute massage, she would extract every possible bit of information from her client.

Meanwhile, I puttered around Poppet, tidying up our displays. My aunt had snagged an exclusive with a very pricey French cosmetic line that I planned to feature in our digital brochure. Afterwards, I scanned the headlines in *the Harbor Bay News* searching for information about Teagen. Her death was the biggest story to hit our little town in many years, and readers would be hungry for every scrap of information. Although the item appeared below the fold, it was quite unmistakable. A discreet notice featured the following announcement:

"A memorial service for Mrs. Teagen Doyle will be held at the Town meeting hall at six PM in three days' time. All residents of Harbor Bay are invited to attend what promises to be a joyous event. The family requests that you wear bright colors to honor Teagen's vivid and enduring spirit."

Joyous event? That sounded odd in view of Teagen's untimely exit from this world. Apparently, her body had still not been released by the medical examiner pending further tests. Benny Soto, whose talent for leaking information was exceeded only by his irascible nature, informed Gemma that further toxicology tests had been ordered at the insistence of Mr. Doyle.

I pondered that for a moment. Every mystery novel that I read emphasized that the victim's character was the key to solving the case. Kim said that Teagen lived in a fantasy world shaped by Hollywood scripts and movie themes. If true, she would never consider the downside to risking her own life. I recalled that canister of powdered caffeine in her cupboard. Perhaps that was a test run, a dress rehearsal, so to speak. It had worked perfectly: frantic scene, Brendan and Roddy swooping down to rescue her, and Madge taking charge with the EpiPen. If only I knew who had prepared that seduction supper. The list of suspects was meager. I hoped that Kim or Aunt Violet might have unearthed a clue or that Gemma might suggest an answer. An unexpected insight emerged when Letty Briggs finished her treatment. My partner was a miracle worker; I'd seen her handiwork before. In this instance, her client had been transformed from a drab wren to a proud peacock. Letty's complexion glowed, and her posture was runway perfect. No slumping or downcast eyes on that lady. No sir!

"I feel great," Letty said. "Rejuvenated. Sign me up for another one next week."

Gemma made no attempt to be modest. She pocketed the generous gratuity from her client and gave her a friendly hug. Before leaving Poppet, Letty selected several pricy items from the new French line and virtually skipped out the door.

"Wow! You sure hit a home run today," I said. "Now tell me. What did you find out?"

Gemma's coy look frustrates me. Sometimes I yearn to slap it off her face, but I restrain myself in the interests of good business relations. Instead, I played the waiting game. When I deprive her of a starring role, she ultimately gives in.

"Okay. First, Letty has a bad track record with men." Gemma turned my way. "You understand that, Marky. Anyway, she's a two-time loser: two divorces, and Lord knows how many broken affairs. She's sworn off romance for the time being."

"Understandable," I said. "But not relevant to Teagen's death."

Gemma sometimes resembles a Cheshire cat. I knew that grin all too well and finally coaxed her for more. "What else? You're saving the best for last. I know it."

"Letty went to some fancy college in the East. Real hoity toity to hear her tell it. Anyhow, that's where she met Marge."

"Wait a minute. I thought they were cousins."

"Wrong," Gemma said with an air of triumph. "Letty was Ronald Stone's cousin. She comes from the money end of the family. Madge was a scholarship kid."

"Interesting. Makes me appreciate Madge even more. What does Letty do with herself all day other than support Madge's charities?"

Gemma thought for a minute. "Well, she loves to cook. Culinary arts or something like that, and she gardens. Got a master gardener certificate or a landscape architect degree. I forget which."

I recalled the carefully cultivated shrubs and flowers surrounding Madge's estate. If that was Letty's handiwork, it was indeed masterful.

"Did she mention Teagen at all?"

Gemma hesitated. "She didn't say much about Teagen, but I got the sense that she wasn't a big fan. When I mentioned Brendan, though, she kind of freaked."

"Interesting. Could Letty have cooked up the seduction special? She apparently loved to cook, and Teagen may have asked as a favor."

Gemma shrugged. "Maybe, but I think you're reaching. Face it, Marky. That hussy got what she deserved, even if the Professor is guilty."

"Gemma! Don't even think that about Roddy. He's no killer. Besides, what would he gain from killing the proverbial golden goose?"

She rolled her eyes. "I don't know about any goose, but I watch all those reality TV shows. Crime of passion, they call it. Happens all the time."

Kim and Aunt Violet joined us and served as peacemakers. Neither one offered any suggestions, although they listened carefully to my theory about Teagen accidentally overdosing.

"She was capable of pulling that kind of stunt," Kim said. "Anything to get attention. It's just so macabre."

Neither one believed that Letty Briggs was involved. "Letty had no great love for Teagen," Violet said. "I'm positive she'd balk at getting involved in one of her schemes."

Violet and Kim exchanged looks. "I guess it's no big secret," Kim said. "Letty was once in love with Brendan. Absolutely mad for him."

"They were practically engaged until Teagen entered the picture," Violet added. "That shattered Letty. She had two unfortunate marriages afterwards and then…"

Gemma leaned forward. "Come on. Don't leave us hanging, Violet."

My aunt seldom gossiped. She considered it bad form and unworthy of a lady. In view of the situation, however, she relented and finished Letty's sad story. "She had a breakdown. According to Madge, Letty swallowed some pills and had to be hospitalized. I blame both Brendan and Teagen for that. They behaved disgracefully, flaunting their affair in front of her."

Kim shook her head. "So, you see it's highly unlikely that Teagen would ask, or Letty would agree to engineer that scheme."

"Looks like you struck out again," Gemma told me. "Better hang up your deerstalker. Isn't that what your hero Holmes used?"

I took the high road and ignored her comment. "Okay. Who made that special meal? Any suspects we haven't already excluded? Think hard."

While we were chattering, two customers entered Poppet. Fantasia gave a warning bark and bared her teeth as Brendan Doyle swept in, accompanied by someone I knew all too well. Both men were tall, well-built, and full of swagger. By objective standards, they were handsome and charismatic. Unfortunately, there were other less savory aspects to their characters. Both were brimming with bravado. They epitomized the Masters of the Universe so vividly portrayed by author Tom Wolfe. Brendan was two decades older than Killian, but they were brothers under the skin.

"Ladies, I trust we're not disturbing you," Brendan said. "I believe you know my attorney, Killian Blaine." He focused his specious smile on Kim and Violet, pointedly excluding me and Gemma.

Kim and Violet nodded, acknowledging both men. Killian Blaine lasered in on the flowers decorating our front counter.

"What a charming display," he said. "Someone must be very special." His imperious gaze pinned me to the wall.

Violet smothered them with kindness. "How can we help you, gentlemen?"

Brendan explained that they wanted a gift for their hostess, Madge Stone. "Something elegant, just like that lady," he said.

While my aunt showed him an array of Creed fragrances, I gave Attorney Blaine my full attention. "We carry a wide range of men's products," I said, smiling sweetly. "Sometimes mature skin requires a special moisturizer."

Nothing fazed him. He chortled and gave me his vulpine grin. "Very amusing, Ms. Davis. I like a woman with spirit. More evidence of your rapier-sharp wit, I see. Perhaps you can give me some samples of these magic potions."

Gemma gasped, but I was undeterred. "Of course. Please, follow me."

He lowered his voice. "You're more lovely than ever, Marky. I can't get you out of my mind. You haunt my dreams."

"Hmm. You looked happy enough at the Met Gala last month. I saw a picture of you on *Page Six* wrapped around that model. They said you two were engaged."

"Just another client," he said. "Public relations bunk, nothing more. Besides, that photo didn't get my best side." He leaned closer. "Glad to see you're still following my exploits. That gives me hope."

He was baiting me, and I refused to succumb. Instead, I scooped up several samples of an exclusive men's facial line and placed them in Poppet's customized bag. "We just started carrying RETROUVE. It's pricey but a very effective anti-aging product. I'm sure you'll like the results."

Killian leaned over the counter and faced me. "I'll buy everything in this store if it makes you happy." As I gave him the samples, he touched my fingers, sending a jolt of electricity coursing through my body.

"Let's stop fencing," he said. "Have dinner with me, Marky. Please. I'm tied up with Brendan this evening, but tomorrow, any time, any place. I must see you."

"You realize that I'm involved with someone," I said.

Killian scoffed. "That Professor? Please. He's not your type at all. Way too passive. Brendan told me all about him." He lowered his voice to a mere whisper. "You need a man who challenges you. Someone like me who can match you stride for stride and appreciate you for your courage and strength."

"Are you volunteering for the job?" I asked. "I suppose you have references."

We locked eyes, each of us unwilling to yield. Killian might have useful information. Information that could help Roddy. That's what I told myself when I agreed to meet him the next evening. After all, what harm could one dinner cause? The spell was broken when Brendan hustled over and called his friend. "Come on, buddy. Madge is waiting."

Killian joined him, but not before winking at me as he left.

"Wow," Gemma said afterwards. "Talk about your energy boost."

Kim laughed. "I know. Testosterone overload. Those two could light up the sky."

"Ha," I said. "More like Dante's ninth circle."

Violet put her arm around me. "Take it easy, Marky. Poppet made a profit on them, and Madge got a lovely bottle of Creed—Spring Flowers. I know she loves their products."

"Marky got something special too," Gemma smirked. "Dinner with the divine Mr. Blaine. That guy is bonkers for her. I can tell. He'll edge out the Professor in no time."

Kim raised her eyebrows. "What will Roddy say?"

I shrugged. "He should be glad. I'm only doing it for him."

All three women laughed gleefully.

* * *

When Roddy phoned me that evening, our conversation was brief and strained.

'I'm staying in Ann Arbor for the next few weeks," he said. "Unless the cops haul me back to Harbor Bay. No one at the university suspects me of anything, but I think it's best to stay close."

"Of course," I said. "Keep in touch."

There were no expressions of love or fidelity. I got the distinct impression that Dr. Roderick Park was taking a permanent sabbatical—from me. I didn't brood even though I still cared for him. He had brains, brawn, and a sweet nature, but his passivity during the Teagen affair had disappointed me. Was Killian Blaine that wily lawyer right about this? Was I condemned to a life of single blessedness while awaiting the elusive perfect mate? Gemma would scoff, but Aunt Violet had an uncanny ability to read my emotions. When I called her, she immediately suggested that we do something fun.

"In Harbor Bay?" I asked. "Rather limited options, wouldn't you say?"

"It just so happens that a pal of ours is hosting a cocktail hour that promises to be delightful. So, scoot. Put on your party clothes and get ready to shine."

Violet finally relented after I begged her for more information. It seemed that Doogie Kinkaid, that man about town and fount of all news, was celebrating a sale that netted him a fat commission.

"Count on plenty of great food and lively conversation. You know Doogie. He'll have the scoop on Teagen's last adventures."

When I hesitated, Violet dangled more bait. "Didn't you say that Doogie was hiding something? We can double-team him if you like. Nothing can stop the Davis duo when we're on the scent."

I succumbed as she knew that I would. Why be a housebound drudge at twenty-six when there were so many adventures for the asking? Besides, I had a subtle pale pink slip dress that sat, lonely and unloved, in my closet. Time to rescue it and my flagging spirits.

The sound of Violet's horn summoned me at precisely seven pm. She nodded her approval as I skipped to the Mercedes and pirouetted.

"That's my girl. You look elegant, Marky. And that Pashmina shawl adds the finishing touch. Well done!"

When my fashionista Aunt gave her seal of approval, my confidence soared. Violet looked rather nifty herself, swathed in a whirl of silken splendor in buttercup yellow.

"Who's on Doogie's guest list?" I asked. "The usual crowd, I presume."

Violet nodded. "He described it as an intimate gathering of kindred spirits. I wrapped some of that French room fragrance as a gift." She gave me a steely glance. "Don't worry. Madge has her hands full with Brendan and Killian. You won't run into them tonight."

Doogie's home was a beautifully maintained brick townhouse in the historic district of Main Street. Every detail from the coffered ceilings to the dentil moldings was carefully curated. Delicate Queen Ann pieces mingled with sturdier modern choices that could accommodate a man of Doogie's girth. The walls were awash with the color of the year, Origami White, accented with splashes of aubergine. I'd never studied this space before, and I was awed.

Our host greeted us with warm hugs and a gracious smile. "Ladies, what a pleasure. As the poet said, "Beauty is its own excuse for being.""

I preferred Keats' version to Emerson's. "Beauty is truth, truth beauty," said he, and I aimed to extract truth from Doogie Kinkaid or die trying.

"How literate you are, Doogie. You quite confound me." Aunt Violet patted his cheek and swept into the gathering. I hung back, feeling shy in this elite grouping of guests, many of whom I recognized but had never met before.

"Where's your handsome professor?" Doogie teased. "They're not measuring him for the noose just yet, no matter what Brendan says."

"You have a talent for overstatement, Mr. Kinkaid. Roddy returned to the University with the concurrence of Chief Miles. He has classes to teach, remember."

"Now, now. Don't be hostile, dear girl. I'm one person who truly misses Teagen Doyle. That woman could light up any room with just her smile. Too bad she left us. Teagen had big plans for Dr. Park and for you, too, of course." He herded me into the kitchen, where tempting canapes were arranged on a Herend platter. "Help me with these, Marky. You don't mind, do you?"

"Where's your kitchen staff? Didn't the caterer send anyone?"

Doogie laughed. "Caterer? Surely, you're joking. I prepared everything myself. Cooking is a passion project with me." He plucked an Hors-d'oeuvre from the platter and popped it into my mouth. "Here. Try this."

"Sublime," I said, smacking my lips. "And caviar too. This reminds me of Teagen's seduction supper. Roddy praised the food, although the ending left much to be desired."

Doogie's normally rosy cheeks paled, and for a moment I thought he might collapse. "What…what are you suggesting?" he said in a whisper.

Time for direct assault, I told myself. "You helped her. You were her secret chef. Teagen couldn't even boil water, but she kept that charade about Le Cordon Bleu alive."

The big man hurriedly downed a flute of champagne. "Please, Marky. Not now. You don't understand. I promise to tell you everything tomorrow. It was an accident, I swear. The whole thing was a prank that went wrong. She begged me to help her carry it off."

At that moment, an energetic brunette bustled into the kitchen. "Your guests are looking for you, Doogie. Here, let me help with those treats." She grabbed the Herend platter and disappeared in a cloud *of Chanel #5.*

Doogie made his escape, but not before repeating his promise. "Tomorrow. Lunch at the Patisserie. Don't tell anyone else. It'll be our secret."

Chapter Eleven

That lunch never happened. A corporate group with ten women descended upon Poppet, requesting an array of services and flashing plenty of cash. I texted Doogie, apologized, and asked to reschedule for the next day. He was unavailable for lunch but suggested that we meet at his place that evening before Teagen's memorial service. It was slated for seven pm and promised to be a memorable occasion.

The next four hours were a flurry of massage, mani-pedi, and makeup tutorials. Just before closing time, Gemma ordered me to vamoose. "You have a hot date tonight, remember. He's used to models and debutantes. Don't let us down."

Violet agreed. "We can handle any foot traffic, Marky. Wear that turquoise sheath from Dolce-Gabbana. It suits you perfectly." She reached into her tote and produced a silk pouch.

"Here, I thought this might complement your outfit."

Gemma gaped at the earrings inside. "Wow! These must have cost a mint."

"Not really," said my aunt. "I have a friend at Bulgari, and he sent me these. They're called Viper Serpenti—how perfect is that for a dinner with Mr. Blaine?"

I was speechless. "Oh, but I couldn't. They're exquisite." The earrings were rose gold, molded with a spray of pavé diamonds in snake form. Each of the scales was precisely crafted to replicate it's namesake. I'd never seen more enticing jewelry.

Violet brushed off my protests. "Nonsense. I was saving it for your birthday, but there's no need to wait. Trust me, Killian will know what they are. A man like him is accustomed to lux things." She wagged her finger my way. "But keep him guessing. Don't tell where they came from."

I wasn't nervous. After all, a dinner date with an acquaintance was hardly a big deal. When Killian called for me, he looked me over stem to stern. The predatory look he gave me was disquieting. I channeled Aunt Violet and forced myself to remain calm. If he had any romantic notions, he was doomed to disappointment.

"You look lovely, Marky," he said. "Elegant." He lasered in on my earrings. "Quite a nice touch. Bulgari, I presume. Someone must be very generous. Odd. I didn't think assistant professors made that kind of salary."

"You'd be surprised," I said, smiling sweetly.

He shook his head and escorted me to his car, which was sprawled in front of Poppet despite a no-parking sign. It was the ultimate luxury vehicle from Mercedes, a brazen display of wealth and privilege.

"Still driving the Maybach, I see. Wait a moment—this one must be new."

He grinned and ducked his head. "Yep! When this model was released, I just couldn't resist." He opened the passenger side door and tucked me into the incredibly soft leather seat. "After all, why not? You know I'm a car buff."

I had to admit that it was infinitely superior to my humble Jeep Wrangler. But the Jeep suited me and my station in life. I had no need or desire for something fancier.

"You're somewhat of a snob, Miss Davis," he said. "Disapproval is written all over your lovely face. You probably consider me a money-grubbing lawyer who flaunts his wealth."

Had he read my mind? I fought to restrain the blush that crept up my neck. "Not at all. I admire success. My aunt is a prime example of ability and drive. Roddy, too."

Killian raised his brows. "Well, no matter. Let's not quarrel. Since this is our first official date, I want it to be something special for a very special lady. I thought we'd drive to Petosky. There's a great restaurant there that I think you'll enjoy."

Petosky was a lovely city, only twenty miles from Harbor Bay. I'd never dined there before, but I knew it was renowned for gourmet fare. As we drove down Route ninety-two, I glimpsed the first buds of Spring and a peak at Little Traverse Bay. Killian's choice of music, a blend of classic rock, soul, and romantic ballads, surprised me. I'd expected something flashier, something that proclaimed his knowledge of current musical fads. I leaned back in the glove leather seat and closed my eyes. The strains of John Denver's, *Jet Plane,* lulled me into a gradual slumber. Oddly enough, I heard Killian accompanying him, softly singing every word. I awakened just as the Maybach eased into the parking lot of *Palette Bistro.*

Killian gently touched my shoulder. "We're here, Sleeping Beauty. Our dinner awaits."

Losing self-control in front of him was humiliating. I shook myself and apologized.

"Fine date I am. Please excuse me, Killian. We were so rushed today that I was exhausted. That song…it's one of my favorites. I love it."

He spoke softly. "I do too. That's something else we have in common. And don't make excuses around me, Marky. You don't need to. Ever." The tender expression on his face left me confused and wary.

Remember, Marky. This man is a notorious player who woos and discards women like crumpled tissues.

Fortunately, the valet interrupted what promised to be an awkward scene. He gulped when he saw the Maybach, treating it with the reverence normally reserved for a sacred relic. Killian Blaine recovered his snarky grin so quickly that I thought I had imagined the tender side of him.

After we were seated, we ordered drinks. He opted for a Grey Goose martini, but I settled for Perrier. Killian noted my choice and immediately pounced.

"Abstaining, are you? Afraid I'll take advantage of you?"

I shrugged. "You flatter yourself. I'm used to fending off mashers."

His response was immediate. "Mashers, is it? Love your use of archaic language. You're quite a change from the vacuous dates I usually have. Intellect is part of your charm."

I scanned the menu, savoring each delectable item on offer. I was ravenous, quite unwilling to feign indifference or lack of appetite.

"Hmm. That Forest Floor Soup sounds amazing," I said. "So do the Serrano wrapped dates."

He lowered his reading glasses and smiled indulgently. "Go for it. I admire a woman with a healthy appetite. So many models and actresses starve themselves and smoke or use drugs to compensate."

Was he taunting me? After all, he was accustomed to glamour girls, not a cosmetic shopkeeper and failed artist like me. Suddenly, Aunt Violet's words again echoed in my brain—*Don't sell yourself short, Marky. You are a talented artist, successful business owner, and practically engaged to a man many women lusts after.*

I laughed merrily, trying to ignore how appealing he looked in reading glasses. "Need any help with the menu? It's so difficult to read small print in this dim light."

Killian chuckled. "Oops. Got me again, Miss Marky. You certainly keep a man on his toes. I think I'll order the beef tenderloin. At my advanced age, a man needs plenty of protein. What looks good to you?"

I dabbed my mouth with a napkin. "Salmon sounds fine. I don't eat red meat or pork for ethical reasons."

That amused him. "Commendable, Miss Prim and Proper. However, you're carrying a very fine Italian handbag made of leather, I see, and those stilettos with the red soles are Louboutin, are they not? Inconsistent, wouldn't you say?"

I bowed my head. "Okay, you caught me. But at least I'm trying." I put my elbows on the table and looked him squarely in the eyes. "Let's get serious. I need your help. Roddy had nothing to do with Teagen's death, but I'm afraid they'll pin it on him or at least tarnish his reputation. A murder charge could be a real career killer even in academia."

"You're wise to be concerned. Brendan is convinced that your professor murdered his wife, and Brendan carries a lot of weight with the authorities."

"Pooh! I watch plenty of true crime shows, and the spouse, particularly the husband, is almost always the culprit. Maybe he protests too much to quote the Bard. Teagen and Brendan fought constantly, and I've heard he was planning to divorce her. Maybe he thought murder was cheaper than alimony."

Killian suddenly morphed from charming companion to stoic solon. "I've seen nothing that implicates Brendan, who, by the way, is my client as well as my friend."

"You don't practice criminal law. Why not consider all the possibilities?"

"Like what?"

I took a deep breath and plunged into the maelstrom. "I think that Teagen deliberately spiked that meal."

Killian scoffed. "Why in the world would she do that? Are you suggesting she committed suicide, Marky? That's patently absurd and libelous. Teagen Doyle was too self-centered to end her life."

I grabbed his elbow. "No. Just hear me out. Teagen was a drama queen, right?" He nodded.

"What if it was a ploy to gain Brendan's attention. I think she staged that whole scene so that Brendan and Madge could swoop in and save her. She had a dress rehearsal with powdered caffeine a few days before. Apparently, this time she overdid it."

He gave me the gimlet eye. "What proof do you have?"

"Nothing that would convince a jury—yet. But I'm working on it." I told him about Teagen's sham cooking skills and her need for a confederate. "I confronted Doogie Kinkaid last evening, and I think he's about to crack. He practically admitted that he cooked the meal, but denied adding the allergens. If he didn't do it, he knows who did."

Killian yawned. "Let me know when you sweat it out of him. He may need a good attorney."

I wasn't finished. "Did Madge say anything last night? After all, she knew Teagen better than almost anyone except Letty."

When our entrees arrived, we stopped sparring and tucked in to a delicious meal. Killian

attacked his blood red steak with a zeal that astounded me. I took small bites of my seared salmon and slowly chewed, savoring its delicious taste.

After dinner, he signaled our waiter. "Let's order a digestif." He held up his hands. "Strictly as a finishing touch to our delicious meal. Come on.

Loosen up." He ordered a single malt Macallan Scotch neat.

"What would you suggest for me?" I asked. "Nothing too strong."

"I wouldn't even consider it. Try Chartreuse. It's French and made from flowers, herbs, and berries, plus, it's color is a striking green very much like your eyes."

I gulped, unable to think of a suitable response. He'd probably perfected that line and used it on many women. "Okay. I'll try it."

When our drinks arrived, I sipped mine cautiously. The color was enticing, and the taste pleasing.

"Well?" Killian asked. "What's the verdict?"

"Tasty, but it packs quite a wallop." I moved closer and stared at him. "By the way, it case you haven't noticed, my eyes are blue. You must have confused me with one of your other conquests."

Nothing flustered that man. "Green, blue, or blue green. No big difference. They still sparkle."

"Enough about my eyes. Let's focus on Teagen's death."

"Her murder, you mean?"

"Whatever. Teagen always bragged about her EpiPen. Said it was her savior. Here's my question: why didn't it work this time?"

He shrugged. "Who knows? ¿Quién sabe? Isn't it more important to find out where those allergens came from? Brendan said it was dairy and nuts. She was violently allergic to both."

"Right. They got into the meal somehow. That's why I want to question Doogie."

Killian's expression was grim. "Sorry, Marky, but your boyfriend had the best chance to spike the food. Even if Teagen asked him to it's still manslaughter at the least."

"What about those tinctures she was taking? Nobody tested them, and they can have side effects. It says so on the internet." I got a sudden brainstorm. "What do you know about Letty Briggs? I heard that she hated Teagen. She's no fan of Brendan's either."

His response was noncommittal. "Lots of maybes, Marky. I think you're reaching. Madge said that Roddy was, in her words, 'totally captivated' by

Teagen."

I swallowed way too much Chartreuse, causing me to cough violently. Killian slapped my back, a bit harder than he needed to. "Are you okay? You're like a tigress protecting her cub. Does Dr. Park really mean that much to you?"

I stammered something totally forgettable that reflected my own ambiguity about Roddy and the state of our relationship. He was a paradox, intellectually strong but a tad wimpy when it came to practical matters. I suspected that his mother and sisters had pampered him all his life, and his legion of female fans had indulged his every whim.

"Roddy is brilliant," I said. "I admire a man like that."

Killian smirked. "I'm attracted to those same qualities in a woman, no matter what you read in the tabloids." He learned forward. "But I also like a woman with spunk and talent. Like you."

Forge ahead, I told myself. Don't get flustered by this man.

"We inhabit very different worlds," I said. "Let's settle for being friends. Besides, I think you'd be challenged by solving Teagen's death. We can do it together. A competition. of sorts. You know, see who's the better detective." I paused. "Unless you're afraid to lose."

"I never back down from a challenge, Miss Davis, and I seldom lose." He downed his scotch and rose. "But let's be clear. I think your fiancé or boyfriend or whatever is guilty. If I find proof, I'll go straight to the cops. No exceptions." He pulled back my chair and helped me to alight. "And we share all information. That's only fair."

"Agreed. The same applies to your pal and client, Brendan Doyle."

On our ride back to Harbor Bay, we plotted a strategy. Our first test was the meeting with Doogie Kinkaid the next day.

Chapter Twelve

Since Killian was busy with preparations for Teagen's memorial, I tackled the meeting with Doogie alone. We'd agreed to meet at his townhouse an hour before the big event. For some reason, I felt a sense of unease. It wasn't fear. I'd known Doogie for ages. He was garrulous but essentially harmless. He'd make a killing in real estate, not by murdering his client. Besides, the big fellow was one of the few folks around who seemed to genuinely love and admire Teagen. Even Madge and Brendan, her closest confidants, seemed more carefree without her, as if a tremendous burden had been lifted off their shoulders.

Gemma spent the first hour of the workday grilling me about my date. I tried to brush off her pointed questions, but she was relentless.

"Tell me everything," she begged. "Did he make a pass at you or play it cool?"

"Neither. We had a wonderful meal and discussed Teagen's case in a civilized manner. Remember, I'm practically engaged to Roddy."

She gave me a look of disdain. "Like that would discourage a hottie like Killian Blaine. I tell you the guy's crazy about you."

When my aunt joined us, Gemma tried to enlist her aid. "Come on, Violet. Aren't you the least bit curious about what went on? Marky won't even give me a hint."

"Some things are private, Gemma. We've got to respect Marky's boundaries." Violet gave me that look of forbearance that always filled me with guilt. Before long, I completely caved.

"He was quite charming," I said. "Very complimentary."

"I knew it," Gemma said. "A guy like that expects to score right away."

"Gemma!" Violet scolded. "Marky knows how to handle a man, even one as sophisticated as Mr. Blaine. Tell us, did he share any theories about Teagen's death?"

I shook my head. "Not really. He and Brendan both think that Roddy's guilty. Of course, he couldn't provide any real motive other than Madge's opinion that Roddy was obsessed by Teagen."

That silenced even Gemma. When Violet spoke, she sounded puzzled. "I'm surprised that Madge feels that way. Surely, she considered the possibility that it was an accident. Dr. Park barely knew Teagen. He certainly had no reason to harm her, and he's scarcely homicidal."

"What about the money angle?" Gemma was always the practical one. In this instance, she made a valid point. "How much did she offer Roddy? I bet it was a packet."

The contract I'd signed with Teagen specified that if any unforeseen event not attributable to an action on my part terminated the agreement, I would still be paid. Too bad I'd voided that when I returned the document to Teagen. Roddy's situation was different. He'd accepted a flat fee of one hundred thousand dollars. for appearances and unspecified other duties. That sum meant a lot to a fledgling professor still saddled with student loans. Teagen's demise freed him from those duties but didn't abrogate the contract. Some people, Brendan Doyle among them, would call that a motive.

"Money, that filthy lucre. Even the Bible warns against that," Violet mused. "Perhaps other people benefited from Teagen's death. I wonder if Mr. Blaine could be helpful with that angle. You know, insurance policies and the like. He could evaluate the state of Brendan's empire. There's some speculation about it being shaky."

"Forget that" I said. "Killian made it clear to me that Brendan is both his friend and his client. He clammed up the moment I mentioned the husband as the potential suspect, even though every true crime show highlights that."

We agreed that this was a matter for Kim to broach with her husband. Despite his churlish nature, Lionel was a genius when it came to money matters. As a partner in Teagen's Tinctures, he had access to all the financial information. The matter was ticklish, however. If there was a key person policy on Teagen, Lionel also stood to profit financially from her demise. That made him a suspect, although a rather unconvincing one. Lionel was a planner, not a doer. He might conspire with someone else, but he would leave the dirty work to others.

"So, you've added Killian to our team," Gemma said. "Not a smart move, Marky. How do you know we can trust him? He might run back to Mr. D. and spill all our secrets."

I'd pondered that myself, but somehow, I knew I could trust Killian—in business matters at least, if not romantic ones.

Violet considered the matter before speaking. "I think Marky's right, Gemma. We need someone who's close to Teagen's side. Mr. Blaine could be very useful."

"Hmm. I could think of a dozen better uses for him," Gemma teased. "Okay, what's our next move?"

I explained my plan to question Doogie. Gemma immediately jumped in, eager to join me.

"Let me help," she begged, her eyes gleaming. "I can rough him up if he won't cooperate. That boy will get the massage of a lifetime."

"Absolutely not," I said. "Subtlety is the key here. He'll never talk if you badger him."

Violet decided to question Madge about her sudden aversion to Roddy. "She and Teagen were close, almost like sisters. I'll test our theory about an accidental overdose with her."

Gemma agreed to do double duty: monitoring Chief Miles's actions through Benny and exploring the topic of EpiPens with an EMT pal from our local hospital.

As I rushed to dress for the evening's events, it suddenly occurred to me that Roddy, the person at the center of the entire mess, was uninvolved and seemingly oblivious to the dangers he faced. He had texted me hours before stating that, in view of Brendan Doyle's animus towards him, he thought it was advisable to "sit this one out."

Violet's warnings rang in my ears. Was I plunging into something out of obligation or affection? I had few maternal instincts, but Roddy's utter cluelessness aroused the need to nurture him. Had our relationship devolved into a case of pity versus passion?

* * *

The newspaper notice asked everyone to wear bright colors to reflect Teagen's vivid spirit. I'm no hypocrite. Teagen Doyle was a spoiled, self-indulgent woman with a mile-wide mean streak who trod on anyone foolish enough to oppose her. Still…as a business owner under public scrutiny, I yielded to propriety. I compromised by donning a modest lemon-yellow frock with a fitted jacket accompanied by grandma's pearls. It suited the occasion without proclaiming any faux love for Teagen. When I exited Poppet, a surprise awaited me. There, sprawled over two parking spaces, was the Maybach and its grinning owner.

"What are you doing here?" I asked. "I'm late for an appointment."

"No need to get testy," Killian said. "I decided to join you. After all, we're partners in this caper, aren't we?"

"Absolutely not. Doogie won't talk if you're lurking about. Besides, what possible excuse can you give for being there?"

As usual, he had a ready reply. "Doogie lives and breathes real estate, and I am a potential customer. When he sees my bank balance, he'll salivate all over me."

"Don't be crude. He knows you're from Chicago."

"True, but I've decided that Harbor Bay would be the perfect weekend retreat for me. I have a boat that could cruise down here on Lake Michigan with no problem."

He was impossible to discourage and infuriating besides. I bowed to the inevitable and hopped into his car.

Before we left, Killian leaned over and touched my shoulder. "You look captivating in that outfit, Miss Davis. a Spring buttercup."

"Some gardeners call buttercups weeds," I said. "Or noxious pests."

"Well," he said, "If the term fits…" His expression changed. "As you frequently point out, I am a decade older than you. I've accrued quite a bit of wisdom in those years, and believe me, I can read a person's guilt or innocence like a child's primer. Doogie will be putty in my hands."

He made a valid point, one that I couldn't dispute. Killian was known for brokering shrewd deals and for his business acumen. Having another person evaluate Doogie's reaction might prove invaluable. Reluctantly, I agreed to his presence with the proviso that I lead the discussion.

Our plan was disrupted, however, by the presence of another guest. Letty Briggs, wearing a stunning ivory sheath with delicate scalloping, turned a tearstained face toward us and whimpered.

"I'm sorry to intrude. I needed a friend, and Doogie was kind enough to oblige." She gathered her purse. "I should leave."

"Nonsense," Killian said. "I won't complain if another lovely lady joins us. What say you, Kinkaid?"

Doogie ducked his head to avoid my eyes. "Of course. Let's chat a bit and drink a toast to Teagen. Then we can head over to the memorial. I've made some special canapes in her honor that I think you'll enjoy, Marky." He led me to the kitchen, where a platter of delights awaited.

Doogie lowered his voice to a near whisper. "Sorry for the disruption. I had no idea she'd

turn up. I'm not avoiding you, Marky. You'll see. I would never have hurt Teagen. It was all a mistake." He seemed sincere, but I detected a whiff of relief in his manner.

"No problem. Tomorrow—lunch at Patisserie. Be there. No excuses."

"Oh, my I smell something so divine that I feel transported back to Paris." Killian Blaine appeared at the kitchen door, where he'd probably been eavesdropping.

Doogie brightened. "Just a simple charcuterie—duck rillettes, corniches, and black pepper pate. They were her favorites. And champagne, of course. She was partial to Veuve Clicquot le Grande Dame."

Killian winced. "The widow. How tragic that she favored that variety in view of her untimely death."

Doogie gulped and bustled out the door, holding the tray. I scooped up utensils and plates and followed behind him. Killian cradled the champagne in his arms as if it were an infant. He eyed the Baccarat flutes on the table and smiled. "How appropriate. Teagen would have approved."

We filled our plates and gathered around the dining table as our host offered a toast. "For Teagen, a bright light extinguished far too soon."

Letty Briggs coughed when it was her turn. I stepped in, giving an honest if not heartfelt tribute. "To Teagen, a visionary who never gave up."

Killian nodded at that. With his talent for duplicity, he appreciated it in others. "As Keats observed, a beautiful thing will never die; its loveliness increases. It will never pass into nothingness."

Letty cried, "What a lovely tribute. Were you one of her admirers, too, Killian?"

"Only from afar, madam. Brendan and Teagen were my friends."

"I guess it's my turn," Letty pursed her lips. "Shakespeare said it best. Maybe he knew someone like Teagen. 'Woe, destruction, ruin and decay... death will have its day.'"

We gaped, frozen in shock as Letty flung her Baccarat flute into the fireplace and fled the room.

Chapter Thirteen

We stayed silent on the brief ride to the civic center, each of us mired in his own thoughts. Letty's tantrum, not to mention her destruction of a flute of gorgeous crystal, had totally unnerved me. I'd excluded her as a suspect, but now I reevaluated that decision. According to my aunt's account, Letty and Brendan Doyle had been in love until Teagen appeared on the scene. Some wounds never heal, especially wounds of the heart. Had Letty seized a chance to dispose of her rival and punish her former lover?

Killian parked his prized auto in a secluded spot to avoid the dings made by lesser vehicles. Before opening the door, he hesitated. "Dollar for your thoughts? Inflation, you know."

"I'm flabbergasted. You know the whole tribe, so tell me. Is Letty a viable suspect? She seems so downtrodden that I just excluded her."

"Hmm," Killian said. "You violated rule one of the murder manual, Nancy Drew. Be careful, or you'll lose your detective's badge."

"What rule did I break?"

He taunted me, but then relented. "Rule number one—suspect everyone. That includes Letty, Brendan, Doogie, and even your own Sir Galahad, Roderick Park. Since I was three hundred miles away, you may exclude me."

I knew he was right, but it galled me to admit it. "You forgot my primary suspect, Teagen herself. I'm positive that she engineered the entire drama, excluding her death, of course."

A court of law demanded proof. I was nowhere even close to that yet, and Chief Miles was under pressure to make an arrest or at least clarify what happened. My meeting with Doogie might lead us closer to that.

"A word of caution," Killian said. "Keep your suspicions to yourself tonight. Brendan will explode if you drop any hint of them. My advice is to observe, not talk. Most of your suspects will be there, paying lip service to the bereaved."

We separated at the door. I joined Aunt Violet, Gemma, and Kim while Killian claimed a front row seat next to Brendan Doyle. As I expected, the room was packed with townspeople and assorted members of the press. In death as in life, Teagen Doyle made good copy. Brendan spared no expense in decorating our usually austere space with tributes to his wife. Baskets of orchids surrounded a larger-than-life portrait of Teagen, and white gloved attendants gave each audience member a long-stemmed white rose and an engraved bag with samples of Teagen's tinctures.

All in all, it was a tasteful and well executed performance that the deceased would have heartily endorsed. I suspected that Madge, that arbiter of good taste, was the architect of the event. Left to his own devices, Brendan would have opted for something more garish.

Gemma elbowed me and whispered. "Doesn't Benny look sexy in his dress uniform? That boy has the body of a movie star."

"Who? Lassie?"

"You never give him a break," Gemma whined. "He's gonna solve this case and show everyone up."

Unfortunately, Benny also had the brain of a gnat. I doubted that he could decipher a grocery list let alone a complex murder. I pointed to Josephine Soto, seated two rows across from us. "Look who's giving you the dragon stare, my girl. Watch your step."

Gemma forgot our spat and ducked her head to avoid scrutiny. The thought of any contact with Benny's mother terrified her.

I scrutinized my aunt Violet. marveling at her ability to look elegant and respectful at the same time. She wore her signature lilac color with the French flair I'd come to expect and paired it with a subtle pair of Manolo Blahnik pumps.

"How did your meeting with Doogie go?" Violet asked. "I noticed that you had an escort with you tonight."

I scowled and lowered my voice. "Total disaster. I'll fill you in later."

At precisely six-thirty, Killian Blaine approached the podium. He cleared his throat and welcomed the crowd. Gemma stared at him, taking in every well-tailored inch of his person.

"Goodness, that man is hot, Marky. He may even be hotter than the Professor."

"Hush," Violet said, patting Gemma's knee. "The show is about to begin."

Killian welcomed the crowd and extolled the many achievements of Teagen Doyle. A professionally produced slide show featured Teagen's memorable appearances in television and movie roles, ending with her final video flogging Teagen's Tinctures. Someone had tactfully omitted Roddy's portion of that production. As I watched the audience reaction, I was startled to see Chief Aubrey Miles in full uniform, seated in the back row. As usual, her placid exterior concealed whatever emotion she was feeling, although I noted that her bright eyes swept the room with vigilance. Benny, who was stationed against the wall, looked poised to spring into action at the slightest provocation.

"Very slick," Gemma said, after it concluded. "Your boy knows how to grab a crowd."

"He is not my boy! I am involved with Roddy, as you well know."

Gemma scoffed. "Huh! Why didn't the Professor show his pretty fact then? Too chicken?"

Violet shushed us before I could respond. Killian stepped aside as Brendan Doyle mounted the stage steps and clutched the microphone. I had to admit that he looked diminished, very much the grieving widower despite his superb Savile Row suit.

"My wife was my life," he said, his voice so low it could barely be heard. "She had the beauty and energy of a dozen women, and never once surrendered or admitted defeat. I will miss her all the rest of my days." Brendan dabbed at his eyes with an exquisitely made linen handkerchief. "Her like will never be seen again."

I heard a few sobs among the audience after that poignant homage. Killian rose to console his friend, enveloping him in a hug. Suddenly, the spell was broken in spectacular fashion when Letty Briggs jumped to her feet.

"Tell the truth, Brendan. You hated her. You called her a monster many times when you lay in my arms." Letty sobbed. "I'm glad she's dead and so are you."

At first, there was stunned silence, followed by gasps of surprise and outrage from the audience. Madge moved swiftly to control her cousin, and Doogie gently ushered Letty out of the room. Brendan Doyle was speechless, but fortunately, Killian was not.

"Tragedy strikes all of us when we lose someone. Keegan was above all a compassionate friend who would have understood and forgiven that unfortunate outburst." Killian paused, "Now, I ask you to join in singing one of her favorite songs, *Hallelujah*."

The curtain parted, exposing a pianist and a vocalist whom I recognized from one of those television competitions. She began a soulful rendition of the song and invited us to participate. Initially, most people were reluctant, but ultimately, they joined in. The program ended on that somber but glorious note, leaving few dry eyes in the group. Letty's tantrum was forgotten or ignored, and Teagen's face flashed before us in a triumphant smile.

* * *

"What a show," Gemma said. "Better than a horror movie."

"I promised Kim that we'd join her at her place for a drink," Violet said. "Good place for a post-mortem as well. Lionel rushed off to confer with Brendan and Killian, so we'll be alone."

Despite the beautiful spring weather, we piled into Violet's Mercedes. I reminded myself that a killer might be roaming about, and I was without my usual walking partner, Fantasia. The Stevens manse was an impressive beachfront home on Lake Michigan with décor that reflected Kim's exquisite taste and Lionel's capacious checkbook. We adjourned to the lakeside patio and arranged lounge chairs around the fire pit.

Gemma had never been there before, and she was clearly impressed. "Wow. This is some place, Kim. Benny and I could be happy here."

Kim was flustered by the compliment. "Thanks. I love my home. Lionel keeps urging me to sell, but it holds too many memories to give up."

The look on her face told me that Kim was recalling her late son, who had been run over as a teenager by a callous drunk. She regained her poise and wheeled a serving cart with drinks and snacks from the kitchen.

"Shall we drink a toast to Keegan?" she said, pouring each of us a cognac.

Violet nodded. "Why not. Despite everything, there was much to admire about her."

"Phooey," Gemma said. "Not according to Letty Briggs. Quite a performance, wouldn't you say? Good thing Benny was there, or we would have had to break up a riot."

Once more, I marveled at my partner's capacity for self-delusion. Benny Soto was far more likely to cause a fracas than calm troubled waters. Was that a testament to true love? I'd never been that besotted about any man, even Roddy. No wonder I was once again on my own.

I turned to my aunt. "Was it true or was Letty just being dramatic?"

Violet and Kim exchanged looks but didn't comment. It felt like a conspiracy of silence.

"Come on, you two, fess up." Gemma skipped the niceties and went straight to the main event.

Kim shrugged. "It's possible. Brendan wasn't a faithful husband. Teagen knew that and so did her friends, but it might have been wishful thinking on Letty's part."

Violet agreed. "Letty never got over Brendan. She blamed Teagen, but let's face it, Brendan was culpable too. In fact, he was a big part of it. He saw Teagen and went for a bigger prize than poor Letty. He replaced Madge in the same way, although they remained friends."

I replayed the scene at Doogie's house for them. Gemma gaped, Violet sighed, and Kim shook her head. Letty Briggs had a lot of anger bottled up inside. If Teagen was murdered, Letty rose to suspect number one on my list. I wondered what Madge would say about the entire episode.

"Letty loves to cook," I said. "She might have spiked that seduction supper knowing Teagen would go into shock." Surely Roddy had been vindicated by her outburst, or maybe I was as delusional as Gemma.

Kim poured herself another cognac. Gemma and I chowed down on the fruit and shrimp platter.

"Let's approach this logically," Aunt Violet said. "You're indulging in wishful thinking. dear Niece. It's unlikely that Letty could have gotten even close to that dinner. Teagen gave her a wide berth, for good reason as it turns out."

Once again, she was right on target. If Teagen hadn't salted that meal herself, someone very close to her must have done so. That didn't bode well for Roddy, although Brendan was still in the running for chief villain.

"I plan to confront Doogie tomorrow," I said. "He's an accomplished cook, and he acted like Teagen's servant. He knows something, and he's been dodging me ever since she died. He practically admitted cooking the meal." I told them about the nasty scene at Doogie's with Letty that evening. "I swear that woman is unhinged. Even Killian agrees with that."

Gemma couldn't resist commenting. "Oh, he did? What else does Mr. Blaine have to say?"

I averted my eyes. Kim and Violet were too well-bred to comment, but their expressions said plenty.

"Killian plans to buy a house here. At least that's what he says. You can be sure that Doogie will shadow him every chance he gets."

Kim agreed. "He certainly can afford it. He made the *Forbes* and *Chicago Magazine lists* as one of the city's wealthiest. Naturally, Brendan's wealth surpasses his, even though Teagen plowed through money at a record pace." She smiled. "I got the scoop from Lionel. You know how obsessed he is with such things."

My aunt seldom discussed finances. She referred to friends or acquaintances as 'comfortable' or very well fixed. Both descriptions indicated someone who rose far above my humble status.

"I believe that Killian has a Gold Coast condo on Lake Shore Drive. Quite a lovely area and very pricey. Madge considers him quite a catch." Violet glanced my way. "You should be flattered by his attention, Marky. He has a long list of conquests."

I launched into a diatribe about lotharios who regarded vulnerable females as fungible assets to be acquired or discarded at will. When I finished my rant, Gemma gave me an eyeroll.

"Big deal. That's the way of the world, especially for a rich, hot guy. If I weren't engaged to Benny, I'd love to be on his radar. Didn't your pal Shakespeare say something about protesting too much?"

Violet clapped her hands. "Splendid! You're amazing, Gemma. Personally, I believe Mr. Blaine is genuinely smitten with Marky. She's a match for him in brains and wit, not to mention talent. But enough teasing. We haven't made much progress on Teagen's death."

"The authorities called it 'suspicious' but didn't classify it as homicide," Kim said. "At least not yet." She plucked an envelope from her tote bag. "Here., I got this from a contact in the medical examiner's office. Please don't mention it to Lionel. He'd have a fit."

"What's the difference?" Gemma asked. "Coroners like on television, or medical examiners."

I knew the answer from my previous duels with death. Teagen's body was sent to the Grand Traverse Medical Examiner for processing. Coroners weren't always physicians, but Michigan law dictated that certified forensic pathologists had to investigate suspicious deaths.

"Brendan screamed to high heaven about wanting a complete autopsy," Kim said. "They contract with Western Michigan University. It's a highly regarded facility. We already know the immediate cause of death—anaphylactic shock from ingesting large amounts of dairy and nuts."

Of course, what we didn't know, and couldn't prove, was how those allergens got in Teagen's food. It sounded suspicious, and Roddy was still vulnerable, especially with Brendan pressuring every one of his contacts to act.

Kim's Newfoundland Dulles gave a mighty woof that announced Lionel's return. That was our cue to exit the party and head home. Fantasia needed her nightly walk, and I had a lot of variables to consider. I decided to contact

Roddy the next day. He needed an update on the murder inquiry, and I badly needed an update on our relationship.

Chapter Fourteen

Sleep eluded me that night. After counting sheep and deep breathing failed, I sprang up and sat at my computer. Fantasia gave me a puzzled look and returned to her bed. At least one of us had some common sense.

My call to Roddy went straight to voicemail. We hadn't spoken in several days, and he had ignored my urgent texts. It was painfully apparent that he was either ghosting me or trying to avoid hearing unpleasant news. Neither possibility thrilled me. I decided to forge ahead and maintain my normal schedule.

I prepared to confront Doogie even if it meant making a scene and losing a valued customer. Thirty minutes later, when I received a text, I took a deep breath, expecting it to be Roddy. Alas, that was not to be. Doogie once again rescheduled our meeting. He begged forgiveness and mentioned that he was showing a property to a very important client—Killian Blaine. "I found him the perfect spot, and he's keen on finding something special. Please understand. I can't afford to disappoint him. Come to my place after your store closes," he said. "Please. I'm not avoiding you. I promise."

Once again, Killian Blaine had inserted himself into my life. The man was hell bent on annoying me. That morning brought several additional challenges. Gemma had an emergency dental appointment, a scheduled delivery of Oribe products failed to materialize, and an irate client demanded a refund after smashing a pricey bottle of fragrance.

I handled each crisis with aplomb and managed to subdue my growing anxiety about a certain Professor. As usual, Aunt Violet's presence soothed my sagging spirits and helped me to regain a sense of perspective.

"I spoke with Madge today," she said. "Letty calmed down after taking her medication and was thoroughly ashamed of herself." She paused. "I mentioned our theory about Teagen accidentally dosing her own food."

"You did? OMG! How did she take it?"

My aunt's smile was a gentle reproof. "I was tactful, of course. Panache, Marky. It seldom fails. Always the right approach. Madge and I just discussed possibilities. Nothing more. Of course, she knew about the cooking scam. It was a big joke between the two of them—Teagen the Cordon Bleu diplomate who couldn't boil water."

I was puzzled. "Did Madge know who prepared that meal?"

"She said no, but I wasn't convinced. Madge was emphatic about one thing. Teagen would never have knowingly endangered her own life. She was far too self-absorbed." Violet bit her lip. "But there's one thing I think you should know. According to Madge, Teagen and Roddy got quite close."

I closed my eyes to avoid my aunt's look of compassion. "How close?"

"Teagen told her they were intimate. She praised his skill. Called him a master of erotic arts or words to that effect. Probably an exaggeration."

How misguided was I? I'd thought this day couldn't get any worse, but it certainly had. Teagen Doyle knew plenty about men, and she was right on target about Roddy. The man had energy, imagination, and the equipment to match.

I fought back tears. "So. Was she serious about him?"

Violet laughed. "Heavens no. He was merely a diversion to Teagen, a momentary detour into pleasure. She enjoyed her little flings."

I gripped the edge of the table to steady myself. "I guess Roddy should be pleased if he could satisfy such a lover."

Violet wasn't finished. "One more thing. Apparently, Teagen said Roddy was obsessed with her. She tried to end their liaison, but he wouldn't listen. I'm afraid Madge told that to Chief Miles, too."

I tried to assess the situation rationally and dispassionately, but I failed. We had only Teagen's word for it that anything had happened. Roddy swore that he'd fended off her advances, and I'd believed him. Now I was not so sure.

My aunt put her arms around me. "Men can be foolish, Marky, especially when they're confronted by someone as determined as Teagen. Don't give up on Roddy just yet."

My response was contemptuous. "He said he felt sorry for her. Compared Teagen to his mother for heaven's sake."

We both got a laugh out of that as I vowed to scrutinize Mrs. Park more closely if I ever got the chance. Perhaps she was a femme fatale. Mothers had come a long way since apron-clad June Cleaver in "Leave It to Beaver."

My iPhone dinged yet again. This time it was a text from that ubiquitous lawyer, Killian Blaine. His message was concise. "Sorry I disrupted your plans, but you'll love my new digs."

Wow! How would I feel having him as a neighbor? Of course, he would spend most of his time in Chicago. Perhaps like Teagen, he considered his romantic forays as mere diversions, brief interludes of no real value. No matter, I had no intention of being his or any other man's side hobby. I quickly fired off an impersonal text. "Welcome to the neighborhood. Harbor Bay is a very friendly community."

When Gemma returned from the dentist, her jaw was slightly swollen, and her mood was surly. "I need a root canal," she grumbled. "Double level of pain in that. Too bad money doesn't grow on trees."

I was too engrossed in my own issues to comfort her. "Grow up," I said. "Modern dentistry doesn't hurt except for the bill. Besides, you have insurance."

Gemma reared back. "Wow! Aren't you the grumpy one? You'd think you were the one having her mouth torn up instead of me."

I brushed aside her gripes. "Don't be a drama queen. I'm the one in pain."

That stopped her in her tracks. "Oh yeah? Tell me more."

I explained the latest developments in the Roddy saga, sparing none of the salacious details. Gemma wasn't shocked. In fact, she was full of ribald comments and speculation. "I don't blame Teagen for setting her sights on him. After all, her hubby is no kid. He may not have been up to the job even though he looks spry enough."

"That's no excuse for Roddy's behavior."

"Stop pouting. You said yourself that the Professor gets an "A plus" in lovemaking. It probably didn't mean a thing to him. Men are like that. Some women, too."

"Well, it means something to me. What if Benny did that? You wouldn't be so forgiving."

As usual, Gemma got the last word. "Are you kidding. If he nosed around a hussy like Teagen Doyle, I'd put him out of commission for a long time. Maybe forever."

I folded my arms and stomped off to find Fantasia. She was my boon companion, the one constant in my tumultuous life. I embraced the collie, fastened her harness, and embarked upon a brisk four-mile walk. The breeze over Lake Michigan was invigorating. It allowed me to strategize about my confrontation with Doogie. If he'd just unloaded a prime property, Doogie would be voluble and willing to speak candidly about his part in Teagen's death. I examined my motives. Why bother prying into the case? One way or another, my affair with Roderick Park was over. Finished. He could rot in prison for all I cared. Maybe abstinence was the right path for me to follow. Work and painting would occupy my days and lonely nights. Perhaps I could audition as a vestal-almost-virgin if any slots were available.

I finally admitted that ego motivated me. Pure hubris. I'd always loved solving puzzles, and Teagen's death intrigued me. The perfidious Professor didn't kill her. I was certain of that just as I knew that he wasn't obsessed with her. If she were a politician, pundit, or lawmaker, maybe. But a middle-aged B-level actress—no way. Someone else who knew her habits had eliminated that tiresome woman. Doogie was the key, and one way or another, I'd unearth his secret and unlock the puzzle.

* * *

Doogie closed shop at six, so right before then, I skipped out the door of Poppet, determined to confront him mano a mano. Despite Gemma's pleas, I elected to go solo with only Fantasia as backup. This was no time for girl power or feminine solidarity. I was prepared for battle, but not for the person who lurked at the curb.

"Going somewhere in such a hurry?" Killian Blaine's dulcet tones didn't deceive me at all.

"Why do you ask?" I deftly evaded his arm. "You'll have to excuse me. I'm pressed for time."

"Indeed." He raised one eyebrow in a brazen display of cynicism. "Doogie told me you were persistent. He was polite, of course. I'd call you pushy."

The man infuriated me. "Fortunately, I don't care what you think. Can't you find some anorexic client to console?"

He chuckled. "Ah, come on. Truce. Let me join you. A lawyer might come in handy if you get in a brawl. Afterwards, we could breeze by the place I just bought. You'll love it. A waterfront paradise overlooking Lake Michigan."

He dangled just the right bait to intrigue me. Lakefront homes were priced in the stratosphere. Even the humblest abode commanded over one million bucks. I was curious, although not envious. Killian had earned his success. Mine would come in time.

I checked my watch. "Okay. Let's go. I don't want to give him a chance to weasel out of it." I nodded toward his Maybach. "Fantasia's coming too unless your car isn't dog friendly."

"Not a problem. At least one of you will behave like a lady." In a show of faux gallantry, he helped both of us into his vehicle. Fantasia settled in like the aristocrat that she was. I avoided his gaze by staring out the window and gritting my teeth.

Killian sped toward Doogie's house, ignoring all speed limits and narrowly avoiding a collision with a jaunty senior citizen driving a Corvette. When we arrived, I trotted up to the front door and boldly rapped. In typical Doogie fashion, his doorknocker was a pricey San Michele brand with elaborate carvings. Although he didn't immediately respond, I wasn't concerned. His Lexus was parked in the driveway, and the front door was ajar. Despite the times and headlines highlighting grisly crimes, most people in Harbor Bay still tempted fate by leaving their doors unlocked. Not me. I learned from my wise Aunt Violet to trust but protect myself.

"We're here," I yelled, calling his name. "Right on time." I could hear the strains of Mozart on his sound system and the beeping of the microwave oven. The scent of wood burning in the fireplace provided a homey touch.

Killian stepped in front of me. "Let me go first. After all, I'm a paying client. He won't prosecute me for B&E."

"He's probably in the kitchen," I said. "Ever the good host."

Killian moved cautiously toward the kitchen. "Hope he doesn't own a gun."

"Doogie?" I scoffed. "His mighty mouth is his weapon. Come on. Don't be a coward. Here. I'll go in."

I flung open the kitchen door, backed up, and uttered a plaintiff cry. No more bon mots or gourmet treats from Doogie Kinkaid. He lay on his back in a pool of blood, with a meat thermometer plunged into his chest.

Chapter Fifteen

I'd seen corpses before. That didn't make it easier, especially when the body in question belonged to a dear friend. No fainting or wailing allowed, I braced myself against the Wolf stove he adored and took a deep breath.

Killian bent over and felt Doogie's pulse. "Body's still warm," he said. "I only left him an hour ago, so we must have just missed the killer."

"What's that in his hand?" I asked. As a devotee of endless crime novels. I knew better than to touch anything, but that didn't stop me from looking.

"A pen. Mont Blanc, to be precise. Too bad he couldn't write the name of his murderer."

I stifled a sob. "Doogie was an ardent stylophile. Maybe that was a clue."

"What?"

"A lover of all things pen. He belonged to the Pen Collectors of America, attended their conventions, and wrote articles for their newsletter *The Pendant.*"

"Hmm," Killian sniffed. "Harmless enough hobby, I guess." He grabbed his iPhone. "Time to call the authorities. Chief Miles can handle all this."

He tapped his contact list and was immediately connected to the chief's office. I backed out of the kitchen and eased into one of Doogie's capacious wing chairs, mouthing a silent prayer that Benny Soto was not on duty. Aubrey Miles would assess the tragedy calmly and professionally. Benny would likely blame me.

Amid chaos, Aunt Violet was my rock and first refuge. I dialed her number and breathed a sigh of relief when she answered. My first explanation was muddled.

"Slow down, Marky, and tell me what happened. Is Doogie dead? I suppose it's not such a shock. He had several health issues."

"You don't understand," I gasped in a shaky voice. "Doogie was murdered. Stabbed in the heart with a meat thermometer. Killian called Chief Miles, so I guess it's safe to tell Gemma."

The sound of police and ambulance sirens suddenly echoed through the tranquil neighborhood.

"They're here," I said. "Gotta go."

Killian strode quickly through the living room and opened the front door. Chief Miles, accompanied by Benny Soto, nodded to both of us and assessed the situation. Benny kept his hand on his holster as he eyed Killian and me. His stance said it all: one false move, and we were toast.

"Come this way," Killian said. "He's in the kitchen. We haven't touched anything."

Aubrey Miles asked us to step outside while the forensic team plied their grisly trade. Having worked numerous homicides in Detroit, she had to be familiar with violent death and knew that everyone and anyone was a suspect until proven otherwise.

Although the coroner's van was parked at a discreet distance behind the Maybach, a gaggle of mostly elderly neighbors was already assembling. Their behavior was muted by a distaste for vulgar curiosity, although they spoke quietly among themselves and observed every detail of the proceedings.

One dowager who was a frequent customer of Poppet buttonholed me. "Is Mr. Kinkaid all right?" she asked. "Such a fine man and a generous neighbor." She clutched my hand in a surprisingly strong grip. "Please tell me."

I sputtered several weasel words that didn't deceive her for a moment.

"He's dead, isn't he?"

"Unfortunately. Mr. Kinkaid passed away not long ago." I didn't tell the entire truth. The word 'murder' was too painful to utter. She mopped her eyes with a handkerchief and left to spread the word to her friends. They'd learn the full story soon enough when Chief Miles and her staff interviewed them.

I panicked when I recalled that Fantasia was still in Killian's car. "I have to get her out," I cried. "She may be frightened."

Killian scowled. "That dog has more poise than most humans I know, but here's the key fob. Go get her if it makes you happy."

Fantasia alighted from the Maybach as if she were a movie star approaching the red carpet. I hugged her neck a bit too enthusiastically, causing her to yip in pain.

"Abusing animals, are you?" Killian popped up behind me as if he were an evil genie or a devil. "Not what I expected of you."

"Go away," I said. "Doogie was a dear friend, and I'm devastated."

"Not too distraught to stop snooping, I bet. Tell me. Who's at the top of your suspect list now? You really should be careful. Someone around here has no compunction about killing. You might be next on the agenda. I'd hate for anything to happen to you."

"At least Roddy can't be blamed. He's still in Ann Arbor."

Killian's expression was hard to read. "Is that so? Doogie told me only today that the Professor would once again be his houseguest. In fact, he expected him to arrive at any time."

That floored me, but I managed to retain my composure. Sangfroid, Aunt Violet called it, a useful French expression for staying poised. Unfortunately, I didn't deceive Killian.

"You didn't know, did you? Do I detect trouble in paradise?" His snide attitude irked me.

"Not at all. We're merely taking a pause, not that it's any of your business. As for suspects, I wonder where your bosom pal Brendan Doyle was today. Doogie might have prepared that meal, but Brendan had plenty of opportunity to spike it. I've heard that his business empire is on shaky ground. You must wonder how much Teagen's insurance policy was and who was the beneficiary. Not to mention that you're not in the clear either. You were the last person to see Doogie, except for the killer, of course. Cops always suspect someone like that."

Killian's manner changed from arch to angry. "Brendan's bunking down at Madge's place. Why don't you ask him yourself? I dare you."

We faced each other like pugilists, preparing for the main event. Neither one of us blinked, backed off, or gave an inch. Ultimately, he thrust open the passenger side door and stalked over to the driver's side. "Get in," he barked. "I'll drive you home unless you're afraid to ride with a possible killer."

I gave him my sweetest smile. "Not at all. Fantasia and I can take care of ourselves."

****

He drove in the opposite direction from Poppet, and for a moment, I was worried. *Remain calm I told myself. He can't dispose of you and a big dog without someone noticing.*

Killian must have read my mind. He gave me a wolfish grin that was both smug and snarky. "Scared you, didn't I, Miss Marky. Fear not. I promised to show you my new property, and I always keep my promises. Don't worry. Doogie gave me a key when I signed the papers."

He drove straight to Lake Shore Drive and parked in front of a spacious modern structure located on a high bluff that overlooked Lake Michigan. I was dazzled but kept that feeling to myself.

"Lovely," I said. "Great views of the lake."

"Come on in," Killian said. "I bought it fully furnished. Not quite to my taste, but with the help of a talented artist, it could be brought up to standard."

I ignored that remark, fastened Fantasia's harness, and followed in behind him. The house was spectacular, finished with exquisite detail and perfectly sized for comfort.

Killian shrugged. "I'll have to have a dock built for my boat, but otherwise it suits my needs. A local architect designed it for himself, so it has all the upgrades. Four acres of privacy, too."

That was an understatement. From the chef's kitchen to the great room with its huge fieldstone fireplace, this house was anyone's dream.

"You should see the master bedroom suite. I'll gladly show it to you." He leered at me, eyes bright with mischief.

"Some other time perhaps." I turned toward the front door. "Congratulations. Doogie's

final sale was a tribute to him. Too bad the Doyles weren't as fortunate."

"Will you back off the Doyles! Your boyfriend is probably in the clear now, so what's your problem?"

Killian was angry. His icy stare and clenched fists proved that. Fantasia sensed the tension. She issued a low growl and moved in between us. On rare occasions, good sense deserts me. Instead of cowering or ignoring the issue, I chose defiance.

"Don't you get it? This isn't just about Roddy or Teagen anymore. A good, kind man, who happened to be a dear friend, was just brutally murdered. Doogie confessed that he prepared that seduction supper, but he had nothing to do with spiking it. Someone else, someone he trusted, did that. He planned to tell me everything tonight."

Lawyers love to argue even when their case is weak. He put his hands out in mute appeal, as if hoping for a favorable verdict. "Let Chief Miles handle that. Tell her what you know or think you know and back off." He paused. "I don't want to see you get hurt." He reached out and caressed my hand. "I care about you, Marky. Can't you tell?"

Tenderness was an aspect of Killian Blaine's character that was foreign to me. Before I could respond, we arrived at Poppet, and there on the doorstep sat an unexpected visitor.

"Looks like you've got a guest," Killian said without a trace of emotion. "I'll say good night." He leaned across and thrust open my door. I tumbled out and freed Fantasia from the back seat. "Thanks," I mumbled, feeling awkward and numb. Who knew that Roderick Park would show his face after ignoring me for days?

Roddy watched as the Maybach sped away. "Marky, we have to talk," he said. "I have a confession to make."

Chapter Sixteen

I stepped away from Roddy. Was he guilty of murder or some lesser crime? Either way, I needed to protect myself.

"It's a nice evening. Let's sit here and discuss things." I motioned to the wicker bench outside Poppet. He gave me a puzzled look but reluctantly complied. Fantasia sat between us, providing a furry bulwark against attack.

"This is a surprise," I said. "Unexpected but certainly welcome. I suppose you heard about Doogie."

Roddy gulped before answering. "I found out the hard way. When I went to his place, the cops had it surrounded. One of his neighbors gave me the story." He shook his head. "I can't believe it. Doogie of all people. We'd spoken only this morning."

He deftly dodged the topic at hand as if delay would soften his message.

"Okay, let's stop fencing. Did you kill Teagen or Doogie?"

Roddy's face grew ashen. "I can't believe you'd even asked me that. Of course, I didn't harm anyone."

His reaction was so strong that I tended to believe him. "Okay then. What's this confession all about?"

He couldn't face me directly, but he mustered a weak reply that said enough. "I wasn't entirely honest about my relationship with Mrs. Doyle." Roddy bit his lip. "We…that is, I…allowed things to escalate. Naturally, I take full responsibility."

I folded my arms, narrowed my eyes, and stared. If he was expecting womanly compassion, Dr. Roderick Park was sadly mistaken. "You had an affair with her?"

He hesitated. "More like a dalliance. It only happened a few times, honest, Marky, and it didn't mean anything to me."

He obviously didn't get it. His "dalliance" meant plenty to me. "Madge Stone told the chief that you were obsessed with Teagen. Couldn't get enough of her. That doesn't help your case." Since I felt particularly aggrieved, I added another comment. "Teagen praised your performance, though. Great publicity."

He regained his composure and took my hand. I saw once again the dashing Professor who had won my heart with his brains and beauty. It pained me to remember that.

"Think, Marky. Why would I kill her? Besides, all I did was enjoy that meal. I didn't touch a thing. She'd already paid me for my role in Teagen's Tinctures. I didn't know about her allergies either. She never even mentioned dairy, and nuts, and I certainly didn't taste any in that supper." His eyes pleaded for understanding and forgiveness. He was innocent of murder—that much I knew—but his perfidious conduct with Teagen was another matter entirely.

"Look, Roddy. I'll help you any way I can. Teagen was no loss to the world, but Doogie was. I won't allow his killing to go unavenged. Not if I can help it."

He picked up his suitcase and held out his hand. "For heaven's sake, be careful. You're not a cop or some kind of superhero. Maybe you'll forgive me in time. I admit I was a fool, but it didn't change the way I feel about you. I miss you, Marky." He stiffened. "Unless you've already found my replacement."

I stayed statue still; my expression firmly fixed in neutral. Roddy bent over and kissed my forehead. "I'm staying at the Bay House Inn for a few days. Chief Miles wants to interview me. Call if you want to talk."

"Okay." I took Fantasia's lead and walked slowly into Poppet, knowing that our relationship had just ended.

* * *

Benny Soto appeared the moment I opened Poppet the next day. His officious manner was on full display as he twirled his nightstick and gave me a savage frown. Gemma was oblivious to this pretend drama. She rushed to his side, hugging her lover boy with undeserved fervor.

"What do you want, Benny?" I was groggy from lack of sleep, in no mood to indulge his tough-guy antics.

"Chief Miles wants you right away," he growled. "You'll have to come down to the station. Now."

I yawned and checked my watch. "Naturally, I want to cooperate with Chief Miles. Please inform her that I'll gladly meet with her—after I consult my attorney."

From the look on his face, I could tell that Benny was gobsmacked. He sputtered something vile and stepped my way. I pasted a pleasant smile on my face, but didn't retreat. Fortunately, a confrontation was averted by the timely arrival of my aunt.

"What's this, Benny?" Violet asked, "Did I miss something?"

Benny mumbled a greeting and swiveled her way. "Chief Miles wants Ms. Davis in her office pronto. She refuses to go."

"I'm sure this is a misunderstanding," Violet said. "Let me phone Aubrey and straighten it out." She speed-dialed a number, exchanged pleasantries, and explained the situation to the chief. "Here, Benny," Violet said, "Chief Miles wants to speak with you."

As he listened, his flushed face told the tale. Deputy Soto morphed into a reasonable police officer who politely requested me to drop by the cop shop at my earliest convenience. After mustering his tattered shreds of dignity, Benny exited Poppet with Gemma trailing after him. He brushed her aside, jumped into his patrol car, and sped away. Score one more for the home team!

Aunt Violet turned away as if to hide her smile. "What did I miss? I heard that Roddy showed his face last evening."

Naturally, Gemma didn't hesitate to comment. "He has his nerve. Everyone knows he was knocking boots with that hussy. Benny told me so."

"No comment," I said with a shrug. "I'm focused on Doogie. He deserved better."

"The killer used a curious weapon," Violet said. "It suggests a crime of passion or opportunity, not premeditation. I'm positive it came from his own kitchen."

"Passion? Doogie? Get real." Gemma snorted. "Not unless it involved food or real estate. I think he planned to spill his guts to Marky, and that got him killed."

I had to agree even though it intensified my guilt. Someone conspired with Doogie, not to poison Teagen but to spike her allergies. Knowing him, he probably told the culprit and paid the price for his candor.0

"That Letty Briggs could be the one," Gemma said. "I don't trust her. Besides, wasn't she over at Doogie's the other night? Who knows what he told her?"

Before I responded, another customer waltzed into Poppet. Killian Blaine wore a spotless white polo shirt and form-fitting jeans. I pretended not to notice, but the effect was disconcerting. My unflappable aunt greeted him with a pleasant smile.

"Nice to see you, Mr. Blaine. How may I help you?"

He returned her smile with one of his own. "Actually, I've come to offer my services—as chauffeur. I'm meeting with Chief Miles, and she mentioned that Ms. Davis was also on her list. Since we were together when we found the victim, it made sense."

I hesitated until he added one more bon mot. "Besides, she may need a lawyer at her side, and I want to be of service."

"I'll have you know…" Anger and another emotion I couldn't define made my cheeks burn.

Aunt Violet raised her hand short-circuiting my tirade. "Sounds like a good plan. We can handle things here, Marky. Run along."

After I buckled my seatbelt, Killian couldn't resist a final taunt. "I saw your Professor at the Harbor Bay Inn this morning. He didn't look happy."

"He knew Doogie and liked him. Who wouldn't feel sad?"

"A fair point. Our chat with Chief Miles should be brief. How about sharing lunch afterwards? We could plot our strategy."

Refusing lunch would seem churlish, and I had to. admit that I was starving.

Besides, it wouldn't hurt to hear his views. "Sure. Why not?"

Deputy Soto was staffing the front desk. He had shed his surly manner in favor of a more customer-friendly approach. I suspected that he, like most people, was intimidated by Killian or that he was still smarting from our earlier encounter. We were immediately led into Aubrey Miles' office. She rose and waved us into the two visitor's chairs that faced her desk.

"I'm sorry that you lost your friend," she said. "Finding him must have been a difficult experience."

Her kindness brought tears to my eyes. I envisioned Doogie lying in the kitchen, clutching his beloved Mont Blanc.

"Pardon me," I said. "I feel responsible for Doogie's murder."

She raised her eyebrows and leaned forward. "Really? How so?"

I told her of my suspicions and Doogie's vow to explain everything. Killian added that during their business dealings that day, Doogie seemed untroubled, almost jubilant.

"You see, I knew Doogie had prepared that final supper. He admitted as much but said it was supposed to be a big joke." I closed my eyes. "Someone got him to do it. Either Teagen herself or a confederate. He would never have hurt Teagen. He adored her."

"Interesting," said Chief Miles. "You said his body was still warm."

Killian agreed. "I took his pulse and held a mirror to his lips. Ms. Davis was too distraught to touch him."

"I was in shock," I said. "But I noticed the pen in his hand. Maybe it was a clue."

"Perhaps," she said.

I wondered if the woman always spoke in monosyllables or if that was a clever cop trick to make voluble suspects like me blab.

"I still think that the seduction supper was a ruse, something to arouse Brendan Doyle's jealousy. You know that he was a rake, a libertine—a philanderer of the first order. I bet Teagen used Roddy as bait so that her husband would care for her."

Killian snarled a response. "Dr. Park was very cooperative, so it certainly seemed to work. This is all supposition, Chief. Bottom line: two people are dead under suspicious circumstances."

"Well said, Mr. Blaine." She turned my way. "Is there anything else I should know? Was Teagen Doyle popular or did she have enemies?"

Before I opened my mouth, Killian intervened. "She was a recent arrival here. I suggest you ask Marge Stone about that."

"And Letty Briggs," I added. "She and Teagen went way back. They had history. Letty and Brendan were a hot item before Teagen muscled in. You heard her at Teagen's memorial. And Letty was close to Doogie. We saw her there that very night of the memorial."

"I knew both of the Doyles for years," Killian said. "They were a charismatic couple with big egos and complicated lives. Don't infer too much from that."

"I won't." Chief Miles asked both of us to dictate and sign a statement.

Before leaving us, she turned to me. "Miss Davis, a word of warning. I know you've been involved in several murder cases, but please listen. A killer, possibly a double murderer, is within our community. Leave the detective work to professionals. Don't interfere. I can assure you we know our jobs."

* * *

"You heard her," said Killian Blaine as we enjoyed our lunch at Bistro Bis. "You're no match for a killer with a meat thermometer."

"Very droll. The chief is new to Harbor Bay, but I am not." I tucked into a delicious dish of pike dumplings while he deboned a trout. "This is fantastic. The Chef d' cuisine is a special pal of my aunt's from Paris."

"That's one of my favorite cities," Killian said. "I'd love to take you there someday."

He was using a diversionary technique, a very enticing one as it happens. I gritted my teeth and forged on. "I've been to Paris many times with my aunt. It is a magical place. Now…strategy. We agreed to plot strategy." I speared a dumpling before continuing. "Let's go back to basics. Who profited from Teagen's death?"

"Suppose we start with motives instead." He adjusted his napkin, trying mightily to look earnest. "I've invited a guest to join us for dessert. Three heads are better than two, I suppose."

That aroused my suspicions. Did he intend to sidetrack me by injecting a stranger into the discussion? Right on cue, Madge Stone stepped into the restaurant and took a seat at our table. She'd abandoned her understated garb for a powder blue pantsuit that flattered her complexion and intensified her eye color. As Madge settled in, I detected the delicate scent of Creed Spring Flowers, the same fragrance Aunt Violet had selected for her.

She was gracious despite the somber topic we discussed. "I invited Brendan, but he couldn't make it," she said. "Still grieving. Teagen's death hit him hard, and now Doogie's murder. It's terrible. I can't believe it."

We paused while the waiter took our order for drinks and dessert. I succumbed to temptation and agreed to sample the crème Brule. Madge skipped the sweet stuff and ordered an espresso martini. Killian opted for a Negroni, with a splash of prosecco instead of gin. I'd never tried that, but the name sounded wickedly delicious, rather like the man who sipped it.

Madge's face grew flushed from either alcohol or emotion. That whiff of vulnerability prompted me to pounce. Carpe diem and all that.

"Doogie prepared Teagen's last meal. He promised to give me all the details on the very night someone murdered him." I gave Madge the gimlet eye. "Someone he trusted asked him to do that. As a joke, he said, but we know better."

Madge reared back as if I had struck her. "I don't know what to say. Are you suggesting that Doogie poisoned Teagen? I hope you don't suspect Brendan. He adored his wife even though he didn't always show it."

"Doogie was no killer," I said, "But he knew who was. How else can you explain his murder?"

Before she responded, Killian intervened. "Marky isn't accusing anyone, Madge. We're merely speculating. Let's face it. The range of suspects in a small town like Harbor Bay is rather limited."

Madge took her time finishing the last drop of her martini. I half expected her to lick the glass, but she restrained herself.

"No one here really knew Teagen, not well enough to kill her. She was vigilant about avoiding allergy triggers. Dairy and nuts are in many products, so she couldn't afford to be complacent. Besides, the EpiPen should have saved her. I injected her myself, and I'm a former nurse."

"Why didn't it save her?" I asked. "People said that she always bragged about it. Called it her secret weapon."

Madge shook her head. "They don't always work. Usually, but not always. Teagen usually carried a backup for safety's sake, but she used it the other day. She must have ingested an extraordinary amount of dairy and nuts. I can't understand it."

I gnawed at that problem like Fantasia with a marrow bone. "Who do you suppose asked Doogie to make that meal? It had to be someone he trusted." I ignored Killian's glare and pressed on. "What about your cousin? Letty was at his place a few nights ago, pouring her heart out about something. She and Doogie seemed rather close."

Madge dabbed her lips with a napkin. "I don't feel comfortable speculating about my friends or family. I'm surprised you'd participate in this charade, Killian." She leaned forward and jabbed her finger at me. "As I recall, your fiancé, Dr. Park, is the prime suspect. He was enthralled with Teagen. Made quite a pest of himself. Teagen told me that several times."

I ignored that jab and soldiered on. "Letty hated Teagen. We saw that at the memorial service. Maybe she wanted to win Brendan back. I understand they were once engaged."

She rose, clutching her purse to her chest like a shield. "I'm very fond of your Aunt, so I won't share this nonsense with Brendan. But be advised, Ms. Davis, that if you pursue these baseless allegations, I will consult my attorney."

Her reaction galvanized my fighting spirit. Wealth and position didn't insulate her family or friends from suspicion. "I'm sorry you feel that way, Mrs. Stone. But remember, Teagen hired me because she feared for her life, and Doogie was a dear friend. I owe both a debt."

Madge Stone's eyes bulged with either anger or disbelief. She stomped off without saying another word to either of us.

* * *

We rode back to Poppet in stony silence. Killian was either brooding or sulking, and I was slightly stunned by the encounter with Madge. When the gloves came off and the veneer of class and privilege eroded, she was as much of a street fighter as Gemma.

"Thanks for lunch," I said as I hopped out of the Maybach.

"Never a dull moment with you." Killian made no attempt to prolong our outing or suggest another meeting.

Since I'd never envisioned having a relationship with him, his attitude didn't bother me one bit. I strolled into Poppet with my head held high. Aunt Violet was chatting with two out-of-town matrons, and Gemma was busy giving one of her famous couples' massages. That freed me to find Fantasia and take my good girl for a much-needed walk. As we strolled toward the lakefront, I saw Gemma's friend Emil, the paramedic. The timing was perfect. I decided to pose the EpiPen issue to him. He was lanky, some called him a string bean, with sparse black hair arranged in a bad combover. Appearance aside, he was reputedly smart and good at his job.

"You deal with EpiPens, don't you?" Emil nodded. "Help me out with this puzzle. I need an expert opinion. Teagen Doyle should have been saved by hers. She injected herself or tried to when she first felt ill. Why wouldn't those pens have saved her?"

Emil scratched his ear and pondered that question. "Curious," he said. "A second injection within five or ten minutes of the first one usually works. Should have saved her. We run into that sometimes, but not often." He bit his lip. "Now if her pens were empty or expired…" He shrugged. "Bad stuff can happen." He suddenly grew suspicious. "Hey, wait a minute. Everyone says it was an accident."

Now it was my turn to shrug. "Don't believe everything you hear."

Teagen's death was no accident. Doogie's murder proved that.

As I ambled back to Poppet, I received an astounding text message from Kim.

"The reading of Doogie's will is scheduled for Friday. Lionel said you should be there. Apparently, you're mentioned in it."

That puzzled me. It seemed premature to read the victim's will so soon after his murder. Cold and unfeeling. On the other hand, lawyers weren't known for their solicitude, and Lionel Stevens was one cold fish. I was puzzled by my inclusion, even though I adored Doogie and considered him a pal. When we entered Poppet, Gemma was waiting. Her rapid movements told me that something big was afoot.

"Don't take this the wrong way," she said. "Your Aunt is checking things out."

I resisted the impulse to shake the stuffing out of my pal, choosing instead to gently unhitch Fantasia's harness. "What's going on?"

For once, Gemma calmed down and gave a concise account. "Benny just told me. They hauled Roddy Park back down to the police station for questioning."

"Good heavens, why? I thought they cleared him in Teagen's death."

Gemma's downcast eyes told a different tale. "You don't get it. They think he killed Doogie, too."

I was dumbstruck. "Why? He planned to bunk with him again. They were friends. Besides, Roddy wasn't even in Harbor Bay when it happened. He told me so."

"Think again. Doogie's security cameras caught that handsome mug on the afternoon of the murder. Face it, Marky. Your guy is in deep doo-doo."

It made no sense. I longed to cover my ears and scream. Roddy was no killer, even though he could shade the truth when it served his purposes. He had no motive for killing either one of them. Motive. Killian and I had planned to discuss that. Now that we were incommunicado, I had to rely upon Gemma, Kim, and Aunt Violet, my faithful co-conspirators. Girl power had triumphed before, and it would once more. At least for Doogie's sake and yes for Roddy's too, I hoped so.

Chapter Seventeen

Kim blew into Poppet like an errant wind. Her impeccable bob was disheveled, and her nail polish chipped. She glanced around the store and beckoned to Gemma and me. "Come closer. I have news!"

"Okay," Gemma said, "Come out with it."

Kim lowered her eyes and hesitated. "I should feel guilty, but it was all in a good cause. When Lionel went golfing, I snooped in his office. He always locks his desk, but I know where he hides the key."

I tried not to imagine the worst, but it was hard not to. Had Kim discovered something that implicated her husband? On second thought, I doubted that. Lionel was a crusty lawyer who revered caution above all things. He'd never take that kind of risk.

"I found his will," Kim said.

"Lionel's?" Gemma and I spoke as one.

"No, of course not. Doogie's will. Lionel was his attorney." She swallowed. "Guess who's a beneficiary? I think they call it a legatee."

"I bet it's Letty, or maybe Madge." I said, "They may be wealthy, but that wouldn't stop them. Never enough, as they say. Besides, Doogie probably had plenty of assets."

Kim had a strange look on her face. "You're wrong," she said. "He listed a number of charities, but his residence was willed to you, Marky."

I stared at her, stupefied. Surely, I had misheard. Why would Doogie leave me anything, let alone his gorgeous home? "Me? You must be wrong, Kim."

Gemma pounced immediately. "Marky's an heiress! Of course, that also makes her a suspect, doesn't it? They'll think she was in on it with the Professor." She grinned. "Better call that Chicago stud after all. You may need a good lawyer."

I plopped down in one of our fauteuils to steady myself. "Why would Doogie do that? We were pals but hardly bosom buddies."

Kim squeezed my shoulder. "He explained it in his will, Marky." She reached into her tote and found her notebook. "I copied it word for word. Doogie said he admired your talent and tenacity—his very words. He also praised your kindness to him."

I was speechless, unable to do anything but weep for a friend I'd lost and a man I'd liked. When my aunt entered Poppet, she stopped short. "What's this? Has something happened, Marky?"

Kim explained the situation, although she downplayed her role. Violet was unflappable as always. She raised her eyebrows when she learned of my legacy, but seemed unperturbed.

"How very generous of Doogie," she said. "His home is a showplace, and I can't think of anyone who would take better care of it than you, Marky."

"There's something else," Kim said. "You must agree to love and care for Algernon."

"Huh?" Algernon was Doogie's prize Persian, an aloof creature with patrician tastes. "Of course I'll gladly take him, although Fantasia may object." I'd always loved cats, those wonderous creatures whose piercing gazes often discomforted me. Algernon was particularly gifted at making mere humans cringe under his scrutiny, and no one other than Doogie met his high standards.

"She'll adjust," Gemma said. "Heck for that kind of dough I'd take him in myself." She narrowed her eyes, "Kind of suspicious under the circumstances. Puts Marky in the bullseye. Suppose they think she and the Professor planned the whole thing? You know, like in that movie Bonnie and Clyde."

"Nonsense," Violet said. "She was nowhere near his house when Doogie was murdered. Mr. Blaine can certainly verify that. And since Teagen's death is linked to Doogie's, it's even more preposterous to suggest any involvement by either Marky or Dr. Park."

"Its gotta be worth a bundle," Gemma smacking her lips. "Money is always motive number one."

Kim consulted her notes. "One million eight hundred thousand, to be precise. Lionel had the property valuation among his papers." She furrowed her brow. "Please don't mention this to anyone until the formal reading of the will. Lionel could get in trouble, and Lord only knows what would happen to me."

"Don't fret," Violet said. "We'll keep it secret." She gave my partner a stern look. "From everyone. Right, Gemma?"

Gemma got the message. No sharing tidbits with Benny or anyone else. She crossed her heart but omitted the 'hope to die' part. Considering that we were facing two murders, I considered that a wise move.

My head spun with too many theories and too few clues. I still believed that Teagen and Doogie's deaths were linked, but I couldn't figure out what the motive was. Someone had conspired with Doogie to fix Teagen's last supper. Someone who then deliberately spiked the entrée with allergens, knowing that Teagen would become gravely ill. The EpiPen hadn't saved her. She'd used her backup needle two days earlier and hadn't replaced it. That led to a perfect storm of events that felled the sultry vixen and subsequently Doogie, the unwitting accomplice.

When Chief Aubrey Miles called, I wasn't surprised. It was the fitting climax to a most troubling day. Gemma panicked, clutching her heart in a faux swoon.

"Don't go alone, Marky. She might trap you. You know how you always blab when you're nervous."

"I have nothing to fear. I'm innocent." My brave stance didn't deceive Violet. She merely stood up and gathered her purse.

"No harm in having a witness, is there? Besides, I'm sure Aubrey won't mind. She seems like a very balanced person. Gemma can hold down the fort here."

I agreed after mounting a very half-hearted effort to dissuade her. "Okay. I'll act surprised when she mentions Doogie's will, though."

As we left, Gemma made a final parting shot. "Don't worry, Marky. You'll look great in jail stripes. Orange in the new black, as they say."

* * *

Chief Miles was calm and courteous when we met with her. If Violet's presence was unwelcome, she gave no sign of it. At first, she shuffled some papers on her desk until she plucked a sheet of heavy vellum from the pile.

"How well did you know Doogie Kinkaid, Miss Davis? Were you best friends?"

I stuttered as I tried to formulate a coherent reply. My aunt's gentle pat on my knee helped to right the shaky ship. "We were friends. Plus, Doogie was a valued customer at Poppet, and he helped us find the storefront several years ago."

Aubrey nodded pleasantly. "I see. There was never anything intimate between you?"

That shocked me. "Oh no! Doogie was a perfect gentleman. Besides, I don't think he was interested in sex. He had plenty of female friends, though."

Violet cleared her throat. "Pardon me, Chief, but where is this leading?"

"For now, we're merely having a discussion. I suppose he told you about his will," said Aubrey, acting very much like a police officer. "You've been given a handsome legacy."

At this point, I yearned for the formidable presence of Killian Blaine. He would have easily run interference for me and backed Chief Miles down. I recalled a bit of lawyerly wisdom he'd once imparted to me: when confronted by the cops, don't lie but don't volunteer anything. That was a tough assignment for someone like me who had always been teacher's pet and a good little girl catering to authority figures.

"I only learned about my bequest after his death. Believe me, I was astonished. Why do you ask?"

Violet locked eyes with Aubrey Miles. They both knew the answer straight away.

"Motive, Miss Davis. It goes to motive. Someone murdered Mr. Kinkaid

154

up front and personal in a most brutal fashion. It has been my experience that love and money top the list of motives."

My voice squeaked when I spoke. I loathed that sign of weakness but was powerless to stop it. "Do I need a lawyer? Am I under suspicion? I was nowhere near Doogie's house until after his murder. Just ask Killian Blaine."

Once again, Violet eased into the conversation. "Do you intend to charge my niece? If not, tell us what you suspect."

Nothing flustered Chief Miles. Her face wore that same complacent smile I'd seen before. It frightened me, unlike the bluster and bravado of Benny Soto.

"You also had access to Mrs. Doyle's premises, I believe."

"Yes. She hired me to paint her portrait." I gripped my aunt's hands. They were rock steady and ice cold.

"You severed that relationship before her death. Why was that?"

I gulped. "She was too busy, and my schedule was packed as well."

Her eyes had a predator's hard stare. Cop's eyes. "People say she stole your fiancé, Dr. Park. Is that true?"

I never weep. Hardly ever. But this was one time when I fought hard to suppress tears. Roddy's betrayal, combined with Doogie's murder, took a heavy toll on my emotions. I summoned every ounce of courage and faced the truth.

"He dumped me, Chief, and I saw a different side of Dr. Park. It was Teagen's doing. Doogie had no part in anything. He agreed to tell me who convinced him to make that final meal for her, but the killer got to him first."

"I see." She glanced at her computer. "Did anyone else hear him say that?"

I shook my head. "I doubt it. We were alone in his kitchen."

No reaction from the chief. She merely continued her inquiry. "Dr. Park came back to Harbor Bay on the day of the murder. He was seen at the victim's home on two occasions. Before you arrived and later. Were you aware of that?"

I wavered between silence and speculation. "He mentioned it. I didn't know before that, and he said he arrived after Doogie's murder. He saw the police vehicles and left."

She raised an eyebrow but didn't contradict me. Once again, Aunt Violet ran interference.

"Is Dr. Park in custody? Has he been charged?"

Aubrey Miles shook her head. "Not yet, although you should know that he is a person of interest. Some people think that you are also involved, Miss Davis."

"Me!" I felt like a pawn in a low-rent melodrama. "Brendan Doyle tells everyone that. I suppose you've examined those EpiPens. What if someone tampered with them? That, plus the planted allergens, spells murder in my book. Besides, I wouldn't put much stock in anything Brendan Doyle says either. He's the logical suspect. The spouse always is." I tried to tamp down my outrage but couldn't. "If he's so bereaved, why was he canoodling with Letty Briggs? We all heard her at that memorial service."

That made the chief smile. "Canoodling, is it? I'll have to jot that one down. Thank you for your candor. You've given me much to consider. I'll contact you again as things progress." Once more, she beamed that Mona Lisa smile my way. No longer did I find it charming. It now seemed downright creepy. As Violet and I exited, we encountered the odious Benny Soto. His curled lip and triumphant look were almost too much to bear. For Gemma's sake, I ignored him and trudged toward the waiting room. There, we encountered a motley crew milling about. Brendan Doyle's ruddy complexion was a product of either excessive sun, rage, or incipient stroke. When he spied us, he snorted something vile, wagged his finger, and turned his back. Brendan was accompanied by his boon companion, who was as immaculately turned out and composed as ever.

"Marky and Miss Violet. This is a surprise." Killian Blaine rose and took my hand. "We need to talk," he whispered. "I'll phone you later."

They were joined by Madge Stone and Letty Briggs, both of whom greeted my aunt warmly and snubbed me. I held my head up high and exited with as much grace as I could muster. My brave façade crumbled when we reached Violet's Mercedes.

"What just happened?" I cried. "This feels like Jabberwocky."

"So true," Violet said. "We are indeed seeing through the looking glass."

She grinned. "Who's your candidate for the Red Queen? I can guess the identity of the white knight."

I was no fan of Lewis Carroll, but in this instance, I indeed felt like the benighted Alice. Unfortunately, this was real life, not Wonderland. My vote for the evil red queen was undecided—both Madge and Letty fit the bill. Brendan Doyle was typecast as the Mad Hatter.

"You look deflated, Marky. That's not like you." My aunt deftly pulled out of a tight parking spot. "Come on. I have just the prescription to cheer you up. Kim and Gemma are meeting us for lunch at the Patisserie. We'll drink wine and ingest a scandalous number of calories."

I yearned to bury my head under the covers, but refusing such a kind gesture would be churlish. Besides, stuffing my face with delectables might be just the cure I needed. It had always worked for me as a child.

Kim and Gemma were seated in a secluded booth when we arrived. From the glow on her cheeks, I knew that my BFF had already consumed some wine. Gemma seldom drank alcohol, especially at lunchtime. When she did, she quickly lost control.

"What happened at the jail?" she asked, all wide-eyed. "Benny said you got grilled by his boss."

"He's making that up," I sniffed. "He wasn't even in the room."

Kim was too refined to probe, but she followed every word.

"Chief Miles was very thorough," Violet said, "but I don't believe for a moment that she suspects Marky of any involvement. Still...we should put our heads together."

"Motive," I said. "The chief mentioned love and money."

Gemma jumped right in, "Sounds like Brendan Doyle, at least the love part. Teagen flaunted her affair with Roddy, and no guy likes that."

Kim agreed. "It's no fun being cuckolded. Of course, Brendan was no angel either. Teagen probably knew he was involved with Letty. I'm afraid your Dr. Park was merely a pawn, Marky."

Can a woman be cuckolded? If so, Brendan and I had something in common. I paused and scanned the menu. Sole Meuniere, one of Julia Child's favorites, was also tops on my hit parade. I could taste its delicate flavor and savor the lemon sauce accompanying it. Almost as good as romance. Almost.

"Wake up, Marky," Gemma brayed. "You're dreaming. Get with it, girl."

She was right. With trouble looming, there was no time to brood.

"I'm stuck on the money motive," I said, turning to Kim. "Did you uncover any 'key person' policies on Teagen's Tinctures?"

Kim kept her eyes firmly fixed on her plate. "After some pillow talk, Lionel opened up about that. There was a policy—five million dollars payable to the principal investors in the event of Teagen's death. I guess that's a motive."

"What?" squawked Gemma. "I know half a dozen thugs who would off you for less than that. A lot less."

Violet lowered her voice. "Who are the principals, Kim?"

I held my breath, dreading to hear the names and shocked at the idea of Lionel and Kim engaging in anything remotely sexual. Cuddling with Lionel was akin to cozying up to a grizzled gator. Kim wasn't happy, but she did her duty. "Lionel was one of the investors, of course, and Brendan Doyle, Madge Stone, and…" she hesitated before finishing. Gemma immediately pounced on her, demanding full disclosure.

"Who else, Kim? Come on, spill it." Gemma breathed fire.

Kim spoke in a monotone. "Killian Blaine was the other one."

That shocker left me speechless and dampened my appetite. Just when I'd weakened the tiniest bit, treachery reared its ugly head. Killian Blaine never mentioned his financial stake in Teagen's Tinctures. He joined Brendan and Madge as prime suspects, at least from a financial angle. I excluded Lionel. Knowing that fastidious fellow, I was positive that he would avoid anything as violent as double homicide. Financial skullduggery was another matter entirely. For Kim's sake, I hoped that I was right.

"Looks like lover boy has a big fat motive," Gemma teased. "You said he just laid out big bucks for that house. Maybe Teagen paid for it with her life."

Violet frowned at her. "No need for accusations, Gemma, although Mr. Blaine was on the scene for one of the crimes. Chief Miles cited another potential motive:love. Brendan and even Letty fit that description.

Unfortunately, Dr. Park is also in the mix." She turned to me. "Have you spoken to him recently, Marky?"

I shook my head. "I'm not sure I even want to. Our romance, such as it was, is finished. Teagen saw to that. Plus, he lied to me, or at the very least, omitted telling the truth. He said he went to Doogie's place one time that day, but that's not true."

An uncomfortable silence overtook us as Roddy became the pachyderm in the room.

"Look," Kim said. "I know he's no psychopath. but maybe he got in over his head, and things escalated. That can happen."

Aunt Violet and even Gemma stayed silent. That was more disquieting than a public brawl. I knew in my heart that Roddy was innocent of murder. He was a curiously innocent intellectual who became infatuated with a fading glamour girl. He liked Doogie; in fact, they had become friends. I refused to picture him thrusting that meat thermometer into the poor fellow's chest.

"Wait a minute," I said. "Doogie's killer got up close and personal. How else could he or she have jabbed that thing into him? Roddy has no culinary skills and probably wouldn't even know what a meat thermometer was."

Gemma folded her arms and gave me the fisheye. "You're reaching, Marky. Maybe Doogie ragged him or tried to blackmail him. That murder weapon was probably lying right on the kitchen counter. Anyone could see how sharp it was." She took her knife and stabbed downward. "Poof. End of story."

Kim uttered a faint cry. "It's too horrible to think of. I shouldn't say this, but Teagen deserved her fate. Doogie was a decent person."

I closed my eyes, trying to analyze the prime suspects and their proclivities. Brendan Doyle was aggressive and determined to have his way. He would easily eliminate any person or thing that was an obstacle to him. Killian…he was certainly bold enough to act, but more likely to kill his competitors in the boardroom than the kitchen. I was scarcely objective about him, or Roddy, and I knew it. My judgment ranked scarcely a notch above Benny Soto's.

Violet poured each of us a glass of Pellegrino. "You mentioned Madge and Letty. Are either of them strong enough to overwhelm a man? Doogie was a large fellow, after all."

We mulled over that question. Kim observed that anyone might launch a surprise attack, especially in a frenzy. "I keep recalling Letty's outburst at the memorial service. She was teetering right on the edge of hysteria."

"Yeah," Gemma agreed. "Didn't you say she was at Doogie's place the other night when you and the Dreamboat got there? Shows she knew her way around the kitchen. She wanted Brendan, and let's face it. The chick is unhinged."

I nodded helplessly. There were too many threads in this puzzle to untangle. We skipped dessert, and each went our separate ways without resolving one thing.

Chapter Eighteen

Roddy ambushed me when I took Fantasia on her morning walk. I knew he wasn't dangerous, but caution triumphed over caring as I motioned to a nearby bench. Jogging gear camouflaged his muscular physique, but I noticed that he had lost pounds and vigor in the past few weeks.

"I'm innocent, Marky," he said. "Tell me you believe me. Please. I'm not sure anyone else does."

I steeled myself for a confrontation, despite his pleading look. "Why did you lie to me?"

He ducked his head, a sure sign of guilt. "About what?"

"Oh, let me count the ways. You went to Doogie's twice that day, Professor, not once. They've got you on tape."

"I already explained that to Chief Miles. The first time I realized that he was probably at work, so I phoned him. His secretary said he was out with a client and would meet me later at his house. I never went in. Just stayed in the car. You can check that with her if you like." His tone changed from docile to defiant as he continued. "So, I drove out to the lakefront and ate lunch." He reached into his pocket. "Here's the receipt if you want to check that too."

Conflict was never my strong suit, especially with someone I cared for. Then I recalled the glint in Aubrey Miles' eyes when she questioned me. Like it or not, Roddy and I were yoked together in this case, his motive tied to love or passion and mine to financial gain. Love and money—the twin pillars of most murders. I shivered thinking of the future.

"Chief Miles suggested that you and I were co-conspirators," I said. "Oh, she was very polite, but I still got the message. My legacy from Doogie was a bombshell."

Roddy wrinkled his brow. "Legacy? What are you talking about, Marky?"

I explained, making it clear that it was unexpected, if not entirely unwelcome. "Not that I'm the only one to profit. That pales in comparison with the insurance payout for Teagen's Tinctures. Brendan Doyle stood to collect plenty from that and probably her other life insurance policies."

"Is he your prime suspect? That doesn't make much sense to me."

"Why?" I bristled at his tone. After all, I was doing all the heavy lifting in this case while Roddy wallowed in self-pity.

"Think about it. Brendan really loved his wife, even with all the drama and affairs. Divorce is cleaner and less risky than murder. Besides, Teagen told me herself that she would never leave him. It was a weird setup, but it worked for them."

When jealousy, that green-eyed monster, rears its ugly head, things get ugly. Suddenly, my heart overrode my brain, and I lashed out. "Is that what she told you in the throes of passion? Not very romantic."

He flushed. "I won't discuss it. She told me that, and I believed her. Why would she lie?"

I could think of a million reasons, but pride forbade it. "Consider this," I said. "Maybe he did love her, and that dalliance with you was the last straw. You're a fan of the Bard. Think *Otello*."

Roddy was comfortable analyzing theories. He'd been a star on the Michigan debate team and was masterful at dissecting his opponents' arguments. "You're always big on character, and you've seen Brendan in action. Do you really believe that he'd hatch an elaborate plan to kill Teagen? Far more likely to throttle her to death in a fit of rage."

I couldn't dispute his reasoning. Whoever dispatched Teagen was clever and insidious, two characteristics I could not ascribe to volcanic Brendan Doyle. There was a feline quality to Teagen's death. Doogie's demise smacked of panic and opportunism.

"Okay. Who's number one on your hit parade?"

He paused for a moment before answering. "I understand that Killian Blaine just purchased a lakefront property. Very pricey."

"Don't be absurd. He's flush with cash."

Roddy curled his lip. "Lawyers are a greedy bunch. Never enough money or fame."

Fantasia saved me from replying by jumping to her feet and emitting a fierce growl. When Brendan Doyle bounded up, I tightened her lead.

"What's this?" he snarled. "Two co-conspirators hatching more schemes?"

Roddy rose and stood toe to toe with his tormentor. "Slander suits can be troubling, Mr. Doyle. Be wise to remember that."

Brendan puffed up like an irate cobra. "Why, you gigolo—I'll put my fist in that pretty face of yours so help me." He curled his fists and lunged toward Roddy. Brendan was an accomplished street fighter, but unhappily, he was no match for a wushu expert twenty years his junior. Roddy deflected his blows and launched a kick that left Brendan reeling.

Hostilities halted when Letty Briggs appeared on the scene. She uttered a cry and ran to Brendan. "You beast! You've hurt him."

"Not nearly enough," said Roddy. "Tell your boyfriend to cut it out, or there'll be trouble." He nodded toward me. "Come on, Marky. Let's go."

I scurried after him, leaving Brendan Doyle dazed and confused. Letty Briggs stayed at his side, dithering and murmuring words of comfort.

* * *

Roddy's show of spunk surprised and delighted me. It marked the return of the man I'd grown to admire and love. Violence doesn't resolve conflict, but seeing Brendan Doyle, stripped of his bully boy trappings and reduced to a dazed old man, was gratifying. I'd yearned to pulverize him myself, but I excelled in verbal combat, not fisticuffs.

"I hope you're not disappointed in me," Roddy said. "Violence is against wushu principles, but in this case, it was warranted."

Control yourself, I thought. Discipline, not drooling, is the right move.

"No problem," I said. "Brendan Doyle got his comeuppance. Curious, though, that Letty Briggs was on the scene. Think about it. Brendan was hers before Teagen appeared. Maybe she decided to remove that obstacle and slide back into his life."

Roddy made a face. "What about Doogie, though? You said he was friends with Letty. Would she murder him?"

I shrugged, "She's erratic. Crazy even. If Doogie told me the truth, that would spoil her whole plan. I could imagine her grabbing that meat thermometer and plunging it into Doogie in a fit of rage." The more I thought about it, the better I liked it. How would Chief Miles react to my theory? I decided to run it by Aunt Violet first.

"Chief Miles asked me if I was in love with Teagen." Roddy bowed his head.

"And you said…?"

"Ah, Marky, everything happened so fast. I admit I was flattered, even though she was an older lady. It was kind of a heady experience for an average guy like me. You know, having a celebrity fawn all over you." He gulped. "But love? No way."

"According to Madge Stone, you were obsessed. Her very words."

"She's wrong." Roddy's voice was very definite. "Honestly, you'd think she was Mrs. Doyle's mother or keeper the way she hovered over her. That night, when everything went to hell, Madge pushed me aside and grabbed the EpiPen. I guess she was a nurse or something."

"Think hard. How did Brendan react when he saw Teagen dying?"

Roddy gave me a quizzical look. "Are you kidding? He went berserk. Screaming and yelling. I thought for a minute that he was having a heart attack, his face got so red."

I closed my eyes, trying to visualize the scene. "Teagen bragged that she kept two EpiPens at the ready. Her secret weapons, she called them. You gave her the first one, right?"

He nodded. "I had a hard time finding it, but it was in that fancy bag she carried. She was gasping for air by then, but she jammed that thing into her thigh."

"Didn't it help? It's supposed to have adrenaline or something in it."

"I wasn't much good to her. I tried to give her CPR, but then Brendan and Madge burst through the door, and everything went haywire. He was hysterical, raving and ranting like a madman. Madge told me to call 911 while she found Teagen's backup EpiPen. Thank goodness for her. She was calm and seemed to know what to do. The ambulance came quickly, although it seemed like hours." He gritted his teeth at the memory.

"She was an RN before she married. I guess that training never leaves you." I paused, thinking of the nightmarish scene. Had Brendan Doyle's antics been a distraction or an honest reaction? "What made those two turn up?" I asked. "Seems kind of fishy to me."

"Chief Miles told me they'd gotten a call from Doogie. At least Brendan did. That's why he charged over. Cell phone records verified that."

Doogie! That confirmed my suspicions that he was part of the plot. No wonder he seemed so guilt-ridden and unwilling to talk. His killer acted boldly and viciously to silence the voluble realtor before he blurted out the truth. Sadly, Doogie had unwittingly supplied the weapon that ended his friend's life. Someone spiked that meal with enough dairy and nuts to ensure a murderous meltdown. Someone who had no problem dealing the death card to two people.

"Doogie loved to cook. Apparently, he was about to whip up something tasty for us. Roast chicken, they said. That would explain the meat thermometer. No chance for Salmonella under his watch. No, sir!"

Roddy sighed. "Last time I was there, he was fooling around with that thing. Twirling it and acting the fool. I warned him. Told him to be careful. He just laughed until I took the darn thing away."

Doogie didn't fear his killer. That much was certain. Otherwise, why display such a convenient murder weapon right under the killer's nose? Once again, I pondered Aubrey Miles' words—love and money. Everyone said that Brendan loved his wife. Maybe he was too ardent. Maybe he loved her to death like Otello. Letty loved Brendan and might easily justify eliminating his wife as fair play. Poor Doogie got in the middle of someone's game and paid the price.

"Come on. Let's discuss this with my aunt," I said. "She always puts things into perspective."

Roddy reached for my hand as we wandered back to Poppet, but I evaded him rather deftly. He hadn't redeemed himself yet. Maybe he never would.

An unwelcome surprise awaited us when we reached my store. Benny Sotto, cuffs dangling and scowl threatening, pounced as soon as we crossed the threshold.

"Not so fast, buster," he spat. "You're not going anywhere except to jail."

"Are you insane?" I cried, blocking Benny's path. "Go away. Try your cheap tactics elsewhere." One glance at Aunt Violet's face sobered me up. She made no effort to stop him or to intercede.

"He's got a warrant," Violet said. "Best to cooperate."

Benny flung a paper in my face and grinned triumphantly. Roddy didn't move. He stayed frozen with his mouth agape.

I finally mustered enough strength to ask. "What's the charge?"

"Murder," Benny said. "Guess whose fingerprints we found on that meat thermometer? You know, the murder weapon."

I had no patience with guessing games, especially when the answer was all too clear. For once, even Gemma was stunned into silence. Her ghostly complexion contrasted vividly with jade green eyeshadow and scarlet lips.

"I'm innocent," Roddy cried. "Doogie was my friend."

"Tell it to the judge." Benny roughly clasped Roddy's wrists in handcuffs, and before leading him away, he issued one final taunt. "Better be ready, Ms. Davis. Next time, you'll be the one in cuffs."

I was dumbstruck, but my aunt moved quickly. She grasped her iPhone and dialed the number of Lionel Stevens. After explaining the situation, Violet hung up and heaved a sigh. "That's just a temporary measure. A Band-Aid until Dr. Park finds suitable counsel. Lionel doesn't practice criminal law."

"Surely it's a mistake," I said. "Roddy spent days there. He could have touched that meat thermometer any time. You know how disheveled Doogie's kitchen was."

Gemma gave me the death stare. "Come off it, Marky. Roddy's linked to both murders. If I were you, I'd call in the big gun. Killian Blaine."

"Don't be absurd. He's not a criminal attorney. Besides, who knows what role he played in this whole thing?" I turned to my aunt. "I'm right, aren't I?"

For once, she agreed with Gemma. Violet spoke in measured tones, pouring oil on troubled waters. "It wouldn't hurt to ask him, Marky. Don't let your pride interfere with good sense. Mr. Blaine might be helpful."

Timing is everything, so they say. When my phone buzzed, I saw the name I both hoped for and dreaded. Killian's voice was conciliatory, unlike his normal snarky tone.

"We need to talk, Marky. I've missed you."

I hesitated, trying mightily to summon my most impersonal tone. "As it turns out, we were just mentioning your name. I need your advice."

"Delighted. I'll swing by in ten minutes. Are you at your store or your new home?"

"Meet me at Poppet."

Gemma was openly eavesdropping. I ignored her look of triumph and addressed my aunt. "Killian will be here in ten minutes."

Violet nodded. "Good move. Just enough time for you to freshen up."

* * *

She was right, of course. How could I play Mata Hari or a femme fatale in wrinkled sweats and faded lipstick? I scurried upstairs, took a quick shower, and revived my flagging curls with a shot of Oribe's dry shampoo. After donning a cinnamon-colored midi dress, sandals, and jewelry, I was ready to confront the man who just might save Roddy's life.

He was lounging in our parlor, sipping Perrier from a Baccarat water goblet, and chatting with Aunt Violet. When I entered, Killian looked me up and down and nodded his approval.

"I knew you'd be a bit late. Not a problem. I've enjoyed a civilized chat with your charming Aunt."

He ignored my stony stare and blathered on. "So, Professor Park has been arrested. What a shame. Just when I thought the coast was clear."

Violet rose, smiling at us. "I know you two have much to discuss, and I'm expecting a women's group to arrive any minute." She slipped away with feline grace while I rather clumsily held my ground.

Killian consulted his watch, an elegant wafer-thin Patek Calatrava with an alligator strap. The timepiece was exquisite, but knowing its price and rarity, I bristled. Why did everything about this man raise my hackles?

If he observed my reaction, he chose to ignore it. "Let's see," Killian said. "We have time for either a late lunch or an early dinner. What's your preference, m'lady?"

I shrugged. "Either. If we have time for a serious talk. I'm worried and not afraid to admit it."

Killian's manner softened. "Of course. Believe it or not, I'm rather handy in the kitchen. How about going to my house for dinner? No strings, I promise. We can relax and hash out whatever's troubling you."

My first inclination was to refuse, but good sense and good manners prevailed. After all, I asked for help. Rejecting his offer would be boorish.

"Okay," I said. "You probably know most of it anyway." Killian surprised me by gently kissing my hand in the continental manner. That gesture sent a chill straight to my nether parts, but I quelled my emotions. No time for self-indulgence while Roddy languished in a cell.

He escorted me to the Maybach, cautioning me not to catch my hem in its door. His behavior smacked of old-fashioned courtesy, not sexism, and I confess it felt good. Comforting. We didn't say much on the short drive to his home. Leaning back into the sumptuous leather seats and absorbing the sweet sounds emanating from the Bose speakers lulled me into a near-fugue state. Killian had to tap my shoulder when we arrived.

"Wake up, Sleeping Beauty. Your feast awaits."

His home looked even more imposing in the sunlight. I visualized the changes I would make to this edifice if it were mine. *Cool down, girl. Follow your agenda.*

"How about eating on the veranda?" Killian asked. "We can watch the sailboats on the lake, inhale fresh air, and drink in the sunset."

"Fine. I'd like that." He busied himself in the kitchen while I enjoyed the view. When he returned, Killian brought a tray containing a bottle of Krug nestled in a Bacchante wine cooler with two flutes.

"Very nice," I said. "Lalique?"

He nodded and stared boldly at me. "I've always been partial to beautiful things. Can't resist them, particularly when they're paired with brains."

Time to change directions, I told myself. I sipped the Krug and explained Roddy's plight.

"His fingerprints could have easily gotten on that meat thermometer any time. Roddy admits he handled it. Besides, he's young and strong. Why choose that method when he could have easily overpowered Doogie?"

Killian got a strange look on his face. "Ah, yes. Your Professor knows martial arts. Brendan told me about that dustup."

"Dustup, ha! Brendan ate dirt, and he deserved to. Roddy should sue him for assault."

His lips twisted in a grin. "Calm down. I'm not impugning your boyfriend's skills, just his innocence. You must admit he has motive."

I changed tactics. "Put that aside for a moment. Brendan and Letty have plenty of motive, too. Even Madge benefited financially."

He tilted his head, giving me a quizzical look. "How so?"

I powered down and launched into an analysis of motive. It was a masterful display; one any attorney should have appreciated. "Brendan was either jealous of his wife's activities, or alternatively anxious to collect his share of that big insurance policy you all share in. He's highly leveraged and could use an infusion of cash."

"I was waiting for that to come up," Killian said. "Yes, four of us will get a sizable settlement from that insurance policy. At the risk of sounding brash, I must remind you that all three of us are quite comfortably fixed. One million dollars, while always welcome, is certainly not a game changer or motivator."

A full court blush stained my cheeks. Once again, he had put me firmly in my place and knocked me down several pegs. Had my lowly economic status affected my thinking, or was he obfuscating the issue?

"Okay, how about Letty? I know her family is wealthy, but she's fanatical about Brendan and an obvious nutter. Remember, she'd horned into

Doogie's house when you and I were there. Doogie didn't understand women except in business. Letty could have easily beguiled him into preparing that meal." I sipped the Krug and sighed. "Marvelous brew. Mead of the gods."

"I remembered from last summer that you favored it." There was a look of shared intimacy in his mesmerizing eyes. They appeared less frigid today. An effect of global warming, perhaps, or several flutes of champagne?

I plunged back into the issue at hand. "Chief Miles just about accused me of conspiring with Roddy! That bequest from Doogie made her suspect me."

"Surely not," he said. "Of course, you had no great love for Teagen after she seduced your fiancé. Women have killed for less."

That made me squirm. My voice rose several octaves. "You don't get it. Roddy isn't my fiancé. Not anymore, but I still care about him as a friend."

"Ah," he said. "A spot of good news after all. Do I have a chance, Marky? Please say yes."

His arrogance infuriated me. "Cut that out. I know all about you, Mr. Killian Blaine, Esquire. Don't think I'm one of those credulous creatures you squire around."

My response appeared to delight, not deter him. "Before we start, let me fill in the blanks. I am thirty-six years old, never wed, and very wealthy. I occasionally date models, actresses, and trust fund babies, but that's mostly in the line of duty. You're very different, Ms. Davis. Frankly, you captivate me. Have from the first moment that I saw you last summer. In other words, my motives are pure." He put his hand over his heart and bowed. "I would never hurt you."

I am seldom dumbstruck, but this was one of those times. His words floored me until I recalled that Killian had waited six months to contact me. Hardly the actions of a smitten man. After taking a deep breath, I managed to eke out a response. "Thanks for the update. Now stop clowning and get serious. Am I in trouble? Should I get an attorney? Chief Miles is under pressure to find someone, anyone, who killed Doogie. Include Teagen's death in that, too. I am totally innocent."

Killian rapped his fingers on the marble tabletop. "No need to lawyer up just now. The chief was probably just casting a wide net. She grilled Brendan, Madge, and me rather thoroughly, too." He laughed. "You know, Aubrey Miles is one slick cop. She had no hesitation in tightening the screws despite Brendan's squawks about all his political connections. With Madge and me, she hammered in on financial gain. Brendan wasn't so lucky. After Letty's little performance at that memorial, Brendan had no choice but to admit his affair."

"How did Letty react?"

"The usual. Flood of tears and pleas of innocence. Madge interceded, warning the chief that Letty was emotionally fragile and under a doctor's care. That didn't make much difference. We were all read our Miranda rights at which time I advised my colleagues to remain silent."

There it was—love and money. I wracked my brain, knowing there was something I had missed. Some crucial clue. I knew that Teagen's cause of death was listed as "undetermined," although it was attributed to anaphylactic toxicity. Doogie's autopsy results were pending. In view of his injuries, there wasn't any doubt that it would be classified as homicide.

"I still think Doogie left us a clue. That pen. What if he was referencing the EpiPen? Has anyone analyzed that? Teagen had two of the things. She used one, and Madge injected the second one into her later. Maybe they were intentionally tampered with."

Killian paused before answering. "That's a good point. The police probably bagged and tagged those pens, although with Deputy Soto on the prowl, one can't be certain. Are you suggesting that Teagen's death was orchestrated to appear accidental?"

I nodded. "It's certainly possible. Just think. Someone gets Doogie to prepare that seduction supper and makes sure to salt it with dairy and nuts, knowing Teagen will go into shock. Her allergies were no secret, and she told everyone about those EpiPens. When they didn't work, most people would figure it was a tragic accident."

"Hmm. Simple and elegant. You realize, I suppose, that Roderick Park is still in the frame. He stayed with Doogie, so he had access to his home. He could easily have tampered with those EpiPens as well."

"I just thought of something. During that caffeine overdose incident, Madge used one of those EpiPens. Maybe Teagen didn't replace it. You're advised to always have two of them at your disposal. What if she used the wrong one?"

Killian shrugged off that comment. "I guess I could check with Brendan or Madge. That still wouldn't absolve your boyfriend, though. If his fingerprints are on Doogie's murder weapon, things don't look good for him."

He distracted me by bringing up one of my favorite subjects: food. True to his word, Killian produced a restaurant-quality meal. We dined on broiled whitefish with native corn, grilled asparagus, and mushrooms. After I demolished every savory bite, he grinned.

"I told you I am a man of many parts. Utterly civilized."

"My aunt said the same thing. You've earned her seal of approval."

"High praise indeed. How do I convince you?" His eyes glittered with a hint of mischief.

"Help me with this case. We make a good team, and you have access to Brendan's side of the house. He doesn't like me much. Seems to consider me the enemy."

Killian held up his hands in surrender. "Okay. But only if we share information. No cheating." We shook hands to seal the bargain. Afterwards, he escorted me back to Poppet and zoomed away without even a chaste kiss. I wasn't disappointed. Not really. After all, the man had said there were no strings. If he found me desirable, he certainly resisted any amorous impulses quite easily. As I climbed into bed, another thought gripped me. Killian bragged about his culinary skills. Could he have prepared Teagen's fatal meal?

* * *

My sleep was troubled, and when the alarm sounded, I was tempted to roll over and ignore it. Unfortunately, the dulcet tones of Aunt Violet put paid to that notion.

"Rise and shine, dear niece. Remember, they're reading Doogie's will this morning. All eyes will be on you, so you'll want to look your best." She handed me a delicate porcelain mug. "Here. Drink this espresso. Caffeine works wonders."

"Ugh. Do I have to go?"

The firm set of her lips and her steely gaze answered that question quite emphatically. "Most of Doogie's pals will be there, including Mr. Blaine. You must do your duty."

I groused some more but ultimately bowed to the inevitable. For such a somber occasion, most people wore black. Widow's weeds they had once been termed, but I recalled how much Doogie loved color. Yellow and red were his favorites, the colors of Provence, his beloved vacation spot. To honor him, I chose a red coatdress, adding a yellow scarf for a splash of color. When my aunt looked me over, she nodded her approval.

"Excellent choice. Mr. Kinkaid radiated joy and a passion for life. No need for gloom and doom." Violet herself wore a cranberry concoction that flattered her complexion and emphasized her excellent figure.

We left Gemma in charge and motored over to Doogie's townhouse, now mine, for the official ceremony. His will had specified that location, and it seemed fitting, especially since it was the scene of his final performance.

Lionel Stevens chaired the proceedings. He nudged us into the dining room where Kim, Madge, Letty, Brendan, and Killian were already seated. Violet urged me to hold my head up high and ignore any bad behavior. I followed her lead and pasted a smile on my face as I scanned those around me. Letty wore a wrinkled navy skirt suit that had seen better days. Once again, I marveled at the incongruous behavior of this woman who possessed considerable wealth but chose to downplay it. Madge redeemed the family honor by garbing herself in a crème-colored dress with delicate scallops on its hem. The widow had established a pattern of wearing either white or a derivative to both Teagen and Doogie's events. I had to admit I liked her style. Brendan, Killian, and Lionel wore dark suits that were appropriate for this somber occasion.

Lionel acknowledged us all and immediately cut to the chase. A large flat-screen television dominated the front of the room. That puzzled me at first until he announced that Doogie himself would be reading his will. Aha! A video will. How unusual—very much like the man who orchestrated it.

Letty moaned when Doogie's image appeared on the screen. "How macabre. Must we be subjected to this charade?" She bowed her head and buried her face in her handkerchief. Madge consoled her cousin by hugging her and murmuring something in her ear. Brendan's scowl made no secret of his distaste for the proceedings, but Killian's bold stare suggested that he relished every bit of drama. Lionel was his normal dour self, and Kim wisely stayed in the background playing her part as hostess.

Doogie gifted his audience with a big smile. *"I presume if you're all gathered here that I have shuffled off this mortal coil, as Hamlet would say. No matter. Life has been good to me, and I have no regrets or at least very few."* He leaned forward and wagged his finger at us, the invisible audience. *"Teagen's death devastated me, especially since I played a part in it. Oh, it was inadvertent. I trusted someone who promised that it was all staged. A big joke. Turns out the joke was on me. I adored Teagen and would never have done anything to harm her. For that, I sincerely apologize. I plan to explain my actions to Marketta Davis tomorrow evening. She has a keen mind, integrity, and a thirst for beauty. That's why I'm willing my home to her with the proviso that she always cares for Algernon, my dear and constant companion."* As if on cue, the pampered Persian leapt on the dining room table and fixed us with a stony stare. Letty immediately shrieked and moved closer to Brendan. Madge, Killian, Violet, and I stayed still, waiting for the next shoe to drop. Violet gripped my hand under the table and squeezed it. Despite her placid expression, my aunt's fingers were ice cold. Doogie then disposed of more assets, willing his collection of vintage cookbooks to Letty and his pen collection to Madge. He requested that Violet establish a foundation in honor of Teagen that would award scholarships to aspiring student entertainers. Doogie reserved a handsome sum of seed money for that effort. The balance of his estate went to the local animal shelter and feline rescue. He concluded by thanking each of us for brightening his life with our friendship.

When Lionel switched off the monitor, there was silence in the room.

Letty buried her face in her arms; Madge bowed her head, and Aunt Violet dabbed at her eyes with a monogrammed handkerchief. All three men remained stoic. An emotion they might have felt was masked by steely resolve. As for me, I tried mightily to process Doogie's final testament without surrendering to sorrow. Time for that later, when I was able to collect my thoughts in private. As we filed out of the room, Killian tapped my shoulder.

"We need to talk, Marky. I'll call you tonight."

"Fine." I dodged Brendan's stormy scowl and Madge's look of revulsion. Letty staggered toward the front door as if she were traumatized. She ignored me and everyone else in a frantic effort to escape.

Lionel beckoned to me before I left. "Naturally, the estate must go through probate, but you're free to inspect the premises whenever you like. Kim can give you the keys."

I nodded and joined Aunt Violet for our trip back to Poppet. We were both eager to trade impressions, although we waited until the madding crowd had passed to do so.

Violet heaved a big sigh. "That was quite a unique experience. Trust Doogie to put on one final show." She smiled. "It was so typical of him, trying to entertain his guests."

"Ugh! I thought it was ghoulish. Doogie must have filmed that the day before he died."

"Don't you appreciate the dramatic flourish?" Violet sounded amused. "He confirmed your suspicion that he was Teagen's secret chef. Too bad he didn't finish the story."

Knowing Doogie, he was probably trying to insulate his co-conspirator. That effort to protect his faux friend had backfired.

"Chief Miles needs to hear that," I said. "It validates my theory and exonerates Roddy."

"How so?" Violet's expression was skeptical.

I explained that even Doogie, trusting soul that he was, would have been suspicious if Roddy asked him to prepare that meal. "Remember, Teagen's cooking skills, or lack thereof, were known only to a few close friends. The rest of us thought she was a whiz in the kitchen."

"That makes sense," Violet said. "Teagen wanted to impress Dr Park." She furrowed her brow. "That narrows the list considerably. Brendan, Madge, Doogie, and Letty knew, of course. I doubt that Mr. Blaine was involved. Not his type of thing at all."

I realized that an important part of the puzzle remained unsolved. Tampering with the food was suspicious, but the culprit had no idea that the EpiPen wouldn't save Teagen. Unless…the same person had tampered with those devices. It was a conundrum. I yearned to discuss it with my crime-solving partner, but was too cowardly to contact him. Let Killian Blaine make the first move. If that didn't happen, I would speak with Aubrey Miles by myself.

Gemma pounced as soon as we entered Poppet. "Did you hear?" she asked. "Big news!"

She began to pace, arms waving wildly.

"Calm yourself, Gemma." Violet knew how to handle my emotional buddy. "I'll brew some tea, and we can have a civilized discussion. We have news to share, too." She prepared tea the British way, eschewing the use of teabags for loose tea leaves. Fortnum and Mason Royal Blend was her favorite. By the time the water was heated, the kettle warmed, and the tea brewed, Gemma had powered down to an almost normal level.

"You go first," Violet said to Gemma.

"Okay. Benny just called me." She grinned. "He was all upset, poor baby, but I'll make him feel better."

I interrupted, "Is this about Roddy? Is he okay?"

Gemma glared at me. "I was getting to that. Give me a break, will you? Anyway, it seems that Benny may have jumped the gun a bit. You know how decisive he is."

I could think of several less flattering descriptors for her fiancé, but I refrained from sharing them. Impulsive, reckless, and foolhardy came to mind. I motioned for Gemma to continue.

"Is Dr. Park still under arrest?" Violet asked, sipping her tea.

"That's the problem. Chief Miles wanted to question Roddy, not necessarily arrest him. Benny got that wrong. The Professor called some big deal from the University of Michigan Law School, who made a stink. Lawsuits, racial discrimination, and some other bad stuff. They had to release him, and the chief made Benny apologize."

Picturing that scene made me smile, and I ducked my head to avoid giving myself away. A check of my phone confirmed that Roddy hadn't contacted me. No calls, no texts, no hope. I swallowed my pride and focused on the future. I needed to speak with Chief Miles, pronto.

Violet shared our news with Gemma after cautioning her to keep it confidential.

"OMG," Gemma said. "You were right on target, Marky. Doogie was Teagen's secret chef. Now the big question is who put that bad stuff into the meal?" She bit her lip. "Personally, I think Brendan and Letty cooked up the whole thing." She paused. "Pretty clever, wasn't it? Cooking up murder? Remember, we know that he was shagging Letty, and she is a first-class nut-case. Who knows how far she'd go?"

"Be careful about what you say," Violet said. "We have no proof."

She was right, of course, but that did explain the twin motives of love and money. I recalled Letty's wild look at Teagen's memorial. Brendan didn't deny her claim or mount much of a defense.

"I have an idea," Violet said. "I'm part of a civic group meeting tomorrow. Nothing exciting, just the usual pre-tourist checklist. Madge and maybe Letty should be there. Let's see if I can sound them out about Doogie's will. We can discuss the endowment he tasked me with."

I knew my aunt's talent for extracting information from the unwary. She would have made an exemplary spy had she so chosen. Mata Hari on steroids.

Gemma was eager to help. "Letty's scheduled for a massage tomorrow afternoon. She may blab something worth hearing." She turned my way. "Better make yourself scarce when she comes in, Marky. She can't stand you."

That remark stung. I was always the good girl, beloved of parents and teachers. When did I become persona non grata?

Violet nodded. "Good thinking. I suggest that you meet Kim at Doogie's place. Search it thoroughly in case the authorities missed some clue. They can hardly object after all. You're his designated heir."

I sent Kim a text explaining the goal of our mission. She responded immediately. *"Count me in! I'll get the key from Lionel and meet you at noon."*

Kim's transformation from timid hausfrau to co-conspirator was something to behold. Her stodgy husband barely recognized the confident woman she had become. But, oddly enough, he now seemed to appreciate her more.

Fantasia gave me her special look, reminding me that she needed sustenance and exercise. I attached her harness and headed for the bike path. It was deserted in mid- morning as exercise freaks, businesspeople, and students had already scurried off to their jobs. Birds, blooms, and baby carriages still abounded, however, making this verdant haven feel safe. I wasn't oblivious to danger. After all, a double murderer was still on the loose, and my detective efforts were well known in Harbor Bay. I relied on Fantasia's unerring senses and decided that a modest jog was still in order. That's when it happened. I lost my balance and sprawled headlong into a briar bush. Despite the tumble and blow to my pride, I was dazed but otherwise unhurt. Fantasia tried her best to provide canine comfort. Unfortunately, her efforts weren't enough. Licking my face and bloodied knee didn't help me untangle myself. It took strong arms, pulling me upward and out of the brush, to extricate me. To my chagrin. those strong arms belonged to none other than Brendan Doyle. My savior snickered as he surveyed my disheveled state.

"Getting your exercise, I see, Ms. Davis. Here. Sit down on the bench."

I ignored the sarcasm. After all, the man had been helpful, and considering our previous encounters, that surprised me. I toyed with slapping the smirk off his face, but opted for gratitude.

"Thanks for your help. I'm not usually so clumsy."

"Not injured, I see." Brendan sounded disappointed. He plopped down next to me, mansplaining big time.

"I suppose you're tougher than you look." His expression was as frosty as his tone. "My Teagen was easily hurt. Oh, she hid her feelings, but I knew her best. I loved her."

Silence seemed golden in this instance. Brendan Doyle had a strange way of showing devotion. According to Kim, Letty was only one of many romances the man had while married to Teagen. She was no angel either, and I doubted that she was the tender soul her husband described. In my experience, she was tough as nails and determined to get her way.

"You let her down," he said, baring his teeth. "You and that gigolo you brought into her life. She should never have gotten involved with the pair of you." He teared up. "That killed her."

I don't always use good sense, and emotion can easily overrule my mind. Brendan Doyle's pious platitudes and scurrilous charges were just too much to bear. I turned to that pitiful wreck of a man and spoke my mind.

"You're wrong about me and Dr. Park. Teagen approached us asking for help. She worried about her safety and, for some reason, thought that I could help." I ignored his mottled cheeks and smoldering rage and soldiered on. "Furthermore, it was you that she feared. You, Mr. Doyle. Your wife thought you planned to kill her."

Brendan Doyle was accustomed to cowing his foes, especially females. His bulging eyes and gaping mouth proved that. For a moment, I considered making a break for freedom. Fantasia would protect me, and, even injured, I felt I could outmaneuver this aging hulk. His next action put paid to that plan. He grabbed my shoulder and squeezed it. Hard.

"Take that back," he spat. "How dare you! You're nothing but a failed artist and minor shopkeeper. Why, I could buy and sell you ten times over."

I should have felt frightened, but for some reason, I didn't. Surely, he wouldn't risk injuring me in a public space. That was my story, and I stuck to it despite the increasing pressure on my shoulder.

"Take your hand off me, Mr. Doyle. You've assaulted me. I won't hesitate to have you charged." I smiled. "You might just need all that cash you brag about when I sue you."

Who knows what might have happened if Madge Stone hadn't wandered by. Madge, the guardian angel, immediately assessed the situation and intervened. Yet again, her composure awed me. Madge ignored the obvious and acted as if we were three pals enjoying a jaunt in the park.

"Why, Brendan, here you are. I decided to join you for your walk. Exercise clears away the cobwebs, you know." She bent down to hug Fantasia, then turned to me. "Marky, I owe you an apology. I've been unforgivably rude to you since we lost Teagen. It's all been such a shock that I forgot my manners."

I nodded, managing a wan smile. Something told me to keep quiet while this scene played out.

"She lied," Brendan wailed tearfully. "Teagen wasn't afraid of me. She loved me."

Madge put her arms around him, cradling him as if he were an infant. "We both loved her, but you know how Teagen could be. She loved her drama. Don't blame Miss Davis. I know for a fact that Teagen approached her."

"She brought that gigolo into our home."

I couldn't restrain myself. "I'll have you know that Dr. Park is a respected professional employed by a major university. He had a signed contract to promote Teagen's Tinctures. Nothing more."

Madge shot me a warning look. "Yes, yes. That's true. Teagen's death was a tragic accident."

"What about Doogie?" I asked. "That was no accident. That meat thermometer didn't stab him accidentally. Did you know he prepared that meal for Teagen, Mr. Doyle?"

"Certainly not. My wife was an accomplished cook. Wasn't she Madge?" He pleaded with her to agree, but Madge ducked the issue.

"Teagen had many talents. We all can agree on that. Chief Miles is a very competent officer. Let's leave the detective work to her." Madge glared at me. "Don't you agree, Miss Davis?"

"You're right. I have confidence in the chief." I extricated myself from Brendan Doyle's grip and called Fantasia. "But Doogie was my friend, and I want his killer found. Whoever killed him will pay for it."

Brendan Doyle erupted yet again. "You're nobody. Stay out of our business."

He was a shattered hulk of a man relying on position and money to impress. His words didn't even sting. Revenge was sweet, and I enjoyed his outrage when I gave him a sugary smile.

"Oops! I've neglected my duties. Time to return to Poppet. After all, we minor shopkeepers can't ignore our customers."

I leapt to my feet, called my dog, and scooted back to safety.

* * *

"What's your problem?" Gemma asked. "You look like hell."

"Thanks so much for your support. Buzz off."

Aunt Violet frowned. "What's wrong, Marky? Mr. Blaine has been looking for you."

I explained the kerfuffle at the park and Brendan Doyle's antics. "He's unhinged. Maybe homicidal. I'm tempted to report him to the chief."

"Hmm." Violet gave me a hug. "I'm not sure that's the best course of action. Why escalate the tension? Besides, you've seen Brendan at his worst. Do you really believe he's capable of concocting such a sophisticated scheme?"

"Yeah," Gemma said, shaking her head. "He'd probably just clobber Teagen or strangle her. Not a deep thinker that boy."

Aunt Violet cleaned my mangled kneecap with an astringent that stung. She ignored my protests and focused on the positives.

"Don't be childish, Marketta. Sit still. Reminds me of how you acted when you were a little tot." She applied a Band-Aid, pronounced me good to go, and checked her watch. "Aren't you meeting Kim today?"

"Yikes!" I'd forgotten all about it in the heat of the moment. I whisked up to my apartment, bathed, and readied myself for the next adventure. Apparently, it was my day for popularity. Killian had left several messages on my phone, and a certain Dr. Roderick Park had as well. I ignored both. Relationships and the men behind them were simply too taxing when a murderer went free. Perhaps if I pledged a life of celibacy, focusing on my business and painting, I would gain clarity of thought. In Shakespeare's time, a woman could hie herself off to a nunnery, but that was no longer an option. Besides, my childhood had been scarred by unpleasant memories of nuns wielding rulers and ranting about eternal damnation. There had to be a better solution.

After feeding Fantasia, I harnessed her and clambered into the Jeep. On the short trip to Doogie's place, I replayed the bizarre scene with Brendan Doyle in my mind. Was the man really unhinged, or was he merely playing a part? He ran a vast business empire and was reputedly quite adept at doing so. And why was Madge trailing behind him as if she were his caretaker? Were her nursing skills once again coming to the fore, or did she know something about the two suspicious deaths in Harbor Bay?

Kim had preceded me to my new home and was waiting outside. I parked along the curb and spent a moment studying the lovely townhouse. Hard to believe that it was truly mine. I was so lost in thought that when she tapped on the window, I shrieked. It was a modest, very genteel sound, nothing to alarm my new neighbors.

"Marky, what's wrong? Violet phoned me about your accident."

"Sorry. I'm kind of jumpy. I keep expecting Brendan Doyle to pop up again."

Kim opened the door and squeezed my hand. "Don't worry about him. You have a bodyguard with you, I see. Time to introduce Fantasia to Algernon."

I'd forgotten all about my new family member. Fantasia had no problems with felines, but I feared that the pampered Persian might feel otherwise. We followed Kim into the hallway and stopped short. Algernon was perched on the top of the newel post, glaring balefully at intruders. When he spotted Fantasia, every hair on his body stood up, and he hissed.

My beautiful collie wagged her tail and ignored his bad behavior like the patrician that she was. Meanwhile, Kim and I went into the living room, sinking into the plush down of the sofa.

"Do you plan to keep everything the way Doogie left it?" Kim asked. "I feel him in every room of this place. He loved finding just the right antique or collectible."

That alerted me. "Let's make sure the door's locked and the security system is switched on. Come to think of it, why wasn't the alarm activated when his killer came in?"

Kim shrugged. "That's no big deal. Most people don't activate it during the day, especially when they're home. Besides, don't you agree that he knew his killer? Probably wasn't surprised at all."

That was the sad truth. Doogie, the eternal optimist, saw only the good in his friends. I'm positive that he thought the person who approached him had nothing at all to do with harming Teagen. That assumption sealed his fate.

Entering the kitchen took all my courage. I tried mightily to blot out the memory of Doogie, prone on that prized Italian stone floor, with blood seeping out of his chest. Never again in this lifetime could I look at a meat thermometer, let alone use one.

"Have you spoken to Roddy?" Kim asked. "I'm curious, not trying to pry."

"He left me a message, but I ignored it. Let him stew for a while. Killian, too." I noticed that Doogie's collection of vintage recipe books was neatly arrayed on a shelf. At some point, Letty would be able to claim them. As I idly thumbed through a beautifully illustrated edition of French recipes, I stopped short.

"Hey. Check this out." I pointed to a page with folded corners and grease spots. "This looks like the Seduction Supper menu."

Kim leaned over. "Nothing about dairy or nuts in this. I know for a fact that Doogie followed directions slavishly. Refused to add or subtract anything that wasn't in the recipe."

That meant that the killer added the deadly ingredients to the mix. No wonder Doogie was so upset. "Wait a minute. Maybe that's why he gave his cookbooks to Letty. It was a clue."

"How so?"

"I'm positive that Letty arranged that whole thing, at least the meal prep."

Kim's eyes widened. "That makes sense. She hated Teagen. Maybe she wanted to hurt her but not kill her."

"Or maybe she was in cahoots with Brendan Doyle. Letty seems very suggestible."

We then debated whether to contact Aubrey Miles. I opted to plunge ahead but Kim urged caution. "Why interfere in police business, Marky? No good will come of it."

A sudden noise startled us as someone rattled the doorknob.

Kim wheeled around and clutched a large cast-iron frying pan. "Were you expecting anyone else?"

I shook my head and tried to control a mounting sense of panic. Doogie's kitchen boasted an array of chef's knives and a lethal rolling pin. I reached into the drawer and chose a nine-inch blade. Knives terrified me, but so did facing a potential killer without having some type of weapon to defend myself.

"Hush. Pretend we're not here." I whistled for Fantasia. "She'll charge if someone barges in. Get your cell phone out. Hide behind the pantry and get ready to dial 911."

Kim's lip quivered, but she complied. Each moment felt endless as we awaited the unknown. When the front door swung open, I crouched in the kitchen, prepared to strike. Then a familiar voice called out.

"Hello. It's Aubrey Miles. Harbor Bay police."

Chapter Nineteen

I almost wept with relief. Chief Miles approached us cautiously, wearing a puzzled smile.

"Put down the knife, Ms. Davis. I didn't mean to scare you." She turned. "You too, Mrs. Stevens, unless you're planning to cook something. No need to panic."

I tried not to babble, but it was hard not to. "We're checking out the place. Lionel told us it was okay."

Kim jumped in. "It belongs to Marky now. Doogie left it to her in his will."

"We didn't take anything." Why did I sound so defensive? I should have realized there was no danger. Fantasia hadn't sounded an alarm.

Chief Miles motioned us to follow her. We filed out like obedient children during a school fire drill. No talking, feet straight ahead.

"One of your new neighbors reported prowlers, so I decided to see for myself. Mr. Stevens left a key with my deputy." Her manner was friendly though not familiar, a professional cop at work. I stared at the Glock holstered at her side. It was a menacing fashion accessory that I could do without.

I gulped and summoned my courage. "We were just discussing you, Chief."

"Oh?" She raised her brows, still friendly but cautious.

Kim flashed a timid smile. "You probably heard about Doogie's will. We think…that is, Marky believes, that he left some clues to his killer."

Chief Miles folded her arms in front of her. "What were they?"

I explained about the cookbooks and Doogie's admission that he prepared Teagen's final meal. "Weird take on the Last Supper," I quipped.

That remark was unfortunate. I suddenly recalled that Aubrey Miles was a daily communicant at Holy Childhood of Jesus Catholic Church on Main Street. From the way she narrowed her eyes, it appeared that she considered my jest to be sacrilegious or even blasphemous.

"Mr. Blaine already reported that to me," she said. "Of course, we don't know who added the dairy and nuts to the food, or who instigated the entire mess."

Aha! Killian Blaine, my so-called partner, couldn't wait to spill the news and show me up. Another reason to avoid the perfidious creature.

I shared my theory about Letty Briggs. "Everyone in town heard her at the memorial service. The woman is unhinged. Personally, I can't imagine any woman lusting after Brendan Doyle, but to each her own."

Another tight smile from the chief. "There's one piece of information you don't have. Since it will become public knowledge soon enough, I'll tell you. Mrs. Doyle's death was no accident."

"I thought she died from anaphylactic shock," Kim said.

"True enough. But our forensic people found that someone had deliberately tampered with both of her EpiPens. They were empty. Totally ineffective."

I forced myself to slow down and think before speaking. "What about the nuts and dairy in that food?"

"They were certainly hazardous, but according to the medical examiner, proper injection with her EpiPens would have saved her at least until she was treated at the hospital."

All sorts of thoughts raced through my mind. Had someone deliberately dosed Teagen's food and then disabled her EpiPens? Did that same killer eliminate Doogie before he could reveal his or her identity? Who could be that cunning or that evil?

"But Doogie," Kim said. "Why kill him?"

Aubrey Miles had apparently lost patience with amateur sleuths. "I think that's obvious, Mrs. Stevens. Someone was tying up loose ends. Let that be a lesson to both of you."

She glared at us with that cop stare, a cold, soulless look that portended doom for its target. "Let me be clear. This murderer is smart and determined. Let the professionals deal with the case and stay out of it. I don't need any more corpses on my watch." She whirled around and stalked toward the exit. Before she left, I summoned my remaining store of courage and called out.

"What about Dr. Park and me? Are we still under suspicion?"

"Everyone is a person of interest until I make an arrest. And in Michigan, we take obstruction of justice rather seriously. It's a felony under the state penal code. Check it out with your husband, Mrs. Stevens, or with Killian Blaine. Both of you are teetering on the edge."

She didn't exactly slam the door, but Aubrey Miles gave it a very firm push. Afterwards, Kim and I exchanged shellshocked looks. That soon gave way to peals of laughter.

"Lionel will hit the ceiling," Kim said. "Just thinking of his wife as a felon. Although I'd look okay in prison orange, don't you think? Bright colors suit me."

"Ah, Kim, you'd look great in a potato sack. On the upside, the notoriety might boost sales at Poppet," I quipped. "You know, being a criminal has some cachet. The good matrons of Harbor Bay may find me interesting now."

I couldn't wait to share the news with Gemma and Aunt Violet. Before leaving, I noticed that Fantasia and Algernon had reached a type of detente. They lay side by side, neither touching nor fighting. That lesson in peaceful coexistence was something for me to consider. After locking up the townhouse, I sat back in my Jeep and dialed the number of Killian Blaine.

Chapter Twenty

He answered immediately. "Nice to see you're not ghosting me, Miss Marky."

That man never missed an opportunity to taunt me. I swallowed the biting comment on the tip of my tongue and opted for a neutral response. "Very amusing. I just spoke with Chief Miles."

"How is Aubrey? Nice woman. Very smart."

"You told her about Doogie's will, didn't you, partner? So much for sharing. If that's your idea of cooperation, I can do without it."

"Whoa. I'm an officer of the court, remember. It's my duty to cooperate with law enforcement. Besides, you didn't answer my call."

"Ha! When it suits you or your client, you're Mr. Helpful. Did Brendan Doyle tell you he assaulted me today? I'll bet you didn't share that with Chief Miles."

"Calm down. Madge told me it was just a misunderstanding. Brendan is the excitable type, you know. Acts before he thinks sometimes."

When a man tells a woman to calm down, it's often male code for tamping down female hysteria. I refused to play his game by reacting. "You have been a busy bee today, Mr. Blaine. Here's a tip. Madge acts like Brendan's caretaker, not his friend. Take anything she tells you with a pound of salt. and tell your pal to leave me alone or face the consequences."

"Ooh. Feisty females turn me on. Do you have dinner plans? You've aroused my appetite."

"None that concern you." On that note, I ended our conversation and hurried back to Poppet.

* * *

Gemma was unavailable. I recalled that she had scheduled a fifty-minute massage for Letty Briggs and would be occupied most of the afternoon. Aunt Violet had recently returned from her visit with the ladies who lunch and was eager to share information. We retreated into our salon, away from prying eyes and big ears. Despite my jittery nerves, I made a beeline for the espresso machine. Caffeine is my drug of choice, a constant friend in an unpredictable world.

"You first," I said, sipping the heavenly brew.

She shrugged. "Okay. Madge gave us the lowdown on Brendan's behavior and said that they would be liquidating Teagen's Tinctures very soon. She didn't flinch when I asked about the financial issues. Admitted straight away that the investors would be compensated by insurance." Violet grinned. "You'll find this interesting. Brendan has decided to relocate permanently to Harbor Bay and concentrate on writing his memoir."

"Terrific. There goes the neighborhood."

"Wipe that sour expression off your pretty face and tell me your news."

I gave her the full story, complete with our panic attack and discussion with Chief Miles. It was one of the few times I'd seen my aunt flabbergasted.

"My stars," Violet said. "That's more insidious than I'd imagined. Poor Doogie. He had no idea what he was dealing with. Talk about the lamb to the slaughter." She frowned, as if recalling our dear friend was painful.

"I guess we're back to square one," I said. "Someone hated Teagen enough to orchestrate an elaborate murder plot. Too bad Doogie got in the way."

Violet patted my shoulder. "Take Aubrey's warning, Marky. Stay out of it. If you and Dr Park have been cleared, I see no reason for you to endanger yourself."

For once, I disregarded her advice. "You forget one thing, dear Aunt. Doogie. I won't let his murderer get away with it. I owe him that much. I suppose I should return Roddy's call. He needs to know what's going on."

Violet gave me a sly smile. "What about Mr. Blaine?"

"Don't even mention that serpent's name to me. He's out of the picture."

She busied herself with arranging a display of Creed fragrances. "Hmm. I wonder. He's a man who knows what he wants and usually gets it. Believe me, he wants you."

"Phooey! Killian can just go back to those vapid creatures he usually dates. They're right up his alley. He says feisty females turn him on, but I think he prefers the compliant type."

At that moment, the door to Gemma's treatment room opened. Letty Briggs flounced out looking more energized than I'd ever seen her look before. Her eyes sparkled and even her cheeks showed a noticeable glow. She ignored me but spoke directly to my aunt.

"Gemma is a genius, Miss Davis. I feel transformed to another plane." After scheduling a session the following week, she floated out the door on a cosmic high.

"That woman is nuts," I sniffed. "Totally bonkers."

Gemma appeared, laden with towels and linens. "Oh, I don't know about that. She called me a genius."

"Proof positive." I seldom snarled at Gemma, but her cheeky attitude annoyed me.

"She's right about that," Violet said. "Everyone raves about your magic fingers."

"Especially Benny," Gemma crowed. "That boy can't get enough."

I'm no prude, but perhaps my own lackluster love life made me cranky. "Stop the trash talk and tell us what you learned. You must have gotten something out of Letty in ninety minutes."

Gemma struck a pose. "It wasn't easy, but once she relaxed, she spilled her guts. I'll tell you one thing—that girl is wild about Brendan. Every time she said his name, she practically drooled."

"Ugh! How repulsive." I got a mental image of Letty cowering at Brendan Doyle's manicured toes. Not a pretty picture. "Did she mention Teagen or Doogie?"

"Not really. She expects Brendan to marry her, if you can believe it. Has her wedding dress picked out and everything. She showed me a picture of it on her phone. Fancy-smancy—not my type at all. Something from Vera

Wang." Gemma sighed. "Benny likes simple things, and his mother sure does."

Simple was the perfect descriptor of Benny Soto. I kept that thought to myself to avoid antagonizing Gemma. "What about Teagen and Doogie?"

Gemma hesitated. "Letty felt bad about Doogie. Said he was her only friend except for Madge. I asked about that special meal, and she said Teagen got what she deserved."

"Anything else?" asked Violet.

Gemma turned away, pretending to fold linens. We'd been pals since kindergarten, and she couldn't deceive me. I knew when she was hiding something.

"What aren't you telling us?"

"Letty said that Teagen didn't like you, Marky. That's why she went after Roddy."

"Why? I never did anything to her."

My aunt spoke up. "Jealousy, my dear, pure spite. You are young and beautiful. Teagen envied that and tried to hurt you."

"Yeah," Gemma agreed. "Letty said Teagen tried for Killian Blaine, but he brushed her off. She figured all that stuff about her life being threatened was an act."

"Unfortunately, she was right about that after all." Violet gathered her things. "I have a dinner engagement, so you'll have to excuse me."

"I guess we'll see your picture on *Page Six* or in *The Reliable Source*," I teased, mentioning two prominent gossip columns. Violet gave me an enigmatic smile and sailed out the door.

I attended to two new customers who scoured our shelves for the perfect lip and nail colors. My preferred brand, *Chanel*, is pricey but very durable. Neither woman blinked at the cost, and soon I rang up several items that made our bottom line sing. As closing time neared, I summoned my courage and phoned Roddy, secretly praying it would go to voicemail.

His voice, deep and dreamy, sent a quiver through my body. *Be strong!* I told myself. *Picture him with Teagen.*

"Marky…it's good hearing your voice. I've missed you."

"How are you doing?" I asked. "I have some good news. At least I hope it's good."

If I stuck to business, this call would be less painful. I was too cowardly to confront anything personal.

"My attorney says things are looking up. At least they haven't charged me, and the University is standing behind me. I've been too busy with my classes to worry."

When I told him about the news from Chief Miles, Roddy's reaction stunned me. He seemed indifferent, almost dispassionate. It was either a sign of innocence or ignorance.

"I heard about your legacy," Roddy said. "Wonderful. I hope you'll show me around when you get settled."

I didn't respond. Couldn't. My feelings for him were uncertain, and the specter of Teagen Doyle loomed large.

"Let me ask you this," I said. "Who do you suspect? Who could be capable of such a heinous crime?"

"I don't know. Teagen was a law unto herself. She damaged lots of lives and made some enemies. But Doogie didn't feel that way. He told me he'd do anything for her."

"Someone deliberately tampered with her EpiPens. That requires access to her and her medication."

Roddy paused. "Yeah, but Teagen always left that stuff lying around. She was careless. Anyone could have grabbed them. Even I knew where they were. But so did all the others."

Our conversation was stilted, awkward, two strangers navigating a narrow path.

"Okay. I'll keep in touch. Let me know if you think of anything. Maybe Doogie gave you some clue."

Before I hung up, Roddy spoke again. "Be careful, Marky. If something happened to you, I don't know what I'd do. My feelings haven't changed. They never will."

* * *

Gemma was unapologetic. "I heard you and the Professor," she said. "Hot stuff."

"You eavesdropped!"

"Of course. How else would I know what to tell you? Boy, Marky, you have all the luck. Two hunks fighting it out." She beamed. "Personally, I'd go for the big dog—Killian Blaine. Of course, the Professor has looks and brains too. Hard to choose."

Gemma was difficult to discourage and impossible to change. I tried to refocus her energy on murder. "Forget the romance. Neither of them interests me."

She raised an eyebrow and changed course. "What about that will of Doogie's? Didn't he give any hints at all?"

I wracked my brain but came up empty. "It was straightforward. But I think he figured out that EpiPen angle. Remember, we found him clutching his Montblanc. That must mean something. It was his dying act."

She wasn't convinced. "Maybe he tried to write a note. The name of his killer or something."

"Maybe, although there wasn't any paper around. I thought Doogie was naming his killer, but I suppose that doesn't make much sense either."

Gemma checked her watch. "Got a hot date tonight so I must spruce up. Benny's Mom is at some big church conference, so while the cat's away..." She licked her lips in a vulgar gesture, locked our front door, and sprinted away. It pained me to admit it, but I envied my pal. Gemma's life was filled with simple joys. She didn't allow complications such as murder or infidelity to sidetrack her. Maybe I should follow her lead.

I realized that I was hungry. Starving. The day's frenzy destroyed my peace of mind but not my appetite. Harbor Bay boasted several five-star restaurants, including *Junoon,* that featured exquisite Indian fare. It was pricey, but I told myself that I deserved a treat. After making a reservation via OpenTable, I rushed upstairs and prepped myself for a solo night on the town. I selected a saucy saffron colored pantsuit and paired it with matching stilettos. After applying a dose of texturing spray to my hair and refreshing my makeup, I felt enlivened and a tiny bit brazen. Marketta Davis, coquette and hussy in training. I pirouetted, viewing the results in the full-length mirror. Not bad!

Fantasia stared dolefully at me but seemed to approve. Aunt Violet had always stressed that there was no reason to feel daunted by dining alone. After all those days when women needed an escort had long passed. I told myself I was an independent woman, fearless and primed for adventure, not a loser who couldn't get a date.

That streak of bravado ended when I stepped out my door. Killian Blaine lounged against his Maybach, like the lord of the manor.

"Aha!" he said. "I hoped I'd catch you." He boldly eyed me from stem to stern. "You look especially lovely in that color, Marky. Who's the lucky man?"

"No one you know," I said. "You'll have to excuse me. I have a dinner reservation." I pushed past him. "By the way, we have strict anti-stalking laws in Michigan. Better brush up on them, counselor. As you said, you are an officer of the court."

He scoffed, chuckled, and did everything in his power to annoy me. Did this man thrive on rejection?

"You're really something, Ms. Davis. Someday, on our twentieth wedding anniversary, we'll laugh about all this. You'll see."

That remark left me temporarily speechless. I recovered quickly, however, and made a cutting reply. "In your dreams, Counselor. In your dreams." I scurried to my Jeep before he could spew further nonsense. As I drove to Junoon, it occurred to me: Killian had either proposed marriage or renewed his quest to bedevil me. The latter was certainly more likely.

Junoon was a pleasant surprise. The décor, subdued but elegant, featured traditional Indian colors of red, yellow, and saffron. A gleaming bar area alight with crystal glasses and bottles of exotic liquor flanked the interior. Diners could recline on padded banquettes or choose more intimate tables. When I arrived, the host seated me immediately at a secluded table for two, far away from the heavily trafficked areas. As I perused the menu, an unexpected trio arrived and was seated nearby. Brendan Doyle, Madge Stone, and Letty Briggs strolled in and claimed a choice spot. Letty still sported the glow from her bout with Gemma. She looked svelte and rather sexy in a sleeveless raspberry dress that flowed to her ankles. Its eye-popping cleavage revealed more of her than I'd ever noticed before. and encouraged Brendan Doyle to openly leer at her across the banquette. Madge showed her usual restraint and good breeding by once again choosing a silk pantsuit in palomino gold. Initially, they huddled together speaking in hushed tones. Was it kismet or just plain luck? Either way, if I concentrated, I might learn something valuable. I used the menu to conceal myself, praying for a cloak of invisibility. Where was Gemma when I needed her? That girl could lip-read with the best of them. Knowing Brendan, I expected drama and was not disappointed. He and Letty were a combustible duo who cared little for propriety or the comfort of others. They ordered a round of drinks. I decided to follow suit. Why not live dangerously by ordering a Kaapi, which my server assured me was their superior take on an espresso martini? The cost of the prix fix menu made me gulp, but I resolved to be brave. By choosing the less pricey two-course version, I saved both calories and cash. Meanwhile, Brendan's voice rose in volume as he slurped down some exotic mixture. I leaned in, managing to hear at least some of the conversation.

"You're mad. woman! What makes you think I'd ever consider marrying you?" He wagged his finger at Letty. "Teagen always said you were a psycho."

Madge grasped his arm, but it didn't stop him. "Go back to the nut house where you belong, why don't you."

I geared up for what promised to be a rousing spectacle. Guests at the surrounding tables openly gaped as the drama continued.

Letty flushed cherry red. "After all that I did for you. How can you be so cruel? I love you, and you said you loved me."

Brendan leapt up, dislodging a water goblet. "Bah! We had a roll in the hay. That's all. Teagen was the only woman I ever loved."

At this point, Letty was openly weeping. "You said if she was gone, we'd be together. I counted on that. Bought my wedding dress."

He snarled a response. "Get out of my sight. You disgust me."

In all the excitement, I forgot to hunker down. When Brendan Doyle spied me, he charged toward my table like a mad bull, his features contorted in rage. "You! You were spying on us! How dare you!" He raised his hand and might have struck me but for the intervention of an unlikely savior.

Killian Blaine slid into the seat opposite me and looked quizzically at his friend. "Is something wrong, Brendan?" He took my hand and kissed it. "Sorry I'm late, darling. Please forgive me."

"You're with *her?*" Brendan asked. His puzzled expression told me the big dolt was trying unsuccessfully to process things. Frankly, I was somewhat bewildered myself.

"Where else would I be but with my fiancée?" Killian gave him a bland smile and a wink.

I tried sipping my Kaapi and nearly choked. The entire crowd was riveted on our melodrama. By tomorrow, all of Harbor Bay would be atwitter, and my faux engagement would be topic number one.

At first, Brendan Doyle seemed rooted to the spot. He ignored the protestations of the harried Maitre'd and finally stalked toward the exit. Meanwhile, Letty and Madge stayed frozen in place. Killian summoned our waiter and coolly ordered a Charbray Clear martini. He perused the menu as if nothing was amiss.

I'm no connoisseur of vodka, so I had to ask. "What's a Charbray Clear martini? I've never heard of it."

The chance to flaunt his superior knowledge pleased him. "Any vodka lover will tell you that Charbray Clear is primo. It's a small operation run by a family of purists from Ukiah, California. No charcoal filtration, just pure heavenly hints of apples and almonds." He sighed. "Sublime."

"Thanks for the info. I'm always eager to learn."

That remark was a mistake that Killian immediately seized upon. He moved closer and whispered in my ear. "There's plenty more I'd love to teach you, Miss Marky, if only you'd agree."

I moved away. "Grow up and stop clowning. You don't fool me one bit."

Killian was unperturbed. He studied his menu instead. "Oh, that three-part prix fixe looks delicious. Have you ordered yet?"

I nodded and hastily assembled my thoughts. "I suppose I should thank you for—"

"For saving you? It was a pleasure. I'd always be there to save you." His eyes twinkled, looking warmer than I'd ever seen them. More sapphire than icy. The effect was not unpleasant. "I've known Brendan for twenty years. He loses control quite easily, but he'll calm down soon and feel very ashamed."

"He's a savage. The man has no manners and even less discretion."

Killian agreed. "When I saw your Jeep and his Bentley, I knew there might be trouble. So voila, here I am. Your knight in shining armor."

I lowered my voice to whisper level. "What's this about our engagement? Everyone in here heard you."

Nothing flustered that man. "Sounds like a fine idea, don't you think?"

"Absolutely not."

He squeezed my hand again. "Would it be so terrible? I'm considered quite a catch in some circles."

My head was spinning. Things were getting way out of hand. "I'm not your type. Besides, what about Roddy?"

"Phew! You need a strong man who appreciates you. Your Professor let you down." He leaned over. "Besides, you haven't the slightest notion what my type is. I told you I admire smart, talented women, and that describes you perfectly."

The arrival of our meal forestalled further discussion. I savored the fried eggplant chaat and fish curry while he devoured salad, langostino, and lamb chops. Avoiding dessert would have been wise, but I'm a sucker for rice pudding. Their creamy rendition did not disappoint.

"Still have a hearty appetite, I see." His grin took some of the sting off those words.

"Don't worry. I'll pay my own way."

Killian laughed and produced an Amex Centurion Card. "Allow me. I need the points."

Naturally, the server bowed and scraped to that distinctive black card and the man who carried it. Killian signed the check with a flourish, then turned to me.

"Now confess. What did you hear tonight? We're partners, remember."

I described the scene between Brendan and Letty. "She practically confessed to murdering Teagen. Naturally, she didn't mention Doogie, but I'm positive that she did that, too."

He swiveled around as Madge Stone approached our table. She appeared untroubled by the kerfuffle, composed and unflappable to the end.

"I'm surprised to see you here," she said, addressing Killian. "Marky witnessed our little upheaval, I'm afraid. Nothing major. Just Brendan being Brendan."

"You caught us in the midst of a celebration," Killian said. "Marketta and I are engaged."

That caught Madge Stone flatfooted, and I relished her reaction. "I didn't know," she said after a pause. "Congratulations."

"Is Letty okay?" I pressed my advantage. "She said some odd things about Teagen's death."

Madge bristled at that. "Letty is sensitive and prone to hysteria. Always has been. Don't take anything you heard literally. She had nothing to do with Teagen's death. Nothing."

"You've probably heard the news," I said. "Someone deliberately tampered with those EpiPens. Small wonder that Teagen died. Doogie probably found out and was murdered for his trouble."1

"Nonsense," Madge said. "She was very careful about them. That's just senseless gossip and speculation. I'm surprised that you said that."

The goodwill I'd felt toward Madge began to erode. Instead of a kindly humanist, I now saw a bossy patrician with a superior attitude.

My smile was letter perfect, but it told her I didn't believe a word she said. She excused herself and rejoined her cousin. Soon afterwards, our server appeared bearing a bottle of Krug.

"We didn't order that," I said.

The server pointed to Madge. "From that lady. To honor your engagement."

I felt a full-body flush inching up my leg, but Killian was delighted. He saluted Madge and did that whole oenophile bit by swirling, smelling, and tasting the champagne before approving it. Most men who try that look pretentious at best and foolish at worst. Killian handled it with aplomb.

I seldom drink, but I'm a fool for fine champagne, especially Krug. When our flutes were filled, he lifted his aloft and made a toast.

"To the woman of my dreams."

I greedily sipped the heavenly wine, ignoring his facetious comment. Tomorrow would come soon enough, bringing with it an avalanche of gibes from Gemma. Aunt Violet would be subtle but understandably curious. Both deserved an explanation.

"Madge acted very defensive," I said. "Could be she's part of the cabal. After all, she got a hefty share of that insurance payout."

Killian laughed in my face. "It isn't money. You may find this hard to believe, but Madge Stone rather fancies me. Seeing us together must have been a blow."

It was my turn to scoff. "Get serious. She's way older than you."

"Age is no barrier where love is concerned. Think about that, Marky."

"I'd rather think about Doogie and whoever killed him. We haven't made much progress, and neither have the cops."

He sighed after repeating the same tired warning that my aunt and Gemma droned on about—leave it to the professionals. It made sense, but I couldn't let go. It felt like abandoning Doogie, that gentle giant who had made me his heir. He was counting on me, and I wouldn't let him down.

Chapter Twenty-One

Killian planted one chaste kiss on my forehead and sped away to his new abode, leaving me relieved but rather disappointed. Had I dreamed this whole engagement thing? It was probably a ruse designed to deceive me and befuddle his pals. He was undoubtedly bored in our little hamlet and chose me as his summer crush. *Not so fast!*

I bounded into Poppet and freed my furry princess from her crate. It was barely ten o'clock. Fantasia deserved a comfort break, and I needed a hearty dose of fresh air to clear my head. A recap of the night's events made me laugh. In one evening, I'd been threatened, proposed to, and fed a heavenly meal. Plus, as an unrepentant eavesdropper, I'd gleaned information that implicated a culprit and her motive for murder. Not a bad night's work for a rank amateur.

I decided to forge ahead and share my latest theory with Chief Miles the next day. After all, she described the two most common motives for murder: love and money. Letty's lust for Brendan was no secret. Nor was his appetite for cash. Together, they formed a deadly duo.

Fantasia strained toward home and the comfort of her bed. As usual, my collie companion showed more sense than her pet parent. I quickly undressed and slid under the silky Frette sheets that my aunt provided. I had just dozed off when my iPhone jolted me awake.

"Thinking of me," Killian purred in a sexy voice, "I can't get you out of my mind."

"You're insane, and I'm exhausted. Go to sleep." I disconnected my phone and slipped back into dreamland.

* * *

Gemma pounced on me the moment that I entered Poppet. Even though I expected it, the onslaught left me reeling.

"Engaged! Why was I the last to know? Don't you trust me?"

I sputtered, trying to explain, but she was relentless. "Benny's mom heard it from one of the waiters. You might as well take out an ad in the *Harbor Bay Times*. Now the entire town will be buzzing." She narrowed her eyes. "I bet he got you some sparkler. Let's see it. Why aren't you wearing it?"

Aunt Violet entered so silently that I barely heard her. The woman was as stealthy as a panther and twice as wily. Her demeanor was calm, her emotions unreadable. That activated my urge to confess everything that happened the prior evening.

"I have news to report," she said. Something, possibly her dalliance with that doting senator, brought an especially becoming flush to her cheeks.

"You're not the only one," Gemma said. "Marky hit the jackpot."

Violet raised her brows but didn't probe. That made me even more uncomfortable. I never could deceive my aunt no matter how I tried. She had an uncanny ability to see into my soul.

"Tell us your news first," I said, stalling for time.

"It concerns Brendan Doyle. The SEC is investigating his firm and him personally for unspecified federal crimes."

Gemma looked puzzled. "What's the SEC?"

"Securities and Exchange Commission. Apparently, his firm is on very shaky ground with them and the IRS as well." Violet paused. "There's talk of a Chapter 11 bankruptcy filing."

That bombshell floored me. Did Brendan need the money from Teagen's Tinctures to survive? If so, that was a compelling motive for murder. Letty was supposedly rich and a soft touch if Brendan needed money. But Letty was no fool. She would demand something in return. If wedding bells didn't ring, Letty might not loosen the purse strings.

"Funny that the hot lawyer didn't tell you that," Gemma teased. "I thought you were partners."

She had a point, but I felt compelled to defend Killian. "He's Brendan's lawyer. Probably can't divulge anything."

Aunt Violet agreed. "It's a delicate situation. I wonder if the investors in Teagen's Tinctures are nervous. Lionel, for one, never likes to lose money. He's very protective of the bottom line."

"Wait till you hear this." I recreated the scene at *Joon*. "I'm convinced that Letty is the killer. She could probably plead insanity and avoid jail time."

Gemma jumped in. "Yeah. Those rich types get special treatment. Not like the rest of us poor slobs."

My aunt reserved judgment. "What does Mr. Blaine advise?"

I shrugged. "He's loyal to Brendan Doyle so I suspect his motives. He's trying to distract me with all this romantic talk. Poor Roddy might be the fall guy."

"No way to talk about your fiancé," Gemma teased. "I'd ditch the Professor if I were you. After what he did—let him twist!"

She was probably right. Still, Roddy met Teagen through me, and I felt responsible for his plight.

Violet patted my shoulder. "You can't save everyone, Marky. No one forced Dr. Park to get involved with Teagen. But I don't believe for a second that he harmed Doogie." She stared at me with the same steely resolve that undid me as a child. "Now tell us about your engagement."

I sputtered and stuttered but managed to piece together Killian's bizarre engagement ploy. Both Gemma and Aunt Violet listened without commenting. The expression on their faces said plenty

"Well. Come on. Out with it. Don't you have anything to say?"

Gemma curled her lip. "Typical Marky. A Dreamboat proposes, and you blow it off. Watch out. You're not getting any younger, you know."

That unfair remark stunned me. I turned to my aunt for comfort, but didn't get it.

"I think Mr. Blaine was serious, Marky. He's been fascinated by you since last summer." She smiled. "Very understandable. You're beautiful, brilliant, and talented. He's accustomed to being pursued by women, but you challenge everything. That's alluring to a man like him."

I was confused, unable to respond. I refocused on the only thing that mattered to me: Doogie's murder. "Don't you suspect Letty, too?" I asked my aunt. "It all fits."

"Perhaps. The Briggs family has a history of mental instability. Letty may well have acted impulsively. I knew her mother well. She was subject to violent mood swings. Not homicidal but troubled."

"Pooh." Gemma folded her arms and frowned. "Face it. She's bat shit crazy. Letty, I mean, not her mom. She told me all about her wedding to Brendan. Dress and all. He probably cooked up that scheme with her."

I couldn't disagree. If Doogie questioned Letty or threatened to alert the police, he might have sealed his fate. He left that stupid meat thermometer and kitchen mitts on the counter for anyone to grab. No wonder the only prints on it were Roddy's. The killer wore those gloves.

"I've got to see Chief Miles right away. She needs to know about Letty."

Violet stood up and gathered her things. "I'll join you. Don't argue, I'm coming."

Her presence bolstered my confidence even though I didn't admit it. Every hero had someone watching her back, and no one did it better than Violet Davis.

"What do I tell Killian if he shows up?" Gemma asked. "I know. I'll say you're pregnant. That always makes a man think."

My look of horror stopped her. Gemma waved her arms and hastily retreated. "Just kidding."

As we were leaving, she received a text from Benny Soto. For a moment, I thought Gemma might faint. Her complexion turned ghostly white, and her mouth flew open. "Wait," she yelled to us.

Violet raced to her side. "What's wrong?"

Gemma's voice sounded weak, quite unlike her normal tone. "They just found Letty Briggs. She's dead. She committed suicide."

Chapter Twenty-Two

"NO! That can't be true." I reeled back, collapsing on a nearby sofa. "I just saw her last night."

"What else did Benny say?" Violet asked. There was a noticeable strain in her voice.

"Not much. Before he finished, Chief Miles called him, and he made tracks. I think she kinda scares him."

Just then, Kim Stevens burst through the door looking more ravaged than I'd ever seen her look before. Windblown hair, mismatched clothes, and missing lipstick told me that she had dressed hurriedly. Despite those missteps, however, she still looked gorgeous.

"Have you heard?" she asked. "Lionel got the entire story from the police. I just can't believe it."

Violet put a closed sign on Poppet's door and led Kim toward our sitting area. Gemma and I followed behind, moving numbly like automatons.

"Some herbal tea would be nice," said my aunt as she nodded my way. "We could all use something to calm our nerves."

I scurried to the kitchen to do her bidding. Chamomile with honey should do the trick. Despite the calories, I opened a tin of DiCamillo's almond and chocolate biscotti and arranged cups and saucers on a Limoges tray. Kim was normally calm and cool, so her narrative must be a bombshell.

They were sitting silently when I reentered the room. Kim's breathing had returned to normal, although Gemma looked ready to explode. Violet poured each of us a cup of tea while we waited for Kim to speak.

"Ah, I needed this," Kim said, leaning her head back and sighing. "When

Lionel told me about Letty, I lost my senses."

Gemma drummed her fingers on the tea tray, a sure sign that her patience was almost gone. "Skip that stuff, Kim, and get to the main event. We're dying here."

Violet frowned at her and intervened. "Who found her?"

"The housekeeper. Remember, Letty was staying in one of the guest houses on Madge's estate. She went in to tidy up and found Letty. She was 'unresponsive' as the newspapers say."

We digested that information for a moment before commenting. As I recalled, Madge's estate boasted two guest cottages that were the size of most people's homes. Brendan and Teagen had occupied one until recently.

"What makes them say it was suicide?" I asked. "Might have been natural causes."

Kim shook her head. "She left a note. A confession. They found an empty bottle of pills next to it."

"Really?" The thought clearly shocked my aunt.

"Unfortunately." Kim edged closer to us. "Believe it or not, Letty murdered Teagen and Doogie."

I recalled Letty's outburst at *Joon*. Had rejection fueled her suicide? Was that emotional, fragile woman really a double murderer?

"Why did she do it? Gemma said she left Poppet in a great mood yesterday." I reminded myself that after Brendan's cruel treatment, Letty had dissolved into tears.

"Yeah," Gemma asked. "Why kill Teagen and Doogie. Especially Doogie. Guess she was a real nut case, after all."

Kim cleared her throat and sipped more tea. "Letty always hated Teagen, and she loved Brendan. She hoped he'd marry her if Teagen wasn't in the way. Doogie's death was a crime of passion. He confronted Letty, and they quarreled."

I realized that both Roddy and I were now in the clear, but at what price? What a sad coda to the saga of Teagen Doyle, whose legacy would only heighten from the publicity. I fully expected to see a *Netflix* movie or *Forty-eight Hours* program highlighting Teagen's life and demise. It hurt to think that Doogie would only be a footnote in this tragedy, doomed to obscurity. My heart and mind felt heavy with the weight of three violent deaths.

"Better call the Professor," Gemma said. "Make someone happy at least."

I clutched my iPhone and staggered up the stairs to my private space. Maybe he'd be busy, and my message would go straight to voicemail. Things would be so much easier that way. I wanted to weep, but tears wouldn't come. Maybe later, when I'd had a chance to process everything.

As luck would have it, Roddy answered immediately. If he was startled by my call, he didn't say so. I explained everything I knew about Letty's suicide and concluded by saying that now we were both absolved.

"Good to know," he said. Once again, his manner was nonchalant as if he was bored by the whole sordid mess. He didn't kill the messenger, but he wasn't effusive either. "Thanks for letting me know, Marky. I'll tell my boss about it. She'll be relieved, I'm sure."

A combination of anger and angst overtook me. What was wrong with this man? Was I deluded to expect a modicum of gratitude or a crumb of affection? After all, three people died, including one who had been a friend to him. Teagen had been more than a friend, but I excluded her from the mix. Maybe Killian was right about Roddy.

He wasn't totally oblivious to events in Harbor Bay despite his indifference. "I hear you've already got my replacement lined up," Roddy chuckled. "Some rich lawyer from Chicago. Good luck. I can't compete with that even if I tried."

My silence spoke volumes. Our conversation ended abruptly with both of us promising to keep in touch. I am a realist in matters of the heart. Any romance between Roddy and me was over. Even friendship was only a remote possibility now. I wished him well as I exited from his life.

* * *

"Why so gloomy?" Gemma asked. "Everything's tied up nice and neat. You can concentrate on your future now. Planning your wedding—"

"Cut that out. I told you Killian wasn't serious. He's a notorious womanizer who wants one more female on the string."

When it came to men, Gemma was the ultimate pragmatist. "Big deal. Enjoy it while you can. Guys like that don't come along every day." She sighed. "I'd love to have him for a boy toy if I didn't have Benny."

"This whole thing with Letty bothers me. She was vulnerable, not vicious. Maybe someone else, like Brendan Doyle, killed her before she talked. I bet Madge knows more than she's letting on."

Kim left to join Lionel. Aunt Violet headed out to address a woman's group, abandoning Gemma and me to handle the influx of customers. Harbor Bay is a hub for gossip, and throughout the day, curious customers wafted in, eager for tidbits about Letty. I fobbed all of them off with a smile and polite denial. Gemma, however, used the opportunity to tout some of our high-end items. Her philosophy was pure Carpe Diem, and our cash register hummed with sales to the curious.

By six p.m., both of us were exhausted. I shortened Fantasia's evening walk, ignoring her pleas for more exercise. Despite the mild temperature and brilliant blue sky, my mood was troubled by visions of Letty Briggs proudly displaying her wedding dress. In my opinion, Brendan Doyle was directly responsible for Letty's death. He was a vicious beast who cared little for the feelings of others. That cavalier attitude made him a perfect match for Teagen and probably explained his success as an entrepreneur.

Killian neither called nor appeared, despite or maybe because of the events of the day. I told myself that he was likely consoling Brendan and Madge as they navigated their way through the vale of tears. There was another possibility, of course. The crafty Mr. Blaine might well be preparing to decamp for Chicago now that the murders were solved. If he remained in Harbor Bay, he would have to face me, a most inconvenient fiancée.

I changed into pajamas and tidied up my apartment. Restoring order always had a therapeutic effect on my mind. It allowed me to recall that I still had a completed sketch of Teagen done in charcoal. In all honesty, it was one of my better efforts. Even my aunt said so. If I returned it to Brendan, it might ease the tension between us and pave the way for more positive dealings in the future. On the other hand, he might well thrash me using the portrait as a cudgel. It was a delicate situation that called for tact and diplomacy, two qualities that I sometimes lacked. *Be brave* said my inner voice. *Be cautious*, said my mind. Unraveling some unresolved issues might lead me to Doogie's killer. That presumed, of course, that Letty was not the culprit. It might also plunge me into danger yet again. I had no illusions about Killian Blaine riding to my rescue. Those fantasies belonged in romance novels, not in real life. *Be your own superhero.* That was my mantra.

My aunt texted me later that evening, telling me to contact her. She kept European hours, which meant that she would be available until midnight. When we spoke, her voice held an undercurrent of excitement.

"I learned something tonight that might interest you."

"Okay."

"Copies of Letty's suicide note are already circulating around Harbor Bay."

"You're kidding! How did that happen?"

"Never mind. I'll send it to you, and you can decide for yourself." Violet was a woman of few words. She bid me goodnight and hung up without any further explanation. I abandoned any hope of sleeping until I read that note. When it arrived, I was touched by its simplicity.

I have done an unforgivable thing that I cannot erase. My hatred for Teagen Doyle never stopped despite the passage of time. She stole the only man I have ever loved, and I made her pay for it. I wanted her to suffer but not die. That was an accident. Doogie Kinkaid was an innocent partner in my scheme. When he threatened to tell Brendan, I tried to stop him. You know the rest. Think kindly of me occasionally. I neither ask for nor expect forgiveness. Letty Briggs

Chapter Twenty-Three

That note made me weep for a forlorn lost soul mired in despair. She had beauty and wealth on her side, but that wasn't enough. Even her final words were typed into an impersonal computer. I sat upright in my chair, unable to sleep or even read a novel. Fantasia understood. She left her bed and placed her lovely head in my lap. Stroking her soft fur was comforting, more comforting than contact with any human. I must have dozed off because before I knew it, sunshine streamed into my room. Another day full of promise awaited me. I said a prayer for the souls of Letty and Doogie but left Teagen to fend for herself. Why be a hypocrite at this stage? After bathing and doing my beauty routine, I selected a bright green pantsuit and got ready to face the day. At least I still had that option. Doogie and Letty did not.

Fantasia, my boon companion, hovered over me, eager to confront the great outdoors. Before leaving, I read Letty's final words one more time. Something about that message bothered me, but I couldn't quite grasp it. To reward Fantasia and assuage my guilt for neglecting her, I powerwalked four miles from home to the docks and back. By the time we returned to Poppet, both of us were more than ready for a hearty breakfast. Fantasia ate her kibble with chicken daintily, but I shamelessly wolfed down my veggie burger. My phone stayed by my side just in case someone called. I didn't expect anything—not really. Saturdays were usually busy at Poppet, and this day didn't disappoint. Gemma swept into the store on the dot of nine, full of exuberance and questions.

"Did you read that confession?" she asked. "Benny showed me a copy.

Sounds like it ties up all the loose ends." She looked quizzically at me. "So why aren't you happy?"

My muddled explanation didn't make sense even to me. "There's something that just isn't right. I can't put my finger on it yet, but I will."

"Phooey. Stop playing detective and cozy up to the Dreamboat. I saw him at the patisserie when I passed by. He was with Brendan Doyle, who looked like hell." She snickered. "Your guy was as perfect as ever. Not a hair out of place."

That answered one question. Killian hadn't skipped town yet. I resisted the impulse to track him down. Far better to focus on stacking the shelves with items to entice buyers. I was especially fond of some new products from the British line, *Philip Kingsley.* They were pricey but magical when it came to hair care.

Our first customer, a well-groomed blonde in her forties, wandered through Poppet before examining our display of *Chantecaille* cosmetics. I'd never seen her before, but with the start of tourist season, that wasn't unusual. I offered to help her select, but she resisted.

"I know this brand," she said with a tight smile, "but perhaps you can answer a question."

"Sure."

"Why did Letty Briggs will her fortune to Brendan Doyle?"

I gasped, as she'd caught me flatfooted. "I don't know what you're talking about."

The blonde whipped out a press pass and introduced herself. "Lena Wells, *Chicago Tribune.* I was told that you were investigating the case."

I shook my head. "Sorry. You've been misinformed. We're shopkeepers, not detectives, and I have no idea who benefits from Ms. Briggs' will. Ask Chief Aubrey Miles."

Her lips twisted in a crooked smile. "Funny thing. I just saw Mr. Doyle, and his attorney said to ask you."

Gemma rushed in to play interference. "I'd contact Madge Stone. She knows everything about her cousin."

Lena Wells handed me an eyeshadow trio from the Cheetah Collection.

"I'll take this while I'm here." She plucked some bills from her wallet, paid, and exited without saying another word.

I was still stunned by her question. Had Letty willed her estate to Brendan? If so that gave him an even more compelling motive for murder. Love and money—her need for love, his for money. Chief Miles' words echoed in my head.

"Can you believe the nerve of that broad?" Gemma asked.

"Hush. She's a customer willing to shell out seventy-five bucks for eyeshadow. Besides, she told us something I certainly didn't know. Did you?"

Gemma shook her head. "I'll check it out with Benny. Hold on." She dashed to the back room, clutching her phone. When she returned, she confirmed the reporter's story. Letty Briggs' estate, rumored to exceed ten million dollars, had indeed been left wholly to one Brendan Doyle, her putative fiancé.

We had no time to discuss things. Several customers joined us, including one who requested a full makeover. That was a potential moneymaker that typically resulted in a fat bottom line. Poppet buzzed with customers and cash that day. Gemma was booked all afternoon doing massages, and Aunt Violet floated in at noon to assist. If she knew about Brendan's latest legacy, she said nothing. Later that afternoon, a surprise awaited me when I returned from walking Fantasia. A glorious display of orchids and lilies from *Forever Flowers*, accompanied by a five-pound box of yummy *Edelweiss Chocolates*, lay on the front counter. Blood rushed to my face despite my efforts to remain unaffected. Aunt Violet said nothing, but Gemma snatched the card from my hands.

"Aha! Listen to this —*to the girl of my dreams, now and forever.* Marky, you have all the luck. On his best day, Benny gets me drug store candy and supermarket flowers." She rubbed her hands together. "Killian Blaine sure knows how to treat a lady."

Instead of speaking, I opened the chocolates and passed them around. Violet chose a cherry cream, but Gemma grabbed three pieces of fudge. I'm partial to truffles. When I bit into one, it produced a sensation of almost orgasmic delight.

"He probably sends this stuff to all his conquests," I said, hoping they would deny it. "It doesn't mean anything."

"Who cares," said Gemma. "Stop squawking and enjoy for Pete's sake."

"She's right," Violet said. "Mr. Blaine is very attentive, as he should be. Value yourself, Marketta, and others will as well."

Naturally, she knew all about Letty's will. Madge had confided in my aunt and Kim when they lunched. "Madge didn't eat a thing," Violet said. "She was so distraught that I thought she might burst into tears. She truly loved her cousin."

"She can stand to miss a few meals," I sniffed. "Middle age spread is deadly."

Violet gave me a pained look. "Be kind, Marky. Madge says that Brendan is a mess. He simply can't adjust to losing Teagen and now Letty."

I couldn't restrain myself. "That man deserves to suffer. I'll bet he's not too upset to scoop up those payouts. Besides, I still suspect he had his hand in Letty's pocket even though he treated her shamefully."

When Killian called, I tried unsuccessfully to play it cool. "Thanks for the flowers," I said. "They're lovely." I stifled a laugh. "Those chocolates are out of this world. Never tried that brand before."

Killian paused. "It's nothing. You deserve to get the best, and Edelweiss produces it. I know the owners. They handcraft every bit of their product. LA insiders swear by it."

I pinched myself to avoid being seduced by sweet words. "Listen, we need to talk."

"Talk away. I'm at your disposal." His voice had a slightly smarmy edge to it.

"In person. Not on the phone."

"Even better. Where and when."

I considered several possibilities before choosing Doogie's townhouse (now mine) for our assignation. Cancel that. This was a business meeting, not an assignation. Killian had valuable insights that I needed to know. It was the perfect setting for our collaboration, the place where the entire Teagen travesty started, the space still inhabited by the spirits of Doogie and

CHAPTER TWENTY-THREE

Letty. Nothing romantic was on offer.

My sole culinary specialty involves the humble egg. Aunt Violet taught me the trick to making a perfect French omelet, one that is elegant and far superior to American fare. In preparation for the main event, I gathered my ingredients—pasture-raised eggs, sweet cream butter, and a wedge of heavenly Parmigiano Reggiano to pair with crusty baguettes. Doogie's kitchen came fully equipped with every gourmet gadget imaginable, so that was no problem. Thankfully, the murderous meat thermometer had been removed by Chief Miles. I knew that my late pal and benefactor would be delighted to have his home involved in this quest. I raised a silent prayer to the kitchen gods that I would do it justice.

It was no use trying to evade Gemma. She spied the ingredients and immediately pounced. "Having a party tonight? I wasn't invited."

I ignored the gibe as I carried my stash to the Jeep. Gemma followed right behind, heckling all the way. "You never cooked for Roddy or any of the others. did you? On second thought, maybe that's just as well."

"Ha, ha. You're quite a comedian. This is merely a strategy session. Nothing else."

She smirked but said no more. Even Gemma knew when silence was golden. I made a quick stop at the Patisserie to snag some of their heavenly lemon tarts and readied myself for what promised to be a pleasant and productive evening.

He arrived promptly at seven o'clock bearing yet another bottle of Krug. I pointed to the cabinet that housed crystal, and while he poured the champagne, sped to the kitchen to perfect our dinner. Despite my misgivings, the omelets were perfect, just enough to satiate hunger without over-indulging. We sat at the lovely walnut dining table, reminiscing about absent friends and potential suspects, before I finally summoned the courage to speak.

"I don't think Letty killed herself or anyone else. When she left Poppet, she was on top of the world or close to it."

He raised one brow and stared my way. "Didn't you just say that Brendan humiliated her at that restaurant? Made her cry. For a sensitive soul like

Letty, that may have been the trigger."

I couldn't agree. Letty and Brendan were used to dramatic scenes, addicted to emotion. This was merely another chapter in their saga.

His tone changed. No more banter when he knew precisely where I was going. "So, you think someone murdered Letty as well as Teagen and Doogie? Rather fanciful, wouldn't you say? I doubt that a triple murderer is roaming the streets of Harbor Bay." He leaned forward and clasped my hand. "Face it, Marky. This distasteful episode is finally over. I know you suspect Brendan of every crime imaginable, but trust me, he's innocent." He grinned, "Of murder if not financial hijinks."

"Tell that to the SEC when they come calling. You're his attorney, I get that. But face facts. He needed an infusion of cash, and voila, he got it. Between Teagen's estate and Letty's, your client has a new lease on his dubious life."

Killian's frown deepened. "You forget something. Brendan is also my friend. He's not perfect, but he's no killer. I know him, and you don't."

The cozy mood rapidly evaporated. We were pugilists, glaring, fists clenched and ready for battle.

"My opinion of Brendan Doyle is based on his behavior toward others, especially women. He's ruthless and rude. I doubt that he has even one ounce of empathy in his overfed body."

Killian's eyes were sharper than shards of ice. "Is that why you wanted to see me? To accuse Brendan of murder? Face it, Marky. This case is closed. Frankly, I hoped it was something more personal that you had in mind." He gently brushed my fingers with his lips.

I pulled away, folding my arms. "Doogie deserves better than this. Just listen for a minute. Suspend judgment."

His expression hardened. "Okay."

I took a deep breath. He would respond to logic, not emotion. "There's one big flaw in Letty's supposed confession. Something very simple."

"Go on."

"It's typed on a computer."

Killian made a derisive snort. "That's it? Your big scoop?"

I steeled myself for resistance but forged ahead. "When I first met Letty, she explained that she never used a computer—carpal tunnel syndrome or something like that. Did everything longhand."

His expression didn't change, but I noted a certain wariness in his manner. "So. What does that prove? Maybe she wanted her final act to be more formal."

"Perhaps, but there's more. That so-called confession was typed perfectly—no errors. It showed skill and practice, not the emotional act of someone about to die."

He paused as he digested my theory. Killian switched to super-lawyer mode, no longer angling for romance. I realized that once again, I had likely sacrificed something valuable.

"Okay. Where do we go from here? I can assure you that Brendan is not a skilled typist, and with spell-check and auto-correct, Letty could have produced a perfect document."

Despite the risks, I couldn't let it go. "Maybe, but he uses a computer for everything. Teagen said so. I'll tell Chief Miles about this. Let her decide what's important."

"Do you want me to go with you?"

I watched him closely. Clearly, he was conflicted about the entire matter. His offer told me, however, that there was a glimmer of hope for us. Maybe he really did care for me.

"Thanks, I appreciate it. I truly do. But you have an ethical dilemma. I don't."

We parted company then, with each of us deep in thought.

###

Aubrey Miles sighed the next morning when I approached her desk. Despite those misgivings, she offered me coffee and remained professional and polite.

"How can I help you, Ms. Davis?"

I'd practiced several approaches but, in the end, opted for candor. Based upon our previous encounters, I knew that Aubrey Miles had an incisive mind and an excellent BS detector.

I blurted out my theory. "Letty Briggs didn't kill herself or anyone else."

She shifted in her chair but didn't react immediately. "And you know this how?"

In retrospect, my computer theory seemed unconvincing even to my ears. I summoned my courage and continued. "You said yourself that most murders involved love or money."

Aubrey nodded. "I did."

"Okay, Teagen and Letty's deaths involved both elements, and only one person benefited from them." I didn't utter his name, but the implication was clear.

The chief gave me that flat cop stare. Friendly airs and small talk were history now. This was serious police business. She folded her arms in the universal gesture that spelled resistance.

"I know you mean well, Ms. Davis, but let me emphasize this—the case is closed. Finis. Letty Briggs took full responsibility for two murders. I'm satisfied and so are the State Police." She spread out her hands in supplication. "I must advise you to leave this matter alone. Otherwise, you risk your reputation and possibly your business. Some people already consider you a crank." Her voice softened. "I realize these past few weeks have been difficult for you. Time to relax, reflect, and let it go." She rose and opened her office door. I had no choice but to leave.

Chapter Twenty-Four

Gemma and Aunt Violet ignored me when I entered Poppet. Both kept their heads down and backs turned as they pretended to review the day's schedule. Someone, probably garrulous Benny Soto, must have spilled the proverbial beans about my ill-fated visit to Chief Miles. It was my task to break the ice.

"Okay, tell me. What have you heard?"

Violet turned around and grinned. "Not much. Your adventures precede you, dear Niece."

Gemma was less restrained. "Benny said the chief booted you out of her office."

"Not true. I left of my own accord. We had a very civilized conversation where I shared my views on the case with Chief Miles."

My aunt merely nodded, but Gemma was unrelenting. "Guess you blew it with the Dreamboat. Kim said he hightailed it to Chicago this morning with Brendan Doyle."

That hurt. I pasted a faux smile on my face and shrugged. "So what. It's a free country."

"It was callous of Brendan," Violet said. "He left all the funeral arrangements to Madge at a very difficult time for her. I think she's planning a small gathering at her place to celebrate Letty's life."

Tastefully honoring a killer's life was a tricky proposition. Madge had probably consulted Emily Post and was up to it. I was certain that Madge would exclude me from that gathering since I was persona non grata. Too bad. It would be a fascinating spectacle.

Harbor Bay had experienced far too many funerals of late. Attendance at Doogie's service had been confined to a few old friends, but the memory of his casket on the way to the cremation chamber still left me shaken. No memorial or celebration of life had been scheduled yet. Violet suggested that we host a gathering for local admirers at his townhouse, and I immediately agreed. Doogie was proud of his home. He would join us in spirit as we honored him there.

My encounter with the chief had been an epiphany of sorts. I vowed to follow Aubrey Miles' advice and accept the verdict. Doogie, Letty, and even Teagen could now rest peacefully without any more interference from me. Did some questions remain unanswered—absolutely. I still suspected the grubby paw of Brendan Doyle was behind Letty's scheme, but proving it was a bridge too far. Time to move on with my life.

It was easier said than done. In the weeks following that resolution, life felt pedestrian and pointless. My prescription for the doldrums was painting. That had always been my refuge and antidote to pain. It didn't fail me this time. I transformed the charcoal sketch of Keegan into an oil painting with a slightly impressionistic air. When it was completed, I asked Violet for her assessment. That took every ounce of courage I could muster. My aunt respected me too much to mouth platitudes. She would give me a frank appraisal of my effort, no matter how much it stung.

I held my breath while she examined the painting. Violet sat in front of it and remained silent for what seemed like an eternity. When she turned my way, I noticed a smile on her face.

"Amazing. This is one of your best works, Marky. Perhaps the best. You managed to capture Teagen's physical beauty while hinting about the layers underneath. What do you plan to do with it?"

Initially, I was too shellshocked to respond. I had steeled myself for disappointment and was unprepared for praise. After heaving a gigantic sigh, I shared my plan.

"I want to give it to Brendan. Sort of a peace offering, although I still despise the big brute. Would that be too bold?"

She thought a moment. "Not at all. Acts of kindness are worth doing even if they're not appreciated. Our Jewish friends would call it a mitzvah. Let me have it framed for you. I know just the place to do it."

The finished product, framed in gold leaf, was sublime, a subtle but elegant tribute to a complex woman. Initially, I hung it in my bedroom, but the specter of Teagen Doyle gazing down at me troubled my sleep. Far better to place it in the tiny alcove in my living room.

Two weeks after he had decamped to Chicago, Killian Blaine reappeared. I knew that he and Brendan had been seen around town, but pride kept me from contacting him. When he waylaid me on my morning walk with Fantasia, I was startled but not surprised. He was casually dressed if any article from pricy Loro Piana could be called casual. His khaki cotton trousers and Caban coat cost more than most mortals' yearly clothing budget. My modest Lululemon sweats fell far short of that standard. I greeted him politely and kept on walking. Fantasia wagged her tail but remained aloof.

"Hold on, Marky. Wait a minute. I need to talk to you." His voice was gentle, not his normal peremptory tone. Killian patted the seat next to him on a bench and sat down. "I missed you." He put his arm around me and moved me toward him. "Don't pull away. Please."

The faint scent of Creed Irish Tweed wafted from him, lulling me into a strange sense of complacency. This man was trouble. He was a rake, a womanizer with an abysmal track record. That was a matter of public knowledge. I knew it, yet I found him almost impossible to resist.

"I thought you'd given up on Harbor Bay."

"Never. Not as long as you're here." He turned my face toward him. I'm no ingenue. I'd been kissed by plenty of men. But Killian Blaine's tenderness and passion set a higher standard. I found myself responding, returning his embrace with a fervor that astounded me. Who knew where things might have gone had an unwelcome party not appeared. Brendan Doyle brashly interrupted us without any apology or hint of civility. Naturally, he ignored my existence.

"There you are, Killian. Come on. We're late for our breakfast meeting, and I'm starved."

His boorish conduct broke the spell. I pulled away and hastily straightened my clothes. "Nice seeing you," I said as I gathered Fantasia's lead.

Killian seemed dumbstruck. He leapt up and glared at his friend. "I'll call you this afternoon," he said to me. "Are you free for dinner?"

No way would I falter in front of odious Brendan Doyle. "Call me," I said with an enigmatic smile. Fantasia and I jogged back to Poppet with a spring in our step.

* * *

Gemma pounced as soon as I opened the door. "Did you see him? The Dreamboat came looking for you, and he was all lathered up."

That comment was both crude and inaccurate. A man like Killian Blaine never lost his composure, at least not totally. I leaned back, reliving that amazing scene in the park and the kiss that we shared.

"Are you okay, Marky?" Gemma felt my forehead. "You feel kind of flushed."

"I'm recuperating from our run. You should try exercising more yourself."

That distracted Gemma, sending her off on a tangent about busybodies spewing unwanted advice. When she wound down, I slipped upstairs to ready myself for the business day. A local teacher had booked two hours for a clinic on optimizing personal appearance. I looked forward to teaching our audience, twenty teenage girls, about skin care as well as makeup application. At their age, very few were satisfied with their looks. Insecurity was only exacerbated by social media and the soul sucking pressure to be both thin and beautiful. I used a slide show to illustrate the many types of beauty in different cultures. Afterwards, I did several makeovers and fielded a variety of questions, including a few about Teagen Doyle.

By the end of the session, both my audience and I were exhausted but also exhilarated. Although each student received free samples, most elected to purchase products as well. As Violet said, these things were a win-win for us and the girls. They would learn some things and spread the gospel of Poppet to their female relatives and their fathers as well.

At day's end, I collapsed into our chaise, propped my feet up, and sipped a soothing cup of tea. That's when he called me. *Calm down, I told myself. This man expects easy conquests.*

Killian's voice was soft and silky smooth. "Sorry we were interrupted today. I was enjoying myself. By the way, I told Brendan to treat you with respect in the future."

"Hmm."

"Are you free for dinner? I owe you one after that delicious omelet you made."

"Sure. That sounds like fun."

He was clearly puzzled by my reaction, or lack of it. "I can pick you up at seven."

"Make it six-thirty. There's something in my place that I'd like to show you." I'd decided to unveil my portrait of Teagen and gauge his reaction. He'd never seen my cozy nest. Very few men had. I was prepared for his look of disdain as he compared the studio to his own ritzy digs. I had a sentimental attachment to the place. It had cosseted Fantasia and me for several years, but with my legacy from Doogie, it was time to move on. Gemma had already asked to rent it until she married Benny Soto. I was ambivalent about that, especially the thought of boorish Benny despoiling my lovely refuge. Aunt Violet suggested that we postpone any decision until Doogie's will went through probate. Since she owned the building and was technically my landlord, her superior wisdom prevailed.

I dashed upstairs to prepare for my date. Fortunately, I had a bottle of Chablis with a respectable pedigree, and some leftover Scottish smoked Salmon to serve my guest. I deliberately chose to wear an understated cream jumpsuit that was refined but not sexy. No need to suggest that I was on offer as an hors d'oeuvres.

Killian was prompt. He arrived on the dot of six-thirty, impeccably garbed in what looked like, and probably was, a Savile Row suit.

"Follow me," I said, leading him up the stairs to my studio. "This won't take long."

He shook his head, feigning disappointment. "Too bad. I've found that things worth doing can take time."

I ignored that double entendre and played hostess. He glanced around my living room and nodded. "Very nice. Cozy but not crowded. It reflects your good taste."

After pouring him a glass of wine, I slipped into the alcove and got the painting. "I have something to show you. Give me your honest opinion."

Killian sipped his wine as he viewed Teagen's portrait. I expected some meaningless compliment or outright dismissal, but I was wrong. He leaned toward the painting and scrutinized every brushstroke. When he finally spoke, I was shocked.

"It's breathtaking, Marky. An astounding piece of work equal to your Aunt's high standards. Congratulations. Your talent awes me."

A flush stained my cheeks as I digested his words. "Teagen hired me to paint her portrait. I felt honor-bound to complete it."

"I'd love to buy it if it's for sale," he said.

"Actually, I plan to give it to Brendan. He doesn't like me much, so he might not accept it."

"Nonsense," Killian said. "Brendan is all Sturm und Drang. Underneath, he's rather a decent chap, believe it or not. I know he'd be touched by this beautiful portrait. He's really grieving for Teagen."

"Maybe you should be the one to give it to him."

Killian grinned. "Fearless Marketta Davis cowed by my buddy. I can't believe it."

"Believe it. I don't like the man, and I still suspect him."

He raised his eyebrow. "Then what's this all about? You could make a tidy profit at any art gallery in the Loop if you sold this."

I hugged Fantasia and gathered my things. "I don't want anything from him. Consider it payment of a debt."

* * *

He behaved like a perfect gentleman, and that puzzled me. Was it a ruse? Was Killian Blaine toying with me, pretending to care when he didn't? After dinner, he planted a chaste kiss on my forehead and departed, with promises to discuss my painting with Madge. No tender touches or words of endearment. He might have been my brother or uncle rather than a lover.

I refused to pout or ponder it another moment. Let Killian play his silly games. I had better things to do. Fantasia needed exercise, and so did I. After changing my clothes, I hummed a sprightly tune, rescued my princess from her crate, and headed for the park. Exhaustion set in after jogging for two miles. Correction, I was exhausted, but Fantasia begged for even more exercise. As I collapsed on a bench, she danced around me, her bright, beautiful eyes shining with expectation. "Sorry, my love. Give me a break." I patted her, begging for forgiveness. It was ten o'clock, and I was knackered. Something or someone had sucked out every ounce of my youthful vitality.

I was engrossed in thought when Aubrey Miles ambled up beside me. I'd rarely seen her in civilian clothes, and the transformation was magical. The chief was svelte as an Olympian, although I suspected that her fanny pack held a weapon that most athletes lack. She stopped and gave me a cheery greeting. "Ms. Davis. Getting your exercise, I see. You know, even in Harbor Bay, wandering around alone at night isn't the wisest thing." She bent down and patted Fantasia. "Although you have an excellent companion with you."

"You solved the murder, so I should feel safe." That sounded waspish, but I didn't care. Chief Miles had dismissed me, and that smarted.

Nothing flustered the chief. She shrugged, ignoring my jab. "Point taken. Watch your step anyway, Marky. You never know who you can trust."

She sped away, leaving me reeling. Was I in danger, and if so, from whom? My heart rate increased alarmingly, and I felt lightheaded. If Brendan Doyle had suddenly appeared, I might have fainted. Fortunately, I regained control by reciting my mantra. *"Cowards die many times before their death. The valiant never taste of death but once."*

Julius Caesar, with an able assist from Shakespeare, said it right. I might not be valiant, but at least I was no coward. I jumped up and beckoned Fantasia. "Come on, girl. We both need a good night's rest."

Chapter Twenty-Five

That next morning, Gemma cornered me. "Okay. Spill. What happened between you and the Dreamboat?"

"Nothing. We talked and ate dinner. Period."

"Ah, come on. Didn't you mix it up a little?"

I glared at my partner. "Certainly not. While we're on the subject, what happened between you and Benny?"

Gemma curled her lip. "Nothing. Nada. His mother stayed with us the whole time. That woman hates me, Marky. I swear she was trying to poison me with that crappy meal."

There was more. I gave Gemma my stern teacher look. "What else? You're hiding something."

Gemma was the strongest person I knew. She never cried, but this time she teared up immediately. "We broke up. Benny and I are kaput!"

I tamped down my joy. "You're kidding."

She shook her head and reached for a tissue. "Nope. I gave him back his ring. Threw it at him."

I wanted to comfort my friend but didn't know how. "Isn't there any hope for compromise?"

"Huh," Gemma spat. "When hell freezes over. Benny wanted us to live with his mother after our wedding. Can you believe it? They'd drag me into court within a month for either divorce or murder. Maybe both."

I'm not a hugger, but in this instance, I put my arms around my friend. "Cheer up. We're both in the same boat. We're independent women living full lives. So, what if men don't appreciate us?"

She sniffled. "I guess."

I fixed both of us a double espresso and added biscotti on the side. When Aunt Violet sailed in later, she eyed us both but wisely said nothing. Just another day at Poppet.

* * *

Zoom meetings leave me dissatisfied and disconnected. Nevertheless, most businesses prefer them during these days of cost-cutting and downsizing. Violet and I spent an exhausting afternoon haggling with two suppliers and one potential advertiser while Gemma handled our walk-in traffic. Violet managed to wrangle concessions from both suppliers in exchange for sizable orders. All told, it was a win-win ending. Afterwards, as my aunt prepared for an evening out with an unspecified companion, I resigned myself to quiet time reading a good book. Before she left, Violet called me. "Marky, I forgot to mention this. Madge invited you to the memorial for Letty."

"Really? I'm surprised."

Violet patted my shoulder. "Don't be so prickly, dear Niece. Poor Madge has a lot on her plate these days. She mentioned your portrait of Teagen. Apparently, Mr. Blaine told her about it, and she thinks it would comfort Brendan. Give her a call when you get a chance."

I knew that was an order, not an option. Violet was the original iron hand in a velvet glove. That approach served her well in business dealings, and it always worked with me. Reluctantly, I dialed Madge Stone's number, praying that she wouldn't answer. As the saying goes, all prayers are answered. Sometimes the answer is no.

She responded at the first ring in that cultured, deceptively mild voice I'd grown to loathe.

"Marky, how nice to hear from you. I spoke with Violet today and asked that you call."

Two could play the nicety-nice game. Let her take the lead.

"Of course, Mrs. Stone. How can I help you?"

Madge hesitated. "Killian, Mr. Blaine, mentioned a gift you had for

Brendan."

"Yes. It's Teagen's portrait. She wanted her husband to receive it. I can stop by this afternoon it you'd like to see it."

"How kind. I planned to visit your wonderful store tomorrow morning anyway to get some supplies." She chuckled. "At my age, one can't leave anything to chance. Would that work for you?"

We ended our chat on a high note, each of us pretending to overlook the hostilities of the past. I had no intention of joining Letty's celebration of life or whatever the term might be for a confessed murderess. The shadow of Doogie's death would loom over the proceedings, making them more dirge than delight. Surely Brendan Doyle would also have the decency to avoid the event. There was the little matter of Teagen's murder to consider.

At closing time, Gemma sidled up to me. "I'm lonely. Want to join me for a drink? We can both drown our sorrows."

Regrettably, my calendar was totally open.

* * *

Gemma's watering hole of choice was a local dive bar on the wharf. Although it had a decent view of Lake Michigan, it boasted few other amenities. She was a regular, so we were greeted with smiles and backslaps by the crowd. When a table opened, we quickly claimed it and placed our order. No gourmet fare here. The Paper Cut catered to a working-class clientele that favored burgers, fries, and pizza. I grinned, thinking of Killian Blaine's reaction to such a place.

"What do you recommend?" I asked Gemma.

"Pepto-Bismol," she joked. "Actually, the pizza is pretty darn good. They serve craft beers, too." She lowered her voice. "Just don't expect Pellegrino or lattes, Princess. This is how the other half lives."

I ignored her and ordered a Margarita with a side of nachos. Both were tasty and packed a powerful punch. Gemma chose a pitcher of beer and a tomato and cheese pizza. As we chowed down, a surprise guest barreled his way into the place.

"Keep your head down," Gemma whispered. "Maybe he won't see you. He's drunk."

That he was. Brendan Doyle blended right into this hardscrabble crowd despite his designer duds. Our effort to hide was futile. The big brute steadied himself, staggered over, and accosted us. "What have we here? Slumming, are you, Ms. Davis?" His speech was slurred, almost incomprehensible.

"I could ask you the same thing, Mr. Doyle."

He loomed over the table and raised his fist to me. "Always a smart remark. Someone should teach you good manners."

Sometimes I speak before thinking. "Who's going to do that, Brendan? You?"

I could smell the liquor on his foul breath as he moved closer. Clearly, the man had lost control of his senses. Panic time. I leaned back as far as I could to avoid the onslaught of his fists or at least to minimize any injuries.

While I cowered in my chair, Gemma jumped up, threw beer in his face, and confronted him. "Back off, bozo. Touch one hair on her head, and you'll spend the night in a cell." She signaled to the bouncer, a muscular Irish lad named Sean, who sped over and grasped Doyle by the collar.

"Out you go, mister. No troublemakers welcome here."

Brendan squirmed and shouted the cliché of the entitled. "Do you know who I am?"

Sean laughed. "Don't know. Don't care. Just leave and don't come back, or I'll call the cops."

He retreated after straightening his beer-saturated clothing and mopping his brow with a handkerchief. I can't deny it. Seeing Brendan Doyle bested by a bouncer gave me a thrill.

The encounter left me shaken. Gemma reacted quite differently. She was enlivened by tangling with the mighty entrepreneur and couldn't wait to crow about it.

"Guess I showed him, the big oaf. For a minute, I thought I'd have to clean his clock." She made a muscle. "Bullies don't scare me. I grew up around them all my life. Never back down or you're doomed."

I bit my lip to keep from crying. Men in my world didn't brutalize innocent women. Or did they? Was I living a fantasy that defied reality? That surprise attack left me rattled and humiliated. Words and paint brushes were my weapons of choice. I was intellectually fearless but a physical whimp.

"Buck up, Marky. Learn to protect yourself." Gemma leaned forward. "Unless, of course, the Dreamboat's around. Come on. Have another Margarita." She signaled the bartender, who brought my drink and an apology. "Sorry for that, lady. This is a respectable place. You two are our guests tonight."

I protested, but Gemma merely smirked. "Thanks a lot. We accept."

Chapter Twenty-Six

Gemma was right. I had to stand up and assert myself to be called a feminist. Brave words, but easier said than done with a monster like Brendan Doyle facing you. I was too ashamed to tell my aunt what happened, but Gemma did it for me. She related a colorful and mostly accurate account of the dustup, painting herself as the avenging angel.

Violet absorbed the information without judging, choosing instead to hug both of us.

"How dreadful. Brendan should be ashamed of himself. Perhaps you should rethink giving him that lovely portrait." She pointed to Teagen's image, sitting on a nearby easel.

That reminded me. "Oops. Almost forgot. Madge Stone is dropping by to view it."

Right on cue, the matron in question strolled in, accompanied by a certain Chicago lawyer. She approached me, arms outstretched. "Oh, Marky, Brendan told us what happened. He's so ashamed. His judgment flies out the window when drink gets the better of him."

Killian's face remained impassive, but Aunt Violet reacted swiftly. "As well he should," she said. She stepped forward, between me and Madge. "I suggested that Marky rethink her generous offer. Brendan doesn't deserve such a lovely painting."

Madge reeled back. "Oh no! Please."

She dove into her capacious tote and produced a checkbook. "Name your price. Brendan must have that painting."

"Sorry, Madge," said Killian. "I already tried. Marky won't sell it."

Some wealthy people believe that they can buy anything and anyone. They're wrong.

"I don't want your money, Mrs. Stone." I turned away and left the room with Killian trailing behind me.

"I should have been with you last night," Killian said. "Brendan wouldn't try that crap in front of me. I'd kill him if he hurt you." I shook my head. "He threatened me, and I froze. That's a fact. Gemma came through, though. She's far braver than I could ever be."

He drew me to him. "I warned Brendan to leave you alone. Don't blame yourself. You can't always be brave. Nobody is. Besides, you don't have to pretend around me. Not ever."

I saw the longing in his eyes and changed the subject. "Madge invited me to Letty's memorial. I won't go, of course."

Killian nodded. "Understandable. What about the portrait?"

I shrugged. "Let me think about that one."

"I've got to leave for Chicago this afternoon, but I'll be back in a few days. We could have dinner…and breakfast, too, if you're willing."

There was no mistaking his meaning, and suddenly I felt emboldened. "I'd like that. Exercise always makes me hungry."

He kissed me with unexpected fervor, and I responded in kind. No more playing hard to get for this girl. *Bravery was underrated.*

That pleasant interlude ended abruptly when an unwelcome voice called out. "Ready, Killian? I must leave." Madge stood there, hands on hips, glaring at us. Was she envious or merely out of sorts? The scowl on her face spelled trouble for someone.

To her credit, Madge swiftly changed course and became pleasant. "I hope you'll reconsider about the portrait, Marky. Call me if you do. Brendan will be gone for the next few days, and it would be a wonderful surprise for him."

Killian squeezed my hand and followed her. Before leaving, he turned back and blew me a kiss. I was thankful that Gemma didn't see that. She'd be certain to equate simple flirtation with undying love. With my dismal dating record, I dared not hope for that.

* * *

Violet didn't pressure me. Quite the opposite, she avoided any mention of Madge, Teagen's portrait, or Brendan Doyle. Gemma was less restrained. She expounded at great length about the sins of the uber-rich and their treatment of underlings. I neither agreed nor contradicted her. Long ago I'd learned the secret to dealing with Gemma— stay silent and let her rant. After a decent interval, I changed the subject to one of her favorites—Benny and his monstrous mom.

"Have you spoken with him lately?" Violet asked. "I saw Mrs. Soto at the florist's, and she looked positively radiant."

Gemma snarled. "Really? I can't believe that."

Violet's smile was enigmatic. "Actually…when she left, the florist told me that Mrs. Soto has a beau. One who sends her flowers."

"No way," Gemma said. "Who'd date the bride of Frankenstein?"

"Hey," I said. "Don't knock it. Less heat on you and Benny that way."

Gemma brightened. "You may be right. But what about this painting? Does the Creep from the Deep get it?"

I didn't answer. Upon reflection, I was utterly sick of everything involving the Doyles and their pals. By disposing of the painting, I could sever any connection to them. With one notable exception, of course. Killian Blaine. He'd gotten into my mind and my heart. This time, I vowed to take a risk. The words of Christina Rosetti's beautiful sonnet *First Day* rang through my mind. I vividly recalled every touch, every time, every word we'd exchanged, even the acerbic ones. That vulnerability frightened me to death. No man, even Roddy, had ever done that to me.

Violet touched my shoulder. "Are you alright, Marky? You seem a million miles away."

"I bet she's thinking of the Dreamboat," Gemma sneered. "Tell the truth."

"Don't be silly. I've decided to honor my promise to Teagen. Brendan Doyle can have her portrait and be done with it. I'll contact Madge this evening."

"Very wise," Violet said. "Let it go. You're the better person."

Gemma folded her arms and growled. "Better, smetter. That stuff is for preachers, not us. Make them suffer."

I waited until closing time to call Madge. When she heard my voice, this doyenne of doom was all charm and noblesse oblige.

"I'm thrilled with your decision, Marky. Shall I send someone over to collect the painting?"

"I'd prefer to hang it myself. The setting must be just right. You know how fussy we artists are about our work."

"Of course," Madge said. "Would tonight be convenient? I'll meet you at the guest house around eight if that suits. Don't worry about Brendan. He's in Chicago with Killian."

When I hung up, Gemma confronted me. "You're not going over there alone." As usual, she was unapologetic about eavesdropping. She folded her arms and glared. "I'm going with you. Some muscle might come in handy if that bully boy shows up."

No argument could sway Gemma when she'd made up her mind. Besides, I could use some moral support when dealing with Madge. Despite my brave talk, her aura of impenetrable wealth and privilege intimidated me.

"Fine. I'll pick you up at seven-thirty. Be on your best behavior."

After refreshing my makeup and changing into a red linen shift, I loaded Fantasia and Teagen's portrait into my Jeep and headed for Gemma's house. For some reason, icy fingers of doubt assailed me as we neared the gated Stone estate. When I came here the first time, I'd been awed by the beauty and grandeur of the property. Now it seemed as cold and remote as the owner herself. Three frequent guests had died violently: Teagen, Doogie, and Letty. Was this lovely setting jinxed or merely a figment of my imagination?

"Why so quiet?" Gemma asked. "You're creeping me out." She scanned the carefully curated shrubs and gardens surrounding the main house. "Boy, this place is really something. No wonder Madame Madge is so stuck up."

I ignored her and pulled up in front of the guest house, a spacious dwelling of at least three thousand square feet, in the Provencal style. Its façade of pale limestone was topped by a red tiled hipped roof. The effect was at once charming and subdued, a complement to the more ornate Chateau style of the main house.

"Wow," said Gemma as she gaped at the place. "If I were her guest, I'd never leave. So, this is where Brendan Doyle bunks."

I opened the car windows for Fantasia's comfort and settled her in her crate. Then, using particular care, I lifted Teagen's portrait out while Gemma carried the bag with hammer and hanging hooks. The main door was unlocked, but Madge was nowhere to be found.

"Where is she?" Gemma asked. "Isn't this some kind of crime—breaking and entering? Maybe we're being set up."

"Hardly. I'm sure she'll be right along. Let me text her." I messaged Madge telling her we had arrived. Rather than stand outside, I opened the door and went inside.

The interior décor was perfect, a soothing blend of French country style in muted shades of yellow and red. Wide wood plank floors and plaster walls completed the look. The sofa surrounding a fieldstone fireplace was plush, the type of comfortable seating a man, even a Neanderthal like Brendan Doyle, would appreciate.

"I think I'll hang Teagen's portrait above the fireplace," I said. "See if you can find a step ladder. They might have one in that tool shed outside." As we drove in, I'd noticed a small limestone structure, perfectly matched to the guest house.

Gemma scurried off on her errand while I found my measuring tape. Proper placement was key when showcasing a painting. While studying the wall, I noticed a study equipped with massive bookshelves and a lovely bureau plat that adjoined the main room. I peeked inside, imagining the Doyles using this space to read or relax. To my surprise, an array of familiar writing instruments was splayed out on the desk. Doogie's beloved pen collection. He had willed it to Madge as an act of remembrance to a treasured friend. I blinked back tears as I recalled the Mont Blanc pen he had clutched in his dying hand.

"There you are. A bit of snooping, Ms. Davis?" Brendan Doyle crept up behind me so stealthily that I shrieked.

"I was admiring Madge's good taste," I stammered. "Trying to find the right spot for the painting."

"Ah, yes, the portrait of my dear wife. You've managed to capture her beauty, I see. But not her malevolence. Teagen was a heartless bitch; more devil than darling. She possessed me, tormented me. But I couldn't let her go." He took another step toward me. "Do you have any idea what that's like? Heaven and hell in one beautiful package. Madge told me you were trouble. Fancied yourself a detective." His smile was fixed, as artificial as his gleaming teeth. In his hand, he clutched my hammer. "Here. You'll want to use this." Suddenly, he swung it aloft. "Or maybe I should do the honors."

Be brave, I told myself. Act normal.

"Madge said you were in Chicago," I said. "Sealing deals, making money. Doing whatever you magnates do."

He laughed. "Killian's attending to that. I'm a man of leisure now."

I edged toward the door. "I'll just leave this portrait with you and be on my way."

As I fled, I ran into a solid wall of flesh. Madge Stone, looking stoic and sinister, blocked my path. "Not so fast, missy." She grabbed my arm. "We must stop her, Brendan. Give me that hammer."

He looked puzzled. "Whatever are you talking about?"

Madge glared, her mouth set in a grim line. "Don't you see? She knows."

"I don't know anything," I babbled. "My aunt is expecting me. I must leave."

Brendan Doyle turned toward Madge, wrinkling his brow. "Are you crazy, woman? What does she know?"

"Don't you see? I did it for you, Brendan. So that we can be together at last. I've loved you for so long, and I know you love me." She was pleading now, very near tears.

I should have been quiet, but I couldn't control myself. "You killed them all," I cried. "Three lives gone. Doogie was your friend, and Letty was your cousin." I didn't mention Teagen.

Madge scowled at me. "I didn't have a choice. Doogie fixed that meal, her so-called seduction supper, and I added the finishing touches. What a joke. He never suspected a thing until you badgered him. It's your fault that he's dead."

I now knew why Doogie clutched that pen. His final act was a clue to his killer, a link to Madge, the friend who murdered him. Brendan Doyle didn't move. He stayed frozen, unable to process things. "But you tried to save Teagen, Madge. You used her EpiPen. I saw it."

They seemed to forget my existence. At least I hoped so. As they spoke, I inched closer to the door.

"I emptied those EpiPens beforehand, Brendan. It was easy enough to do. Then I could swoop down, play Madge the savior, and make sure that she died."

"And Letty? What was her crime?" For once, Brendan Doyle, man of action, was stymied.

Madge snarled a response. "That nitwit wanted you too. She thought you loved her. I had to put a stop to her foolishness. I've waited so long for you, Brendan. Now we can finally be together." She held out her arms, waiting for an embrace. I reached the study door, carefully, stealthily creeping toward freedom.

Brendan leapt up, his face crimson with rage. "I never misled you. You knew I loved Teagen. She's the only woman I ever loved. Ever could love. Not you or your goofy cousin."

Madge's face lost all color. Tripple murder didn't faze her, but rejection devastated her. "They weren't good enough for you. You must understand, Brendan. We can leave here. Eliminate that clerk and be happy." She moved to his side. "Teagen betrayed you, but I never would. I killed for you."

In an instant, the unthinkable happened. Brendan Doyle swung the hammer at her head with all his strength, dealing Madge a massive blow. As her crumpled body hit the floor, I made my escape. He didn't try to stop me. I doubt very much if he even noticed me. Brendan stood over the corpse of the evil woman who loved him, crying Teagen's name.

Chapter Twenty-Seven

A surprise awaited me when I bolted out the front door. Gemma, armed with a shovel, stood guard as two Harbor Bay police cruisers and an ambulance pulled up. Chief Miles unholstered her Glock and cautiously approached Madge's guest house.

"I had you covered," Gemma crowed. "Heard the entire thing." Her russet curls waved wildly in the breeze, and her eyes blazed with excitement. "Never expected him to go all caveman, though." She paused as Chief Miles led a shaken Brendan Doyle out to her squad car. EMTs rushed to Madge's side, but there was little they could do. She was gone, that fount of altruism. She would no longer spread largesse around the community. Too bad she was a heartless killer.

"How did you know?" I asked my partner and savior.

Gemma snorted. "You always accuse me of interfering. Bet you're glad I did this time. I called the chief when I saw Brendan go into the house. Then I grabbed that shovel in case things got rough."

I forced myself not to cry. Instead, I hugged my friend so fiercely that she yelped.

"Hey! Watch your step. Don't damage the merchandise."

Our reunion ended abruptly when a familiar voice rang out. "Chief Miles wants both of you down at the station. Now!" Who else but Benny Soto would intrude at such a moment? Everything about that man raised my hackles, but he didn't intimidate me one bit.

"We'll be there after I speak with my aunt and get Fantasia settled."

Gemma piped up. "Yeah. She'll want to talk to her attorney, too. You remember him, Benny. Killian Blaine."

That name made Benny blanch. He waved his nightstick in a futile attempt to control us, but backed off. Gemma and I ignored him and slowly strutted to my Jeep. That's when my iPhone chimed.

"Are you all right? I just heard." Killian's voice sounded strained. "I'll be back first thing tomorrow. Don't talk to the cops unless I'm there. Brendan hasn't been charged yet."

His voice comforted me. I wouldn't admit that to him, Gemma, or anyone else, but it did.

"Okay."

"Don't worry. I'll make everything okay. Promise. I'll take care of you."

Had he lost his senses? I'd just watched a woman's brains get splashed all over her priceless Persian carpet. Things would never be okay again if that image remained. Then I thought of Doogie, dying slowly and painfully in his own kitchen. She did that. Madge, who pretended to be his friend but was really a ruthless murderer. Now that gruesome image of her didn't trouble me anymore.

"I'll be waiting," I told Killian.

"Was that the Dreamboat?" Gemma asked.

I nodded. "We should call Aunt Violet. Kim, too." I felt exhausted, barely able to steer my car. "Will you dial their number?"

Violet answered immediately. Despite my garbled account, she pieced together the basic elements of the tragedy. "I'll get Kim and meet you at Doogie's place," she said. That seemed fitting, as if my dear friend were still a part of the discussion.

When we arrived, they were already seated in the dining room around that lovely marble table. Four friends who had each played a part in this saga toasted its finale. Kim sat at one end, blinking back tears. Gemma stood near the kitchen door, bouncing back and forth on her toes with excitement. As usual, my lovely aunt was utterly composed. She uncorked a bottle of Krug and poured five flutes.

"Is someone else joining us?" Kim asked.

Violet smiled. "He's already here. This flute is for Doogie. You know how he loved champagne." She lifted her glass and made a toast. "To absent friends and those still with us. À Votre Santé."

* * *

Despite everything, I slept soundly that night. Well before sunrise, I roused Fantasia and set off on a brisk walk. It was barely daylight, but there was no danger. Harbor Bay had been cleansed of the evil that plagued it. I felt surprisingly free, full of energy and optimism. After a vigorous two-mile jog, I was winded and collapsed on a bench. That's where he found me.

Killian, attired in a bespoke suit, dazzling white shirt, and Rep tie, completed the look with hornrimmed glasses. Frankly, the sight of this lawyerly version of the man was breathtaking. He wasted no time. Instantly, he embraced me and softly stroked my hair, murmuring words that comforted both of us.

"I didn't know," he said. "I never suspected Madge was capable of such things."

"She fooled most people, even my aunt. Funny thing, I was never comfortable around Madge. She was always Mrs. Stone to me, someone on another plane far above me. Another weird thing—even at the funerals, she always wore white. Yeah, the widow wore white."

Killian explained that Brendan was under a doctor's care pending further action by Chief Miles. "He's almost catatonic. Barely recognized me. I told you Brendan was basically a decent guy. This whole thing traumatized him."

"You think! That 'decent guy' beat Madge's head to a pulp. Of course, she deserved it, but still…"

Killian got that stubborn look on his face. "He truly cared for Madge. Considered her a friend. He had no idea that she was in love with him. He lost control when she admitted to killing Teagen."

"She didn't just own up to it. She bragged. I heard her. Brendan might be traumatized, but I'll bet he'll still take her money if he can. That would end his business problems."

He sighed. "Let's not fight. I'm still his business partner and his friend.

Even though I can't represent him in any criminal proceedings, I'll help him all I can."

I noticed that a few joggers and dog walkers had entered the park. That reminded me of my appointment with Chief Miles.

Reluctantly, I moved away from Killian and prepared to leave. "Oops. I must change clothes and head for the police station. Can't let Benny Soto track me down."

He held his hand out, traffic cop style. "Wait. I'm coming with you. I promise not to interfere, but you need a lawyer to protect your rights."

I'm a realist, so I had to wonder—was he protecting me, or his buddy? "Gemma will be joining us," I said. "You understand that I won't lie to protect Brendan even if it hurts his case."

Killian stiffened. "Nor would I ask you to. Don't question my integrity, Marky."

We walked back to Poppet in silence with Fantasia serving as a furry Maginot line. No more sweet words or cozy conversation ensued. When we reached the store, Killian decided to drive by himself. "I'll meet you there," he said, using the curt tone I was all too familiar with

"No problem." I hurried inside and made a beeline for my apartment. After bathing, grooming, and dressing myself, I regained perspective. If truth-telling severed ties with Killian, then so be it. A relationship built on lies would never last anyway.

Gemma immediately noticed my hangdog look. I never could deceive her, try as I might.

"What's your problem?" she asked. "We've got to make tracks before they send out the posse." She glared at me. "I bet you had a fight with the Dreamboat. Don't tell me you blew it again."

I ignored her and marched out the door toward my Jeep. "Come on. You're wasting time."

Our interview with Aubrey Miles was relatively painless. Killian sat in the back of the room wearing that opaque, inscrutable expression so beloved by attorneys. We didn't speak. We didn't even make eye contact. Chief Miles asked both of us to recount everything that happened at the guest house that awful afternoon. Gemma enjoyed her turn in the spotlight, especially since Benny Soto lurked on the far side of the room opposite Killian, glowering. I stared straight ahead and gave as accurate an account as I could. Ever since that day, I had replayed every second of the ill-fated visit in my mind. It haunted my dreams, became my nightmare.

When asked about Brendan Doyle, I took a deep breath. From the corner of my eye, I saw Killian tense up.

"Madge admitted that she murdered Teagen, Letty, and Doogie. Bragged about it. She had no remorse at all. Brendan seemed shocked. It was obvious to me that he had no idea what she'd done.

Madge said she eliminated them so that she and Brendan could be together. She planned to murder me as well. Brendan was holding the hammer I'd brought to hang Teagen's portrait. As she approached him, he swung the hammer he was holding and struck her. I ran out the door."

After a few more questions, Chief Miles asked me to sign my statement. The case would be referred to the prosecuting attorney for Emmet County, who would determine any charge against Brendan.

Gemma and I clambered into my Jeep and headed home. Killian followed his own path, probably to his lakeside villa. It really didn't matter anymore.

* * *

That encounter left me shaken and subdued. A sheath of ice encircled my heart, numbing me to any emotion. Gemma was oblivious, but Aunt Violet understood. She tapped on my front door bearing a tray with two snifters and a bottle of Grand Marnier Cognac.

"I believe you could use some of this," she said. "You've had a difficult couple of days."

"You might say that." I explained everything that happened, from Killian's behavior to our interview with Chief Miles. That opened the floodgates, and I wept uncontrollably for several minutes. Violet sat silently, allowing my tears to ebb.

"You did the only thing possible, Marky. I'm confident that Mr. Blaine understands that. Move on and let the legal system deal with Brendan. He'll be represented by the best talent money can buy."

She was right, of course. Aunt Violet always was. Weeks passed into months as Madge Stone's death slowly faded from the headlines. Brendan Doyle was reportedly sequestered in a seaside mental health facility in West Palm Beach that offered restorative care in a luxurious setting. After viewing their list of impressive amenities, I was tempted to sign up myself.

Anonymous sources leaked details of Madge's foul deeds to the media, thus ensuring that the true character of the triple murderess was unveiled. No one mourned or defended her, and the prosecuting attorney quietly decided against prosecuting her killer. Under the circumstances, however, Brendan was ineligible to inherit the massive estate that she'd bequeathed him. I was happy about that, especially since the secondary legatee was the Little Traverse Bay Humane Society.

Killian kept his distance. He neither called nor appeared on my doorstep despite my secret hopes. Once again, his dating exploits were chronicled on all the gossip sites. I ignored them, but Gemma kept me up to date on his every move. The Stone case was sensationalized by one of the national true crime programs, so for a time, Harbor Bay was once again in the news. I declined all attempts to involve me. Naturally, Gemma did not. Professor Roddy Park gave a brief interview in which he heaped fulsome praise on Teagen Doyle. Killian surfaced when he provided an impassioned defense of his friend and colleague Brendan Doyle.

"Wow," Gemma said. "He looks better than ever. Still a Dreamboat." She glared at me. "The Professor is still hotter than hot, too. Boy, how could you let both get away? What a waste!"

I couldn't answer her question. Didn't try to. I focused my energy on the move into Doogie's townhouse and the business boom at Poppet. It seemed as if every tourist who visited Harbor Bay stopped in to get a peek at our little store. Poppet's bottom line profited from the increased traffic, so I was happy to keep busy. Mad Madge and Teagen had done us an unintended favor.

After wrestling with myself, I decided to place the portrait of Teagen with

Violet's friend, a respected Detroit art dealer. I was proud of my work, but that painting was a vivid reminder of a gruesome chapter in my life. Let someone else appreciate its artistry and the beauty of its subject. The gallery hosted an elaborate launch party at the Dalton Hotel in Birmingham, which Gemma, Kim, and I attended with my aunt. We made it a festive occasion, despite the circumstances surrounding Teagen's end. I was gratified and humbled by the crowd that the showing attracted and elated to learn that my painting had sold quickly at a mind-boggling price.

"I told you how talented you are," said Violet. "There were several respected art critics at the show, and they were impressed. Their opinion will mean a lot to your future."

Her praise was balm for my soul. The past few months had made me question my life choices and path forward. I hadn't asked to be involved in Teagen's sad saga. On the other hand, I hadn't resisted. The appeal to my ego had been too strong to ignore, so I owned some of the consequences. Roddy got embroiled in it because of me and his own concupiscence. Who knows where our relationship would have gone without the Teagen factor? I didn't dare explore my complicated feelings about Killian Blaine. They felt too raw and painful.

Months later, when Gemma galloped into our sales floor, I knew something major had occurred. She brandished a copy of *Hour Detroit,* a glossy monthly publication that featured fashion, food, and art trends. Her excitement resulted in a stream of jumbled, indecipherable speech that confounded both me and my aunt.

Violet waved Gemma to a chair. "Sit and catch your breath. Now, what's so urgent?"

My pal pointed to the magazine's cover. That cover took my breath away. The headline read, *Teagen's Final Tip—A tale of passion, money, and murder.* My portrait of the late film star filled the page. My hands shook as I thumbed through the magazine, seeking the article.

"Read it to me. Please." I handed it to Violet, who calmly and dispassionately recited it word for word. The account contained almost no new information apart from an update on Brendan Doyle's health. He had left his Palm Beach refuge "completely recovered" and announced a planned foundation honoring the restorative powers of Teagen's Tinctures. His attorney, Killian Blaine, would oversee the project.

"Ha," Gemma spat. "A likely story. He'll soon be back to his old ways. Brendan, I mean. The Dreamboat already moved on."

Aunt Violet grasped my wrist. "Listen to this, Marky. They mention your portrait and say it is in the hands of a private collector. That's quite a plug from a prestige magazine like *Hour Detroit.*"

"I guess."

Gemma leapt to the computer and immediately ordered twenty-five copies of that edition. "Hey," she said. "This is big stuff. We should celebrate."

Violet nodded. "I agree. Let me call Kim."

I reluctantly joined them for dinner at Junoon, the same Indian Restaurant where Killian made his faux proposal. My appetite waned, but I maintained a brave front for the sake of my friends. That evening, I wore the same saffron sheath that I'd worn the last time. It was a grim reminder of my foolish past and a statement of future resolve. Romance was off the table for Marketta Davis. Never again would a man control me or hold my emotions hostage. Brave words indeed. Unfortunately, based on experience, they seldom translated into deeds. Oscar Wilde said the essence of romance is uncertainty, yet I yearned for the unattainable.

Kim touched my hand. "You're not brooding, are you, Marky? We're celebrating your success tonight."

"Don't mind her," Gemma said. "Every time a guy dumps her, she acts that way. It'll pass."

I couldn't help responding. "What are you? The voice of experience, Miss formerly engaged Watts."

"Ouch!" she said. "You got me good. I guess both of us are love's losers."

Suddenly, the atmosphere in the dining room changed. As if by a cosmic force, men squared their shoulders and sat up straight while women tried mightily not to gape. I dared not look because I'd seen it happen before.

"OMG," Gemma gasped. "He's here."

Kim glanced toward the entrance but said nothing. Aunt Violet patted my hand. "Steady, my girl. He lives in Harbor Bay part-time. You're bound to run into him occasionally."

Killian Blaine was instantly shown to a choice table for two. My heart sank as I envisioned some glamorous starlet as his companion. Instead of speaking, I buried my head in the menu pretending to study it. *Take a deep breath, I told myself. Don't humiliate yourself.*

Our server soon approached us bearing a magnum of Krug. Violet gave him a quizzical look. "I don't recall ordering this?"

"From the gentleman at the corner table, madam." He nodded toward Killian Blaine.

I was paralyzed, didn't move a muscle. So typical of Killian to flaunt his wealth over the plebeians. My aunt waved her thanks with a gracious dip of her hand.

"Wow!" Gemma said. "That guy has class." She raised her flute and proposed a toast. "To that almost famous artist, my pal and partner, Marky Davis."

Violet agreed. "A votre Sante," she said. "Hear, hear," Kim echoed the salute.

I knew he would join us. His tactics were so transparent, and subtlety was simply not his style. I saw him approach out of the corner of my eye. Still the heartthrob, immaculately tailored and barbered.

"Ladies, forgive me for intruding. I saw the issue of *Hour Detroit* and wanted to add my congratulations." He stared at me with those sapphire eyes, sending an unmistakable message. It took effort, but I maintained a stony silence, substituting an enigmatic smile for words.

Ever the diplomat, Kim asked. "Won't you join us?"

Killian demurred, adding that he was meeting a client. Then in an instant, he was gone.

"You blew it again," Gemma said. "You must love being alone. I bet that client is some hot chick. A man like that doesn't eat by himself."

"This is our celebration," I said. "No additions needed. Forget Killian Blaine." I proposed a toast to woman power and our mutual successes. Each of us had overcome obstacles both personal and professional, and that alone was cause for celebration. Kim suggested the two-course premier tasting menu, which we could sample and share. I knew *He* would choose the three-course version. Everyone agreed, and we soon indulged in an array of tempting dishes topped off by an after-dinner cordial.

Meanwhile, Gemma kept a weather eye on Killian's table. She reported that his dinner companion was male, a fortyish fellow with little hair and plenty of girth. That pleased me. We ended our dinner on a high note and piled into Violet's Mercedes for the short trip home.

Fantasia had waited patiently for her evening walk. Accompanied by my aunt, I freed my beautiful collie from her crate and gave her a well-deserved turn around Harbor Bay. The streets were deserted, and the evening was balmy. The star-studded sky featured a full moon, harbinger of good things on the horizon. Violet paused to stare up at that moon.

"You know that he'll contact you. He practically devoured you tonight."

I shook my head. "We have nothing to say to each other. I'm sick of men playing games with my emotions."

She shrugged. "Suppose he's serious. Perhaps you should listen to what he has to say."

I seldom contradicted my aunt because she was usually right. This time, however, was different. "As Gemma would say, he kicked me to the curb. No amount of champagne or flowers changes that. Killian loves asserting dominance over others, especially women. No more."

Violet laughed. "You can be prickly, dear Niece. Don't let pride be your downfall."

"How did you handle things like this?" Violet had a string of romances over the years about which she volunteered very little information. Even now, mature men were panting after her. I yearned to know her secret.

"I was rather a free spirit, Marky. Sometimes, overthinking things works to your detriment. I just threw caution to the wind and let nature take its course."

With those words of wisdom, Violet turned toward home. "Time to get our beauty rest. Even Fantasia looks tired."

* * *

I felt a tad woozy the next morning. Champagne, cognac, and sumptuous food were not my normal fare. After a bracing shower and shampoo, I recovered sufficiently to face the workday and prepare for whatever it brought. I was on my guard in case *He* appeared. Despite my precautions, there was no sign of Killian Blaine. Gemma reported that he was hosting a large gathering of business types at his home that weekend. Her impeccable source was the local caterer who happened to be Gemma's second cousin. In a small town like Harbor Bay, the tradespeople were well versed in most gossip, and familial relationships ran deep.

On the bright side, I'd been offered several commissions since that big splash in *Hour Detroit*. Portraits were not my ideal subjects, but after consulting with my aunt, I accepted two from the Grosse Point area. The extra cash and notoriety were welcome additions to my bottom line. I nourished a faint hope that someday I might still forge a career as an artist.

One afternoon, I visited the Boz Boutique, hunting for the perfect birthday gift for Gemma. She loved the custom pieces featured there, and the price points fit my modest pocketbook. As I window shopped, a familiar voice beckoned me.

"I hoped I'd run into you," said Killian Blaine. "Care to join me for coffee?"

He'd ditched his formal attire in favor of casual chic or the designer version of it. On him, jeans and a Cuccinelli spa hoodie carried the day quite nicely. I noticed that his lush brown hair was now collar length and slightly damp, a pleasing change that I applauded. Some things about him never changed. As we exchanged looks, the challenge in his eyes was unmistakable. I'm no coward. I managed to grin and accept his invitation. Besides, the Pâtisserie was deserted at mid-afternoon. I was thankful for that blessing because it meant that fewer eavesdroppers with wagging tongues would be there, eager to carry tales.

Killian reached across the table and took my hand. "I've missed you, Marky. So much."

"Really? I must have lost your messages."

His rueful chuckle was disarming. "Serves me right, I guess. Never a dull minute around you. I'm always playing defense." He brushed his lips across my fingertips. "Let's stop fencing. I want to see you, be with you."

Aunt Violet's advice rang in my ears, but so did Polonius's advice to Laertes. *"To thine own self be true."* Time to look straight at his face and speak plainly.

"Look, Killian, I'm no plaything. Not like those other women you squire around."

He sighed. "You don't get it. No one else counts. They're just placeholders. Half the time I can't even recall their names. It's you I want. You've taken over my soul."

"Huh!" I said, pulling my hand away. Did he think I was naive, another credulous creature under his spell?

"Just give me a chance. How about coming to dinner at my place tonight? I promise to whip up something special." He had a winning smile, designed to stir and steal female hearts. It worked just fine on me.

"Okay. I'm free for dinner. What time?"

"I'll pick you up at eight."

"Don't bother. I'll drive myself." I finished my drink and rose. "See you soon."

* * *

Steady, Girl, I told myself. *Keep your competitive edge.*

I dressed and groomed myself with extra care that evening. A black silk halter top and slacks gave my ensemble a casual but elegant touch without looking seductive or staged. It took effort, but I'd evaded Gemma and my aunt that afternoon by busying myself at Poppet. Why bother explaining what I couldn't understand myself? At the appointed time, I leashed Fantasia and climbed into my Jeep. That old Tennyson saying, "Into the Valley of Death rode the Six Hundred," felt apropos, although this was hardly the *Charge of the Light Brigade,* and Fantasia and I were scarcely facing death. Maybe I needed a new slogan.

Killian's weekend home stood out amongst a neighborhood of similar lakefront villas. I noticed that he'd done some elaborate landscaping that complemented the surroundings perfectly. Correction. He'd hired someone to do the menial task. Either way, the effect was pleasing.

He answered the doorbell instantly, wearing crisp linen clothes and Gucci loafers. A hint of Creed's Royal Oud wafted up from his collar.

"I see you brought your bodyguard," he said, as he patted Fantasia. "It's a treat hosting two lovely ladies. Come on in."

He'd adjusted the lighting, nothing too obvious, just soft and inviting. For a time, we sat on the velvet sofa, sipping wine and discussing inconsequential things. Strains of familiar music filled the room. The selection of sweet, seductive tunes from long ago surprised me. Ballads, such as "Lady," "I Will Always Love You," "First Time Ever I Saw Your Face," and the ultimate love song "At Last," floated from his sound system. I shivered more from emotion than temperature.

"If you're cold, I can turn down the air conditioner." He moved toward me, putting his arms around me. When he kissed me, I forgot my resolutions and returned his embrace. Things were getting out of hand. I fought to return to some sense of normalcy.

"Those are some of my favorite songs. I'm surprised that you like them."

Killian shook his head. "You don't get it, do you? Those tunes remind me of you every time I play them." He rose and took my hand. "Here. Let me show you something."

We entered his study, and there it was. My portrait of Teagen Doyle hung across from his exquisite Louis V bureau plat just above the marble fireplace. At first, I was speechless, unable to summon any coherent response.

"*You* bought my painting?" I stammered.

He laughed. "I confess. Believe me, it wasn't an easy proposition. I had to fight off several other collectors."

"But why? You can afford a listed artist. Just about anything you like."

There was frustration and amusement in his expression. Killian threw up his hands. "It was my way of having a little piece of you. Something to hold on to. I had to have something of yours."

I took a deep breath. None of this made sense.

"That engagement scene at the restaurant wasn't a stunt. I'm in love with you, Marketta Davis. I've searched for you for such a long time. Do you…could you feel the same way about me?"

This was no time for evasion. *"Cowards die many times before their deaths…"*

Over the years, I'd made so many missteps with men. I glanced up at Killian and nodded.

One chapter in my life was finally closing as another, more exciting door opened.

"Yes."

About the Author

Arlene Kay crafts mysteries with clever plots, intriguing characters, and a whiff of romance and a dose of humor. She is the published author of 14 novels featuring traditional, romantic suspense and cozy themes. A former Senior Executive with the Treasury Department, Ms. Kay has now renounced her bureaucratic ways and focused on murder (writing). Her writing seminars have earned her a host of fans who enjoy lively instruction and sharp commentary.

AUTHOR WEBSITE:
   arlenekay.com

SOCIAL MEDIA HANDLES:
   Arlenekay.com; Arlene Kay author:

Also by Arlene Kay

Intrusion

Die Laughing

The Abacus Prize

Swann Dive

Mantrap

Gilt Trip

Swann Songs

Death by Dog Show

Homicide by Horseshow

Murder at the Falls

Murder at First Blush

The Mascara Murders

Murder Masque